Max Hennessy was born John █████████████
colourful, multifarious career wr████████████
of Hennessy and Mark Hebden. █████████████
and air force and had first-hand experience in the Second
World War. In addition, Hennessy became a cartoonist, a
journalist and a history teacher. Finally turning to full-time
writing, he established himself as a master of the war novel,
mixing the realities of war with bravado and high adventure.
Max Hennessy's novels draw heavily on his own experiences
allowing the reader to witness an imaginative, versatile
writer of real flair.

MAX
HENNESSY

BLUNTED
LANCE

HOUSE OF
STRATUS

This edition published in 2001 by House of Stratus, an imprint of Stratus Holdings plc, 24c Old Burlington Street, London, W1X 1RL, UK. Also at: Suite 210, 1270 Avenue of the Americas, New York, NY 10020, USA.

www.houseofstratus.com

Typeset, printed and bound by House of Stratus.

A catalogue record for this book is available from the British Library and the Library of Congress.

ISBN 1-84232-877-8

PART ONE

The Civil War
In America
by
Major-General
Sir Colby Goff, GCB.

Sitting on a rock on the Jebel Surgham overlooking the Nile at Omdurman, Lieutenant Dabney Augustus Rollo Goff studied the book he had taken from his saddle bag. It was always with him. What his father had set down of the war in America seemed of enormous help to a subaltern uncertain of his skill and dubious of the ability of his commanding officer.

The Old Man, he thought warmly, was not only more than a little articulate, he was quite a boy. And, at the age of sixty-two, still was. Willing to drop a rank to lead the cavalry under Gatacre, his junior in years and military position, in the force commanded by Horatio Herbert Kitchener, Sirdar of Egypt – who was junior even to Gatacre – he was at that moment inside the zariba, the barricade of timber and thorns the army had built round the mud-walled village of El Egeiga, awaiting on this second day of September, 1898, the arrival of the Dervish army of the Khalifa. And, Dabney decided, he wouldn't have very long to wait either, because faintly in the distance he could already hear the elephant tusk war-horns beginning to sound in a chorus that was being taken up in the shriller, brassier notes of cavalry trumpets and the drums and fifes of the British infantry standing to arms with their backs to the River Nile.

The mooings from the south – like the sound of cattle distressed by lack of water – had lifted the head of Dabney's sergeant and he was staring over the rocks of the ridge they were on, a deep frown on his face, all ears and eyes and nervous concern. As he turned, his gaze fell on Dabney's book and he grinned because he knew as well as everyone else what it was.

'Just reading what the general would 'ave done, sir?' he asked.

Dabney smiled. 'I'm sure he'd have had some answer, Sergeant.'

One of a spray of officer's patrols thrown out by the 21st Lancers, they waited quietly, anxious despite their training. They had cantered out of the zariba in darkness, their instructions to watch the advance of the Dervish army, all a little concerned about the unseen black-skinned figures that might spring up from among the rocks wielding broad-bladed spears, and all more than glad to see the daylight.

'They'll not come now,' the sergeant decided. 'It'll be tonight. They'll come in the dark.'

'I wouldn't be too sure of that, Sergeant,' Dabney said. 'They're a bit of an unknown quantity.'

In front of them the sandy plain stretched away from the river with its fringe of starveling grass and thorn bushes. It was one of the most inhospitable places in the world. You woke in the morning in the same hot wind that sent you to sleep, your eyes, nose and throat choked with sand, the folds of your clothes filled with dust; and to add to your pleasure there were always spiders, scorpions, camel thorn, boils, ulcerated throats, heat apoplexy and enteric fever. Even the horses caught sunstroke.

The desert was almost salmon in colour and it was already beginning to shimmer and dance in the heat. The hot restless breeze was rattling away in the distance like an approaching train, nagging at the thick thorny bushes by the Nile which looped and turned its muddy course round the army so that wherever you looked it seemed to be there.

'What's that, sir?'

Even as the sergeant spoke, Dabney saw the Dervish army. They had known all along where it was and during the hours of darkness the one thing they had been afraid of was that it would come when it was hard to tell the direction of the attack. Now, though, as the light paled, they saw the dark mass in front, like a great shadow across the rosy-buff waste of sand, enormous masses of men joined together by thinner lines, like tendrils, while behind and on the flanks the reserves had been halted, like dark blurs and streaks across the desert.

'Jesus,' the sergeant said quietly, peering over his horse's back. 'There's a lot of the bastards!'

'Yes, Sarge.' The voice came quietly from among the rocks. 'And they've got their rib-ticklers with 'em. You can see the sun on 'em!'

It was true. The Dervish army seemed to be lit by a curious glow that came from the first rays of light catching the polished blades of the spears they carried.

For savages, the Dervishes' formation was surprisingly professional. There were immense numbers of them, their front nearly five miles long, and ahead of them emirs, scouts and patrols moved. Their cheering was still faint, but it came to the Jebel Surgham like the sound waves or the tumult of the sea before a storm.

'They're coming this way, sir! It won't be safe here much longer.'

The sergeant sounded a trifle uneasy and Dabney stuffed his father's book into his saddle bag.

'No,' he agreed. 'Time we were getting back. Mount the men, Sergeant!'

As they cantered back, another patrol from further north joined them, led by Winston Churchill, of the Hussars. The horses looked far from their best because, while the infantry had been brought most of the way to Omdurman in barges, the cavalry had been obliged to make their own weary way, and the long march alongside the chocolate-coloured water of the Nile had brought a serious deterioration in the condition of the mounts.

Churchill looked eager and ready for action, however. 'Hello there, Goff,' he rasped in his strong lisping voice. 'Been getting a view of the Mahdi's tomb?'

Dabney smiled. Neither of them belonged to the 21st, whose men they were leading, and both had pulled strings to get themselves attached for the campaign.

'Drill's good,' Churchill observed as they rode alongside each other. 'Kitchener's going to get his battle after all.'

There was a feeling in the 21st that Churchill was too big for his boots, because he was a nephew of the Duke of Marlborough and Randolph Churchill's son. He was considered to be bumptious and said to collect campaign medals because he intended to go into politics, and a season of having fought for the Empire would do him a lot of good. It was well-known that Kitchener disliked him, because he detested newspapermen and, in addition to his duties as a soldier, Churchill was representing one of the London dailies.

In front of them now were the brown masses of the British and Egyptian infantry, with a fringe of cavalry dotting the plain in front. Churchill's hand moved as he gestured at the vultures wheeling in the brassy sky above them.

'*They* know,' he said.

He drew rein, turned in the saddle and stared back over the plain to where the Dervish mass was still moving towards them.

'Well,' he said, 'it confounds all the optimists who insisted they'd come last night. Smith-Dorrien didn't want a night attack.'

'Smith-Dorrien,' Dabney pointed out, 'like my father, was one of the survivors of the massacre at Isandhlwana. Neither of them are keen on hand-to-hand fighting. They prefer to keep 'em at a distance.'

The zariba looked strong enough as they approached it. The previous night had been brilliant as the rain had stopped and the soldiers had been nervous, but there had been nothing but breeze and shadows and, in the distance, the ominous throbbing of drums and the moans of elephant tusk war-horns. They had been roused before daylight, grumbling after an uneasy sleep full of nervous muttering and peering into the darkness. There had been the usual hawking, spitting and lighting of pipes, as they had rubbed chilled bones and dressed by the light of the moon, throats raw from the perpetual wind and the everlasting sand. They were all now hoping the Dervishes would attack them. With the same hope of standing in defence, doubtless the Dervishes were hoping the British would attack *them*.

As the patrols moved back, the infantry were checking their rifles and the artillery were busy over their guns, the one thought in every man's mind 'Were they going to have to fight their way into Omdurman?' Dabney's father had been at the relief of Lucknow and Dabney had often heard him tell of the confusion of battling through the narrow streets.

The army, which had just begun to form up outside the zariba, ready for yet another move forward, were with-drawing again now behind the hedge of thorns. As the patrols rejoined the Lancers, Martin, the colonel, insisted on written reports. There was little to tell him save that the Dervishes were on the move and that if he stayed where he was he'd damn' soon know they were. But Martin was a fussy man, determined that his newly-raised regiment, which had never been in battle before, should somehow in this campaign collect its first battle honour to decorate its drum cloths. Dabney's father didn't trust him too much.

'A damn' sight too much tally-ho,' he had said quietly to his son.

As Dabney dismounted, the sergeant appeared.

'What about water, sir?'

A veteran charger champed its bit because of a bridle sore, and the farrier, a single horseshoe on his sleeve, moved round it, checking for cuts and bruises. Horses were good and bad. Some were trained, some not. Some were perfect, some were devils. One was a star-gazer, one a slug; another had a cold back, a devil for the first few minutes of every day and able to throw its rider whenever it chose. But a man's life depended on his mount and they had to be carefully watched.

'Let 'em drink,' Dabney said. 'But see they don't get too much.'

He glanced towards Kitchener, who was standing just in front, a tall man younger than many of his subordinate commanders. He had succeeded to the command of the Egyptian army to the dismay of rivals who had thought it might be theirs, but had since managed to win most of his enemies over with his competence. Sitting his horse nearby, watching over the heads of the infantryman, was Dabney's father, General Goff. He was trim, built more like a jockey than a soldier, slim, a perfect light horseman still despite his age and grey hair. Dabney smiled warmly as he watched him. The old man had not played with him much as a child, as the fathers of other boys played with them, and, leaving the business of the family to his wife, had not even seemed to notice him much. But he had managed nevertheless to gain the whole-hearted respect and admiration of his son in the same offhand way with which he had always held the respect of his soldiers – as if he didn't consider it necessary to try.

As he stared across the burning plain, his face moist under the brassy sun, Dabney could see the shimmering waves of heat, the faint outline of Omdurman and the yellow-brown bulge that was the Mahdi's tomb. It represented the reason why they were there. There had been a lot of talk of 'British interests' and 'making Egypt safe' but the real truth, he felt sure, was pure vengeance. His father had been with the force that had arrived just too late to save Gordon, who thirteen years before had been butchered with his garrison at Khartoum just across the river from where he now waited, and he suspected that in Kitchener, who had also been involved, there was an itch to put right that defeat.

The Mahdi was dead now but the troops facing them across the tawny desert were the same men who had followed him, the men who had stormed Khartoum, massacred Hicks' men at El Obeida and broken the square at Abu Klea, and he wondered if Kitchener's military skill measured up to his ambition. If it didn't, the whole lot of them would be lying dead on the sand before the day was out.

Kitchener was watching the plain, dour and arrogant – but obsequious, so Dabney had heard, to anyone who might advance his career. His beefy face was red from the heat of the sun, his pale eyes and opulent moustache making him look somehow more like a sergeant than a general. Churchill's description of him had already got around. 'He may be a general,' he had said, 'but he's never a gentleman.'

All the same – Dabney studied his Commander-in-Chief carefully – you had to admit the man's skill. Under his tuition, the despised Egyptians had become a force to be reckoned with and he had managed to transport his army across four hundred miles of desert to the threshold of the Khalifa's capital. His military railway and his movement up the Nile of his fleet of gunboats was a remarkable achievement by any standard.

Kitchener was talking to General Goff now, pointing towards the Dervish army. Among the men behind them was General Goff's orderly, Sergeant Ackroyd, dark and lugubrious like his father, Tyas Ackroyd, who had served General Goff as orderly, manservant and general factotum for years and now, at over sixty and limping a little from rheumatism, was running the Goff home as butler. The Ackroyds had gone to war with the Goffs for generations but Tyas Ackroyd had always been more than a mere servant; and his son, Ellis, the sergeant behind General Goff, was a great deal more educated than his father and, with a little help from the General, was making sure *his* sons were more educated even than he was.

Dabney shifted his feet in the hot sand. He'd be sorry to see the Ackroyds sever the connection they'd had with his family for so long. Originally they'd been labourers on the Home Farm at Braxby, and the general and old Tyas had fished and swum together in the Brack long before they'd departed together for the Crimea. Ellis would probably be the last to act as servant to anybody. They were far too independent–minded a family, something that was already showing in Ellis' son, Tom, who, at the tender age of eleven and itching to be apprenticed to an engineer, was already learning all about the new-fangled petrol engines.

The thought led him to think about home. His sister, Helen, had startled them all by marrying a German and seemed quite happy to be translated to a Continental background. Within months, his other sister, Jane, had married the son of the farmer next door and seemed equally happy to be translated from a military to an agricultural heritage. Robert – ? Robert, his elder brother, he decided, was a bit of an ass. He had wangled himself a job on Gatacre's staff and he was well-suited there because Gatacre was considered to be a bit of an ass, too.

Robert, Dabney decided, would suit his chief well. Robert loved the trappings of the army more than the army itself and Dabney often considered he wore uniform less for the fighting than for the ceremonial.

Perhaps being part of a military family was to blame, because in the last decade or two cavalry officers had tended to drape themselves in a self-conscious arrogance that came less from their skill than from their splendid uniforms, and Dabney had long had the feeling that the mess of the 19th Lancers, the Regiment, – *his* regiment – was far from being a repository of original thinking. Robert *was* an ass. He made his mind up with a young man's cheerful indifference to the right and wrong of it.

Aware of Churchill staring at him, he realised he'd been smiling to himself. Churchill was a funny customer, he thought, coming down to earth. But, ebullient, brash and far from popular though he was, there was still something about him and, though he criticised everybody, all too often he was right. Perhaps, Dabney thought, it was because he saw Churchill differently. Among the strings Churchill had pulled to get himself attached to the 21st was the one held by General Goff, who had known his father, so that with Dabney he managed to be more relaxed. And nobody could deny his experience because, despite his youth, he had seen action on the North-West Frontier and had got himself into Cuba to watch the rebellion there against the Spanish. In addition, his mother, like Dabney's, was an American, which had given them a lot in common, and he had been more than once to Braxby to pick the brains of General Goff for his literary efforts.

Dabney glanced at his father again. The contemporary of so many great men, it was odd to think he was still on active service. Evelyn Wood was no longer on the active list. Buller was confined to a War Office role. Even Wolseley – once England's 'only general' – was in eclipse these days and little heard of, Commander-in-Chief of the Army at last after years of intriguing.

The distant noise, the muted buzz that Dabney had heard from the Jebel Surgham – the sound of a swarm of bees in summer – came again, filtering across the plain, mingling with the beating of drums and the mournful wail of horns and changing gradually to a cacophony of human voices. A few officers were standing outside the zariba, looking like a group of racegoers awaiting the appearance of the field round Tattenham Corner. A man laughed. It was high-pitched and nervous, and a sergeant, equally strained, told him to be quiet. Then an officer galloped up to Dabney's father, saluted and smiled. 'They're coming on beautifully, sir! About two miles away now!'

The battle they had all been expecting seemed at last to be on them. Dabney glanced at his father again as he peered across the desert. He'd been roughly Dabney's age when he'd ridden with the Light Brigade at Balaclava. *That* had been a disaster in the making even before the trumpets had sounded.

As Dabney turned towards the front again, he saw a white speck appear on top of the ridge.

'There they are!'

What he was looking at took on the shape of a banner, then he saw another and another, until the whole ridge, a moment before stark and bare, seemed furred along its edge as hundreds of men and hundreds of flags began to line it. The whole ridge to the north was covered by teeming black dots. There was a strange unreality about the scene. The enemy host was marching forward, rank on rank, and it was possible to pick out from the roar of thousands of voices the ceaseless chant of the Mohammedan prayer – La illa Lah Muhammad rasul Allah.

Glancing behind him, Dabney could see the boats carrying supplies and ammunition deployed along the banks of the Nile with the barges that were to carry the wounded. Kitchener was staring across the sand, his head forward, his pale eyes and squint faintly menacing behind the bull's horns of his moustache.

By this time, among the mass of Dervishes, Dabney could see the emblems of the more famous Emirs – the bright green flag of Ali-Wad-Helu; the dark green of Osman-ed-Din; the sacred black banner of the Khalifa himself, heir to the great Mahdi, on its right a vast square of men under an array of white flags. Using his field glasses, he could even pick out the individual leaders themselves, in front of their troops. There were plum-skinned Arabs and yellow men with square bony faces and tightly-ringleted black hair, bent men, straight men, old men, young men, boys even, all advancing together in a cheering excited mob which nevertheless marched quickly and steadily and kept its formation, every single one of them with hatred in his heart and a desire to kill. The sight made his heart thump. These were the men who had killed Gordon and they were inspired by their old victories and embittered by their more recent defeats.

The Dervish left was beginning now to stretch out towards the Kerreri Hills, the centre moving directly towards Dabney, the right edging to the south. This southern wing, under its hundreds of white flags, decorated by texts from the Koran, was perfect in its formation.

There was a surprising clarity about the battlefield, every stone and grain of sand sharp in the light, each one with its sun-touched side and its little curve of shadow. But it was silent. No one seemed to speak. Not a gun fired. In the stillness a horse whinnied and a man cleared his throat noisily, nervously, as men did before a race.

'If we don't win this one,' someone said – and in the silence his voice was clear and frightening in the implication of his words – 'then God help us. It'll be Isandhlwana all over again.'

t w o

The battlefield remained silent. The guns had still not spoken. But the excitement was growing almost too much to bear as they watched the horde of black figures approaching, and there was a murmur and an excited surge forward.

'Stand still,' an officer snapped. 'Your turn'll come!'

As he spoke, about fifty yards short of the zariba two puffs of red sand lifted into the air as the Dervish artillery opened fire. Immediately, one of the field batteries began to bang away, followed at once by more explosions and a roar as the gun-boats anchored in the river behind joined in the barrage. The smell of cordite filled the air and great clouds of smoke appeared along the front of the British and Sudanese brigades as battery after battery opened on the Dervishes between the Jebel Surgham and the Kerreris, the sound of the cannonade echoing and re-echoing among the clefts and spires of the hills.

Though the aim of the British guns was excellent, the exploding shells seemed to send no more than a ripple through the vast horde in front. Then the whole Dervish army seemed to discharge their weapons in a vast feu-de-joie, and a huge section began to peel off from the main line of advance and head for the zariba. The British soldiers waited, front rank kneeling, rear rank standing – just as the Highlanders had received the Russian cavalry at Balaclava, General Goff remembered.

The Dervishes were still moving in good order, the whole division crossing the crest into the plain. The shells were striking them at a rate of twenty to the minute now, bursting in their faces so that the white banners began to topple in all directions and the mass began to crumble into groups under individual leaders. The tumult increased, the Maxims stuttering away, a field battery in action on a small rise, the gunners busy about their pieces, the officers standing on boxes of army biscuits to stare through their glasses at the effect their shells were having. The ragged line of men was still pushing forward, struggling ahead in the face of the pitiless fire, the banners swaying and tossing like waves in a stormy sea, the white-robed figures collapsing in dozens among the spurts of smoke from their own rifles and the larger puffs from the bursting shrapnel.

The infantry were firing steadily and stolidly, mercilessly, without hurry, taking pains to be accurate, empty cartridge cases forming heaps alongside each man. As the Dervishes drew nearer, they became fewer, but the rifles were growing hot now and were being exchanged hurriedly for those of the reserve companies, while the Highlanders were beginning to empty their water bottles into the jackets of the Maxims.

Crumbled by the shells, the Dervish horde hesitated, then came on again in a final despairing struggle. The angry sound of their voices was now a roar, blood-curdling in its volume and intensity. Though their fire was wild and mostly going high over the zariba, a few men were hit and reeled out of the line, and an officer's charger crumpled to its knees, blood pouring from its nose across the sprawling man's tunic and breeches. Then, at around five hundred yards, the forward march changed to a run. For a moment the Dervishes were obscured as the wind dropped and the smoke from the Egyptians' Martini-Henrys drifted across the front, so that it seemed they might just break into the line. Peering forward into the smoke, waiting for it to lift, General Goff saw it

15

disperse at last to reveal only a few men still struggling forward in a group round a banner, until finally they, too, were sent sprawling to the sand.

It seemed to be over and Kitchener, worried as always about the cost, was calling for a cease fire and complaining about the waste of ammunition. A few bullets still whistled into the zariba from a group of riflemen who had gone to ground behind a small ridge in front, but there was no real danger now. The guns had smashed the attack before it had even got going, and an army of almost twenty thousand had shattered itself against the disciplined fire. At least six thousand men lay in front, dead or wounded, sprawling and still, or trying painfully to crawl away. The cloud of white flags had all disappeared.

'There's more to come. We've only been approached so far by the wings of their army.'

The General turned as his chief of staff spoke. Lord Ellesmere, he remembered with a sudden strange switch in time, had been a mere boy with a shocking case of acne when he'd first met him. He had turned out, however, to be a handsome man and a splendid chief of staff with the traditional asset of all good chiefs of staff – a memory like an elephant. He was now noted as one of the cleverer men in the army and his promotion had not been acquired simply because his father was an earl.

'Where are they, Ned?' the General asked.

'I gather the main mass is still hidden behind the hills, sir, waiting its opportunity to see us off.'

'Who says?' the General growled.

'It came from the 21st Lancers. Churchill, I think. The Sirdar thinks he's talking nonsense.'

'I don't,' the General said. 'That young man has a strange habit of being right.'

But nothing seemed to come of the rumour and Kitchener began to study the city to the south. A few minutes later a galloper approached from where Gatacre was stalking up and down, a lanky shape like a stork with nerves. It was Robert, and the General eyed him warily. He had summed up his elder son long since. Robert's idea of living was to inherit wealth and live off it for the rest of his days, if possible adding to it by marrying into the Cosgro family.

Since the Cosgros had lain across the General's path throughout his life, brooding, difficult and stupid, it wasn't a thing he looked forward to.

'They come in bunches of a dozen,' he had often said, 'and there isn't much to choose between any of 'em.' Old Cosgro, the present Lord Cosgro's father, had been a bit like Kitchener, arrogant with his inferiors, obsequious with anyone who might help him up the ladder. Claude, the second baron, had served with the General in the 19th Lancers, and was as fat, lazy and stupid as all the Cosgros with that streak of malicious meanness in him that always made them dangerous. Aubrey, his younger brother, had been broken by the General in Zululand for cowardice. It didn't make for friendly relations.

'Hello, Robert,' the General said briskly, far from willing to be warm because the business had come into the open as they had camped at Atbara.

Nobody had been very happy at Atbara. The weather had broken and the wind had shifted and, on the river, sails had been lowered and the boats anchored as clouds of dust began to drive over the camp, making the night hideous and existence miserable. Then, as rain had begun to fall and they were all covered with a coating of mud, soaked and shivering as boats were dismasted and clothing and tents were whirled away, it was typical of Robert that he had picked the worst possible time to put forward his wish. His face rock-hard, the General had stared at him with contempt.

'You're a damn fool, boy!' he had snapped. 'Nobody but a fool would marry into *that* family. The girl's father's a fool, her mother's a fool, her brother's a fool, and until he did away with himself her uncle was a fool, too.'

Robert's manner now was one of sullen wariness as he confined himself carefully to delivering his instructions, a square young man, blunt-featured without the intelligence in his face that Dabney had.

'From General Gatacre, sir,' he said. 'The Sirdar wishes the cavalry to reconnoitre the Surgham Ridge and the ground between the zariba and Omdurman. He's worried the Dervishes will get into the city and dig themselves in. They're to prevent it.'

Calling Ellesmere forward, the General began to dictate his message, making it as clear as possible because he wasn't sure of the Lancers' experience. Experience had a habit of filtering down through the generations and the 21st were too new to the game and so far had not been blooded in battle. The officers were resentful of the motto the rest of the army had given them – Thou Shalt Not Kill – and were too anxious to win themselves a battle honour. In his concern, he was painstaking, remembering only too well how a badly-worded message had destroyed the Light Brigade, and very nearly himself, at Balaclava.

Robert was still alongside and, in an attempt to heal the breach between them, the general turned to him. 'Would you like to take it to the 21st?' he asked.

'Of course, sir.'

'Make it clear to them they're not to get themselves into trouble. They're not to become heavily engaged. They're only to reconnoitre the Surgham Ridge and the ground beyond.'

Robert was frowning, his mind on his own problems, and for a moment the General wondered if he were listening.

'You have that clear?'

'Of course, sir.'

The 21st were standing by their horses and, as the firing continued to die away, the General saw his son approach the colonel. There was a brief conversation and an outstretched arm, then he heard shouts and saw the regiment mount.

As they started to trot forward, patrols broke away, ready to gallop towards the high ground, while the regiment followed in a mass – a square block of men on small horses – in Christmas tree order, hung all over with water bottles, saddle bags, picketing gear and tins of bully beef, all jolting and jangling together, all the polish of peace gone, soldiers without glitter.

The firing had died away completely now and the army had relaxed. As the Lancers passed close to the General, they were in files, dusty-brown figures with flaps of cloth attached to their sun helmets so that they looked vaguely like Arabs. Two patrols had pushed ahead of them, moving among the dead and dying of the first attack and the limping riderless horses that galloped aimlessly about.

The crest of the ridge was unoccupied and southward towards Omdurman the plain was covered by a broad stream of fugitives, wounded and deserters flowing towards the city, blurred by the mirages the heat threw up so that some of them seemed to be staggering in mid-air or wading through pools of water. As the heliograph started to flash from the ridge to give the numbers, the main attack developing to the north came to a complete halt and the General and his staff trotted forward. The horsemen on the ridge resumed their advance, then, as a spattering of fire came to the ears of the men on the plain, they saw the Lancers' advance guard check their forward movement, turn and gallop back to the main body.

'What the devil are they up to?' The General's eyes narrowed. 'Don't say the damn fools are exceeding instructions.'

From where he sat his mount in the sand dunes, Dabney watched his brother near the Colonel. He was holding on to his horse, which was caught by the stir and movement and was curvetting briskly, and was gesturing towards the Dervishes. As orders came back, the patrols cantered ahead again and the regiment began to move forward after them. As they went, they passed Robert slowly riding back, his brows down, his face set and sullen.

'What's in it for us, Robert?' Dabney called.

'Action,' Robert called back. 'You're to go for the enemy.'

The first patrol was back within minutes to say the plain looked safe from the other side of the hill. A moment later the other patrol galloped back.

'There's a shallow khor about three-quarters of a mile to the south-west,' Dabney heard the officer say.

'Practicable?' The Colonel's head turned.

'Yes, sir. It's between us and the fugitives in the plain. There's a group of Dervishes drawn up in front.'

'How many?'

'About a thousand, sir. Hadendoas, I think.'

Martin smiled. 'I think four hundred horsemen ought to be able to deal with them,' he said.

As they cantered forward, Dabney peered ahead. 'I'd have said there were a lot more than a thousand,' he observed to Churchill. 'And more being pushed in all the time.'

As they left the ridge, the scattered parties of Dervishes melted away and only a simple straggling line of men in dark blue waited motionless a quarter of a mile to the left front. There seemed to be scarcely a hundred of them. The regiment had formed line of squadron columns now and continued to walk forward. The firing from the ridges had stopped and there was complete silence that seemed twice as intense after the recent tumult of battle.

Straining to see through his glasses, General Goff turned. Robert had just reappeared and was waiting by his father, brooding again over the argument they'd had at Atbara. Several times he'd tried to push it from his mind but always it kept coming back. He'd known all along what his father's view of his wish to marry a Cosgro would be, but he hadn't expected it to be quite so firm. When he'd mentioned it to his mother, she'd hummed and hahed and offered warnings but, though he'd known full well that she also hadn't approved, she'd not noticeably demurred.

His father had turned to Ellesmere.

'What's happening, Ned?' he demanded.

Ellesmere was talking to a handsome moustached officer of the Egyptian cavalry.

'Haig here says there are Fuzzy-Wuzzies in a khor out there, sir.'

'And what are the Lancers intending?'

'It's hard to tell, sir.' Ellesmere lifted his glasses. 'I think the Fuzzy-Wuzzies are there to check any further advance. They're drawn up in line in front of them egging them on.' Ellesmere paused and his voice rose. 'Sir, I think the Lancers are going to charge them!'

'By God, they'd better not!' Robert's thoughts were abruptly interrupted as his father swung round on him. 'Did you tell them, sir, that I wished them to exercise caution?'

Robert's face changed and the old man knew he'd forgotten in the irritation of the dispute between them. Directing a glare at his son, he turned to stare to his front.

'I can see a flag beyond them, Ned,' he said. 'No, dammit, two! Jesus Christ and all His pink angels, Haig's right! There *is* a ditch there and it's full of Fuzzy-Wuzzies. God damn it – ' the General's face was furious ' – it's the oldest trick in the repertoire!'

The men of the Lancers' leading squadron had begun to wheel slowly and, breaking into a trot, were crossing the Dervish front in column of troops. Yelling and howling, waving swords and banners, the Dervishes were a mere three hundred yards away now and the blue-clad men were dropping to their knees to fire a ragged volley. Horses and men fell. A riderless animal bolted across the plain, its tail up like a flag, and a man struggled from under his dead mount and began to stumble back the way he had come. Bullets cracked and whined about Dabney's head.

'Left wheel into line!'

As the trumpet sounded above the noise of musketry, the sixteen troops swung and locked at once, without orders, into a long line. There was no hesitation. They were all eager and it seemed that no one waited for the trumpeter who was still blowing as he found himself at the gallop. As they thundered forward, the firing increased and the bullets started up sand and gravel. Feeling it sting his cheeks, Dabney bowed his head to shield his face.

The dark-clad men were still firing in a cloud of light-blue smoke, but the pace was fast and the sound of rifles was drowned by the thunder of hooves on the hard sand, so that it seemed the horsemen would sweep over the line without effort. Dabney had ridden in dozens of point-to-points and this felt exactly the same, with the line of Dervishes in front apparently no more dangerous than the last fence. In a surge of exhilaration, he clapped spurs to his horse and, lifting his sword, pointed forward. Behind him, the line of lances lowered to the Engage.

Then someone near him shouted and he saw they had blundered into a trap. Across their front a dry watercourse had appeared beyond a slight lift in the ground where the plain had seemed smooth and level, and rising from it, coming up like the devil in the pantomimes he had seen as a boy, was a densely-packed mass of white-clad men giving tongue in a high-pitched yell.

Suddenly he remembered what his father had said of the fighting in Zululand – how a fold of the ground had sometimes held a whole impi of warriors. The Dervishes, it seemed, were no less cunning. They were twelve-deep and stretched from one end of the regiment's front almost to the other. There was no chance to check the charge as horsemen and flags appeared and warriors with spears sprang forward to form a cheval-de-frise.

It was Dabney's first time in action and the excitement of the moment carried him forward. Spurring his mount savagely to force from it the momentum to take him across the ditch and out at the other side before he could be stopped, he assumed that, like all infantry before cavalry, the Dervishes would break and run at the last moment.

As the luckless men who had acted as bait were flung backwards by the shoulders of the galloping horses on to the heads of their comrades in the ditch, he found himself in mid-air and looking down on the black faces below. The Lancers went into the ditch like the breaking of a huge wave, and as the riflemen were swept away, the cavalrymen struck the mass of waiting Dervishes with a tremendous crash. Horses were bowled over under the shock and for a whole half-minute no one was concerned with killing, only with escaping from the tangle of struggling men and animals. Terrified chargers kicked and fought their way free. Shaken men, sprawling in heaps, struggled to their feet, and several unseated riders even had time to remount as the impetus of the rest of the cavalry carried them forward. But their pace had been reduced suddenly to a walk and as they scrambled out of the watercourse on the other side, dragging with them a mass of yelling infuriated Dervishes, they left a score of struggling figures behind, and as the mob of men and animals crumbled and separated the killing began.

It broke all the rules of scientific combat. An officer, his helmet crooked, his sword stained, dust on his features, was going for one of the emirs, a tall man in a black-patched jellaba. Riding at a canter, he came to the Engage, his sword outstretched before him, horse and rider in eager anticipation. The Dervish came quickly towards him, swinging a curved sabre. The blades met, the Englishman's sword grinding on the Dervish's handguard, but, as it did so, a yellow-faced man with peppercorn hair rose alongside and, thrusting upwards with a long-bladed spear, took the Englishman under the ribs. The yell of pain faded to a sigh and the British officer rolled from the saddle, to be immediately pounced on by yelling, hacking warriors.

Men who had been flung aside, screaming, impaling themselves on each other's weapons, had now picked themselves up and, reaching for their weapons, began to hit back. A rifle exploded in Dabney's face, so close he felt the heat of the muzzle flash, and he heard a scream on his left and caught a glimpse of a man falling from the saddle. A heavy spear jabbed at him, tearing his sleeve but doing no other damage, then all round him he saw black-faced men in white, patched robes, swinging with huge curved swords at legs and arms and horses' bellies. A bay charger, thrust through with a huge broad-bladed spear, stopped dead half-out of the ditch, trembling, its eyes rolling, an agonised squeal coming from its open mouth, its bowels emptying as it stood legs astraddle, and immediately half a dozen Dervishes were dragging at the rider.

As he went down under a pile of white-robed figures, Dabney desperately discharged his revolver into the struggling mass, but the heavy bullets seemed to have no effect and, as the Dervishes separated, he saw what was left of the horseman in the bottom of the ditch, torn and covered with blood. As the Dervishes turned on Dabney, he dropped the empty pistol and began to fight with his sword. A spearman came at him and, slashing with all his strength, he saw the Arab drop the weapon and stare blankly at the stump of a wrist. Despite the din, there seemed to be no sound. He could see mouths open, yelling, revolvers and ancient muskets going off all round him, wounded horses screaming, and sword beating on sword, but, concentrating on getting clear, his mind would absorb nothing else.

As his horse headed for the opposite side of the ditch a small white donkey appeared in front of him. It was bowled over by the bigger animal but the horse pecked so that he was almost thrown. Immediately there was a yell of triumph but, his heart in his mouth, he managed to drag the animal's head up and scramble clear. Just to his right, several men had entered the ditch at a point where they were faced with a high bank of boulders they couldn't climb and they were wheeling their horses looking for other exits. One of the riders set his mount to scramble up the bank but it fell backwards on to him and both man and beast were immediately covered by yelling stabbing figures in white. An officer – he couldn't tell who it was – scrambled to his feet, the back of his tunic soaked in blood, and began to stumble towards a horse that stood quivering in the ditch, its reins hanging down, severed by a sword stroke. As he ran, a spear took him in the back and he, too, went down. Another officer turned to help but, as he dismounted, he was lost himself in the screaming horde and two troopers had to go to his help as his charger bolted.

As he finally fought free from the ditch, Dabney saw the regiment trying to form up some distance away. An officer, half-fainting with his wounds, was stumbling towards them and, as a group of Dervishes began to follow, a trooper with a clay pipe in his mouth drove across their front, knocking two of them over with his horse and swinging at the others with his lance so that the injured officer managed to reach safety. As Dabney pulled up his panting mount, he realised for the first time that his sword was bent like a question mark.

Other men were cantering up now, their horses blown, but Martin, the Colonel, his revolver and sword untouched, looked as fresh as he had at the moment of setting off.

'I killed a fucking emir!' An excited soldier, his lance bloodied, was yelling. 'I got the bugger straight in the throat!'

The men were rallying quickly to the uplifted swords, pushing through each other to their proper places. Dabney's sergeant, his face hideously slashed with sword strokes so that his nose and cheeks seemed to be flapping loose, was trying through the blood pouring into his mouth, to rally his troop. 'Rally, Number Two,' he was choking. 'Rally on me!'

The ditch seemed to be full of dead and wounded, with far more khaki-dun figures among them than shapes in white robes. Churchill came past with his troop, wild with excitement.

'We should charge back at once,' he shouted at Dabney. 'My people will follow me anywhere!'

The men behind him didn't seem so sure, and as the regiment, cut off by the Dervishes from the rest of the army, faced about and rallied for a second charge, the general battle was forgotten. Riderless horses galloped across the plain and khaki-clad men, their helmets carved through and blinded by wounds, rolled helplessly about, clinging to their saddles. Horses, streaming from tremendous gashes, limped and staggered with their riders, and there seemed to be blood everywhere.

As the Dervish line began to reform, shaking themselves into order ready for another attack, Martin, seeing the damage that had been done, settled for a dismounted action. Drawn up with three squadrons in line and the fourth in column, the Lancers wheeled to the right, galloped round the Dervishes' flank, dismounted and began to open fire with their carbines. Immediately changing front, the Dervishes began to advance, but they had been shaken by the charge and, instead of pressing their attack, they turned again, still in good order, and began to retreat towards the Jebel Surgham.

'Leaves us in possession of the field,' Churchill said.

'And thank God for that,' Dabney breathed.

As General Goff watched the fight disintegrate, Ellesmere came galloping up.

'The Lancers have caught it hot, sir,' he said.

Kitchener was livid. The Lancers had been so concerned with getting into action they had forgotten to warn of the existence of an army behind the Jebel Surgham and as this new horde poured down against the regiments now moving out of the zariba for the advance on Omdurman it was clear the mistake was going to cause difficulties.

'The stupid swabs haven't achieved a damn thing!' he snarled. 'They didn't do what we wanted and they brought no information. They haven't even stopped them attacking MacDonald. What the devil happened? Why did Martin charge?'

'God knows,' General Goff growled. 'They were under fire in column of troops so they ought to have suspected something.'

'Result?'

'It could have been worse. The two flank squadrons didn't suffer much but two troops in the centre were virtually wiped out.'

'Go on.' Kitchener was ominously quiet.

'Enemy casualties trivial. Ned Ellesmere reckons fourteen or fifteen at the most.'

'Good God!' Kitchener's beefy face was purple with fury. 'It's reports I want, not heroes.'

The General frowned. 'It's heroes you're going to get all the same,' he said. 'The great sporting public at home much prefer a cavalry charge to an infantry advance. Reads better in the papers.'

Kitchener's reply was abrupt. He was watching the new attack developing on his flank and his mind was occupied elsewhere. 'What do you know of this damned man, Martin?' he snapped. 'He's obviously no tactician?'

'He doesn't seem to be a very good disciplinarian either,' the General said dryly. 'I doubt if he's even a good stud groom. The Promotion Board doesn't seem to appreciate the responsibility that rests on them when they put duffers in command.'

'Who's his senior major? Is he any good? If he is, remove him! I'm damned if I'll have people running my army who're more concerned with regimental pride than with beating the Wogs. Send him home!'

As Kitchener swung away, the General turned to Ellesmere. 'Got the butcher's bill, Ned?'

'They think five officers and sixty-six men killed or wounded. One hundred and nineteen horses.'

'Out of less than four hundred?' The General frowned. 'What about my son?'

'He's safe, sir. I've seen him.'

'My family seems to have a penchant for coming unscathed through half-baked charges. They'd have done better if they'd made sure the Khalifa didn't escape. I expect he has, hasn't he?'

Ellesmere nodded. 'I gather he was seen riding towards the city.'

The General scowled. A pity he hadn't had with him a few of Beauty Stuart's young officers from Virginia, he thought. Or that madman, Custer; perhaps a few of the Prussian Uhlans who'd done so much damage to the French in 1870. Even his North Cape Horse in Zululand – Irregulars every one of them – had learned the essentials of cavalry fighting, which were not to get themselves killed for the benefit of the newspaper-reading public at home.

As the Lancers came cantering back, they looked tattered and exhausted, men who were lurching helplessly in the saddle held upright by their friends, the blood from their wounds drenching their clothes and streaming down their horses' flanks. For a minute or two of glory, their charge had been very expensive in lives.

Churchill appeared alongside him. 'What did you think of the Lancers' charge, sir?' he asked. 'It was exciting while it lasted.'

'Not for the men who didn't come out of it!'

Churchill's face grew sombre. 'No, sir. Grenfell's dead, by the way. It takes the joy out of the triumph.'

'There never was much joy in war, boy,' the General growled. 'As I'm sure your great ancestor, Marlborough, would have been the first to tell you. Disguise it how you like, it's a shoddy business which only a fool would play at. And only fools do.' He paused. 'Think on that,' he ended. 'It might help you in your career.'

three

Yorkshire was having an off day when Dabney reached home. The clouds were heavy over the hills and the Brack had a leaden look. But Brackdale still managed to look incredibly beautiful, the greenery of the trees mingling with the dry-stone walls that were faintly lavender in the pale light coming over the hills. After the desert it seemed full of colour.

As the trap clattered up to the gates of Braxby Manor, Dabney heaved a deep sigh. It had been his home throughout all his life and every journey away seemed like a sortie from a secure fortress so that he never failed to feel happiness and relief when he returned home.

'Country looks good,' he said.

The groom, an Ackroyd inevitably, clad in tweeds and flat cap, turned his head and grinned. 'That it do, Mr Dabney.'

'How's your Uncle Tyas?'

'Gettin' old, sir. Says his rheumatism plays up.'

Dabney leaned back. It was like rejoining the Regiment to find himself surrounded by Ackroyds again. The whole valley was full of them, sturdy figures all of them, the men stooped from following the plough or straight-backed from following one of the Goffs into the army. At least, thank God, they'd never had to go into the Regiment because of poverty, because this was a prosperous valley where farming was good and his family had always accepted responsibility for their workpeople.

The house came into view at last. As the wheels crunched
on the gravel of the drive, he saw his mother appear from the
stables. She was wearing a grey habit and she hurried
towards him, smiling. As he climbed out of the trap, Tyas
Ackroyd appeared in the doorway to take his bag. He was
wearing black with a striped apron and gloves, as if he'd
been giving a hand with the silver. His long lugubrious face
split into a grin.

'Hello, Tyas. How's the leg?'

'It's the bullet I got at Balaclava, Mr Dabney.'

They both laughed. The phrase was one young subalterns
sometimes used in the mess after a heavy night, and they
considered it funny because Ackroyd's limp really had come
from the bullet he'd got at Balaclava.

'Family, Tyas?'

'The wife's the same, Mr Dab. Gettin' older. Yorkshire
weather don't help. Jenny's married now. Hill farmer out
Ripon way. Ellis you know about, sir. Emmott's an engineer
on the railway.'

'Driving a train?'

'Lord, no, sir. Telling others 'ow to drive 'em. He's in
charge of the works at Doncaster. Ellis' boy, Tom, talks of
bein' an engineer, too. Only 'e fancies these new-fangled
motor cars.'

His mother touched Dabney's hand and glanced at
Ackroyd. 'Better bring some drinks in, Tyas,' she said.

They walked through the house, Dabney, as he always did,
breathing its air, his eyes searching for the familiar spots of
damp. His arm tightened round his mother's waist. She could
never realise just how good it felt, he thought. Omdurman
had been a horrible sight when they had swept into the city.
There had been a great paying-off of old scores following the
Khalifa's defeat, and the bodies of butchered men and
women had lain about the streets and narrow alleys.
The Mahdi's tomb had been damaged by the shelling and

Kitchener, in a rage of vengeance for Gordon, had had the Mahdi's corpse decapitated, and for a while, Dabney had heard, had even talked of having the skull mounted.

He stared about him, looking at the pictures of his ancestors. None of them was very much from the point of view of art, but they represented continuity and order. The Khalifa's capital had been nothing but disorder, his arsenal full of military material of all kinds and all periods, from battleaxes and javelins to Nordenfelt guns and Gatlings captured after the Hicks massacre. There were trophies from Abyssinia and the Congo, Gordon's telescope, the bell of Khartoum church and the Khalifa's carriage, made by Erler of Paris, with upholstery of flame red, yellow and puce. The march in had not been the most orderly because Kitchener had seemed to lose interest after his victory, and it had been Smith-Dorrien who had gained the honour of being first to reach the inner city, by taking his Sudanese down a side street and appearing ahead of the outraged Grenadier Guards who had confidently expected to be in the lead.

As they reached the library, he turned and took his mother in his arms. Coming from slow, easy-going Virginia, she had fitted surprisingly well into the harsher background of Yorkshire where, if the people were warm-hearted, they were also inclined to hide it under a laconic manner. Small, bright-eyed and petite, she had been a beauty in her day, and she was forthright, firm and devoid of humbug. Perhaps that was why his father was still active, he decided, when many of his contemporaries had died or passed into oblivion, spending their lives huddled in the leather armchairs at the Cavalry Club waiting for the end.

'It's good to be home, Mother. Has it been lonely with all your family away?'

'Of course. But Helen brought the children from Germany and Jane's always handy, of course. And my cousin, Micah Love, stayed. He's in London on business for his government.

He's a lawyer, you know. He was sorry to miss your father, because he's fond of him. Your father carried him off the field at Parks Bridge, of course, when he was wounded in the Civil War.'

Ackroyd entered with the decanters and began to pour drinks. When they were alone, Dabney stretched in a chair, his feet towards the fire.

'How is your father, Dab?'

'He'll be home soon. All British officers temporarily employed with the Egyptian army have been returned to England. He was the same as ever. Full of beans. He dined us out in London before we separated. He was bubbling over with energy. Don't know how he manages it. He always seems as sprightly as the youngest subaltern. He sent his love and said he'd be home in a day or two. What's been happening here? The one thing I always missed was knowing what was happening in Braxby.'

His mother shrugged. 'Lord Cosgro's dead.'

Dabney sat up. 'I saw it in *The Times*. Drank himself to death, did he?' He paused. 'You know what Father said? "Poor old Claude. For all his faults he was the best of the lot. I couldn't stand him." '

His mother smiled. After twenty-eight years of married life, she was no longer surprised by her husband's bluntness.

'That's an awful thing to say, Dab,' she said.

'They're an awful family, Mother. They're lazy, cowardly and mean, and I bet Father saw no reason to pretend to be upset. I know what he's thinking: "Thank God, there's one less of 'em." With Aubrey shooting himself in Paris on the way home from Zululand, it's thinned the ranks a bit, and perhaps that's no bad thing.' He looked at his mother. 'Do you think Father ever felt guilty about Aubrey?'

She paused, considering. 'No,' she said. 'He thought he was a coward and that if he'd left him in command he'd have deserted his men again. He'd done it twice before.'

33

'What about the third baron – Claude's son, Walter?'

'He went to live in Paris –'

'That's where Oscar Wilde went when they let him out of gaol. I expect they were together.'

'I always thought Wilde rather a sad man.'

Dabney shrugged. 'I think they all are, Mother, on the whole, and Walter never seemed happy when he went around with Wilde and Alfred Douglas.' He paused. 'Personally I thought Wilde quite poisonous, but also quite harmless, but Walter Cosgro's like the rest of his family. Douglas stood up for Wilde. Walter denied he ever even knew him.'

His mother smiled. 'I think that phase is over now, dear. He's back home. He's taken over the family firm and they say he's good at it.'

'All the Cosgros were good at screwing money out of other people,' Dabney said bluntly. 'And none of them had the slightest idea how to treat their employees. That's why they were such rotten officers. They'd just as soon sack an employee of fifty years standing as look at him. We've always felt responsibility strikes both ways – up *and* down. Look at the Ackroyds.'

Lady Goff smiled at her son. He was handsome in tweeds, young, healthy and full of life, but also full of a young man's arrogance.

'Let's not be too smug, dear,' she said quietly. 'They might all up and leave us tomorrow.'

'Don't you believe it, Mother. The Ackroyds wouldn't walk out on us like that.'

She nodded because she knew he was right. One of the things that had impressed her most when she had first met her husband's family was the correctness of their behaviour and the fact that they paid for belonging to a privileged group by accepting the responsibility that went with it. Nevertheless, she didn't believe in letting them get on to hobby horses, and she kissed her son quickly before he could start sounding off like a Hyde Park orator.

He knew the sign and changed step. 'Saw Robert just before I left London,' he said. 'He's still talking of marrying Elfrida Cosgro. The man's an ass!'

His mother smiled. 'Perhaps he gets it from me, dear. My family was never noted for cleverness. And Robert's a good boy, so don't run him down too much.'

Determined not to listen to what he thought of his brother's choice, she tried to hurry over the subject but he refused to budge.

'Father doesn't like it,' he said. 'If there's one family he doesn't wish to be allied to, it's the Cosgros.'

'There's nothing we can do about it, dear,' Lady Goff said placidly. 'Marriages aren't arranged by parents these days. After all, Helen married a German. A Prussian, too.'

'And wasn't that the surprise of the season?' It was Dabney's turn to smile because Karl-August von Hartmann, contrary to expectations, had proved to be a highly intelligent young man who was clearly going to go far. After Bismarck's wars nobody had had much of a liking for the Prussians, but Karl-August's father had known General Goff ever since the Civil War in America, and for a few days at the wedding, with all the German relations clicking their heels every time they were addressed, Braxby had looked like Potsdam. They had all brought their uniforms and the village had been treated to half the German army and diplomatic corps strutting about, until Graf von Hartmann had taken the more stiff-necked ones to one side and explained. 'British soldiers do not wear uniforms when they can possibly avoid it'.

Dabney's mind was still racing on. 'Would you mind, Mother, if I went over to see Fleur la Dell?'

His mother smiled. 'You fond of her, Dab?'

'Yes.'

'Your father would approve. He was always fond of her father. They were at school together. They rode in the Light Brigade together. He still gets a bit sentimental about him being killed in Zululand.'

'Do you approve?'

'Of course. Will you marry her?'

'Eventually. Pity Robert couldn't find someone like Fleur.'

'The whole family can't marry La Dells, dear. It would become rather boring. How *was* Robert?'

Dabney's face clouded over. 'Same,' he said. He paused. 'I don't think Robert enjoys active service, Mother.'

'Do *you*?'

'There's something about it that makes your blood race. But it has its horrors. The food, for example.' Dabney grinned at his mother, trying to brush aside her worries. 'I just don't think Robert fits. He'll be home soon, too. He met Elfrida in London.'

His mother said nothing and he went on.

'Father was going on about growing old. Says he's had enough of battle, murder and sudden death.'

'How did he bear up? Did the desert wear him out?'

'Less than some of the youngsters. Some of 'em were arriving on a Friday, hoping to fight a battle on Saturday and go home on a Sunday, perhaps with a couple of medals to show for it, and complaining when they didn't.' Dabney eyed his mother. There was a curious quiet excitement inside her, and he guessed something was in the wind.

'You encouraging Father to be off again?' he asked. He grinned and kissed her. 'I'll bet you've got a lover somewhere.'

She smiled. 'I've lived long enough with him to know what makes him happy. He'd die if they sent him home and told him to grow vegetables.'

Dabney admitted the truth of it. 'And now? What is it you've got up your sleeve?'

She smiled and produced a telegram. He stared at it suspiciously. 'What is it? Retirement?'

'You'd better read it.'

He was loath to open it, half-afraid. 'War Office?'

'Yes. Wolseley.'

He gazed at her for a second, then he opened the folded sheet. 'Good God,' he said.

'That's what your father will say, I'm sure.'

He looked up and grinned at her. She smiled back.

'He thought the Sudan would be the lot,' Dabney said. 'But they've made him Inspector of Cavalry. Full General. Well, it gives him a few more years before they put him out to grass. I expect he'll be going abroad, to stir 'em up in all the little outstations of Empire. Will you go with him?'

'I expect so.'

Dabney put his arms round his mother. 'You enjoy campaigning as much as he does, I swear.'

She didn't deny it. 'In India once,' she said, a faraway look in her eyes, 'when the Pathans got into the compound and burned everything they could lay their hands on, your father and I had only a single camp bed between us for several weeks.'

'Was it uncomfortable?'

'I don't know, dear. Your father was in the saddle all day and needed his rest. He had the bed. I slept on the ground.'

'Wonder where they'll send him?'

'Evelyn Wood said South Africa. He says it's South Africa where he'll be most needed.'

Dabney's eyes were gleaming suddenly and he gave his mother a mischievous grin. 'Wonder if he could do with a good aide-de-camp,' he said.

Two hours later, Dabney was waiting in the lane near the house where Fleur la Dell's family lived. Born after her father's death, Fleur was only a few months younger than

Dabney and he had long since decided he wanted her for his wife.

He'd met her first at a meet of the Braxby Hunt. While the adults drank cherry brandy and ate slabs of plum cake among the tremendous bustle of grooms and second horsemen and the cohorts of gleaming mounts, he had seen her at the other side of the crowd, sitting on a fat pony, a dark girl watching him intently. He had been riding a hard-looking dun with a hogged mane and as the fox had broken clear, it had run away with him. As the hounds had given tongue in a covert, with the whip holla-ing from the other side, everyone had bunched in the road, all pushing towards a gate leading to open country, and he had been expelled through it like a cork from a champagne bottle with shouts around him of 'Get out of the way, blast you!' With his horse getting its hocks under it and shooting forward, he had fought to gain control but had been unable to stop and, as the pasture lifted up in ridge and furrow to a blackthorn hedge, he had heard shouted warnings to hold back. By this time, however, he had given up trying, and the horse, which had stopped pulling and boring, had balanced itself and soared over the hedge so that he had been on the spot as the fox disappeared under a wave of tan and white. The Master, standing by his sweating horse, his moustache cock-eyed, his stock hanging loose, had called him over, complimented him on his courage and, rubbing the blood from the fox on his face, had handed him the brush.

Proud as the devil, he had hacked back the twelve miles home with a group of youngsters, among them the dark girl who had watched him so intently.

'They gave me the brush,' he had said.

'Yes, I know.'

'I'm Dabney Goff. Who're you?'

'Fleur la Dell.'

She had answered without shyness and, since she had to pass Braxby on the way to her own home, she had stopped, with several other children – most of them cousins – to eat. She had been the only one who had seemed to understand when he refused to wash his face, and he had never forgotten her, and had always made a point of seeing her, during school holidays, even after he had joined the Regiment, slipping over to her home when he was on leave. She was slim, lithe, intelligent, easy to talk to – and always eager to see him. He knew he was going to marry her, and had done since he was a boy. Sometimes, the rest of the family teased him, but it was like water off a duck's back because he knew the story as well as anyone of how his mother at the age of fifteen had told his father within two days of meeting him that *she* intended to marry *him*. Perhaps, he decided, it ran in the family.

He had had other girl friends, of course, friendships that involved kissing and fondling, but they had never been any more than a youth's exploration towards adulthood, because always in the background there was Fleur waiting for him as he waited for her. The conviction that they had been made for each other was a deep-rooted one. It was irrational and indefensible but he had never swerved from it and, though he told himself often he might lose her, all his life he had assumed that he *would* marry her, and he had often sat alone, half-dreaming, saying her name to himself over and over again – Fleur, Fleur, Fleur – while his brother Robert jeered and his sisters laughed.

He had never experienced with her the intolerable silences he had found with other girls and was never awed, shy, apologetic, afraid of being considered impudent, never held by indecision. The thing had been so natural all the time there had never been the slightest doubt.

Yet also there had never been any deep feeling of sex between them. Though he sometimes dreamed of seeing her as he would see her as a wife, slender, white and naked, he never thought for a minute of trying to force the issue. They had swum in the Brack together, but always with his or her brothers or sisters, they had watched birds and wandered the moors, they had ridden close to each other with the Braxby, Dabney never again wishing to be up at the front, always close by her in case of accidents, terrified that something might happen. He had cheered her successes at school and she his successes in point-to-points, and he invariably felt she was a good deal older and wiser than he.

She appeared unexpectedly from the shadows and reached up to kiss him gently.

'Hello, Dab,' she said quietly. 'I'm glad you're back. Was it terrible?'

He smiled. 'No, Fleur. It was all right. I think I'm cut out to be a soldier. I've certainly never wanted to be anything else.' He paused, lit a cigarette and offered it to her to puff. She did so inexpertly and handed it back.

'We've just heard Father's been appointed Inspector of Cavalry.'

She smiled. 'I expect he'll be good at it,' she said. 'Mother says my father was terrified of him.'

'He'll be going to South Africa. There's trouble brewing there.'

'What sort of trouble?'

'With the Boers.'

'War?'

'It's beginning to look like it.'

'But we've only just finished a war.'

'I suppose it's one of the costs of having an Empire as big as ours. They're always having wars in South Africa. Little ones – against the Kaffirs or the Zulus. Nothing much.'

'My father was killed fighting the Zulus,' she said quietly.

Realising his gaffe, he took her hand and held it tightly then leaned forward and kissed her cheek. It was cool. For a moment she stood still, then she turned and put her arms round him.

'I love you, Dabney,' she said.

'I love you, too, Fleur. And I want you to know it, because I'm going to see Evelyn Wood to try to get an attachment to the 5th Lancers. They're in Natal, and if I can, I might persuade my father to accept me as an aide.'

'Your father's never been a believer in influence.'

'No, but he's a great believer in staff experience. He's always sounding off about the fact that we haven't got a general staff like the Germans.'

She watched him quietly. 'If you get this attachment, Dab, will that mean you'll be involved if there's a war?'

'It wouldn't last long. The Boers are only farmers.'

'I'm afraid, Dab.'

He grinned at her and, holding her close, kissed her again. 'Then marry me, Fleur.'

'Of course!' She seemed surprised that he should bother to ask. 'But not immediately. Mother might not wish it yet.'

'We could elope.'

'No, Dab.' She pecked his cheek. 'Later. You know what they say: Lieutenants may not marry. Captains might. Colonels must.'

'I can't wait until I'm a colonel. Couldn't we get engaged? Couldn't I see your mother and ask her?'

'Let's just leave it as an understanding.'

Dabney sighed. 'Perhaps you're right,' he said. 'There's already enough trouble in the offing. Robert wants to marry Elfrida Cosgro.'

four

South Africa, Dabney realised, was bigger than people thought.

Beneath him, as he swayed and rocked from the motion of the train, the line ran in enormous loops between the rusty kopjes of the Great Karroo Desert. There was little to do but view the scenery and stare through the rain-spattered windows of the carriage at the scattered herds of springbok in the distance searching for the sparse new grass shooting up through the rocky soil.

Back in England, he decided, people had no idea of the size of this country that contributed so much with its gold and diamonds to their prosperity. They always thought in terms of Europe where the distance between towns and cities was short and always interspersed with villages. Here, the country went on forever, mile upon empty mile of stone and scrub where kopjes, huge pink mounds of crumbling rock, rose from the stark plain, and it required six hundred acres to feed one sheep, and a herd of springbok could make the difference between life and death to the flock of some hard-bitten farmer. In Natal the land was green and rolling and the railway line zigzagged up and down through the hills in curves that would have horrified a European engineer. Further north still, it became tropical and dangerous with fevers that struck down both man and beast.

In London, though, they had always felt the world ended at Ealing or Greenwich, at Hoxton or Camberwell, and that anywhere devoid of its murky gaslight simply was not alive. England was still aglow over Victoria's Golden Jubilee and patriotism had run wild at the homage paid by the crowned heads of Europe to the woman who had become the most venerated in the world. The belief that prosperity and wealth were all that mattered was beginning to grow uncertain, however, and there was even a feeling that it was becoming vulgar, and that the Prince of Wales, with his cards and his women, didn't help the image much. Out here, away from the buildings and the theatres, away from *Ta-ra-ra-boom-de-ay* and the swirl of Lottie Collins' red petticoats, things looked different.

The Afrikaners, he had noticed, seemed quite unimpressed by the jingoistic tub-thumping of British politicians. The only thing they seemed conscious of was that British settlers, the hated Outlanders, were trying to usurp power in the Transvaal. He had already become aware of the Boers' distrust for the British and their contempt for the British soldier. Colley's mismanagement of the 1881 campaign had added to their distaste for British interference a deep-seated scorn for the British army's marksmanship, which compared unfavourably with their own ability to shoot the eye out of a springbok without damaging the meat.

Dabney had still been a small child at the time of that campaign and, like every other British schoolboy, had grown up feeling the shame of Colley's defeat at Majuba Hill. He had been led to believe the British were invincible and the story of disaster at the hands of Boer farmers had been hard to accept.

He glanced across the carriage at his father who was sitting opposite, lean-faced, slim, surprisingly young-looking for his age. He was frowning. Looking up, he caught his son's eye on him and Dabney waited warily. He still wasn't sure whether the old man had wanted him as an aide. There were times even when he felt his father resented the trick he'd played, yet at others he had the feeling he was glad to have him, if only for someone to open his heart to, because his tour round the military bases of South Africa had made him few friends.

He had found most of the mounted regiments ineffective in the important tasks of reconnaissance – indeed, many of them seemed to have no idea what reconnaissance meant – and it was clear they considered the wastage of horses on such an unimportant task a disaster when they preferred to save them for the charge with levelled sabre or lance. Despite their objections to the carbine they carried, he had constantly insisted that they learned the duties of interception and had more than once tongue-lashed groups of sullen officers who clearly considered such menial tasks best left to black guides and scouts.

'You'll probably find,' he had snapped at them, 'that you'll never get a chance to charge them anyway. If it comes to war, the Boers' strategy will be to go in for raiding. And they'll be well armed. They always are, and we've heard they've acquired twenty thousand Mausers as well as Creusot guns.'

A cocksure subaltern had interrupted that surely the Boers couldn't be regarded as a serious military adversary and the General had glared.

'If you think that, my boy,' he had snapped, 'then you want your head examining because it seems to have escaped your notice that they defeated the Zulus and wiped the floor with us in 1881.'

How much had sunk in Dabney had no idea. He had a feeling that many people thought his father out of date. Wasn't his nickname Balaclava Bill? Wasn't the Boer military system a laughable confusion, anyway? Apart from the German-trained artillery and the police, weren't their armies merely burghers without uniform or drill? And didn't your Boer never use the bayonet and keep his pony handy so he could run away if things grew too hot?

It flowed off the General like water off a duck's back, and on one occasion, Dabney had seen a beefy red-faced officer who had dared to protest reduced to tears by the dressing down he received.

'There are fools, sir,' the General had snapped, 'damn' fools, and you!'

He had watched, blank-faced, as his father had gone on that, though a cavalry officer probably didn't take well to discipline, he was at least expected to be quick-witted enough to be able to understand what was demanded of him, and had heard him insisting to the 18th Hussars that troopers – *and* officers – should wear their caps with the chin straps under their chins.

'That's why they're called chin straps,' he had snapped. 'What damn good is a man riding at an enemy trying to hold his cap on with his sabre hand?'

To put his point about insisting on orders being carried out he had asked if the men all wore socks as they were supposed to, and, assured that they did, had ordered the colonel to dismount the nearest man and look. Dabney had seen the stare of puzzled disbelief as the man's feet had proved to be naked inside his boots.

'How did you guess, Father?' he had asked.

'Didn't guess.' The old man's smile had been sly. 'He used to be my batman and *I* could never make him wear 'em either.'

Dabney was itching to ask more questions but he had learned to remain silent and listen. An aide existed not to ask questions but to do as he was told, to run errands, and translate his chief's wishes into facts. But if he had any sense at all he could learn an enormous amount that would be useful to him because he was standing alongside experience and wisdom and, no matter what the quality of his general, could learn how to handle things and sort out the bad from the good for his future use.

His father was staring from the window of the carriage now, his eyes narrowed and thoughtful.

'What are you thinking of, Father?' Dabney asked.

The General stirred. 'Jameson,' he said.

Dabney said nothing, waiting. Doctor Jameson's ill-starred raid towards Johannesburg, the Transvaal capital, to seize power from the Boers, had first roused the bitter resentment that was now snowballing into a hatred that Dabney would not have believed possible when he had been in England. There, Jameson had seemed a hero. In South Africa his stature was considerably less, and the resentment the vociferous Outlanders had stirred up had reached a dangerous crescendo.

'That damned raid – ' his father spoke slowly ' – it didn't happen because of the lack of parliamentary representation the Outlanders complained of. It happened because there's gold in the Transvaal and they want to get their hands on it. There are too many businessmen out here itching to make money, and too many politicians who see a little personal glory on the horizon. Milner, the High Commissioner at the Cape, regards the Boer leaders only as humbugs. I rate them rather more highly.'

Dabney sat in silence, thankful that Lord Ellesmere, his father's chief of staff, was laid up in Cape Town with a stomach upset, and that his father had agreed to leave the Cape garrison to him and take only one aide to the meeting that had been called at Pietermaritzburg with Hely-Hutchinson, the Governor of Natal, and Sir George White, who had been sent out as commander-in-chief. He was aware he was getting a very useful insight into military thinking.

'Besides which,' the General said slowly, 'though the British army's been in action on and off for years and there are a lot of victories to crow about, nobody seems to have noticed they were all against untrained savages. Our manoeuvres are still worked out on exercises of a hundred years ago and that sort of thing's sheer folly against the Boers.'

As they descended from the train at De Aar a spider was waiting for them. It was driven by a Kaffir who took their bags and jolted and rocked them along rough cart tracks to a spread of farm buildings in a flat valley between low hills. There were no cattle in sight, but there was a compound full of splendid-looking horses in the shade of a group of eucalyptus trees. Commandant Burger, who had been the General's second-in-command with the North Cape Horse in Zululand, was an old man now and not afraid to offer warnings.

'Your soldiers will have to learn to do things differently, my friend,' he said as they sat on the step after lunch. 'They spend two months of the year training and the rest parading. They also think of Boers as untrained farmers, but every Boer is his own general and he knows the country like the back of his hand. They have no supply problems and unlike your soldiers they are not taught to fight and die. Because there aren't many of them, they have always fought to live and they know when to run away.'

The General nodded, not speaking.

'If war comes,' Burger continued, 'the North Cape Horse will muster as they mustered in 1879 and 1881. Since I shall not be with them this time, though, my son will lead them. Nevertheless –' the old man paused ' – tell your people that they consider your rooinek officers éffète and lacking in staying power. You and I remember one such, meneer.'

'We do indeed!'

The words burst out explosively and Dabney remembered that it had been Burger's horse that Aubrey Cosgro, who had shot himself in Paris, had stolen after the disaster at Tshethoslane.

'The Boers are not lacking in confidence either,' Burger went on. 'And you will have to send the biggest army in your history and maintain it at a terrible distance.'

'Don't underestimate us, Commandant,' the General said. 'If it comes to war – and God grant it won't – the whole British Empire will be behind us.'

The old Cape Boer looked over his spectacles, a shaggy figure with a beard that looked like the nest of a not very tidy bird. 'And don't underestimate the Boers, my dear friend,' he advised. 'It will take time for you to bring your troops from Canada and Australia and New Zealand, and the only problem for the Boers they would present is that it would take a few weeks longer to kill them all. You must remember the Cape is two thousand miles from Durban and the Boers could overrun Natal before you could even get them on to trains.'

The scenery in Natal was green and rolling, and widow birds with long black tail feathers like the crêpe on the hat of an undertaker's mute floated over the green slopes. The windows of the carriage were slashed with rain drops again and there were heavy grey clouds hanging on the hill tops. It seemed to reflect the general's mood. He wasn't looking forward to the conference that had been called.

Pietermaritzburg stood in a basin of smooth rolling downland broken by forests of fir and gum trees and seemed sleepy and dead-alive, and to Dabney surprisingly mellow for a town only sixty years old, its gardens mature, its trees large and stable, the Raadzaal fitting into the background of the wide square it dominated.

One of Sir George White's aides appeared as they watched the baggage unloaded and saluted smartly.

'I have a carriage waiting, sir.'

The drive through the rain-swept town was made almost clandestinely so that Dabney became aware of the efforts the

British army was making not to cause alarm. Surrounded by staff officers and aides, White rose as they entered. He was a tall thin man of much the same age as Dabney's father but he seemed far less active, with a gaunt frame and sunken eyes. When he had broken his leg some time before, he had assumed his active service was over and had been surprised to be sent out in the growing crisis in South Africa to command Natal. He looked old, nervous and doddery.

'Hello, George,' General Goff said briskly. 'How's the leg?'

'All right for everything except running away.' White ran his hand over his bald head and gestured at the men with him. 'You know Hely-Hutchinson, of course. This is Symons.'

General Symons had a curiously-shaped skull with an elongated jaw and soft cheeks. With his hair plastered down across his head and a looping moustache that didn't quite manage to curl up at the ends, he looked a little like a grocer. Colby half-expected him to wring his hands and ask 'What can I do for you, sir?'

Hely-Hutchinson led off with the comment that Milner was very uneasy.

'So he ought to be,' General Goff growled unforgivingly. 'He's done enough to stir up trouble.'

Hely-Hutchinson gave him a sour look. 'He finds it hard to believe that two small republics will take on the British Empire.'

'He obviously doesn't know the Boers,' the General said. 'I remember them for their independence, mobility and marksmanship.'

'*And* corruption,' Symons observed.

The General ignored the remark. He didn't seem to like Symons much, and Dabney remembered that, while Wolseley had been calling for ten thousand more men for South

Africa, Symons had been saying five thousand were more than enough to defend the whole of Natal.

White gestured towards the maps spread on the table. 'What's your view, Coll?'

General Goff stepped across to the map. 'I think they'll invade,' he said bluntly. 'What's more, they think they'll win.'

'They couldn't possibly,' Symons said.

'No,' the General agreed. 'I don't think they could. But by God, they'll probably give us the fright of our lives.'

'It's a worrying situation,' Hely-Hutchinson admitted. 'We can hardly retreat from the north-west corner of Natal and leave it to them.'

'It might save a lot of trouble,' the General pointed out.

'And leave the Colonists to the Boers?'

'They're not savages,' the General said coldly. 'They're a God-fearing people who believe in the sanctity of the family and, despite what the newspapers try to make us believe, they aren't given to atrocities. It wouldn't be for long. We should get it back.'

'We can't let go a part of the Empire.'

'It's big enough. We shouldn't miss it.'

'A retreat would disgust the loyalists in Natal.'

'The most belligerent of whom aren't Natalians at all,' the General snapped. 'They're Outlanders who've bolted from the trouble they've stirred up in Jo'burg.'

White hurried to change the subject, and one of Hely-Hutchinson's young men, a sprig of aristocracy with a high stiff collar and a tight suit despite the heat of the day, gave Dabney a sidelong look and winked.

'If they invade,' White was saying, 'they'll probably be able to muster about thirty-five thousand men. With the reinforcements that are arriving, we shall have about thirteen. Of course, there's an army corps expected by the end of the year.'

'Who's got it?' Hely-Hutchinson asked.

'Buller.'

'Well, he's all right. He's got a good reputation and he knows the Boers.'

'He's also sick of South Africa,' General Goff said sharply. 'He told Lansdowne, the Secretary for War, that if he were ordered to the Cape he'd come back as soon as he could.'

Hely-Hutchinson gave him a startled look. 'Buller?' he said. 'I don't believe it.'

'I do.' Dabney recognised the stubborn tone in his father's voice. 'I've known him a long time. Buller backs away from responsibility and he'll be handling more men than he's ever been called on to handle before.'

'Buller's one of our best men.' Hely-Hutchinson seemed to think he was having his leg pulled. 'And surely we can hold Natal until he arrives? Where are your people, George?'

'Two main groups,' White said. 'Eight thousand at Ladysmith and four thousand at Glencoe, guarding the branch line to the coalfields at Dundee. I'd like to hold the Biggarsberg Mountains but water's scarce up there and I feel we'd be exposed to flank attacks from the Orange Free State in the west and the Transvaal in the east – let alone head-on attacks from both. We'd be wide open to a giant pincer movement.'

'Not sure the Boers are that sophisticated,' General Goff observed. 'Nor are they fools, however. In 1881, our Regulars didn't know whether they were on their arse or their elbow.'

Symons gave him a sharp glance, vaguely contemptuous, as if he regarded him as a has-been. 'From Glencoe my four thousand can strike at any gathering of Boers – particularly with the support of the eight thousand in Ladysmith.'

There was a great deal more argument but the words of Symons and the political weight of Hely-Hutchinson swayed White and he finally agreed uneasily to allow Symons to make his stand in the northern corner of the province. As the meeting broke up, Dabney saw that his father's face was grim.

'Symons is an ass,' he growled. 'He has only two ideas in his head – his bloody duty and doing it like a gentleman. The Boers don't think that way. He'll make a mess of things. He looks like a ferret, anyway.'

Dabney kept his face straight with difficulty. His father's comments often sounded unthinking but the old man had a habit of being surprisingly shrewd.

Symons' troops seemed in good shape, however, and, with polo for the officers and drill for the men, he considered he'd got them fit for anything the Boers might try. Putting on a field day for General Goff, he smiled as the artillery galloped up, unlimbered and fired blanks and the infantry moved forward in four waves.

'A la Gravelotte,' General Goff growled. 'He must be mad.'

There were a few brighter men of the same opinion, and Rawlinson, of the Rifles, a tall balding young man, had no doubts about the danger of pushing north. 'I'd shorten the line, sir,' he said when asked his views. 'Hold the Tugela and withdraw from Ladysmith. The position has no flanks and the Boers will simply ride round it.'

Ian Hamilton, of the Gordons, sensitive, intelligent, and with a withered arm he'd collected at Majuba in 1881 to bear witness to his knowledge of the Boers, held the same view. 'There's still too much of the old contempt for them about,' he said. 'People are even inclined to be boastful, and that's bad.'

Because Baden-Powell, who was at Mafeking in Bechuanaland, had detachments of mounted infantry, they took the train to Durban, picked up a ship to East London, and headed back to De Aar and up north, following the Orange Free State and Transvaal borders. The sky was still full of heavy storm clouds that took the brightness out of the day, and the surface of the veldt was veined and puddled with water among the rocks. As the train clattered over an iron bridge, the river was in flood, a swirling brown torrent far different from the dusty ditch that had been there when they had last seen it. The earth was flushed with green now and stripes of daisies had appeared alongside the track.

'What the Boers have been waiting for,' the General observed, staring through the rain-spotted window. 'Grazing for their ponies.'

As the train followed the shimmering lines north, they could see groups of bearded men in slouch hats riding shaggy ponies in the direction of Johannesburg and Pretoria. They carried rifles and bandoleers, their saddlebags were bulging, and they had strips of biltong and bags of flour tied to the saddlebow.

'Boer commandos,' the general said shortly.

At Kimberley, they found the place under the command of a colonel of the North Lancashires-called Kekewich who was facing the prospect of having to handle Cecil Rhodes, the founder of Rhodesia and one of the most powerful men in Africa. Rhodes himself called on the General at his hotel and invited him to dine. He was a tall man with a high-pitched voice who seemed petulant and spoiled, and to Dabney, he seemed too used to running a country to wish to be ordered about by a mere colonel.

'I could raise you a whole army of mounted men if I wished,' he said sharply.

'Better, I trust, sir,' the General observed dryly, 'than Dr Jameson's raiders.'

It was while they were in Mafeking that they heard the Boers had presented an ultimatum to the British government.

'Points out that voting in the Transvaal's no business of anybody but the Transvaal,' Baden-Powell said. 'Demands arbitration on all points of difference, and insists we remove all reinforcements that have landed since the end of May and that those now on their way here should be turned back. Gives two days' notice.'

War was clearly only hours away as they caught the train south. It was not unexpected, and the Outlanders, who had been the cause of so much resentment in the Transvaal, had been fleeing for some time from the Boers' wrath. The train was crowded with men and women as the exodus became a panic. Every carriage was packed and open trucks had been hitched on the rear, tight-jammed with families heading for the Cape, expecting no comfort in the heat of the day and only bitter cold during the night. As they headed across the veldt the groups of mounted men moving east grew larger, and Dabney was in a state of acute apprehension because he was afraid the line would be cut before they reached safety. The idea of captivity for himself didn't even occur to him in his concern with the disgrace such an event might bring his father.

The General remained unperturbed and even settled himself to sleep. 'Nobody would miss *me*,' he said.

As they steamed into Kimberley, Kekewich met them with confirmation of the news of the ultimatum. 'The telegraph to Mafeking's gone dead already,' he said. 'There's been some incident with their armoured train and some of the track's been torn up. I never thought they'd do it.'

five

Back in Cape Town, they headed straight for the Mount Nelson Hotel where Lady Goff was staying. Lord Ellesmere met them, still looking unwell.

'The Government's rejected the ultimatum,' he announced.

'Thought they would.' The General frowned. 'There's only one advantage, Ned. It might just be the making of us. The Germans are becoming too much of a menace in Europe and I'd rather discover our failings here than outside Paris against *them*.'

Cape Town had been filling up for some time with wives and girl friends who were finding more excitement there than in a dozen London seasons, and the Mount Nelson was already so crowded with wealthy Outlanders who had refugeed from the Transvaal and the Orange Free State it had been dubbed The Helots' Rest.

General Goff loathed it and stared round hostilely. 'These buggers,' he observed, 'seem to think the blasted war's a circus got up for their special benefit.'

As Dabney had expected, his mother showed not the slightest inclination to bolt for home. She kissed her husband and son and announced her intention of helping the war effort just where she was.

'They'll need help with the wounded,' she said.

Almost at once there was news of Boer burghers heading for the front. It caused a certain amount of ribald merriment among the younger officers, because they were known to carry umbrellas and parasols against the sun, and their only military insignia was on their slouch hats which were adorned with the colours of their flags or miniature photographs of President Kruger.

The General's guess about them waiting until the weather broke had been right, however, because they were moving south in downpours which brought on the much-needed grass for their ponies. A police post was the first to fall to them and within a few days they were heading towards Dundee where Symons waited. Almost immediately news arrived that Symons had been killed and White was about to be besieged in Ladysmith.

As Dabney waited with his father on the quayside for the *Dunottar Castle,* which was bringing Redvers Buller and his staff from England, to dock, he noticed that the old man's face was grave and for the first time it occurred to him that his father didn't like war.

With the loom of Table Mountain behind him, shutting off the rest of Africa like a stone curtain, the General didn't seem to be looking forward to the meeting with Buller. The rest of Cape Town was wild with war fever, however, which wasn't in the slightest tempered by the latest news from Natal. The city was gay with flags and bunting, and Adderley Street and the route from the docks were lined with dense crowds.

Dabney knew Buller well. He had stayed more than once at Braxby and he looked stolid and robust with his round red Devonshire farmer's face and large stature. He seemed worried and uncertain and Dabney noticed that his big frame had been allowed to run to fat. Despite what was said about him, despite the confidence that everybody had in him, he didn't have the look of a commander-in-chief.

'Hello, Coll,' he said as he shook hands with the General. 'They told me there have been three battles and that Penn Symons is dead.'

'I'm afraid it's right.'

Buller looked gloomy. 'South Africa living up to its record as the grave of military reputations,' he said.

They drove in an open landau through the hysterical crowds, to see Milner at Government House. Buller shook hands gravely with all the officials lined up to meet him, faintly irritable at the fuss and impatient to get on with the job. Milner, his face pale, handed him the coded telegrams from Natal giving further details of the disasters. He seemed to be terrified of a rising among the Afrikaners of the Cape. He had always believed that the Boers could be frightened into accepting everything he asked of them and now that they hadn't he seemed afraid of losing the war. General Goff didn't feel much sympathy for him. It was Milner's war and he ought to be able to bear the consequences.

'It would be disastrous if the diamond mines were lost,' Milner said. 'Rhodes, too, because he's in Kimberley. We've just had another message from him. He says the place is on the verge of surrendering.'

'Rhodes may be a brilliant financier,' General Goff said, 'but as a soldier he's about as useful as a hysterical nanny.'

'We can't let the diamond fields go.'

'Are you suggesting then that we should let Ladysmith go?'

Milner hummed and hahed. 'We're in a tight spot,' he said bitterly. 'I think we'll have to break up the army corps.'

Buller listened quietly, his heavy face expressionless, but when Milner moved to other matters and turned to his advisers, he drew General Goff aside. 'Now, Coll,' he said. 'Let's hear some sense. What's happened?'

Standing with Ellesmere and the members of Buller's staff, holding a glass of Cape wine and a biscuit spread with pâté, Dabney tried to catch their words.

'White was flanked,' his father said.

Buller frowned. 'Ladysmith's no place to be invested in,' he said. 'It's in a saucer of land and the Boers can get their guns on to the hills. It's also damned hot and dusty.'

'It's none too healthy either. Even less so now, I imagine, with four thousand Boers and eighteen guns within striking distance. They came through every available pass. White told Symons to entrench but it seems he believed he could destroy them as they arrived. He was brought down at Talana Hill.' General Goff frowned. 'Everybody's saying we won the battle, of course, but the Boers did what they usually do and withdrew as soon as their casualties began to mount. I don't suppose *they* considered themselves defeated. Ian Hamilton did well and so did John French. The Lancers caught the Boers at Elandslaagte and knocked them about a bit, but Yule, who took over from Symons, had to retreat to Ladysmith. Then White lost the Irish and the Gloucesters at Nicholson's Nek.'

'Didn't they fight?'

Dabney saw his father's hand move in a gesture of disgust. 'Usual trouble, it seems,' he said. 'The man in command of the brigade just wasn't up to it.'

'What's the transport situation?'

As his father beckoned, Dabney moved nearer with Ellesmere and the others.

'A Director of Railways has been appointed,' General Goff pointed out. 'He's already laid the foundation of a railway administration for the movement of men, horses, mules and supplies. Our objective must be Pretoria.'

Buller frowned. 'The idea was to have a converging drive from Cape Town, East London and Port Elizabeth. We've got forty-nine thousand men when the army corps arrives. Including eight cavalry regiments – among them yours – eight mounted infantry companies and thirty-two infantry battalions. In London they feel we should use the lot together. It looks different from here. We can't let these sieges at Kimberley, Mafeking and Ladysmith succeed.' Buller gestured. 'I'd expected White to hold Natal for two or three months, but now it seems the whole colony will be overrun if we don't do something about it. I'm afraid I'm going to have to divide the troops. One half to defend Natal, the other to be pushed up in the west to relieve Kimberley. Methuen can look after that, Clery can look after the centre, and Gatacre after the Orange River front. Intelligence isn't much help.'

'It never was,' General Goff said bitterly. 'And I wouldn't trust the guides.'

'You'll also find there's a shortage of maps, sir,' Ellesmere said.

'It's something we've tried to rectify,' General Goff pointed out. 'The clarity of the atmosphere here doesn't make up for the lack of information about the lie of the land. We'll be fighting in the dark and that's a futile exercise. At Estcourt they have no maps at all.'

Buller seemed stolidly unmoved, his mind occupied with his problems.

'A Director of Military Intelligence was appointed in 1895,' he said doggedly.

'With a staff of eighteen officers,' General Goff snapped. 'The German Army has a comparable staff of a hundred and fifty.'

'How do you know?'

'You forget my daughter married into a German military family.'

'And that could be an embarrassment,' Buller said, 'if their half-witted Emperor drags us into a war.'

The General acknowledged the fact. 'On the other hand,' he said, 'on more than one occasion it's had its advantages. Great God and all His pink angels, we knew eight months ago we were likely to be at war before the year was out and we've been in this damned country since the beginning of the century!'

Buller, who had been at the War Office himself during the crucial years, tried to defend the system. 'Intelligence has no means of drawing maps,' he said. 'We tried to buy 'em but the man who was handling it died and nothing was done.'

'*Something* was,' General Goff snapppd. 'My son did it. He found maps in the public library and we had them copied and printed. He also found a thousand copies of a map of the Transvaal, which was being produced here for the Transvaal government. We impounded them as contraband of war.'

The following week saw the arrival from Ladysmith of French, the cavalry leader, who had been released with his chief of staff, Haig, to lead the cavalry from the south.

'Last train out.' French was so busy talking he didn't notice Dabney place a glass at his elbow. 'We were hit by a volley near Pieter's Station and when we stopped we were all expecting to be greeted by the Boers. In fact we'd reached one of our outposts and we found a 3-inch shell had gone through the second truck. Good job it didn't hit a wheel or we'd be on our way to Pretoria now.'

French was a short man whom Dabney knew well because he'd commanded the 19th Lancers' sister regiment, the 19th Hussars, and had often been seen at the depot at Ripon. Short-legged and burly to the point of appearing to have no neck, he was a fluent and persuasive talker, but from things his father had let drop Dabney knew he was not regarded as an intellectual genius. He was also supposed to have a liking for women, which was why he was said to be sometimes short of money and, though his reputation as a cavalryman was good, he was rumoured to be weak-willed and petulant when he couldn't have his own way. His chief of staff, the quiet, educated Haig, his looks those of a matinee idol, watched his chief placidly. Dabney had heard that French had borrowed money from him.

They brought information about Ladysmith which was of help, but sounded pessimistic all the same. White, it seemed, was behaving with a curious mixture of rashness and vacillation.

'They're keeping the horses to mount counter attacks,' Haig said. 'But it seems to me if the siege lasts long enough they'll end up eating them.'

By this time, Ladysmith was heavily invested and it was clear that a strong force would have to be sent to relieve it. At Mafeking and Kimberley the Boers appeared quite content to sit and wait and in that area there seemed no great hurry. Then, in November, came news of the destruction of an armoured train from Estcourt and the capture of two officers and fifty-three other ranks, together with the war correspondent of the *Morning Post*, Winston Churchill.

'Well,' General Goff said dryly, 'he always wanted to be noticed.'

Table Bay was full of ships now as the army corps began to arrive. After weeks of playing 'House' and drinking 'Bombay fizzers' – mugs of effervescent sarsaparilla brewed in buckets – and beer in such quantities an enemy could have followed the route to the Cape by the floating bottles, they poured down the gangplanks to be stuffed at once into trains and despatched to the fronts.

'War,' Ellesmere smiled, 'is about to begin in earnest. The 19th Lancers are due any time.'

But when the *Carlisle Castle*, carrying the regiment, arrived alongside in the middle of November, it was found, when the baggage had to be landed, that it was so mixed up in the holds it would take hours to sort it out. Sent down to meet them, Dabney found his brother snarling at a group of bewildered Kaffirs.

'It's the damned crew's fault,' Robert fumed. 'They shoved everything aboard in the wrong order.'

The dispute as to whose fault it was grew hotter, with a furious duel developing between the Colonel, Morby-Smith, and Ellesmere.

'The things we wanted first were shipped first,' Robert snapped as the other two stamped off. 'Now they're at the bottom.'

'Packed your pyjamas at the bottom of the bag instead of the top, eh?' Dabney said cheerfully.

'You can hardly blame the army,' Robert snorted. 'We're not baggage porters.'

'Perhaps we ought to learn to be,' Dabney said mildly. 'We might find it useful.'

They were still trying to sort it out when General Goff appeared. The explanations were hasty and embarrassed and his reaction was exactly the same as his younger son's. 'It seems to me,' he snapped, 'that it might be a good idea to send one or two officers to the docks in future to see how things are done.'

The furious rummaging in the ship's holds had brought the disembarkation to a standstill. The trains to take the troops to Naauwpoort were waiting and whistling incessantly, and in the end a regiment of infantry was put aboard instead, grinning all over their faces and jeering and catcalling the cavalry, while the 19th were ordered to march to Sea Point where a tented camp had been set up for them.

Feeling he must visit his old regiment, General Goff put on his uniform with all his medals to review them.

'And just see you're pleasant to Robert,' his wife insisted. 'He's your son and he's married now to Elfrida, so you've got to accept it.'

In fact, Elfrida had surprised them all with her common sense but the General hadn't yet completely forgiven her for being a Cosgro.

'You can't go on fighting your silly Zulu War for ever,' Lady Goff pointed out.

'It wasn't so damn silly from where I was standing,' the General growled.

'You know very well what I mean. And Elfrida isn't the offspring of your wretched Aubrey Cosgro. She's Claude's child. And she's Robert's wife now and we've got to give them the chance to be happy.'

Morby-Smith was still angry at the confusion over the regiment's baggage and the General was in no mood to be forgiving.

'Not exactly the most brilliant disembarkation in the world,' he observed.

However, the men had a sleek lean look and, eager to see them, he shook his head as Morby-Smith indicated the waiting officers.

'Men first,' he said.

The Regiment was drawn up on foot waiting for his inspection, and he moved along the lines, remembering faces and old actions.

'Trumpet-Major Sparks,' he said, as a resplendent individual with four upside-down stripes under crossed trumpets snapped to attention. 'You made it to the top, I see.'

'Yes, sir,' Sparks agreed. 'Twenty-five years to the day.'

'I remember you joining. You had a black eye.'

Sparks grinned. His uncle had sounded the orders for the General's squadron at Balaclava.

The officers were waiting in the mess tent and Dabney noticed there was a younger Morby-Smith, too, now, the Colonel's son. Robert's potato face flushed as he faced his father. Somehow, he'd missed both his father's and his mother's good looks, but he had a strong body and uniform became him, and there was a staid look about him now.

The General paused. 'Looking forward to the war, Robert?' he asked.

'Yes, sir.'

To Dabney, standing alongside, the words didn't have the eagerness his father seemed to be expecting and he saw the old man give his brother a sharp glance. Robert seemed to realise he hadn't come up to scratch and tried to make up for it with a show of enthusiasm.

'We'll give the Boers pepper, sir, you mark my words.'

'And you mark mine, my lad,' the General said. 'Don't underestimate Brother Boer. One or two people are tending to. Just remember he's crafty. Make sure he doesn't lure you into a trap and give you a bloody nose. I can speak frankly because I'll be going home. The army won't want an elderly inspector general on its back.'

As it happened, it didn't work out like that.

With Buller's army corps broken up and sent to different parts of the country, it began to be clear that the serious fighting was not very far away.

'Supply and transport are now running freely here, Coll,' Buller said, as he stood with General Goff in Cape Town station alongside the train that was to carry him north. 'I think I can now take over the armies in the field with safety. I shall head for the Tugela for the relief of Ladysmith.'

Standing behind his father with Ellesmere, Dabney watched Buller climb aboard. What Buller was being forced by circumstances to do seemed to him, despite his youth, to be entirely wrong. The war could never be run effectively from the banks of the Tugela River.

Buller's head reappeared through the window. 'I shall want the cavalry to go into action at once, Coll,' he said. 'The Boers are mobile and we shall have to be, too. I was hoping the cavalry in Ladysmith could be sent to Colenso to operate on the Boer flanks and rear but John French ought to be energetic enough to foil any attempts to advance into Cape Colony. The one thing we need, Coll, is horsemen. We don't keep up enough of this arm in peacetime. Perhaps we could consider mounting more of the infantry. We have plenty of horses.'

'They aren't yet acclimatised,' General Goff pointed out. 'They left England in their winter coats and they're arriving here green as grass in the heat of the South African summer after being at sea in pretty rough conditions. Now they're being pushed before they're ready into crowded wagons and sent to the front where they'll be overloaded and over-marched. It takes a pretty tough horse to stand that kind of treatment. They should be kept in depots for at least a month.'

Buller frowned. 'We can't wait that long, Coll. Wars cost money.'

The Cape was looking forward to victories, and the army did its best to provide them.

Lord Methuen, in command in the west, worried as he clung to the railway line that ran north along the border of the Orange Free State by the shrill cries of help from Cecil Rhodes in Kimberley, clashed with the Boers at Belmont where he drove them from their position. Striking again at Graspan, he seemed to be advancing with reasonable success, though he appeared to be inflicting more casualties on his own force than upon the mobile Boers who held their position on the hills until the British had reached the foot then bolted down the other side. Then, at the end of the month, he walked into a trap on the Modder River and his men were obliged to lie in the blazing heat of the sun all day, unable to move. Despite their casualties, they were nevertheless ready to resume the fight the following morning, only to find the Boers, following their usual methods, had withdrawn. It was another pyrrhic victory.

By December, however, French was beginning to worry the Boers with his cavalry and the last units of the army corps were being disembarked. Though the hopes of victory by Christmas had long since faded, there seemed nothing to worry about when, as Dabney sat with his father at breakfast, Ellesmere appeared with the newspaper.

'Seen this, sir?'

His face was enough to make the General snatch the paper from his hand. Dabney caught a glimpse of the headlines – 'SERIOUS REVERSE TO GATACRE'S FORCE.'

General Goff looked up. 'What's that idiot been up to now?' he said.

'I took the trouble to find out, sir,' Ellesmere said. 'GOC, Cape Town, received a letter from him saying he'd been misled by guides and found the ground impracticable.'

'That's not enough to create a serious reverse.'

'I've made further enquiries, sir. It seemed he believed he could launch a vigorous attack after a long march through difficult country with troops just arrived from England.'

'Sounds exactly like Gatacre,' the General growled. 'Go on, Ned.'

'Circumstances appear to have been against him, sir. He had about three thousand men, together with a few engineers, artillery and local volunteers. He was trying to throw the Boers out of Stormberg and over-estimated the ability of the new troops. He decided on a night march –'

'Damned hazardous with new troops.'

'Yes, sir. He entrained them at Molteno – in open trucks.'

'In South African sunshine, for God's sake?'

'Indeed, sir. It seems also that neither he nor his staff took the precaution of reconnoitring the roads he intended to follow and he trusted local guides who lost their way. The men were exhausted by the extra distance and were actually in columns of four when they came within range.'

'Good God, will we never learn?'

'Three companies got up the steepest part of the Boer positions but they were too exhausted to be of any use. Those who retired were accidentally shelled by our own artillery. General Gatacre and most of his force were back at Molteno by midday the next day.'

'Casualties?'

'Twenty-five killed, one hundred and ten wounded, six hundred prisoners – mostly caught while they were fast asleep from exhaustion.'

There was a great deal of indignation and anger at Cape Town Castle and they were still wondering what to do about Gatacre when Ellesmere brought news of another defeat. There had been a big battle on the Modder River at Magersfontein where there had been heavy losses, chiefly in the Highland Brigade. It had followed the usual pattern, with the Boers holding the hills, but this time, instead of building their trenches on the heights, they had built them at the foot. With the ground rough and a steady downpour changing the veldt into mud, Methuen, it seemed, remembering previous disasters to night marches, had had his men march in quarter columns so they didn't lose touch with each other among the boulders and clumps of mimosa, and the Scots, caught in the act of changing from one formation to another, had been decimated.

There seemed no light in the gloom, save for a report from Lourenço Marques that Winston Churchill had managed to escape from his gaolers and had made his way to Portuguese East Africa.

'Thank God there's someone who seems to know what he's doing,' Dabney observed.

Another blow came almost immediately. Buller had been defeated at Colenso in an attempt to cross the Tugela and this time the casualty list was even higher and included the son of Lord Roberts, one of the country's most distinguished soldiers. Buller had decided on yet another of the suicidal frontal attacks which had been so successful in the native wars earlier in the century and, thanks to the inexperience and over-enthusiasm of the officers under him, had got the Irish Brigade trapped in a bend in the river and had lost a whole battery of guns. Unnerved, despite the fact that a little moral courage might have changed defeat into victory and relief for Ladysmith, he had quailed before the prospect of more casualties and called off the action.

'Come on, Ned,' General Goff snapped at Ellesmere who had brought the news. 'I can tell by your face that there's more.'

'I fear there is, sir. Hildyard might have rescued the guns after nightfall but Buller refused to allow it, and Lyttelton, who was ordered to support the Irish, was sent too late. Tom Baring, of his staff, has arrived in Cape Town and he says one of the most astonishing features of the battle was that the Boers were so well hidden neither he nor Lyttelton saw a single one of them all day until it was all over. It's a new kind of war, he said. They're using smokeless ammunition and it makes it a fight against an army of ghosts.'

The defeats of Black Week were causing great delight in Europe, and anti-British feeling seemed to be running high everywhere.

'Plain jealousy,' Dabney growled. 'Everybody wants to see the greatest empire in the world humbled.'

Worse followed. Forestier-Walker who was in command at the Cape, had called a conference and as General Goff arrived with his staff, he immediately laid down a sheet of paper.

'I think Buller's gone off his head,' he growled. 'He sent a message to White in Ladysmith suggesting he should make terms with the Boers.'

General Goff snatched at the message, read it and passed it to Ellesmere. Buller's defeatism seemed to have run riot and he seemed to be wanting to besiege Colenso instead of pushing on to Ladysmith.

'Is the man well?' Forestier-Walker asked. 'The army'll be the laughing stock of the whole of Europe. White was so bewildered he heliographed back that he thought the Boers were trying to mislead him. He finally told Buller he mustn't think of giving up. It's the first time I've ever heard of a commander-in-chief being reproved by one of his generals.'

Two days later the news came that Buller had been superseded as commander-in-chief by Lord Roberts and there were a few lighter hearts in Cape Town.

There was no question but that the Boers' tails were up. They were convinced that the war of 1881 was repeating itself. Then, after two insignificant defeats, Gladstone's government had thrown in its hand and given them the Transvaal. This time, however, the government was in a different mood and, with the appointment of Roberts, the decision had clearly been taken to go on fighting.

'He's got Herbert Kitchener as his chief of staff,' Forestier-Walker said. 'They'll make a good team.'

'They'd be better,' General Goff observed, 'if Kitchener were married and Roberts hadn't got the rudest wife in the army.'

The news that escaped from Ladysmith by Christmas indicated that dysentery and enteric fever were increasing and early in the new year with the first days of the new century, the Boers made a determined effort to break through the defences and very nearly succeeded. The rest of the front remained quiet, except for the Colesberg area where French's cavalry was active.

'At this moment,' Ellesmere said, 'French's the nearest thing to a successful general we've got.'

By the time Roberts arrived in Cape Town, General Goff, his job in South Africa finished, was packed and ready to leave for England. Dabney faced his father uncertainly, because he had no wish to go with him.

The General, who was stuffing a case with papers, looked round at his son with a knowing glance. 'I know what you're after, my boy,' he said. 'You want to go back to the Regiment.'

Dabney grinned. 'Yes, sir. I do.'

'Well, I haven't got an active command and I'm due for retirement so I can hardly blame you.'

'Sir –' Dabney hesitated, unsure how to put his case '– I wangled this job –'

'I know damn well you did! And your mother did a little wangling, too, on your behalf.'

Dabney smiled. 'It was never my intention to use it as a cushy billet, though, sir. I wanted to learn.'

'And did you?'

'Yes, sir. A lot. And I'm grateful. But, I have no wish to avoid the fighting. I think I ought to go back to more active duty.'

The General nodded. 'I quite understand. Wait till Bobs arrives, though. He'll want to know what's going on and both Ellesmere and myself have learned to rely on you. I'll let you go as soon as Bobs lets me go.'

Lord Roberts had other plans, however. A small party was thrown for him by Forestier-Walker at the Castle and all three staffs were present.

Roberts shook General Goff's hand and drew him quietly to one side, a small neat square figure with white hair and a white goatee beard, still wearing on his sleeve a black band in memory of his dead son. His impassive face was made striking by expressive eyes which twinkled despite his loss and the seriousness of what lay ahead.

'Hello, Coll,' he said. 'You know Kitchener, of course.'

Standing behind Roberts with an aide, big, solid, heavy-moustached and with cold blue eyes, Kitchener nodded briskly, not an atom of friendliness in his expression.

'I thought I'd better await your arrival,' General Goff said. 'I was just preparing to go home.'

'Not yet, Coll,' Roberts said. 'There's too much to do. White's got to go. Methuen, too. Probably even Buller. I might need you here.'

General Goff gestured. 'You always said a general should be under fifty if possible. I'm older than that.'

'I'm sixty-seven,' Roberts snapped. 'And I need you.'

General Goff's eyebrows rose but he said nothing.

Roberts drew a deep breath. 'White ruined everything by pushing forward and it's clear now we shall need more than just the Regular Army plus the reservists. The Fifth Division's already here and the Sixth and Seventh are on the way, and as you know we're already raising volunteer companies. Militia units are also to be asked to volunteer for service. I think Britain's alive at last to the fact that we can't fight a mounted enemy with infantry. We have to match mobility with mobility. At the moment we seem unable to move away from the railway line. What's your view, Coll?'

General Goff frowned. 'The same exactly,' he said. 'We need cavalry – but the sort of cavalry who're prepared to dismount to fight if necessary.'

'Go on, Coll.'

'So far, it seems to me that quite small parties of mounted Boers are holding off whole brigades of horsemen because they haven't been taught to fight except from the saddle. It's been my task while I've been out here to insist that commanding officers should learn interception but, of course, they're hampered all the time by that half-baked carbine they carry, which is about as useful against a Mauser as a popgun.'

'We can change that. You think that's what we need?'

'I do, sir. But you'll not retrain the cavalry in a hurry. There are too many thick-headed commanding officers.'

'We could unstick a few.'

'You've also got to get rid of the idea they have that fox-hunting and polo are all the training that are necessary.

We're not only the worst horsemasters in South Africa, we're also the worst scouts.'

Roberts was listening carefully and the General went on quickly. 'We've got to get rid of the glitter. We spend more time cleaning up than we do training and, what with burnished mess tins, scabbards and metal mountings, when the sun catches them on the march it's like a brass band arriving. They can be seen miles away.'

Roberts frowned. 'This is a big country, Coll,' he pointed out. 'I need horsemen.'

'Then ask for volunteers from the infantry and teach 'em to ride. You've got to do that before you can risk 'em against the Boers.'

Roberts smiled. He looked hard at General Goff, his eyes twinkling again, the serious expression on his face fading. 'I think, Coll,' he said, 'that you're going to be very busy.'

When Dabney arrived at the Mount Nelson Hotel, his mother was reading a letter from Robert, who was now with General Crawford's column near Donotsfontein.

Dabney grinned at her. 'You'd better start unpacking, Mother,' he said.

'Whatever for?' Lady Goff's violet eyes widened.

'Father's in the war. Roberts wants him to organise his horsemen. He's tickled pink.'

'What about you?'

'I'm to rejoin the Regiment at Donotsfontein.'

Lady Goff looked at her younger son, her eyes troubled. She had already seen too much of war in her life, and Dabney looked so young.

Within a week, in a burst of ferocious energy that left his staff gasping, General Goff's scheme to form mounted schools was on paper. Horses were pouring into the country in enormous numbers and, setting up a camp on grazing ground along the Cape Flats, he assembled them in depots to become acclimatised before shipping them up country.

The mules came in shiploads from America, Spain and Italy and the horses from Britain, South Africa, the United States, Hungary, Canada and Australia. As the depots grew, necessities such as forges, shoes, head ropes, head stalls, fodder and veterinary services were gathered, rough-riding schools were organised and willing infantrymen, already trained as soldiers, were being pushed through the scheme in numbers by the end of fourteen days.

'They'll still not be cavalrymen,' the general pointed out grimly, 'but they'll be able to sit a horse without falling off. And though they'll never be expert horsemasters, with a few good sergeants they'll get by.'

He found a major of the 5th Lancers who'd been wounded at Elandslaagte and contacted Morby-Smith at Donotsfontein to obtain Trumpet-Major Sparks, who was close to retirement age, and, together with Ellis Ackroyd and one or two of the older men he knew, the bewildered infantrymen were chivvied at once with the age-old clichés.

'Sit *in* the saddle, you silly man, not *on* it! And get your legs *round* your mount, don't just dangle the buggers down its side! Now trot and sit straight! Grip with your knees! Head up! Heels down! AND SIT STILL! You're darting about like a fart in a bottle!'

Some of the newcomers didn't take too happily to the rough-riders' ministrations, but at least they were learning to get about the country fast, to dismount and use their rifles, and to hobble their horses and sleep alongside them with an arm through the reins. Firmly believing that the elementary bull's-eye course, considered adequate by the army, was useless, General Goff also introduced such innovations as head and shoulder targets which moved and disappeared, and though a lot of ammunition vanished into the hills a lot more targets were being hit.

Then, with the men learning to fight dismounted, he set about dispensing with some of the things ordinary cavalry carried about their persons, so that they could ride light and move faster for longer distances. His plans were firm. Carbines were exchanged for rifles and horse furniture was revolutionised. Regimental bits were discarded and plain hunting bits substituted. White head ropes and picketing pegs were done away with and replaced by knee-haltering gear. The panelled colonial saddle took the place of the cavalry saddle and a blanket the place of a saddle pad. The pipe clay so reverently sponged on at home was sandpapered off. They were drab soldiers now, even mess tins given a khaki cover.

'Acts of true courage, sir,' Ellesmere smiled.

'Forget all the cavalry dogma you've ever been told,' the General informed his instructors. 'Forget all this business of rising in the saddle. The Boers sit like sacks. Rising just wears out both man and horse over long distances. At home we spent hours learning to trot without stirrups and hold a sword at the gallop. A trot's fit only for a cab horse and riding without stirrups is the best way I know to give a horse a sore back.'

Since Roberts had arrived, a breath of fresh air had blown through the cobwebs and he was already making plans to move north when Buller made another blunder at Spion Kop.

The Boer forces had thrown up half a dozen natural leaders who were already beginning to take the places of their elderly generals like Cronje and Joubert who had fought in the last Boer War. Men like Botha, De La Rey, Martinius De Hoog, De Wet and Beyers were young and moved more swiftly, and they were ruthless enough and intelligent enough not to miss their chances. But, surrounded by an excessive amount of military paraphernalia, Buller had advanced so slowly they were able to watch him every bit of the way.

Spion Kop had ended with another disaster, and a casualty list bigger than for any of the other battles.

Even as the news was received in Cape Town, more defeats followed. At Vaal Krantz, the furious Lyttelton, frustrated by Buller's hesitation, had ignored his orders to retreat from the hill he had captured the day before and had felt his battle won when Buller had ordered a complete withdrawal. Once more they were back where they started, with a great many unnecessary dead and wounded and a public exasperated to learn that yet another hill had been captured and then abandoned. Almost immediately afterwards, Crawford's column, moving between Gatacre and Buller, was caught in the open and driven back in confusion, with the 19th Lancers fighting a rearguard action and acting as whippers-in to a host of stragglers.

'It won't be long,' General Goff told his wife in disgust, 'before British generals won't dare put their noses in the streets.'

It was well known in Cape Town that Roberts was due to leave for the north at any moment with Kitchener. They had been making their plans quietly but there was no visible sign of action and no indication of what they were thinking when a message came to say that Roberts was due to dine at the Mount Nelson and would General Goff make a point of being available for a talk?

The General found Roberts, looking worried and angry, alone in his room with Kitchener, who was wearing his usual bull-at-a-gate look.

'Coll –' Roberts came to the point at once ' – tomorrow I'm going to the front. I shall be boarding the northbound train at Salt River just outside the city. How's your training scheme coming along?'

'Excellently, sir. We shall be turning out plenty of mounted men within another week or two. I was even hoping I might request permission to take some of them north myself.'

Roberts' expressive eyes glinted then he smiled. Without a word, Kitchener poured a drink and handed it to the General.

'I've got a better idea,' Roberts said. He moved to a map spread out on the table and beckoned the General across. 'Instead of rushing up to Natal to relieve Ladysmith, I'm going to go for a flank march along the western railway to Kimberley, then strike out towards Bloemfontein.'

General Goff smiled. 'It's against all War Office doctrine, sir.'

Roberts shrugged. 'It'll relieve Kimberley, silence Rhodes and capture the Orange Free State capital. It'll also draw large numbers of Boers from Natal and reduce the pressure on Ladysmith which, for the time being, can be left to Buller. French will be the spearhead and I'm going to give him some hard work to do. But he'll have the greatest chance he'll ever get with cavalry, because Kimberley must be relieved. I'm going to send him on a detour to cut the railway north of the town. You were with Stuart in the States. You know how it's done. Can French do the same?'

'It's different country,' the General said. 'And water and grazing are more of a problem. But I know the area and, if he makes his plans properly, yes, he can. The Boers are afraid of British cavalry and if he gets them in the open and makes an example of them, it can even have tremendous moral effect.'

'That's what I thought.' Roberts turned from the map. 'Well, Christopher Crawford's column's now near Rosanna. He was near Jacobspoort on his way to take Donotsfontein from the Boers when De Hoog fell on him and pushed him all the way back to Bester's Nek. Awful show. Disgraceful. All this you know. Well, now we've heard he's been chucked out of Bester's Nek, too. We need Donotsfontein, Coll. It's a railway junction and will simplify supplies. Have you got a good man who can take over your scheme?'

'Ellesmere could handle it.'

'Not Ellesmere,' Roberts said. 'I've other plans for him.'

'Well, there's Major Nicholas. He was sent to me because he was hit at Elandslaagte. He's quite recovered now and he's energetic, intelligent and full of ideas.'

'We'll push him up to half-colonel. I have a job for you. But you'd have to drop a rank temporarily. I want you to take over Crawford's column.'

The General's heart thumped in a way that he'd almost forgotten. He'd long since come to the conclusion that he was too old for active service but Roberts, who was older, didn't seem to be and he didn't seem to consider General Goff was either. He offered a warning.

'Crawford's younger than I am, sir.'

'There are some men who were old when they were second lieutenants,' Roberts pointed out dryly. 'You'll need a good chief of staff.'

'I can think of no one better than Ned Ellesmere.'

Roberts smiled. 'That's what I thought. You'll have three battalions of infantry – two of them newly out here, mind, and far from being the best – the 19th Lancers, the North Cape Horse – the outfit you led in Zululand – and units of the Royal Artillery and Royal Engineers. By the time you reach there, you'll also have some local volunteers, who are more enthusiastic than skilled, two more batteries of artillery and a few other miscellaneous groups. But Crawford's scattered them all over the countryside and he never got much unity into them, anyway. It'll be up to you to change all that.'

Roberts paused, looking keenly at General Goff. 'I want someone up there who knows how to handle mounted men, Coll. Gatacre's defeat's left a gap and Buller will never move if he thinks the Boers might fall on his left. I want someone who's willing to probe forward, even get himself attacked, in the hope that the Boers will draw men from Buller so he can be chivvied into a move. I expect you to make an opportunity.'

'Of course, sir.'

Roberts frowned. 'But no more defeats, Coll,' he said. 'We've finished with defeats. The situation's got to change. It's up to you.'

seven

Crawford's column was strung out over several miles of veldt to the north of the little town of Rosanna. As the train steamed in, the General saw horses and wagons stretched across the plain as far as the eye could see. It was hard to decide just what Crawford was hoping to do because there wasn't the slightest chance of surprising the Boers as the column moved laboriously along, fully exposed to the eyes of the scouts who were quite obviously just over the horizon.

A line of ragged trees marked the little town, with, away to the north, the stumps of two small kopjes like broken teeth against the sky. The station seemed devoid of life. A group of black men were dozing like bundles of old rags in the shade near a group of parked carts, their dogs stretched as if dead in the dust. Near the water tower, a few soldiers in grey-back shirts, their necks burned red by the sun, and a few army horses flicking their tails at the flies were all that showed the place was occupied. For the rest, it seemed empty, silent and still. As the train drew to a halt, however, a small cavalcade of horsemen appeared, trotting forward in a small cloud of dust to halt and dismount.

The General frowned. 'Seems a lot of sloppiness around here, Ned,' he growled. 'Chrissie Crawford's let things go.'

As he climbed from the train to the dusty boards that did duty as a station platform, followed by Ellesmere and Ackroyd, the officer from the little cavalcade that had arrived stepped forward and saluted.

'Major Trim, sir,' he announced. 'GSO2 to General Crawford. I was detailed to meet you. General Crawford's with the column.'

'Surely he should be here,' Ellesmere observed tartly. 'He knew General Goff was on this train.'

'It doesn't matter, Ned,' the General murmured. 'It isn't every day you get the sack and have somebody arrive to take your place.'

It had been raining for nearly two days and Crawford's wagons were axle-deep in mud. His column consisted of a long line of cavalry, infantry and guns, interspersed with wagons of all kinds, drawn by teams of sixteen oxen or ten mules, the Kaffir drivers energetically whipping them on. There were wagons carrying ammunition, wagons carrying pantries and kitchens, wagons carrying rations and fodder for the animals that pulled the wagons, and wagon after wagon carrying tents. In between the wagons and the fighting men came an endless procession of those who served on the fringe of the army – doctors and stretcher bearers, signallers with heliographs and flags, bakers, cooks, farriers, paymasters and clerks. There were pontoons, a traction engine, a searchlight, even a balloon.

Everything had been painted the colour of the veldt. The wagons, the guns, the kitbags, the water bottles and other equipment were all khaki – even the quick-firing Maxim guns were wrapped in drab canvas greatcoats. Only buttons and accoutrements shone and, in the heat of the sun, the veldt was drying and the dust clouds that were lifting to the sky were dulling even those.

The infantry were clearly finding the webbing for their greatcoats uncomfortable to wear and many had thrown it away and were carrying the coats en banderole instead, tramping sullenly forward, unshaven and tired-looking, their puttees encasing their legs with tubes of yellow clay.

They were covered with dirt, their uniforms in tatters, and they were loaded down with kettles and firewood for their bivouacs. While the tail of the column was still toiling across the veldt, the wagons of the leading elements were already drawing into a circle, and a hopyard of tent poles was being raised.

'How many wagons do they use for tents?' General Goff demanded as they rode past.

'I can't say sir,' Trim answered briskly. 'A lot, I dare say.'

'I think you'd better find out,' the General growled. 'By tonight. What's the speed of the advance?'

'Can't say that either, sir.'

'That's something else you'd better find out by tonight.'

The column was just descending into a spruit, a sunken watercourse alongside a broken bridge, and two wagons had overturned. Mules were fighting to free themselves from their tangled harness, spare teams of oxen were lumbering up to drag gun carriages out of the mud, Kaffir drivers were wildly flogging their animals, and bored fatigue parties were spreading rushes they had collected in the hope of making a firmer surface for men and vehicles. A cry went up for pontoons and more teams of oxen were hurried up to help with the loads.

'This looks bloody slow and tedious to me, Ned,' the General growled to Ellesmere. 'In future, I want the column split. Infantry and cavalry will not cross where the wagons cross. I see no reason why they should struggle on their hind legs through mud caused by horses, mules and oxen. Make that your first job.'

They reached Heidelberg Springs, where General Crawford had set up his headquarters, just as the sky was changing to green and orange and a last violent red in the west where the sun had set. A few clouds striped the bowl of the heavens with black as it slowly began to take on the luminous light of night. The place was small, and was silent and dead but for a few yellow lights in the windows of the shabby tin-roofed houses. A soft breeze from the veldt carried the low cries of oxen from where the wagoners struggled as the column neared the town. Horses were tethered outside the hotel, snorting softly above the witless chatter of crickets and frogs. Across the dusty square was a store with the single yellow lantern illuminating a group of Kaffirs sitting on the step. Behind it the veldt stretched out in a great prodigality of space, and overhead the tall African stars picked out the scattered gum trees and peppers and the fan of a dwarf palm rusting into thin whiskers, its spikes mirrored in a horse trough where grass grew round a dripping tap.

The bar of the hotel was the biggest single room in the little town. It stretched the full length of the building from the entrance hall to the dining room and the shelves of bottles were interspersed with the skulls of springbok, eland and the magnificent kudu with their ponderous spiral armament, relics of the days when they could be shot at the end of the main street. The men at the bar were dusty and shabby, many of them Boers who were watching the billiard room door, a hotch-potch of glass like the porch of a chapel in coloured cubes and lozenges.

Dismounting, the General tossed the reins to Ackroyd and stamped into the hotel, knocking the dust from the folds of his uniform. Ellesmere and Trim followed immediately. Seeing the uniforms, the owner of the hotel came from behind the bar.

'In the billiard room, sir,' he said.

As the loose panes of coloured glass in the door clashed, the men studying a map spread on the billiard table looked up. In the middle of the group was an elderly officer, tall, thin and lugubrious-looking.

As General Goff appeared, he straightened and became very stiff and still, uncertain, faintly nervous and old-womanly.

It was no wonder General Goff thought, that his troops called him, not 'Chris' but 'Chrissy'.

'General Crawford?' General Goff cleared his throat, aware what an embarrassing business it was relieving a man of his command. Crawford waited, making no attempt to move forward, his face hostile, his expression disapproving.

Very well, the General thought, if that's how he wants it, that's how he can have it. There were half a dozen ways of superseding another officer and, if only for good manners, it was usually made easy by the man who was being superseded. Crawford clearly resented the General's arrival.

'Field Marshal Lord Roberts has sent me,' the General said briskly. 'I'm to take command of the column.'

Crawford blinked. 'I received the information on the telegraph at the station at Rosanna this morning,' he said. 'I'd better introduce my staff – I beg your pardon, *your* staff. This is General Cook, who has the 12th Brigade, and this is General Grierson, who has the 7th. Colonel Windham, my GS01. My GS02 you've already met. This is Captain Pemberton, GS03; Colonel Mortimer, CRA; Colonel Smith, AAQMG...'

General Goff waited silently, nodding as the officers were introduced. He had heard of one or two of them, had even met Cook in India, and had not been impressed. They seemed an indifferent bunch and there were far too many because the troops didn't like to see a lot of red tabs about. He would probably have to replace one or two of them, he decided, though perhaps the unsticking of Crawford might do the trick for him. The poor bugger was obviously too old for an active command.

'I have taken over half the hotel,' Crawford said. 'I have two or three rooms upstairs for my own use and this room for my staff. There are a few things I have to clear up but I presume you will not be wanting me to move out at once.'

General Goff frowned. 'Regretfully,' he said, 'I shall. I propose to start work immediately and I shall need every inch of space I can find.'

'I can arrange for my marquee to be placed at your disposal.'

'I prefer to be here near the telegraph.'

Crawford's mouth tightened. 'It will take time to tie up the loose ends.'

'I trust not.'

Crawford stared back at the General, hatred in his eyes. His throat worked then he nodded slowly.

General Crawford had disappeared by next morning. He had found it possible to tie up his loose ends a great deal more quickly than he had anticipated and had departed in the early hours for Cape Town and a ship home.

During the morning, General Goff called his officers into the billiard room of the hotel and informed them that they were moving towards Jacobspoort at once. There were a few sidelong glances and he decided it needed explanation.

'We're here to chivvy Brother Boer into attacking us,' he pointed out. 'So that the army in front of Ladysmith will be relieved of pressure. But attacking us doesn't mean defeating us and if he won't attack us, then we shall attack him.' He studied the faces of his officers, startled to see how young most of them seemed. 'It's my responsibility to lead this column, but first I want to see it brought up to scratch. This is a time of great emergency. There are people in Ladysmith waiting for relief and it's our job to see that it becomes possible. I expect everybody to pull his weight and I shall accept no excuses.'

He had considered appealing to their loyalty but had decided in the end that a threat might be better. Crawford had clearly let them get away with murder and it was as well to let them know that from now on they were not going to. Chrissie Crawford was out and Balaclava Bill was in control.

Crawford's troops were a mixed lot and the whole column had grown used to easy methods and too much comfort, while the wagonloads of tents were like a red rag to a bull to the General.

'Trim,' he snapped at the aide, 'did you find out how many wagons are occupied by tents alone?'

'Sir!' Trim produced a paper which he laid in front of the General. 'The number of wagons, sir. Also the speed of the advance.'

'What's this?'

'A report, sir.'

'I didn't ask for a report, damn it! I asked you to find out.'

'It's in the report, sir.'

'Well, that's *something*. But in future don't waste your time on bits of paper. They clutter the place up.'

'Sir.'

The General turned to Ellesmere. 'These damn tents irritate me, Ned,' he said. 'There are too many of them. From now on they'll be discarded. Fortunately, in this country even if it rains, when the sun comes out it's hot enough to dry everything at once.'

Trim looked worried. 'Normally, sir,' he said, 'they're only discarded when operations are continuous from day to day.'

The General turned to him. 'That's what they will be, my boy. The troops will learn to sleep under the stars.'

Trim was aghast. 'They won't like it, sir.'

'Then they'll have to lump it.'

'What about officers, sir? They can hardly sleep in tents if the men don't.'

'Exactly. They too will sleep in the open.'

Trim looked shocked. 'Where will they store their baggage, sir?'

The General smiled maliciously. 'They won't have any baggage, Trim. What did we manage with in Zululand, Ned?'

'Forty pounds, sir.'

'Then forty pounds is what it will be here. The rest will be left with the tents.' He beamed at Trim. 'Think how much everybody will enjoy it when we *stop* moving.'

'Sir, I feel – '

The General's eyes flashed. 'I advise you to keep your feelings to yourself, my boy,' he said. 'A general and a column commander is the nearest thing in that column to God, and it's only a man who wishes to commit professional suicide who argues with him. I am not God, and you're not the Archangel Gabriel, but you will *not* dispute my orders.'

Within an hour, the headquarters tent was set up on the scrubby land beyond the group of iron buildings round the station, where the telegraph office was situated. General Goff had a strong suspicion that a great deal of information was being disseminated to the Boers by the bearded backvelders he had seen in the bar of the hotel, and he preferred to have his headquarters where they couldn't pick up titbits of gossip.

It was surrounded by a group of other tents, everything about them khaki because the land and everything on it – the sage bushes, the aloes and acacia thorns, the uniforms – were khaki, too. Even the faces – of both black and white men – were khaki from the dust that lifted every time a foot stirred.

As soon as the tents were in place and a table set down, while the unwitting troops enjoyed their last day of the comfort they had grown used to under General Crawford, General Goff called for regimental returns, the lists of sick and military crimes, and began to frown over interminable reports and telegrams, detailing the tent wagons for food and ammunition and demanding more horses and fresh stores.

Officers' mounts were detached from the wooden hitching rail outside the hotel and tied instead to the rail alongside the railway track, and within twenty-four hours the place had acquired a permanent look, with geraniums planted in old paraffin tins to give a touch of colour to the bleak brown aspect.

Trains began to arrive bringing new stores, frightened horses, half-dead after the journey from the coast, crates of ammunition, boxes of beef, sacks of flour, blankets, bales of compressed fodder for the horses, mealies for the African drivers and grooms, hospital stores and equipment, all trundled in mule carts or sixteen-span teams of oxen to the depot. Occasionally a rider appeared in the distance, dragging with him a cloud of dust that lifted from the veldt like steam, a miasmic figure in the heat and shimmery as a spectre, until he disappeared into a fold in the ground and reappeared a moment later as a messenger from one of the outlying wings of the force. Artillery came up under double teams and fresh infantry arrived from the Cape, weighed down under their webbing, rolled greatcoats, water bottles, Lee Metford rifles and full haversacks, and bulging with the extra rounds in their cartridge pouches. They had travelled in open cattle trucks and were spilled on to the veldt alongside the railway line, bewildered, hot and exhausted.

'They'll do,' the General said, eyeing them shrewdly. 'The junior officers will suffer from the usual stage fright and get into difficulties, I expect, but when the veneer of peace has gone they'll more often than not get out of them. It only requires the spit and polish to go, for the brain to become unglued.' He beamed at Ellesmere. 'It may not be a great war, Ned, but I have a feeling it's going to be a wonderful military spring cleaning.'

His preliminary arrangements made, the General called for his horse and began to ride round the different units of his command.

Morby-Smith, with the 19th Lancers, was delighted to see him. 'I couldn't believe my ears, sir, when I learned it was you,' he said. 'You're just what we need.'

'See you measure up to it then,' the General growled. 'Because you're carrying too much equipment for a start. Half of it's got to go. Horses will be hobbled from now on. And we're no longer drilling for the charge; and the fit of a jacket, the possession of a good seat or a good pair of hands are no longer as important as field craft. And from now on, your job will not be to protect *my* headquarters. It'll be to find out where Brother Boer's are. How are my sons?'

'Doing well, sir. Losby, of B Squadron, went sick and Robert's running it. He's a stickler for detail.'

Robert, the General decided, sounded as though he were a fusspot and Morby-Smith didn't wish to say so.

'And young Dabney?'

'Splendid, sir.' Morby-Smith's reaction was different this time. 'He was clearly chafing as a squadron officer, so I tried him on his own. He's a natural scout, sir, and I persuaded General Crawford to give him a small column of North Cape Horse. He seemed to be doing very well but General Crawford preferred his people close at hand and he was returned to the Regiment.'

The North Cape Horse were next on the list. Composed of farmers and countrymen from the area round Hoeptown, they had done well under the General in Zululand. They were a rough and ready lot and their ponies were shaggy, unlike the sleek mounts of the Lancers, while their equipment consisted only of a rifle, a bandoleer of ammunition, a blanket, a poncho and a saddlebag full of biltong. They were led by Commandant Burger's son, Meyer, and as scouts they were unbeatable.

'You'll be the eyes of the column,' the General informed Burger. 'And I shall make a point of seeing that a few of the Lancers are attached to you to learn the tricks of the trade.'

The word flew round quickly as the General stalked through cookhouse areas, shocked at the lackadaisical methods, and, watched by nervous officers, blistered a few NCOs with his tongue. Service Corps horses were inspected meticulously and officers were informed acidly that this was a mounted war and it wouldn't be won with them in the condition in which he found them. Sergeant-majors were snapped at and veterinary surgeons informed in no uncertain terms that they weren't there merely to hand out horse pills.

Colonels were called to headquarters and told that from now on when the column moved it would move faster, and that when it manoeuvred, it would manoeuvre with a speed it had failed to show when it had been caught on the veldt by De Hoog. The artillery was told to be smarter at their drill. The balloon aeronauts were informed that they were expected to be aloft, not on their backsides on the ground. The 19th Lancers were informed that lances would not win the war because ten to one the Boers would probably never permit them to get close enough to use them, and that therefore they had better make sure that their practice with rifles was also good. The North Cape Horse were informed that, volunteers though they were, they were not expected to behave as if they were on a picnic. The infantry battalions were left in no doubt that they were in need of pulling together and one of the colonels was hurriedly removed from office.

There was a great deal more discomfort than there had been under General Crawford but there was also suddenly a great deal more efficiency and even Trim's disapproving look had vanished. It seemed to be time to advance on Jacobspoort to show De Hoog what they were made of.

It was Dabney who brought in the information on the Boers' whereabouts. Since he had flung General Crawford back,

Martinius De Hoog seemed to have disappeared and the need was for news.

From the 19th Lancers General Goff requested Dabney and a detachment of the best riders, horsemasters and shots for a scouting column. To them he added a squadron of the North Cape Horse which included men who had been raised in the area and knew the country. He was pleased to see their look of efficiency but was startled when Sergeant Ackroyd announced that he wished to go with them.

'Great God in the Mountains, Ellis,' the General said. 'What's my son got that I haven't got?'

'Mr Dabney moves fast, sir. I'd like to be with him.'

The General's eyebrows lifted but he was pleased.

Looking for drifts over the Koro River by which the main force could cross, Dabney's little column worked its way north of Bester's Nek. With them were a group of Bantus known to everyone as The Black Watch, and they lay up in clumps of mimosa during the day and only moved at night. Several times Boer patrols appeared near them and on one occasion they were obliged to bolt, with one man killed and one wounded.

The Boers had moved fast and seemed invisible, but the whole veldt spoke of their presence. The very air was full of suspense for the outbreak of firing, and every clod of earth was an enemy. Plodding on in silence, scouts out in front, at least they were certain that in this barren plain an ambush was impossible. After another mile, Dabney signalled for a halt to look round the horses, then they mounted again and pressed on. The horses were beginning to sweat now and after a while he ordered another pause to check for trouble. A loosened girth was found, and a galling surcingle, then they were off again.

As they disappeared in a fold of the plain, dust clogging their mouths, the horses lathering, Dabney's self-confidence was supreme. He knew he was good at the job in a way that the more conventional officers of the 19th never would be, and he had absorbed everything his father had ever said or written, while the time he had spent in South Africa had cleared his mind of the stiffness of European training. He was self-reliant and more insubordinate than his brother officers, and, unlike them, knew that to keep a good, sleek, hard-riding pony you needed to be expert, among other things, at stealing oats. He had watched his Kaffirs treat wounds with cow dung and, on the occasion when they had been fired on, had seen the surgeon faint when the Kaffirs had removed their foul covering from the wounded man's injury. His men were a tough, self-reliant lot, some South African, speaking Kaffir and the Afrikaner 'taal', some Australian and New Zealand, some British. They were lean, dusty men, their only real uniform the pink puggaree they wore round their slouch hats, and among their weapons were a few long-range Mausers captured from the Boers.

The country fascinated and repelled him at the same time. Hot, sandy, stony and desolate, yet fertile where there was water, it was like a drowsy, yellow-grey monster, dry and scaly, warted here and there with taibosch or prickly pear, or with aloes sticking up like bayonets. Most of the time it was a dust heap covered with flat stones, still and silent, a gauze of purple clinging to the distance and melting away in the sun. The sunsets were awe-inspiring and night came suddenly like a purple curtain pulled across a window, the sun sinking in a golden-green haze shot with crimson and azure. Dawn came with equal speed, the first gleam followed by a saffron glow that edged out of the violet shadows until the hills stood out black against the horizon. As the clouds became edged with gold, they gradually vanished into rosy wisps that dispersed in the brightening sky, and as the stars disappeared beams of light struck upwards and the sun began to flood the plain with day.

It was a mounted man's country and he had learned how to look after his mount. British officers had always prided themselves on their horsemastership but he had found, in fact, that they knew next to nothing. Riding horses in England had not meant looking after them, and those who rode at home invariably had grooms to care for their mounts. Looking wise as a hand was run over a fetlock did not make a man an expert but his father had always insisted on his family caring for their own horses and even Robert, who claimed to hate them, knew how to look after them. The General himself knew more about them than any man Dabney knew and once, when the vet had been unable to get rid of mange in a pony, he had seen him do it with a mixture that consisted chiefly of ointment prescribed for lice.

Picking up the trail of horses near a range of hills known as the Kwathambas, a rocky group laying in a long featureless hog's back terraced by erosion and strewn with red rock, aloes and acacia thorn, among the dusty hoof prints he found the tracks of guns which seemed to confirm that the trail was De Hoog's. Moving forward with nothing but an outlying patrol, he picked up the tracks again just to the south of the hills, and, leaving his men well back out of sight crouching round the fires they had built of dung and the thorn scrub that filled the air with the aromatic smell of acacia, he moved forward at dusk with only Ellis Ackroyd and a man to hold the horses. Hiding themselves in a patch of scrub, they lay down, stiff with cold despite the heat of the day, and waited for dawn. They were across the route where Crawford had been surprised some time before, and in the first light of the new day saw the grave of a British officer nearby, a crude cross with a name burned on it with a heated bayonet, and a pair of feet, disturbed by prowling animals, protruding from the soil.

'There are men on top of them hills, sir,' Ackroyd said quietly, peering through Dabney's binoculars. 'That means we'll have to climb the slopes as usual to dislodge 'em.'

The day was still only a faint promise of gold in the east and it was a pure morning with all the world still and the air invigorating, the early sun turning the rust-coloured peaks of the hills into pink battlements. Africa seemed empty, bare and rolling, and covered with thin brown grass dried by the sun. The ridge in front rose slantwise, rough-edged like a saw where small outcrops of rocks broke through the surface and edged the skyline.

Just behind them their ponies snorted softly, Ackroyd's nuzzling at the dried blood on a foreleg where it had cut it the night before climbing out of a donga. The plain was covered with a thick milky mist that lay like a blanket several feet deep above the ground, above it the ghostly tops of a few trees. After a while they spotted buck, dim ghostly shapes suspended against an invisible background, bodies without legs, heads without bodies; then as they watched, twenty or thirty horned heads shot up where they had originally seen only two or three. Finally, as the mist shifted, they saw the whole herd.

A moment later, as a frightened covey of thickhead birds rose in a clatter of wings, like drops of bright water flung against a stone the buck split apart, swung together like iron filings drawn to a magnet, then began to race across the veldt, sweeping away in a strung-out cloud, a whirlpool of racing shapes, the sun catching the black and white stripes on their tawny sides so that they seemed like a stream running across the empty plain. Over the silence they heard the faint sound of Dopper hymns coming from the base of the hills.

'They're not at the top, Ellis,' Dabney said quietly. 'They're at the bottom. There's a dried river bed there – one of the tributaries of the Koro. I think they're in that and burrowing like ants.'

By the time Dabney returned to the main column, General Goff had moved from Bester's Nek and had set up his headquarters in a farm building with pink stone walls. The Kwathamba Hills ran straight across his front and, with the Boers at an altitude to see any move he made, he was aware that it was going to be difficult to cross the Koro without being involved in a fight. It looked in fact, very much as though he was going to have to fall back on the sort of frontal attack he disliked intensely and, since he would have to be in position at dawn, would have to make a night march, something which had so far not proved particularly successful.

Leaning over his map while Dabney jabbed his finger at it to show the Boer positions, he found he was watching his son more than the map. So that the Boers should not know they'd been spotted, he and his small party had stayed where they were all day, sweltering in the shadeless sun until the sudden African dusk came and allowed them to ride off quietly in the growing darkness. His eyes were alight now with enthusiasm and intelligence and he had already grasped the essentials of the General's plan and its difficulties.

Moving his hand over the map, the General pointed at the Kwathambas. 'Is there any way through these hills?' he asked.

'Yes, sir,' Dabney said. 'There is. There's a gap behind and to the left of where the river bed runs close to the slopes. There's another to the right. They're only narrow, sir, but they're gaps. They've probably chosen the position so they can use them to run as usual if things get too sticky.'

General Goff stared at his son, frowning, then he ran his hand down the line of a hill running south at right angles to the main range. 'What about this hill here – the Graafberg?'

'It's about a mile long and could give excellent cover.'

'These gaps of yours – could cavalry get through?'

'Yes, sir. In single file.'

'It sounds damn' dangerous. Could they do it in the dark so that when the infantry moved forward, they'd be in position to cut off Brother Boer?'

'I think they could, sir.'

'What about lookouts?'

'If they're in trenches at the bottom, there'd surely not be many on top and they'd be looking south where the main column's expected, not north-east where we'd be.'

'We?'

Dabney smiled. 'You'd need me, sir, to show the way. I'd be more reliable than a native guide, and more trustworthy than a local.'

As his son left headquarters, the General stood for a moment staring after the slim, confident figure. What Dabney had suggested was a definite possibility, but it would also be damned dangerous for his son, his favourite son. He stood for a long time staring at the map then he sighed, lit a cigarette and called Ellesmere to the map table.

'Ned,' he said, 'I want you to set up a night march to the Kwathambas. We shall need to be in position before dawn. Let's have the commanding officers in.'

The regimental officers seemed startled at the plan but they had already learned not to object and the more intelligent of them were well aware that, if they were to avoid casualties, they would need to move fast.

'The men will travel light,' the General announced. 'No heavy equipment. No tents. No greatcoats. Just food, ammunition and full water bottles. The men will not smoke after dark, and equipment that's likely to rattle or clink will be tied in handkerchiefs or scarves.'

As he paused, Ellesmere looked up expectantly.

'One other thing. De Hoog's no fool so I want him to believe we're moving to his left, so as to draw off some of his men. One half-battery will remain behind, together with a company of infantry and whatever native bearers we can muster. The ox wagons will move out in a wide sweep into the veldt and join up with the rest of the column tomorrow. They're to make as much noise as possible, shouting and letting off their rifles. They can even light fires. The half-battery will fire its guns.'

He looked at Trim. 'This will be your responsibility, Trim. Think you can look after it?'

'I'd rather be where the fighting is, sir.'

'Have no fear, my lad, you might get more fighting than you expect. Your job will be to make the Boers think we're trying to move over towards Buller and that we've scared ourselves to death as usual with a false alarm.'

As the plan developed, there was a growing enthusiasm among the listening officers.

Giving positions and start times, the General turned to Morby-Smith.

'Your people will move to the left here, throwing out a half-squadron in advance to warn you of danger. You'll take no risks, however, and will attempt to get on this slope here to enfilade the river bed and to be ready to chase the Boers back to Donotsfontein and beyond. They're not to be given a chance to hole up in Jacobspoort. One half-squadron will operate with the North Cape Horse. Who do you suggest?'

'Johnson's able, sir.'

'Johnson it shall be. Lieutenant Goff, who will be acting as guide, will lead them round the back of the Graafberg and the Kwathamba Range.'

When the tent had emptied the General looked at Ellesmere. 'There will be no mistakes, Ned,' he said. 'Everything will be checked and double checked. If we're stopped by Brother Boer, so be it, and I'll answer with my neck, but by God we'll not be stopped through our own carelessness.'

*   *   *

As the bugles sang, the forward march began. By dusk the few tents round the farm had vanished, only bare patches on the earth to indicate where they had stood and nothing but empty bully beef and biscuit tins to show where the force had halted.

The men marched off cheerfully, mouth organs whining to 'Kiss Me, Mother; Kiss Your Darling Daughter', with the Lancers thrown out in a wide screen to watch for Boer scouts.

As darkness fell and the shapes strung across the veldt disappeared into the night, the din Trim's column was making could be heard quite clearly, the silence of the veldt magnifying the rumble of the wagons, the calls of the African drivers and the crack of their whips, the click of metal horseshoes against the stones sounding over the low rumble of the gun carriages. Then suddenly, unexpectedly, there was a faint rattle of musketry and the thud of a gun.

'Trim's been found,' the General said grimly.

In fact, Trim was doing better than anybody had imagined possible, and two hours later a subaltern on a lathered horse came thundering up to the column demanding to know where the commanding officer was. 'Here,' the General snapped. 'What the devil are you making all that noise about?'

'Major Trim's been attacked, sir. He thinks it might be De Hoog himself. He's established himself on a kopje on our left and opened long-range fire on us. Major Trim laagered as many wagons as he could and had the oxen taken down to the river bed for protection but he brought them out again as soon as he could in the hope of continuing the move. Unfortunately, the mules stampeded and set off the oxen and the whole lot bolted. Major Trim feels more men'll be needed to drive the Boers off.'

The General gnawed at his lip, adding up figures in his mind. 'How many supplies have they with them, Ned?' he asked.

'Not many, sir,' Ellesmere said.

'Well – ' the General made up his mind quickly ' – we shall need every man we have to tackle the Kwathambas. We'll have to sacrifice the column, if necessary, to keep up the momentum here.'

He saw Ellesmere pull a face and rounded on him angrily. 'And don't pull that damned face at me, Ned! Jesus Christ in the Mountains, I don't like it any more than you do! But we can't put off the attack to save a few wagons and oxen.' He turned to the subaltern on the panting horse. 'Can you hold?'

'We ought to be able to, sir.'

'Then get back to Trim and tell him there must be no mistake and no surrender. He's to keep the Boers occupied. In any way he likes. I'll try to relieve him by the day after tomorrow.'

As the officer swung his horse and clattered off into the darkness, the General became aware of Ellesmere's eyes on him.

'Are you accusing me, Ned?' he growled.

'On the contrary, sir.' Ellesmere's face was grave. 'I was thinking a decision of that sort shows the mettle of a leader. It must have been a difficult one to take.'

The General studied him for a moment, then he stared to the north-east where Dabney and the North Cape Horse had disappeared. 'Not half so difficult as sending my own son round by the back door, Ned,' he growled.

eight

The two groups of cavalry had moved forward with dusk, leaving the rest of the column behind them. Ahead they could see the Kwathamba Hills and for a long time the two groups moved side by side.

Leading as guide, Dabney rode alongside his brother who was leading a half-squadron in front of the left column. Robert looked grey-faced and unhappy, and for a long time they rode together just ahead of their men, drawn together to talk.

'Do you enjoy soldiering, Dab?' Robert asked suddenly.

Dabney's head turned. 'Of course.'

'Why?'

'Father, I suppose. Grandfather. Great-grandfather. All the other Goffs back to the year dot. I imagine it must be in me. I've never questioned it. Why?'

Robert's head moved unhappily. 'I'm not sure I feel the same way. I prefer desk work to this sort of thing.'

Dabney shrugged. 'There's always a place for a good desk man. Especially these days. The idea of a general staff's growing. This little lot's shown the need for men who can organise things.'

'I don't mean that sort of organisation. I mean as a civilian.'

Dabney's head turned. 'You mean, send in your papers?'

'I've thought of it more than once. Elfrida's not keen on me being a soldier, anyway – frightened and all that – and Lord Cosgro's offered me a position in his organisation.'

'That was merely to get a dig in at Father. It'd please old Walter no end to entice one of the Goffs away from the Regiment.'

'No. It's not that. He said I had the ability, and I think I have.'

Dabney looked puzzled. 'Well, that's a licker, if you like. A Goff in business.'

'Surely to God you're not going to be snobbish about it!' Robert's voice was harsh and irritated. 'The idea that gentlemen don't go into business just doesn't hold water any longer.'

'Oh, gosh, no, old man!' Dabney hurried to correct a false impression. 'I wasn't thinking of *that!* Just of a Goff not being in the Regiment. They've been in the Regiment ever since it was founded.'

Robert gave a little snort. 'Then it's about time they did something else,' he said. 'We're in danger of becoming bores about this bloody Regiment.'

As dusk came, Morby-Smith rode forward to join them. 'I think this is where we part company,' he said, and the two columns separated, two and a half squadrons of the Lancers moving westwards under Morby-Smith, the other half-squadron under Major Johnson, followed by the North Cape Horse, moving towards the Graafberg. As the horsemen bore away across the Boer front, the firing flared up in the darkness to the east. Johnson, at the head of the right column, cocked his head.

'Trim's certainly drawing attention to himself,' he said.

They were hidden now by an area of monkey thorn, mimosa and low trees and scrub, and Dabney suggested they should stop to make sure of their bearings.

'They'll never see us, sir,' he advised. 'We ought to stay here now until the infantry move. They're bound to have scouts out looking for any attempt to get round them.'

Pushing forward on the other flank, Morby-Smith had also drawn rein. Staring ahead into the darkness, he motioned Robert forward with his half-squadron.

'Scout up in the western end of the hills,' he ordered. 'Make sure the way's clear. Make no mistake, though, and be careful. I want you to find us a spot where the horses won't be seen. Some sort of dip where the horse holders can wait, with a rise in front where we can enfilade the Boer position.'

Moving forward with his squadron, Robert shivered slightly. The night was cool and very soon the sky would begin to pale. There was a sliver of moon and, through the darkness, he could just see scanty grass and scrubby bushes. The plain was seamed with gullies and ravines which were offshoots of the dried river bed that the Boers were holding in front of the hills. He didn't consider the job a difficult one but he was terrified of making a mistake. His fear sprang less from the thought of danger than from the knowledge that his father had been an expert scout – he'd heard the story a thousand times of how he'd led a Confederate regiment round a whole Federal cavalry division in the American Civil War and how he'd commanded the North Cape Horse in Zululand – and he was certain that his brother Dabney had the same gift. He himself would never have offered to lead a column round the back of the Boers because he would have been terrified of going wrong, and he was conscious that in the trotting files behind him was Morby-Smith's son.

His little column moved slowly, silent except for the faint clink of harness or sword scabbards. A horse snorted and Robert turned nervously.

'Keep that damned horse quiet,' he snarled in a harsh whisper.

'Sir –' it was young Morby-Smith who spoke '– aren't we a little too far forward?' He jerked a hand. 'I think the rise we're supposed to occupy is over on our left.'

Worried about making a mistake, Robert was resentful of the interruption. 'I know what I'm doing,' he snapped.

Morby-Smith didn't reply and Robert pushed on, worried. Ahead, there seemed to be another slight rise and he was convinced that this, not the one Morby-Smith had pointed out, was their goal. He glanced over his shoulder to his right. There was no sign or sound of the infantry or guns getting into position, and he realised nervously that he was on his own. Waging war in darkness, he decided, not knowing where the enemy was, was a nerve-racking business. Then he saw a chink of light on his right and halted the squadron.

'That must be the infantry getting into position,' he said.

Morby-Smith shook his head. 'Sir, I feel sure we're ahead of the infantry. It couldn't be the Boer position, could it?'

'We can't have come that far, for God's sake!'

The little column halted and the men were told to dismount. Nerves on edge, Robert was dying for a cigarette.

'The men may smoke if they wish,' he said.

'Sir –' Morby-Smith ventured to protest '– I thought –'

'We're all right here.' Robert turned sharply. 'They won't be watching this place, and anyway the order applied to the infantry in front of the Boer trenches.'

A few cigarettes and pipes were lit and there was a quiet murmur as the men smoked, their muttering interspersed with the soft snorting of horses and the scrape and clink as they pawed at the stony ground.

'Soon be daylight.' Robert glanced at the sky. 'Have someone look out for the infantry. When they move, so do we. Any sign of the rest of the regiment?'

Morby-Smith, who was still mounted, stared to the east. 'No, sir. I still suspect we're perhaps a little too far –'

'For God's sake, Morby-Smith!'

'Yes, sir. I'm sorry, sir.'

But as the sky paled and the first flicker of light appeared, bringing with it the reddish-brown colour of the grass and bushes, what Morby-Smith had tried to tell Robert proved to be correct. The light they had seen was in the Boer position and they could see the line of scrub and trees where the infantry were waiting almost half a mile in their rear, with no sign of the rest of the regiment.

'Dammit, where are they?' Robert snapped, aware as he spoke that he was trying to justify his mistake by suggesting everybody else was wrong.

Lifting his glasses, he tried to study the plain. But there was no sign of infantry or guns, or of the North Cape Horse at the south end of the Graafberg. He was just about to lower the field glasses when a single shot came, the echoes clattering among the slopes and krantzes of the hills. Morby-Smith cried out, and, turning, Robert saw him slipping from his saddle, blood pouring from his throat. He tried to grab him as he fell but he was too late and the boy crashed to the ground. Immediately, the squadron was thrown into confusion as the men watched the sergeants, and the sergeants turned to Robert for orders.

The single shot was followed by others and as Robert gave instructions to lift Morby-Smith to the saddle, it changed to a regular fusillade. One of the men trying to hoist the wounded boy clutched his knee as his leg buckled under him, and another staggered back with a grunt, sat down, then flopped over on his back like a rag doll. Morby-Smith slid off the saddle and fell on his head on top of him.

'Mount!' Robert yelled. 'Mount, for God's sake! We've been ambushed!'

He knew he had not been ambushed, because the Boers were still in their trenches several hundred yards away, but had failed to heed advice and led his men too far forward. Behind him, along the face of the slope they occupied, he could see their retreat would be under fire every bit of the way. In his panic-stricken mind, the only thing to do seemed to be to destroy the Boers who were killing his men.

'Mount!' he yelled. 'Draw swords! Squadron into line.'

From a vantage position among the trees, the General heard the first firing.

'What in God's name is happening?' he snapped. 'The infantry aren't in position yet.'

'Sir!' Ellesmere swung round, his binoculars in his hands. 'The Lancers are moving forward.'

'Great God and all His pink angels!' The General reached for his glasses. 'What the hell's Morby-Smith up to?'

'Sir, it's a single half squadron. The rest of the regiment's moving up to support them.'

'For God's sake, Ned, get the infantry moving! Those fools have started before we're ready!'

Furiously angry that his plan had gone wrong, the General watched Ellesmere send a galloper across to where the infantry were waiting among the trees and scrub. Out on the veldt, Trim's little fight was still going on unabated and even seemed to be attracting more Boers, but his casualties, according to the latest information, were heavy and it had required a steady nerve to leave him to his fate to make sure the infantry were at their start line at the right time.

Ellesmere's galloper came back at full speed on a lathered horse. 'The guns aren't in position yet, sir,' he announced.

'We'll have to do without them.' The General tapped the pommel of his saddle in irritation. 'The blasted Boers'll be able to bolt before we're on to them now.'

He lifted his glasses, frowning as he saw the half squadron of horsemen on his left front wheel into line and begin to move forward. The rest of the regiment was galloping up on their right in support and, as the single squadron broke into a gallop, the greater mass of men swung behind them to form a second, longer line.

Looking back, Robert saw that Morby-Smith had got the rest of the 19th into position to support him, but they were a long way behind. In front, he could see puffs of smoke coming from the end of the Boer trenches. There was little to be seen of the men who were firing, however, beyond a small group standing by a group of rocks, and what looked ominously like a gun. Even as he ordered the Charge, he was aware that he had made a mistake but that it was now too late to do anything about it. With his men dismounted, despite the indifferent shooting of British soldiers, he could have silenced the group by the rocks, but the sudden fusillade had panicked him and the only thing he could think of was to attack.

The first glint of the sun appeared between a gap in the hills in the east. It was in his eyes and made it difficult to see the Boers. He drew a deep shuddering breath. They were committed now.

The drumming of hooves increased and at that moment he saw a flash and a shell burst among the horses. From the corner of his eye he saw animals go down and he held his sabre more tightly, his thumb pressing the back of the hilt in line with the blade, alert to grip more firmly at the moment of impact. The hooves about him beat a steady rhythm, but the excitement was getting hold of the riders now and the horses were almost out of control. The gun fired again and there was another crash as more horses and riders went down.

The pace had quickened and they were almost at a gallop, the reins loose, the horses' rumps bunching together.

'Give points!' he yelled. 'Give points!'

He had been concentrating so hard on the single gun, he had not noticed the increase in the musketry and it dawned on him now that bullets were whipping and cracking all round him. Turning to check his command, he realised riderless horses were breaking away across the slope now and several men were already stumbling to the rear on their own two feet.

Then he saw the gun fire again and the flash at the muzzle seemed to coincide with another flash just in front of him. His horse pecked, stumbled forward and wavered and, as he hauled at the reins to keep its head up, its forelegs buckled and it crashed to the ground. Flying over its head, he slid on his side, his sword and helmet gone, the hard shape of his revolver jabbing into his middle until, blinded with dust, his mouth full of grit, he came to a stop against a small boulder.

On the other side of the front, Dabney was watching through his glasses. The half-squadron advancing on the Boer trenches seemed to have disappeared, and the supporting line two squadrons long to be scattering in retreat, a few of the riders taking cover in one of the gulleys and trying to keep up a fire on the Boer trenches.

Johnson was watching the hills for the flash of light from his signallers. In Dabney's opinion, Johnson wasn't the most imaginative of men. Brave, bigoted, hide-hound, a prodigy on the polo field or at steeplechases, he was a firm believer in ceremony and seemed lost in front of the enemy. Yet it was obvious something ought to be done at once because Dabney could see the infantry trying to push forward in a sleet of rifle fire and finding it difficult.

'I think, sir,' he attempted, 'that we ought to be on the move.'

'I've had no signal,' Johnson said.

For God's sake, Dabney thought, a cavalryman was supposed to have an eye for this sort of thing, was supposed to know the exact moment to launch his men! It seemed clear that, with the little attack at the far end of the line brought to a halt and the infantry still struggling, a hammer blow on the opposite flank couldn't be anything else but useful.

'I suspect we might not get a signal, sir,' he said. 'The infantry might not even get going unless we give them a bit of help.'

Johnson looked worried and Dabney gestured.

'With respect, sir, a little pressure here might draw a few of the enemy towards us and that would surely help. The rest of the Regiment seems to have sacrificed themselves on the left, perhaps for the same reason.'

Johnson remained uncertain but in the end he decided to move forward. 'We're going to be under fire from the hills,' he said.

'If we move fast enough, sir, we ought not to get too many casualties.'

'All right. But not too fast. I want to keep the column under control.'

They moved forward warily, Johnson's eyes constantly on his men. Dabney was fidgeting in his saddle, waiting for the first blast of fire, and he could see Meyer Burger trying to speed up the advance. Johnson persisted in a controlled advance however, until, as they approached the southern-most tip of the Graafberg, the Boers on the Kwathambas opened fire. A shell dropped just behind them, then another in front. The next one, Dabney knew, would have the range exactly and he edged his horse forward in the hope of persuading Johnson to move faster. But Johnson was still concerned with his fear of losing control, and he moved his arm up and down to warn against advancing too quickly. By this time Burger's men had moved away from the Lancers and were heading obliquely towards the shelter of the Graafberg.

As the third shell dropped, Dabney was covered with grit and dust and he saw Johnson reel in the saddle. Grabbing the reins and, with Ellis Ackroyd helping on the other side, he kicked his horse to a gallop and shouted to the following men.

'Come on,' he roared. 'Fast as you can!'

They reached the cover of the Graafberg, followed by the North Cape Horse. Burger had seen the shell fall and the increase in speed and had instinctively swung his men back to join Dabney.

Reaching a point where they couldn't be seen from the peaks, they stopped and Ackroyd lowered Johnson from the saddle. His face wore a petulant expression.

'I told you we'd come under fire,' he said angrily and promptly fainted.

Dabney straightened up. As senior regular officer, he seemed to be in command. For a moment, he felt nervous at the responsibility, but the feeling passed.

He turned to Burger. 'Look,' he said. 'Suppose we split the column and push ahead with one half on the forward side of the Graafberg while the rest go round the back.'

Burger stared at the hills. 'It might work,' he said.

By this time, on the opposite end of the range of hills, Robert was aware of absolute failure. To right and left of him in the gulley were what was left of the two and a half squadrons of the 19th Lancers, driven back in a seething mass of clubbed and broken horsemen. Morby-Smith was dead, shot through the head, stretched at Robert's feet in the dust, only a few yards from the body of his son. The soldiers, the straps of their sun helmets on their chins, were lining the edge of the gulley, firing blankly into the distance where it was quite impossible to see anything at all. The horses were further along with the horseholders behind a small rise and there were considerably less than when they had started.

He realised now that he had failed completely to do as he had been ordered and that, as a result, both Morby-Smiths were dead, two other officers and a great many men were wounded, and they had achieved nothing at all. In their present position, the Boers could have held off a whole army corps because the land in front of them was too flat to give any cover once the infantry had left the trees. He could see white stones and bits of rag on sticks and knew the Boers had marked off the ranges; their shooting, as usual, was magnificent, and bullets kept kicking up the gravel so that he had to spit the dust from his lips.

Above, the sky was a deep blue and the sun was increasing in heat. All around him the air was full of the crack and whine of rifle bullets, and he had a suspicion that, not only was the whole regiment being held back by a mere thirty or forty men, but that other Boers were creeping round behind them. He glanced at Morby-Smith, sick with misery. Father and son both dead because of his mistake. He knew he would have to live with it for the rest of his life. As he raised his head, he saw several pairs of eyes on him and he knew what his men were thinking. The Morby-Smiths had both been popular and they were already blaming him.

His sergeant crept up to him, keeping his head well down. 'What do we do, sir?'

'We stay where we are. We can at least keep the Boers busy.'

The sergeant grunted. He was a reservist and had served the whole of his time in the army without being in action. It was bothering him now that his first action might also be his last.

'I think we're cut off, sir,' he said.

'You're undoubtedly right, Sergeant,' Robert said tartly. 'But at the moment there's nothing we can do but hang on. We shall be relieved before long.'

The sergeant didn't seem to share his optimism.

Robert looked along the line of men. They were clearly restless and aware that more of their comrades were dead than ought to be dead. He had a feeling it was something he would never live down. He could see men looking over their shoulders and knew they were worried about being surrounded and captured. One or two of them, even, were making no attempt to fire, but were crouching down as if they considered they were already as good as prisoners of war.

He stood up. 'I think we ought to try to move round to the left, Sergeant,' he said. 'I suspect the Boers are trying to get behind us.'

'Yes, sir,' the sergeant said. 'I think it might even be better if we pulled back a bit.'

'Nobody asked you what you thought, Sergeant,' Robert snapped. 'And don't cower like that when you talk to me. Stand up.'

The sergeant gave him a sour look and straightened up. As he did so, his right eye seemed to explode, spattering Robert with blood, and he flopped back in the gulley and sat staring at Robert with one dead blue eye. As Robert stepped forward, his helmet was jerked from his head and he felt a thump in his upper arm that spun him round and flung him down alongside the sergeant. For a moment, he was dazed, then the medical corporal bent over him.

'It's nothing, sir,' he said. 'Just a flesh wound. It ain't touched any bones.'

His look seemed to suggest that it was Robert's own fault and, biting his lips to prevent himself crying out with pain, it was at that moment that Robert finally decided he wasn't cut out for a soldier.

Watching from the willows, the General, unaware of the bullets striking sparks from the nearby rocks, saw his attack come to a halt.

In an attempt to salvage something, the artillery was struggling up. Dust swirled and a bugle shrilled, then the guns started to fire, the gunners counting aloud after each shot to give the regulation interval. But the Boer trenches had been cunningly sited and the General suspected they weren't achieving much, despite the fountains of earth and stones he could see being flung into the air. As for his infantry, they had come to a full stop. They had risen, their company commanders blowing their whistles, the men firing volleys, and doubled forward, their heads bent to the Mauser fire like a cornfield bending to the wind. But now the advance was halted and he could see the dun-coloured figures hiding behind ant hills and clumps of thorn. The metal storm coming from the hidden trenches stirred the dust in little spurts as if it were alive and there was a steady rearwards trickle of wounded.

Staring across the sun-drenched plain, the General frowned. Finding a scapegoat would help nobody. In the end, the responsibility was his. The army made no allowances for lack of skill or courage in subordinates and the blame always came back to the man at the top.

A Creusot field gun barked from the Boer position and a riderless horse galloped back from where the cavalry had been stopped. A group of infantrymen passed, the sergeants calling the step, a young officer urging them to keep calm. 'Steady, chaps. Don't lose your heads. It's nothing.' A shell landed nearby with a scream and a crash and a shower of fragments that hummed through the air like birds. A team of oxen abandoned by their native driver stood just in front, patiently chewing the thin dewy grass, oblivious to their danger.

Frustrated and bitterly disappointed, the General frowned. 'No more defeats,' Robert had said, and here he was already on the brink of one. He knew what his men would think. Elderly generals. Old hands from old wars who hadn't kept up with the times. But the plan had been a good one, he knew, good enough for him to risk his own son in the Boers' rear. If they didn't start moving soon, there would be no return for Dabney.

Behind the hills, the half-squadron of Lancers and the mounted volunteers were moving at a canter along the lower edge of the slope. A few scattered shots were fired at them from the top, but it wasn't much. Two or three saddles were emptied and a riderless horse stopped, its reins trailing, and began to nibble at the sparse grass alongside the body of its rider.

There was little more than a few hundred yards of the gauntlet still to be run but the fire was growing stronger, and Dabney was beginning to wonder if he were wise to persist. It was obvious someone had committed a frightful blunder on the opposite end of the front, and he had no wish to compound it with another on this side. Yet his father had insisted that there must be no more mistakes, no more defeats, and it was up to him to push himself and his men to the limit.

Behind him he heard the rattle of musketry as Burger dismounted his men and started to enfilade the Boer trenches. The sound swelled as the Boers returned the fire. By this time, the outposts on the Graafberg must have guessed horsemen were moving towards the Boer rear, but he was hoping they'd be round the back before the outposts could draw the attention of the main Boer force, occupied now by Burger and the rest of the column.

On his left the hills opened in a gap and the rolling sound of musketry came louder to his ears. Rifle fire was still spattering down around them and another horse went down with a crash and a jingle of harness. But now, in front of him he could see a cloud of knee-hobbled Boer ponies guarded by two or three men on horses and one or two on foot, standing near a string of wagons.

'Horses, transport, everything,' he breathed.

He turned to the leader of the North Cape Horse and gestured to the gap in the hills. 'There's your spot. Find yourselves a good position and keep 'em busy.'

As the mounted volunteers streamed away, Dabney turned to the half-squadron of Lancers.

'Draw swords,' he said. Swords were out of date but they were silent and on this occasion better than rifles.

He heard the swish as the weapons were unsheathed, and set spurs to his mount. As they thundered forward, the Boers by the wagons looked up and started to scatter in alarmed confusion. A few rifle shots snapped out at them and a man clutched at his chest and rolled from the saddle, then they were among the hobbled ponies. One of the Boers, an old man nearing seventy, turned towards Dabney, his rifle raised and he found himself staring into the muzzle of the gun. But for some reason, the old Boer couldn't manage to pull the trigger, any more than Dabney could bring himself to run the old man through. Instead he whacked him over the head with the pommel of the sword and saw him drop to the ground, then they were among the ponies, cutting at ropes, scattering the horseholders, and in no time the animals were galloping in a loose bunch across the veldt towards the north accompanied by an odd slouch-hatted rider bolting for safety.

As a group of the Lancers set off in pursuit, he yelled at Sergeant Ackroyd. 'Fetch 'em back, Ellis! Fetch 'em back!'

As Ackroyd spurred away, he shouted to the rest of his men. 'Rally! Rally on me! We have other business!'

Eventually all but one or two rallied and they spurred their tired horses to the eastern gap in the Kwathambas. There Dabney found himself almost behind a group of Boer riflemen who were blazing away at a group of hidden British soldiers in a gulley further along.

On his left he could hear the rattle of rifle fire. The Boers on that end of the line were being joined by more Boers, who were running. The North Cape Horse had clearly arrived in position and, dismounted, were pouring in a heavy fire from the rear to drive the Boers along the river bed.

'Dismount,' he yelled. 'Horseholders up!'

As the men swung from the saddles, they were flinging themselves to the ground and starting to fire without being told what to do. They were doing deadly work because they were almost at point-blank range and the Boers had been completely surprised. Glancing over the river bed, he saw Burger and his mounted volunteers appear from among the rocks where they had been hiding and begin to move forward. As Ackroyd rejoined him, he saw the infantry, pinned down just beyond the shelter of the scrub, also rise to their feet and begin to walk forward as the Boer fire slackened.

Then he saw a small neat figure, which he knew to be his father, followed by the taller shape of Ellesmere, spur forward, both waving frantically as they urged the infantry to greater speed. A few Boers, seeing the new danger, began to fire towards the infantry and Dabney realised that it was only a matter of a minute or two before one of the Boer marksmen spotted his father and picked him off.

'Horseholders forward!' he yelled. 'Mount! Draw swords! Infantry, fix bayonets!'

There were no infantry and no bayonets but the Boers had never liked steel, and they were already beginning to edge away. Swinging into a ragged line, sabres sparkling in the sun, the cavalrymen spurred forward, and the Boers started to mill about in confusion. Leaping his horse into the river bed, Dabney began to force his way along it, followed by his trumpeter, his orderly and Sergeant Ackroyd. All round him other horses were dropping down, colliding, swerving, occasionally falling, and a fierce hand-to-hand fight began to take place before the Boers began to scramble out and bolt for the slopes behind.

Halfway along the river bed, he ran into the North Cape Horse who were driving a large number of Boers before them. Seeing the new force of mounted men approaching, jabbing with swords and stamping them into the ground, the Boers flung down their rifles and raised their hands, yelling for mercy.

As the firing died away, the infantry stormed forward and, gathering his men about him, Dabney sent them in a scrambling charge back through the defiles, so that those Boers who had fled up the slopes and were now scrambling down the reverse side found them waiting to cut off their retreat. There was a little scattered shooting then white flags and handkerchiefs began to appear. With their horses gone and their wagons lurching across the plain far to the north in the direction of Jacobspoort, there was little else the Boers could do but surrender.

As Dabney swung away, the 19th arrived from the left, the senior major in command. He looked grim and angry, and as they moved past, Dabney saw his brother. There was blood on his tunic and his arm was bandaged. His face was grey and sick-looking.

'Come on, old man!' he called. 'Now's your chance! Don't stop until you get to Donotsfontein!'

They had rounded up the prisoners when his father rode up. His face was grim and he looked tired and, for the first time in his life, Dabney realised that his father was an old man. As the Lancers swung away, followed by Burger's men, Ellesmere joined the General then, their faces shadowed by the peaks of their caps, they headed to where Dabney stood with his trumpeter and Sergeant Ackroyd, grinning all over his face.

As they met, Dabney saluted.

'I think, sir,' he said, 'that it's all over and that we've won.'

PART TWO

'And that's how it was. That was how we won the Battle of Graafberg.'

Joshua Loftus Colby Goff smiled at his grandfather. To him, the man sitting alongside him in the gig was tremendously old, a small slight man with a fuzz of white hair about his ears, gnarled hands and a straight small body that was everlastingly erect.

'Next day,' the old man went on, 'we broke through to Donotsfontein and everybody came running out to see us. Black men, brown men and white men. The pavements were lined with people, all yelling and cheering like lunatics.'

'It's in a book I've got, Grandpa,' Josh said. ' "How we liberated Donotsfontein." With maps and everything. There's a picture of you and Lord Ellesmere looking at a map and one of father getting his medal.'

Sir Colby Goff looked at his grandson. He looked like another Dabney, small, slight, dark-haired and dark-eyed, his face intelligent, sensitive and full of humour. Because it was his grandmother's birthday and there were to be a bonfire and fireworks, he had insisted on joining his grandfather to help in the preparations.

The day was brilliant, just one more brilliant day in a brilliant period of summer. Every day that summer seemed to have been one long heat-filled delight, full of the hum of bees and the song of birds beneath a cloudless sky. The bonfire stood ready in the middle of the lower meadow behind the house, waiting for the first brand to be thrust into the straw beneath the logs and brushwood, and they had gone down on the thin excuse of making sure everything was ready.

Because his father was with the Regiment and not due home until later, and his mother was preoccupied with a younger sister, the old man had driven over to Josh's home to fetch the boy, promising him they should spend the whole day together. Nothing ever pleased the boy more than being with the old man, and nothing pleased the old man more than the boy's company. It was as if their ages had skipped a generation, because they were incredibly close, had the same interests, laughed at the same jokes, and enjoyed the surroundings of Braxby in exactly the same way. The old man's pleasure came from the boy's interest, and the boy's chief delight was in listening to the old soldier's stories of his battles.

'Was Graafberg why they made you a sir, Grandpa?' he asked.

Sir Colby Goff rested the reins on his knee as he lit a cigar. 'No,' he said. 'Bit before that. But Lord Roberts gave me a Division. Graafberg was the first real victory, y'see. Came at just the right time after a lot of setbacks. Didn't amount to much, though, I suppose.'

'There were a lot of prisoners – as many as at Modder River. Papa told me.'

'But it raised no siege, my boy. Just got Buller moving.'

'They call you "Goff of Graafberg" though, don't they? I've seen it in the papers. The Regiment wears it on its drum cloths. When he stayed here that time, Lord Kitchener said it was the one thing that got the war going again. He said it was why they made you a field marshal.'

The old man gave a wry smile. 'A field marshal's baton's all too often a consolation prize when you retire.'

'Field marshals never retire.'

'No, but the people at the top make sure they don't interfere. We're always on the active list, of course – me, Roberts, Evelyn Wood – but, by God, I wouldn't like to have to fight a war run by a lot of old dodderers like that, would you? All right at organising things, naturally, because we know King's Regulations back to front – you'd have to be a bit of a donkey not to, after the years we've spent in uniform – and that's why they don't put us out to grass like generals. They consider we're experienced enough to be helpful when they need advice, y'see. That's what we are: A military aid committee.'

The boy moved closer in the seat. 'Tell me again, Grandpa. What happened afterwards?'

The old man made himself comfortable, clicking his tongue to set the pony in motion. How much the boy understood of what he told him he had no idea. He never talked down to the child and somehow he felt that a lot of what he said was absorbed.

'Well,' he said, 'when he learned what had happened at the Graafberg, Lord Roberts sent French forward. The Boers were holding a place called Klip Drift and French took a chance and charged straight through the centre of their line. After all that effort, in the end all it needed was imagination of the sort that Roberts had, and the sort of courage French showed. While they were still celebrating, Cronje surrendered at Modder River. Graafberg tended to get forgotten.'

'That's a shame, Grandpa.'

The Field Marshal studied his grandson thoughtfully. Not really, he thought. A lot of men had done a good job that day. His plan had been a sound one and it had come off in spite of Robert's silly blunder and the disaster to the 19th Lancers. No man liked to see his own regiment involved in disaster but it *had* been a disaster, redeemed only by Dabney with

121

Johnson's half-squadron and the North Cape Horse on the other end of the front.

'If father got a medal for Graafberg,' the boy asked, 'why didn't Uncle Robert?'

The Field Marshal lifted his head, jerking himself back to the present. He seemed to spend most of his time these days somewhere in the past.

'You don't give medals for the sort of thing your Uncle Robert did,' he said.

'It was brave.'

'It was also a bit stupid, Josh.'

And it had damned Robert's military career for good. Lord Roberts had not been slow to offer praise both for the Field Marshal's plan and for Dabney's skill at interpreting what was needed, but he had also been furious at the loss of a squadron of desperately needed cavalry, and he had demanded a report. The Field Marshal had not enjoyed condemning his own son but there was no alternative and he had accepted at that point that Robert would never make a soldier and was better out of the army and in business as he seemed to wish.

He frowned, remembering it all with sadness. Damn silly, he thought. Silly enough to leave Robert in charge of a remount depot for the rest of the war where he could do no harm, while Dabney, given a job in Intelligence, had commanded an advance column, scouting ahead of the army and along its flanks, raiding Boer farms for news of De Wet and De La Rey. He had once seen him come in out of the blue, his squadron reduced to a mere forty-two, his soldiers ragged, bearded and sick, half the horses unfit after a hundred and forty miles in six days. But, with methods more suitable to bush rangers than cavalry, they had brought in information which had helped sweep the Boers down towards Portuguese East. With the Graafberg, it had been sufficient for him to pick up a DSO and his future seemed secure.

Just ahead of them, a group of men were walking slowly back to the Home Farm and the boy eyed them keenly.

'Will the Ackroyds come to the fireworks, Grandpa?'

'The Ackroyds always come and Sergeant Ackroyd built the fire. You'd better ask him to make sure.'

As the gig drew alongside them, the men stopped and touched their caps. Ellis Ackroyd, a little greyer now and a little stouter, smiled. 'Bonfire all right, sir?' he asked.

The Field Marshal gave the boy a nudge and he leaned forward.

'It should go up splendidly, Sergeant,' he said. 'We hope anybody who wants to see the fireworks will come along.'

Ackroyd's smile widened. 'That they will, Master Josh.'

'Boys coming, Ellis?' the Field Marshal asked.

'Not Tom, sir. He's with the railway at Doncaster. But Hedley's coming.'

'How's he doing?'

'Well, sir. Thanks to your help. We could never have got him to university on our own.'

The old man grunted, faintly embarrassed. 'Had to do our bit, Ellis. Can't let these clever fellers down, can we? What's he going in for?'

'He don't know yet, sir. Something brainy, I expect.'

As the pony moved on again, Josh sat in silence for a while then he spoke thoughtfully. 'Grandpa, why didn't they make you a lord? Field marshals are always lords.'

'Evelyn Wood never got to be a lord.'

'Why didn't you?'

The old man chuckled. 'Edward VII. When he was Prince of Wales. Started chasing your grandmother round the shrubbery. She was younger in those days and jolly pretty. I told him he'd better stop – and pretty damn' quick, too.'

'Why would he chase Grandma round the shrubbery?'

The old man coughed in his confusion. 'Liked to run races, boy. That sort of thing. Great one for running races with the ladies. Not done in Yorkshire, though. All right for London, but not here. So he went on to Tranby Croft and while he was there a feller was caught cheating at cards. Nasty business.'

The boy was puzzled. At his age, a king could do no wrong, and the old man had to explain.

'He didn't even want to up me to field marshal,' he said. 'But the army insisted. They told him all about Balaclava, y'see, and Tshethoslane and Isandhlwana and a few other places like Omdurman and the Graafberg, and the army can make its feelings felt when it wishes. What I got was a baronetcy. And that'll go to your Uncle Robert who's bound to get one for services to commerce before long, anyway, so you'll have to go through life as a perfectly ordinary person.'

There was a long silence as the pony trotted towards the house. At the front door, a groom, inevitably another Ackroyd, appeared from the stables and took the animal's head.

As they moved to the library, Josh studied his grandfather. He always found it hard to realise that this man who seemed so old and frail had once been young enough and strong enough to have ridden with the Light Brigade at Balaclava. He had often studied the pictures in his books and tried to decide which one of the frantic horsemen braving the Russian shot and shell was the old man. According to what he'd been taught at school, Balaclava had been a victory, but his grandfather always insisted it was nothing of the kind, and that, too, was hard to understand. He glanced again at the old soldier at his side, slight, erect, brisk. History went back through him and, through his father, Josh's great-grandfather, to Waterloo, and through his forefathers, to the victory of Wandewash, after which his great-great-great-grandfather had been given this land at Braxby and two hundred and fifty pounds to raise a regiment of light dragoons –

The Regiment. He never thought of it as the 19th Lancers, which it had become in the years after Waterloo. Just as The Regiment. The Regiment had filled the whole of his life since he had been old enough to think and there had been more occasions than he could remember when he had stood among the spectators near the saluting base, pinching his female cousins and kicking his male ones as they had waited for the green-clad Lancers to march past. The Clutchers, they were called. The Widowmakers. Goff's Greens. Even his name was part of their title.

'Grandpa,' he said abruptly. 'Will there be a war between Germany and France?'

The old man's face looked bleak for a moment. 'God forbid, boy.'

'What if there is? Will England be in it?'

'Doesn't look like it. Everybody else will – treaties and so on – but we haven't got any and we seem for once to be the only ones who aren't touched.'

The boy considered. 'What if we were? Would I have to go?'

'Bit young, boy.'

'How about you?'

The old man chuckled. 'Bit *old*. They'd find a job for me, I suppose – givin' pep talks to young soldiers.'

There was another long silence. 'Grandpa, what if there *was* a war and we *were* in it? Would that mean that Father and Uncle Karl-August would be fighting on opposite sides?'

The old man hesitated. 'It's happened before, boy,' he said at last.

'It'd be a bit difficult if Father found himself face-to-face with Uncle Karl. What about Uncle Karl's father, the Graf?'

'Like me. Bit beyond it now, boy. They'll use *him* for pep talks, too.'

'What sort of things do you tell them in a pep talk, Grandpa?'

The old man considered. 'The meaning of the Regimental motto. How to be patriotic and brave. All that nonsense.'

'Is it nonsense?'

'Sometimes. But it works. Then I'd tell them all about saluting and bearing themselves like good horse-smelly British soldiers.'

'What would the Graf tell the Germans?'

'How to bear themselves like good horse-smelly German soldiers, how to salute the flag and how not to bolt their sausages.'

They both laughed, the boy rolling on the floor, the old man hunched in his chair, his frame shaking silently at the boy's mirth. Then the boy sobered suddenly.

'I wouldn't like fighting against Cousin Constantin.'

'Might never happen, boy. Pray God it won't. War's a terrible thing. I was at Isandhlwana and I rode into the camp and found them all dead –'

'That will be enough of that!' The words came from the doorway and the old man shrank back in his chair, winking at the boy.

Lady Goff studied her husband, her violet eyes disapproving. She was white-haired now but had lost none of her beauty, despite the lines on her face, and none of her shape. The old man's heart filled with pleasure at the sight of her.

She was regarding him with mock horror. 'I expect you're frightening the life out of the child again.'

The boy grinned. 'Not really, Grannie. I like to hear Grandpa's stories.'

'All about battle, murder and sudden death.'

'What's a man's life but battle, murder and sudden death?' the Field Marshal growled. 'Especially if he's a soldier.'

126

The old lady frowned, her eyes unhappy for a moment. 'It won't happen to Josh. He might even decide not to be a soldier.'

'God forbid that he goes into business like his Uncle Robert.' The Field Marshal frowned. 'And if you saw him in the green of the Regiment, you know it'd make your heart turn over with pride.'

'Probably,' Lady Goff conceded. 'Probably with fear also.' She frowned. 'Surely you read the papers? The Kaiser's been waving his sword again.'

The Field Marshal tried to change the subject. 'Bonfire's all ready,' he said. 'Ellis Ackroyd's got the fireworks. Don't it make you proud on your birthday?'

'It makes me feel old.'

'Don't look a day over forty.'

She gave him a quick smile, almost a grin, the sort of smile that had jerked at his heart when he was young and had never stopped since, and it made him think about his son, Robert, once more. He'd heard rumours that he was having an affair in Leeds with the wife of Lord Balmael. Knowing Lord Balmael, he wasn't surprised. Balmael was in the Guards, a dim, stupid, honourable man whose father had been a self-made rough-diamond and whose wife was much the same. But Robert was a Goff, and Goffs didn't go in for that sort of thing. It jabbed at his liver and he tried hard to push it to the back of his mind before it gave him a headache.

'Tyas tells me his rheumatism's bad,' he said quickly.

'So's his arthritis,' his wife said. '*And* his memory. Oughtn't we to have Ellis in the house to take over?'

'Tyas stays as long as he wants to.'

'He dropped the best tea-set last week.'

The Field Marshal grunted. 'He didn't drop me when he carried me off the field at Yellow Tavern with a hole in me leg as big as a cricket ball. For that he stays long as he wishes.'

'I wasn't thinking of asking him to leave, dear. But he's older than you and I felt we ought to have someone ready to step in, in case he decides to retire.'

'I'll see Ellis. He'll know what to do.'

'Very well. In the meantime, I'd better find out what he's done with the tea and muffins. Don't start terrifying that child with your stories of Zululand.'

As she disappeared, Josh stared at his grandfather who winked at him again.

'What shall we talk about, Grandpa? Cricket? Yorkshire are doing very well against Lancashire. Kilner got 93.'

'Did he now? He'll be playing for England, I suppose.'

'Who'll they pick, Grandpa?'

'Hobbs, of course, for a start. And Rhodes. And how about this feller, Coe, who hit 237 for Leicester against Hants? The way I see it, it goes like this.'

He thrust his newspaper at the boy with the team written in the margin,

> *Hobbs*
> *Hirst*
> *Hearne*
> *Coe*
> *Woolley*
> Fender (captain)
> *Rhodes*
> *Kilner*
> *Slater*
> *Jaques*
> *Booth.*

'How's that?' he asked.

'That sounds a good team, Grandpa. They ought to beat anybody.' There was a long silence. 'Grandpa, why is our Regiment called the Widowmakers?'

'Not *our* regiment, boy.'

'We founded it.'

'We raised it. That don't make it ours. We only had it on trust. Lord Ellesmere has it now.'

'Why are we called the Widowmakers?'

'Because we've made quite a few in our day. In the Peninsular, chiefly. Boney's time.'

'Did you fight Boney, Grandpa?'

'Good God, boy, I'm not that old!'

The boy grinned and abruptly switched subjects again.

'Why did Uncle Robert resign his commission?'

The old man blinked and considered, trying to be tolerant.

'Your Uncle Robert decided he wasn't cut out for soldiering. Decided he was better suited for business. Besides, he married your Aunt Elfrida and she wasn't keen.'

'I thought our family never married Cosgros, Grandpa. Cousin Philippa said we didn't. She said there was a feud between us and that you started it. She said you shot one of the Cosgros.'

The old man sat bolt upright. 'Damned if I did, boy! I just sent him home from Zululand. Told him there was no place in the Regiment for him.'

'Why? Was it full?'

'Sort of. He shot himself in Paris on the way home. Couldn't face his family. Didn't measure up. Aut nullus aut primus.'

'What's that?'

'Regimental motto: Nothing but the Best.'

'Is that why Uncle Robert sent in his papers?'

The old man tried to change the subject again. 'You're growing a big chap, young Josh. You'll be able to join the Regiment yourself before long. Know why you're called Joshua?'

'No, why?'

'After the Joshua Pellew Goff who founded the regiment.'

'Then why does Uncle Robert call himself "Cosgro-Goff"? Father's simply "Goff." '

The old man grunted. 'Your Uncle Robert's started getting some damn funny ideas lately,' he growled. 'I fancy that when he was taken into the Cosgro business, he decided he ought to become a Cosgro like the rest of 'em.'

'Sometimes he even spells his name differently – G.O.U.G.H.'

If George were called 'Ball', Sir Colby Goff thought, he'd probably write it 'Testicle.'

'Fashion, boy,' he said shortly. 'Fashion. Great ones for fancy spelling, some people.'

'Tyas Ackroyd says he's not a proper Goff, anyway.'

'Little pigs have pig ears and Tyas ought to be careful what he says. All he means is that your Uncle Robert's not a soldier and the Goffs have always been soldiers. That's all. Tyas is getting too damned old. Like me. After all, Chelmsford's gone. Buller's gone. Wolseley died last year. Only leaves me, Wood and Roberts. Soon there'll be nobody left from those half-baked little wars in the last century except Kitchener.' He saw the look of alarm in the boy's face and decided he was growing maudlin. He sat up. 'Still, the family'll see it through, won't we?' he said briskly. 'Your father's a good soldier.'

'You and I would see it through, too, Grandpa.'

'That we would. We'd not let the Regiment down.'

'Specially if it came to a charge.'

'God bless me soul! Yes. It's the sort of thing the Goffs go in for, I suppose.'

'Hedley Ackroyd says aeroplanes and motor cars will do that sort of thing in another war.'

'Does he, by God? Well, if Hedley Ackroyd says so, probably it's right. I expect he's thought about it. He seems to think about most things.'

'Father says Uncle Karl's coming to stay with us?'

'That's right.'

'I heard him say it might be for the last time. What did he mean?'

'This war in Europe, boy.' Josh heard his grandfather sigh. 'The thing's got a bit out of hand, y'see, and there are quite a few people who might be at each other's throats before the year's out. If it comes, your Uncle Karl will be in it.'

'Will he be killed?'

'God forbid, boy.'

The old man frowned. All the same, he thought, his mouth working, there would be a distinct bloody possibility.

two

The younger children, who had been put to bed in the afternoon to allow them to stay up, were in a state of hysterical excitement by the time Dabney arrived. He strode into the house where they were all gathered and kissed his wife and children, then his mother, then he turned and embraced his father. He was a quiet man but his manner was brisk and commanding and even without his uniform he was clearly someone of consequence. And, despite his slightness, there was an air about him of a man who knew exactly what he wanted and exactly where he was going, aggressively male in spite of his build, his face wearing an expression that was full of strength and ancient wisdom and belied his youthfulness of manner, an air of self-confidence that showed in his every gesture, in the tilt of his head, the set of his feet, the arch of his back, the way he held his shoulders. The Field Marshal regarded him warmly, guiltily aware that he had never made any bones about this being his favourite child.

With his arrival, the family would be complete for the first time in years, because the Hartmanns had arrived earlier in the afternoon from Germany. Dabney was immediately aware of the strangeness of the gathering, because over it brooded the international situation and the awareness that before long the two branches of the family might even be enemies.

His sister, Helen, was clearly worried. She looked well and prosperous, and plump nowadays in the German manner, with a brood of children around her, but she was clearly upset that the international situation might cut her off from her childhood home.

'Will there be a war, Dab?' she asked.

'God forbid!'

'That's no answer.'

Dabney looked up at her under one eyebrow. 'No,' he agreed. 'It isn't. But it's the best I can do. You should tell Karl-August to stop that idiot of a Kaiser talking through his hat.'

'Karl says the British are trying to prevent the German empire expanding.'

'Does he really believe that?'

'I don't think so really. But that's what the Kaiser says. So, it's what the government says and what everybody in Germany says.'

Her husband appeared alongside her, holding his youngest son by the hand. Dabney patted the child's head and gave him an abstracted kiss because he was watching his son, Josh, struggling with his other German nephew, Constantin, in the far corner of the room in a wrestling match. Despite the yells of delight, the faces of the two small boys were twisted into grimaces as they fought, and the thought that they might one day be doing it in real life troubled him.

'How's your father, Karl?' he asked.

Karl-August shrugged, a tall good-looking man going a little grey, his eyes intelligent and brooding. 'Very well,' he said. 'Growing old, of course. Do you think there'll be a war, Dabney?'

Dabney sighed. 'God forbid,' he said again. 'Wars benefit nobody. I hope everybody has enough sense to avoid one.'

'There's a mood in Europe, nevertheless.'

Karl-August was right, of course. The German Emperor was eager for a war to get what he wanted. The French wanted a war to get revenge for their humiliation in 1870. The British didn't want a war because they had all they needed, but they would go to war if they thought they were in danger of losing it.

Dabney's wife, Fleur, was talking earnestly with Helen. She caught his eye and smiled at him over Helen's shoulder and he thought with agony of what she might have to go through if there *were* a war. He had no fears for himself – war was his profession – but once it had been his duty in Cape Town to inform the wife of a brother officer who had been killed by a sniper. Unaware of the message he brought, she had risen smiling to meet him. As she realised he hadn't returned her smile, her eyes had gone strangely dead and empty and when he had told her his news, she had said nothing for a moment, sinking into a chair abruptly, her fingers picking at the material of the arm. Then she had lifted her hands to her mouth and pressed them tightly over her lips as though she were trying to stop herself crying out. Her anguished whisper – 'Oh, God, what am I to do?' – had wrenched at his heart. That, he felt, must not happen to Fleur.

They had been lovers before they had married. She had met him in London when he had returned from Cape Town. Her family had thought she was staying with a friend and the friend had been sworn to secrecy and had promised to lie if necessary. She had waited for him, her clothes neatly on the chair alongside the bed, a slender white wand in the semi-darkness, shy yet eager at the same time, as aware as he was that this was not just a clandestine meeting in a hotel bedroom but a culmination of years of waiting. To them both there had been nothing sordid in it; it was merely a step forward to the state of marriage which they had both believed in and had expected since they had been children.

As they talked and Ackroyd and one of his granddaughters circulated with the sherry, the Suttons arrived, John every inch a farmer, red-faced and sturdy in tweeds, his wife, Jane, Dabney's other sister, looking as if she'd just left the preparations for the harvest supper. Their two daughters drifted at once to where Dabney's daughter, Chloe, was gazing entranced at Helen's youngest child. Then he heard Tyas Ackroyd, bent and old, whisper in his father's ear.

'The Cosgros 'ave arrived, sir.' It sounded vaguely like an alarm.

The Cosgro-Goffs swept into the room in a noisy avalanche, the children hurtling across to join their English and German cousins. The two daughters, May and Ann, took after their mother, plump, pretty in a way that would fade quickly as they lost their youth. The boys were too fat, too smartly dressed, and Dabney saw the eldest, Aubrey, try to join the wrestling match between Josh and Constantin, only to receive a push that made him sit down heavily and back away, unwanted.

Dabney was about to stride across the room and admonish his son when he saw Robert advancing on him with his hand outstretched. 'Hello Dab,' he said. 'How's the army?'

'Ticking along,' Dabney said quietly. Having repudiated the army, these days Robert seemed to enjoy making it sound like an infants' class, as if he considered it a puerile, futile thing compared with the importance of making money. It constantly irritated Dabney and sometimes he was hard put to reply lightly.

His annoyance seemed to sail over his brother's head and Robert turned aside. He never spent long talking to Dabney, almost as if with his contempt there was also a faint sense of guilt. He swung round to his brother-in-law.

135

'Hello, there, Karl,' he said. 'What the devil's your Emperor thinking about, with all these antics he gets up to?'

The behaviour of the German Emperor had baffled Europe for years but Karl-August stiffened, his intelligent face set. 'He is thinking about Germany, I suspect,' he said with a touch of pride. 'As King George thinks about England.'

'Yes, but all this talk of war! Dammit, the world's big enough for everybody and war would play hell with business.'

Not, Dabney thought, with the Cosgro business. They were in wool and now had an interest in Sheffield steel. A war demanding uniforms and guns would make them a fortune.

Robert was growing fat, he noticed, while Elfrida wasn't growing any slimmer. Robert looked as though he didn't expect to be much affected by the crisis that had crept up on Europe. It had arrived almost unnoticed and talk of war had become common coin these days. Everybody was used to the fear of a major conflict, and it was even accepted that suffering and death were part of the European background. Because Europeans had been used to war for thousands of years, it was not considered unusual for men to go off occasionally under their banners and carrying their weapons, their honour in their helmets like a plume.

Dabney looked across at his brother. Not Robert, though, he decided. Never Robert. Robert would never go to war again.

He could hear him now, sounding off.

'Of course, the Franco-Prussian War left a lot of bitterness. You have to admit that.'

'In France,' Karl-August said patiently, 'Germany has as bad a neighbour as it is possible to have.' The German was trying hard to be tolerant of his brother-in-law's views.

'Well –' Robert shrugged – 'of course, whatever happens, we shan't be in. We've had a policy of splendid isolation for years from all your Continental animosities. In any case, with the royal family German and a lot of German families coming over here with them, like this family the country's drawn more to our German "cousins" than towards France, whom we've never really trusted. All the same –' Robert paused to deliver a pontifical rebuke ' – when things were going badly for us in South Africa, there was a great chorus of delight on the Continent and it was led, old man, by your Emperor. He even offered to help Kruger.'

Karl-August smiled. 'I think your navy precluded anything like that.'

'But he's built up his own navy since then, hasn't he? That's why we had to become friendly with France. We didn't want to. After all, they're a pretty scruffy lot and we'd much rather have been friendly with the Germans.'

'You have the Entente Cordiale, nevertheless.'

'It's not a treaty. It doesn't bind us and nobody in his senses in this country would ever go to war for France.'

Karl-August gave a sad smile. 'Nevertheless,' he said, 'I think the whole of Europe is walking on eggs. And if war does come, I have no doubt that it will have nothing to do with anything your government has said or done – or my government either. It will spring from something quite trivial which will set things in motion and then there will be no going back.'

As Dabney stood with one arm round his wife and one round his mother, his father joined them. 'For God's sake,' he hissed, 'get Robert away from Karl-August! He's on his high horse. Karl-August's trying hard to be tolerant but if we allow Robert to go on much longer this blasted war he's on about will break out here in our own drawing-room.'

Lady Goff smiled and, without a word, crossed to Karl-August. Taking him by the arm, she swept him away, leaving Robert with his mouth open, his sentence unfinished.

Deprived of his victim, he turned to his brother and father. 'You know, Father, Karl-August's wrong,' he said. 'Quite wrong. The way he sticks up for that damn fool, William II, is ridiculous. If war comes, it won't be our fault. Who'd get the command, Father? French? He did well in South Africa.'

His father grunted noncommittally. 'Europe isn't South Africa. These days it's magazine rifles and machine guns. To go after a herd of elephants with a machine gun would be a massacre. It's not much different with men. Perhaps that's what made South Africa no damn use at all as a preparation for a European war. That was a sporting war but, as far as Europe's concerned, we'd better forget about sportsmanship, and use everything we've got.'

Robert looked at his father disapprovingly. 'That's strange talk from you, Father.'

The old man shrugged. 'War's a dirty business,' he said. 'Anybody who tries to suggest otherwise is a fool. If we can win while keeping it decently dirty, so much the better, but if we can't then we'd better go in for something a little less clean and aim at winning.'

'Do you think there *will* be a war, Dab?'

Dabney drew a deep breath. 'I think that must be the fourth time today I've been asked that question.'

'Well, what *do* you think?'

'I think there will.'

'Well, we're not involved.' Robert sounded smug. 'We haven't a treaty with any of the other powers.'

Dabney moved away. 'I expect,' he said over his shoulder, 'that someone'll find a way round.'

As the pale summer sky changed to violet and then to deep blue, they all trooped down to the lower meadow, the women and the smallest children in the gig, followed by all the Ackroyds from the Home Farm and the cottages. Tyas Ackroyd and the Field Marshal rode in the big Vauxhall, driven and maintained for the family by one of Tyas' grandsons.

'Drinks all ready, Tyas?' the Field Marshal asked.

'Ellis 'as 'em under control, sir.'

'Food?'

'Hampers already down there. Soup. Pies. Parkin. Toffee for the children. The beer barrel's been broached.'

Since the summer had been so beautiful and the heat had built up, it was still warm despite the hour. By the time the car arrived, everybody was waiting, the children wide-eyed, eager-faced, and excited at being out of bed. Ellis Ackroyd and his wife and daughter were already passing round the drinks, and the older children were gathered in groups chatting, among them Robert's elder daughter, May, Jane's daughters, Philippa and Rachel, and Helen's daughter, Gabriella von Hartmann.

As the flames began to sweep up the pile of logs and brushwood, there were gasps from the smaller children and while they were still staring, three rockets went up together, and a line of roman candles flared into brilliance.

In their light, Dabney watched the faces of the youngsters around him. Among them was an older boy in a Norfolk suit and breeches, his hand touching that of Dabney's niece, Philippa Sutton, his sister Jane's daughter.

'See Hedley got here then, Tyas,' he said.

'Yes, sir. He usually does what he says he's going to do.'

As they moved among the watching children, the boy in the Norfolk suit moved to where Dabney stood with his father.

'Pleased to see you so well, sir,' he smiled to the Field Marshal. 'I've come to report.'

'Report what?'

'My progress, sir. It's thanks to you I'm at university. The least I can do is tell you how I'm getting on.'

The boy had the same look old Tyas had, the same look Ellis had, the same direct manner.

'No need to feel beholden, my boy,' the Field Marshal said.

'Nevertheless I do, sir, and I try to prove I'm worth it. I think I've done well in my exams and hope to get a good second. To get a first you have to do a lot of swotting and I'm not sure that's what university's about. I've preferred to use the time in other ways.'

'What other ways?'

'I've learned to fly, sir. It's the coming thing.'

'Is it, by God?' The Field Marshal's eyebrows shot up. 'That what you're intending to go in for?'

'I might.'

As the boy turned away, Dabney noticed he moved back at once to Philippa Sutton and saw once again that surreptitiously their hands touched.

As they stood watching, the Field Marshal spoke quietly. 'Tell me, Dab,' he said. 'Everybody's occupied now. How are things with the Regiment?'

Dabney shrugged. The Field Marshal was little involved with the army these days. He was ageing fast and he limped badly from old wounds. But he missed the army and he missed the men, and he liked to keep in touch through his son.

'They're in good shape, Father,' Dabney said.

'I'm glad.' The old man frowned. 'We may have need of them before long.'

Dabney nodded. 'Yes,' he agreed. 'But not just yet, I think. There's nothing in the evening paper to alarm anybody. Only some Austrian archduke assassinated in Bosnia, and that won't affect us.'

three

Dabney couldn't have been more wrong.

The assassination of the Archduke Franz Ferdinand, heir to the Austrian throne, had set alight a slow-burning fuse. Believing the assassination the work of the Serbian authorities, towards the end of July the Austrian government issued an unacceptable ultimatum to Serbia and five days later, without giving them chance to appeal against it, declared war. Immediately, in support of a promise made to the Balkan Slavs, Russia mobilised and the following day Germany issued an ultimatum to France, informing her that nothing that had happened was any of her business.

The rumours grew. The war everybody had been expecting had come at last. In Germany, reserves were being called up, escorted to the station by weeping wives and children. And as Germany mobilised, France, her ancient enemy, mobilised too. The streets filled as crowds of men began to move towards the barracks, and two days later the British Fleet was at sea.

Fleur's face was horrified. 'But *we* can't possibly be in the war, Dab,' she said.

Dabney's expression was grim. 'We can now. German troops are massing on the Belgian frontier and we have a treaty to protect Belgium.'

Fleur stared at him with shocked eyes. 'Then you – ?"

'Not only me,' Dabney said grimly, 'but Karl-August, too. I expect Ellis Ackroyd'll have to go, too. He's still a reservist. So, for that matter, will father.'

She looked startled.

'A field marshal's never too old,' he explained. 'I don't suppose he'll have to stand up and be shot at but he'll be busy. Everybody'll be in it in the end.' He managed a smile. 'Such a good summer, too, and Yorkshire doing so well.'

The papers were full of dark and foreboding stories, and breakfast was a silent business.

ENGLAND GIVES UP PEACE NEGOTIATIONS, stated the headline, over the smaller one announcing Germany's invasion of Belgium. Mobilisation, it continued, was progressing with great enthusiasm, and the two sets of allies were squaring up to each other.

Then came a moving letter from Helen. Even the envelope showed the feelings that had been aroused, because some German postal clerk, seeing the address, had scrawled 'Gott Strafe England' across it.

Karl-August was already in uniform, it seemed, uncertain whether to feel despair at the way things had turned out or pride at his country's readiness, and Helen described the trains full of soldiers chalked with 'Nach Paris' and 'Nach Petersburg,' the men inside cheering and singing. She had just returned to Berlin from England; her luggage had been lost in the chaos of the crowds rushing home from the summer holidays and she had heard it had gone to Holland. In the Unter Den Linden, mobs were pacing up and down, singing 'Deutschland Über Alles' and 'Die Wacht Am Rhein.' Here and there a company of infantry or a squadron of horse, wearing their new grey uniforms instead of the old-fashioned Prussian blue, shook hands and accepted food or bottles of wine. She had seen the Kaiser in his car, and the Crown

Prince, and the Socialists were all busy saying it wasn't a people's war.

'I wish to God,' she wrote, 'that it wasn't. There seems little else I can say. Now I am a German and must think like a German. But I am still English by instinct and can't find it in me to hate the land where I was born. This may be the last letter I shall be able to get to you, though I shall continue to try via Holland, where we have friends who might be persuaded to forward them. But just in case we don't manage it, I must say goodbye for the time being.'

The call came to Dabney at Colchester where the 19th had recently moved from Ireland. With only a small volunteer army, the mustering of reserves was different in England. The men arrived quietly, less than willing but not shirking their duty. Many of them were clearly too old and it was obvious at once they would be useless as fighting soldiers.

The remounts were also beginning to stream in and Dabney moved through the stables between a long row of intelligent heads. Swishing well-kept tails had been squared to a hand's-breadth above the hock, coats had been brushed and polished, and hooves oiled as if by a manicurist. Burnished saddles lay on the racks and in the armoury swords and lances were being sharpened and rifles checked.

Running a hand down a fetlock, Dabney turned to the sergeant alongside him.

'Pleased with this one,' he said. 'Good batch, that last lot. But we'll have a different man on the grey mare. His hands are too heavy for her.'

News had arrived that Sir John French had been appointed commander-in-chief of the British Expeditionary Force, and since he was a cavalryman it was expected there would be action.

There was a lot of anxiety that it would be over before they could arrive and that the French would wipe the

Germans off the map, but Dabney had listened too often to his father, and the belief that it would be over by Christmas was not his view. His father had said it would be a matter of years, not months, and he had heard that Kitchener, at the War Office, had said the same thing.

He wasn't sure what to expect. It was still believed that the cavalryman was first and foremost the soldier of the charge and the mêlée and that if he were regarded merely as a mounted rifleman a great deal would be lost. The lance-versus-sword question had always ended in acrimony and most people had tried to steer a middle course between the conflicting ideas on cavalry employment and armament, but the argument had eventually been settled by an army order allowing the Lancers to retain their nine-foot weapon for escort duties, reviews and ceremonial parades, though they were now armed also with a rifle and a sword.

'See that Number 78 gets a rug on him,' Dabney said. 'Mustn't let him take a chill. And find a heavier horse for Soames. He's getting fat.'

The sergeant grinned. 'The war'll get some weight off him, sir, I reckon.'

'I think it will. Let's leave the chestnuts on an extra feed of linseed. Light-coloured horses always seem a trifle less sturdy than the rest.'

Coming to the end of the line, Dabney returned to the squadron office and stood in front of the shelf containing his books. Chief among them was his father's work, *Cavalry Studies*. He picked it up and opened it. The Old Man, he decided, had absorbed well the lessons of America and the Franco-Prussian War and had ignored Zululand, where he had made his name, because he: regarded it as a tribal war and of no consequence to European thinking.

'The answer to the rifle,' he read, 'is not the sword or the lance, but another rifle, in the hands of a man who uses his horse to move rapidly from one cover to another.'

Dabney pushed the book back on to the shelf. Unlike most cavalry leaders, his father had not slipped into the facile belief that simple rapidity of movement was the answer to the rifle and the machine gun. He was a believer in the horse, but only for speed. It was worth bearing in mind.

As he turned, there was a knock and Ellis Ackroyd entered. He looked red-faced and uncomfortable in uniform.

'Colonel's compliments, sir,' he said. 'He'd like to see you for a minute.'

'Right, Ellis. I'll go along straight away. How're you finding being back in the Regiment?'

'Bit of a wrench, sir.' Ackroyd smiled. 'I'd just got used to being back at Braxby. But it's not too arduous. They don't expect an old man like me to get into danger. They're going to give me the orderly room when Sergeant Addison goes to France.'

Dabney smiled back. 'You'll be keeping the reinforcement cadres coming, I expect,' he said. 'Just try to push into 'em some of that field knowledge you pushed into me as a small boy. Ferreting with you was of great value when I reached South Africa. I found I could get nearer to the Boers than anybody without being seen. How was your father?'

'Gettin' old, sir.'

'Tom?'

'Wants to join some transport unit.'

'And Hedley?'

'Talking of joining the Flying Corps. Says he'll show us a thing or two.'

The adjutant was just leaving the colonel's office when Dabney arrived, and instead of Lord Ellesmere he was surprised to find George Johnson standing by the desk, a bundle of papers in his hand.

'Ah, Dabney,' he said. 'There's been a change. Lord Ellesmere's been upped to brigadier. Brigadier Lowson in Jamieson's division of the First Corps has gone sick and they've given him the job. He's very happy because, unlike some, he's not been pushed off to a yeomanry brigade. They're given me the regiment in his place.'

Dabney looked at Johnson. He was a tall thin man with a long neck and protuberant adam's apple. While he had always admired Ellesmere, privately he didn't consider Johnson a clever soldier and he had suffered more than once from what he felt was a narrow-minded jealous streak. For some reason, Johnson believed the credit for the Battle of Graafberg belonged to him not Dabney, and that Dabney wore the ribbon of a DSO which should have been his.

Johnson was still talking. 'Lord Ellesmere, of course, was sorry not to be leading the Regiment into action but his loss is my gain. We shall be in France in three weeks, I imagine. As senior captain, I want you to take over my squadron. You'll find it in good shape, I think. I hope you'll make sure it stays that way. Your promotion will be in the Gazette in a day or two. Then, since I'm trying to see that everyone gets a visit home before we leave, you'd better try to slip away for the weekend. I suspect we're going to be busy.'

The Yorkshire countryside looked better than Dabney had ever seen it and, with the news that he had received, had a strangely personal feel about it. It was his, this land, and he suddenly felt he wanted to cling to it.

Fleur was at the station with the children in the car to collect him. Her eyes were moist and there was a bleak look on her face. His hand touched hers as he climbed in beside her.

'It might not happen,' he murmured.

Josh pushed his head between them. 'Are you going to the war, Papa?' he demanded.

'Looks like it, Josh.'

'Bring me back some souvenirs.'

'What would you like?'

'A German sausage would do.' As the boy fell back, hooting with laughter, Chloe piled on top of him and the two of them fought and wriggled on the back seat, Chloe at least uncertain what she was laughing at.

Reaching home, Dabney hurried the children off for their tea and took his wife in his arms. She seemed to scent disaster, trying to hold back her tears.

'Oh, Dab,' was all she could say and even so her voice sounded strangled.

He held her against him, trying to give her courage. 'Steady, old thing,' he said.

'Why does there have to be a war?'

'Because there are stupid, ambitious men in the world.'

'I'm not sure I can handle this, Dab.'

'Of course you can. Your mother did. My mother did. You will. You have to, for the sake of Josh and Chloe. You've got to put on a brave face. If you look frightened, they'll be frightened. You can't allow that.'

'No. Of course not. I'll try, Dab. I'll try.'

That night as Dabney lay along the edge of the bed, Fleur seemed to be asleep. The news of his impending departure had left her wretched and he tried not to wake her but lay straight-limbed, staring at the ceiling.

Inside him there was a terrible anxiety for his family. In South Africa he had had nobody dependent on him, no one who really mattered. Fleur had been safe in the bosom of her family still, cared for, occupied with her home. Now her home was his home and her cares were their children, and things were very different.

The newspapers still insisted the war would be over by Christmas, but intelligent people he'd spoken to had said that not only would it not be over by Christmas but that it would eventually cover the whole of Europe. Already Belgian cities were in flames and people were dying there. The newspapers carried atrocity stories which he didn't for a moment believe but he guessed Fleur had read them and was terrified for him and her children.

He shifted slightly and she stirred. 'Are you awake?' she whispered.

'Yes. Couldn't sleep.'

She turned quickly and moved into his arms, her body close to his so that the warmth of her flesh flowed into him.

'Will it go on for long, Dab?'

'Shouldn't think so,' he said at once, trying to reassure her. 'Nobody can afford long wars these days. They cost too much.'

'Will they let you come home? It's only France, after all.'

'Yes, they'll give leave, I expect.'

'I have to feel we're close.'

'We've always been close. All my life as long as I can remember.'

'I can't imagine what it will be like with you in France and me here. We've only been separated at odd times before.'

There was a long silence and she moved closer, so that he could feel her heart beating and feel her warm breath on his cheeks.

'Make love to me, Dab,' she whispered. 'Please.'

He turned towards her and kissed her, slowly, tenderly. 'You don't have to say please for that, Fleur.'

The following day Dabney drove over to Braxby Manor to see his mother. She was on her own and he had a feeling that she had aged a little in the last few days. He told her the news of his promotion but it brought no comment and she showed him the letter from Helen, waiting in silence for his observations.

'It's a pretty rotten world, Mother,' was all he could find to say.

Her eyes filled with tears. 'Suppose you come face to face with Karl-August.'

'The chances are pretty slim, Mother. In any case, I suspect it'll be a long-range war and there won't be much face-to-face stuff. Where's father?'

'At the War Office. He and Lord Roberts and Evelyn Wood have formed a committee with one or two other senior officers. He doesn't think it'll do much good but he agreed to serve. He thinks he'd be much better stumping the country encouraging men to join the army. What about you? Will you be going?'

'I think we shall *all* be going before long, Mother. I suspect it's going to be as big as that eventually, and any who slip through the net now will be caught later. Father thought several years and I believe Kitchener thinks the same. There's talk of raising a hundred thousand volunteers for a period of three years or until the war ends.'

'Will they get them?'

'It depends how they make the appeal. They'll need more than just the types who normally enlist. All too often *they* joined up for a good meal and a pair of boots because they hadn't got a job. I think this time they'll need to appeal to men with jobs who're prepared to give them up for a while. They're going to open up recruiting offices in every town, I hear.'

'When will you go?'

'Johnson thought within three weeks.'

In fact, Dabney was standing on the quayside at Le Havre in less than a fortnight.

The reservists and the remounts had poured into the depot smoothly and for once no one was arguing about the indents for equipment. Long before the call came to entrain for the coast, the 19th Lancers were ready, three squadrons of men and horses, complete with wagons, ammunition and supplies.

Dabney had made a point of reading and rereading his orders, meeting the reservists and inspecting every animal. When everything was ready, he decided it was safe to meet his father for lunch and pick his brain.

The Cavalry Club was as quiet as it always was, and still remarkably free of uniforms. Dabney had had a busy morning. He had been to the War Office, where he had arranged with his father to meet him, then he had visited his tailor. The old man behind the counter had known him since he had been a subaltern at the time of Omdurman.

'I'm delighted to hear of your promotion, sir,' he said, making a note of the crimson and blue of the DSO and the Sudan and South African campaign medals. 'I'm sure it was well deserved and your father, the Field Marshal, will no doubt also be pleased.'

As always, the club seemed unmoved by the events in Europe and it was impossible to hear the traffic moving outside. Dabney stopped to look at the pictures which he'd known, he felt, for most of his life – Rupert's charge at Edgehill; the 21st Lancers at Omdurman; French's charge at Klip Drift which had carried him through to Kimberley; the Marquess of Anglesey, who had commanded the cavalry at Waterloo; the great Duke of Wellington, curiously mild-looking for a man of such astringent comments; and Captain Oates, of the Inniskillings, who had offered his life in an attempt to give Scott a little more hope in the Antarctic.

His father was in the smoking room, sitting in a deep leather armchair, studying a sheaf of papers. To Dabney's surprise, he was in uniform. He hadn't seen his father in uniform for a long time, and the blaze of colour above his left breast indicated just how much active service he'd seen.

'Dab,' he said, putting down the papers and rising. 'What's all this about?'

'Nothing,' Dabney said. 'Goodbye for a while, that's all. We're waiting for orders.'

'It won't be long. I've just come from the War Office. How's the Regiment?'

'Ready. To the last button.'

The old man looked pleased. 'Seen your mother?'

'Yes. She's not happy, of course, any more than Fleur. She'd heard from Helen in Berlin.'

'Poor Helen. It's harder for her than the rest of us. We may not be very clever but we're her link with England. See Robert?'

'No. But I hear he's offered himself.'

'He won't go. He'll put on a uniform and prance about a bit, but he won't go. Perhaps it's best. He's more use making sure we get the weapons.' The Field Marshal paused. 'This war will be a disaster, Dab.'

'Sir?'

'It should never have happened. The politicians panicked, and before they knew what was happening the whole of Europe was acting like lemmings. I hope the French plan's a good one and I hope we don't get lost in it, because the BEF's not very big and we're fighting for our very existence. It's Britain and Germany who're facing each other, you know. France's become a side issue, and either Britain or Germany has to go down.' The old man paused, his expression troubled. 'And "down",' he went on, 'will be a long way down. That'll make it a long war because, under those circumstances, neither side's going to acknowledge defeat until the very last moment. So, if you're ever in command don't put all your eggs in one basket.'

'Nobody's going to enjoy being kept in the rear, sir.'

'Don't worry, they'll all be in it, given time. I'm not sure John French has grasped the enormity of the problems which confront us. Not so sure, even, that he's the man to have the command. There's a weakness in his character and his outlook's narrow. Haig's already had a word in my ear that he has his doubts about him. Since he's likely to be his successor if it comes to a change, it's not surprising. The army's full of intrigue.'

Dabney listened quietly until the old man had finished. 'How about you, Father?' he asked.

'Out to grass. Roberts is insisting on going to France to follow his beloved "boys." We're trying to dissuade him. He'll only be in the way. Dammit, he's over eighty and, field marshal or not, Bobs or not, the army won't want to be occupied looking after a frail old man who refuses to give up trying to be an active soldier. I'm staying home where I can be of most use. I was born before Victoria came to the throne. I remember the Duke of Wellington patting my head. He liked children even if he couldn't stand his wife. I didn't learn about Waterloo from the history books, Dab, I got it first hand from my father. There's no place in war for men of my age.'

There was a holiday spirit about the BEF as it embarked. Despite the appalling discomfort in which they travelled, they cheered and sang and shouted 'Are we down-hearted – NO!' at the grey waters of the Channel, while the name of the commander of the German right wing had produced a song which so delighted them they persisted in singing it all the way across.

'We don't give a fuck
For old Von Kluck – '

They weren't all young. The British army was small and it was relying a great deal on its reservists, and there were middle-aged faces and large moustaches among the pink-cheeked youngsters under the cheese-cutter caps. On their chests were ribbons for campaigns some of their comrades had never even heard of. They were tattooed, with all the usual crosses, bleeding hearts, unclothed women and 'Death rather than Dishonour,' and more than a few of them had crime sheets as long as their arms. But they were full of spirit and full of experience; the only trouble was that there were so few of them. Many were glad to be back as a change from unemployment, but there were as many again who were disgusted at having to leave their families to the meagre help offered by the government.

It was easier for the officers. There was lunch on board, and the landing at Le Havre was as efficient as careful planning could make it. The population was already going mad as they filed down the gangway, both men and women kissing everybody within reach. Wine was flowing and the officers were scuttling about like lunatics confiscating bottles and pushing away the persistent French who were trying to thrust them on the far from unwilling soldiery.

The long train journey to the front seemed occupied chiefly with feeding men and horses, a task that was not made easier by the fact that nobody seemed able to speak French. Dabney himself could speak excellent German because he had often spent his holidays with his German cousins but it was of little use to the French peasants who flocked round to see what the British army looked like. However, Leduc, who was his squadron second-in-command, came from the Channel Islands, and could translate.

Union Jacks were everywhere as they detrained in a small town in the north to a scale of hospitality they had neither expected nor ever seen before. Dabney could see already that some of his men were beginning to get drunk and Johnson called him across.

'Get rid of these damned French women,' he snapped. 'We've got to stop this drinking. The youngsters don't know how potent wine can be on a warm day. When we move off, we'll move on foot.'

'That'll startle the French, sir. They're used to seeing cavalry moving with a bit of dash.'

'And ending up facing the enemy with exhausted horses. Our way will save the horses and sober the men.'

They fed and watered in market squares where Uhlan patrols had looted the wine shops in the first days of the war, then began to move along a cobbled road through a drab area of mines and manufacturing. Somewhere ahead things were growing confused and there were constant delays. When the delays didn't come from the front where some unit had come to a halt as their line of march was crossed, they came from the rear with cries to slow down to give the tail-end time to catch up. Horses were everywhere. There was no mechanical transport, not even for the generals, and though they had got into position with extraordinary speed, they were now reduced to the pace of Napoleon's men because the railways were delivering troops faster than they could march away from the sidings, and the armies were growing congested.

Everybody was alert with excitement, the officers crouched over their maps at every halt, studying the countryside for areas where mounted action could be considered.

'Too many barbed wire fences, small fields and muddy ditches,' Leduc grumbled. 'We'd never get going.'

Riding at the head of A squadron, Dabney turned from time to time to stare backwards where the lance points glittered in the sunshine above the fluttering red and green pennants. Up ahead he could hear the rumble and mutter of artillery where the forward elements of the BEF were in contact with the Germans. Around him, every field seemed to be full of men and horses and wagons, and the road they were on was jammed with more wagons and guns. Column followed column, rumbling carts, stumbling men, and horses staggering with exhaustion, riders dozing in the saddle, slowly bending further and further forward over the saddle horn until their noses almost touched it in sleep. Thousands of mules with tossing heads and wild eyes trudged back from carrying up supplies.

Then they began to see batteries among the trees and occasional tumbled houses. When darkness came, they turned into a field. It was too dark to see what they were doing and they bivouacked silently, without attempting to make themselves comfortable. In Dabney's mind there was a certainty that very soon they would be in action and, after making sure both men and horses had food and drink, he stumbled off to a tumbledown barn where Ellis Ackroyd, still with the regiment despite the promises he'd been given, had found shelter. It smelled of damp and mice and by this time Dabney felt mummified with the dirt on him, unshaven, tired and stiff with riding. He pulled a pile of straw together and lay down on it. Somewhere in the distance he could hear the roar of artillery and the occasional rattle of musketry, and through the chinks in the broken boards of the barn, could see a flickering light in the sky where the guns were at work.

Things had happened so fast he found it hard to believe that it was real and kept feeling that he would wake up to discover it was a nightmare. Then he heard Ackroyd's voice and realised that Johnson had appeared. He was holding a scrap of paper in his hand and was telling the orderly to make tea.

'What is it, sir?' Dabney demanded.

Johnson crossed to the group of sleep-dazed officers. 'Rouse the men,' he said. 'We'll have time for tea but little else. We're to move forward into Belgium. The French attack in the Ardennes has come to a halt. It appears to have been a disaster and they've had heavy casualties. One of General Lanrezac's aides told me. He was trying to get the BEF on the move. We're all moving to the left because there seems to be nothing there to stop the German right. The whole French army's shifting front to meet them and the BEF's to take up a position to the right of D'Amade's group and the left of the French Fifth Army.'

'Where, sir?'

'Some mining town just over the border.' Johnson glanced at the paper in his hand. 'Mons. That's the name. Mons.'

four

They moved forward through the sweltering heat of the next day, pushing the tired horses along, flank patrols working the parallel roads. For some time now they'd been moving steadily east, and the squadrons had been broken up. Reconnaissance patrols had been sent out, brought back in panic as Uhlans were reported, then sent out again in different directions as the weird sensation of not knowing where the enemy was made the men in command nervous.

They were in full marching order, each man's possessions a saddle with two blankets under it, one for the horse, one for himself. On the offside of the saddle was a leather rifle bucket with a flat round metal mess tin strapped to it with a feed bag containing seven pounds of oats, on the nearside a leather sword frog and a pouch containing spare horse shoes, a folding canvas bucket for the horse's water and an emergency ration of more oats. Now, in addition, there was a bewildering panoply of additional gear – with, round the horses' necks, bandoleers containing extra ammunition. The horses themselves had gone ungroomed for days and, far from galloping, as their condition fell away it was all they could do to raise a spiritless trot.

Johnson was not with the regiment. He had been to see the major-general in charge of the division and had not yet returned, and as they moved on again they were halted by a battery of medium artillery jamming the road. While Chapman, Johnson's second-in-command, was still arguing with them, Dabney gave orders to tear down a barbed wire fence and the regiment moved past in the field alongside.

Leaving the wagons behind to rendezvous at Carville, they moved on at increased speed but an hour later ran into a transport column moving towards the rear and had to wait until the wagons were turned off the road so they could continue. An aeroplane passed overhead, whirring like a sewing machine, a frail box-kite-like affair of wires and white canvas through which the sun shone, outlining the struts like the veins of a butterfly's wings. It made Dabney think of Hedley Ackroyd.

It was long past the time when the horses should have been watered but all the time the brigade major was chivvying them on.

'The horses are going to suffer, sir,' Leduc complained.

'We're in a war, Tim,' Dabney said. 'I'm afraid they've got to.'

They pushed on again, the sergeants trying to encourage the men to sing, but they were tired and it was hard work. Dabney was aware now of his own exhaustion and sat straighter in the saddle to stay awake.

There was still no stopping beyond a short halt in a village of which no one knew the name. The inhabitants had retired behind drawn curtains and somewhere in the distance there was the loom of a pit slag heap. A sergeant reported that the horses were beginning to go lame and that one or two had girth galls. There was nothing they could do about it. Then Leduc appeared to announce that C Squadron seemed to have vanished in the dark.

The sound of firing grew louder. At midnight, they passed a heavy battery in an orchard and one of the guns fired as they clattered by. An orange flash lit up the gleaming steel of the barrel and they saw camouflage nets leaping in the momentary glare.

Dabney's horse was staggering with weariness as if it were drunk when Johnson appeared through the darkness and turned them off the road into a large meadow.

'There are cattle troughs in the corner of the field,' he said. 'Get your horses watered and fed.'

Lanterns gleamed in the darkness as they dismounted. One man, stiff after the ride, hobbled round his horse, hanging on to the saddle to keep himself upright. As Dabney moved along the lines, he saw that some of the horses were already lying down. Nobody asked about tents or bothered to tie groundsheets together to make bivouacs, but concentrated on hanging the nosebags on their mounts and preparing food.

Ellis Ackroyd handed him a mug of tea, heavily laced with rum that coursed through his veins to bring life back to his stiff limbs.

'Get the horses on their feet, Ellis,' Dabney said. 'Water by troops. And start now. It's going to take a long time but we must be close to the Germans by this time and we don't want them catching us unprepared. They seem to do their shelling of villages during the morning so I expect we'll be moving at dawn.'

Ackroyd grinned. 'Always dawn,' he said. 'Why not eleven-thirty? After coffee?'

As daylight came, they struggled to their feet, still stiff and not much refreshed after only two or three hours sleep. The rations had come up and they were just about to eat when the first shells arrived.

Whistling troopers, their braces over their hips, were grooming, watering and feeding their horses or cleaning rifles and saddlery. Other men, stripped to the waist, were washing and shaving in the canvas buckets that were used for the animals. A few officers in portable baths were removing the dust. Tea was being brewed and there was the appetising smell of frying bacon in the air. As he went about his business, Dabney became aware of a growing shout and lifted his head. Others heard the sound, too, and stopped what they were doing. The sound increased to a scream and there was a tremendous crash as a salvo of shells fell in the next field. Horses stampeded at once, followed by dismounted men, their faces all covered with lather. It looked like panic but was in fact no more than the swift reaction of cavalrymen useless without horses.

No more shells fell in their immediate vicinity but there was a series of crashes near a clump of woods to the rear and they saw smoke begin to rise.

'They must be after the battery,' Leduc said.

Though the shelling stopped, there was a great deal of bitter swearing because they were all itching to give their best and found little to cheer about. They had half-hoped for wide rolling country ideal for an exhilarating knee-to-knee gallop, but around them were only endless smoky villages, surrounded by slag heaps, railway embankments and the usual profusion of barbed wire.

They were standing by their horses on the Carville – Mortigny road ready to move when another salvo of shells landed some distance away. A corporal came running.

'Colonel's compliments, sir. Will you see him?'

Johnson was standing with his orderly and the adjutant. He looked worried. 'You ready?' he asked.

'In every way, sir.'

'Then you'd better move ahead. That damned shell sent splinters as far as B Squadron and Hawker was hit. It's not serious but he'll have to go to the rear. With C Squadron not yet turned up, you'll have to continue in the van. I want you to move north through the village, putting out patrols. We expect to run into the Germans.'

After so little sleep, within a couple of hours men were already dozing in the saddle again. The horses were also tired and it was clear that much more of this sort of thing would halve their numbers because the confused orders that had sent them hither and thither on abortive reconnaissances were too hard on the reservists who, soft from civilian life, were beginning to feel the strain.

As they edged forward, there were sulphurous exchanges between the different branches of the services which bumped into each other to cause immovable road blocks, and generals, purple in the face with rage, argued with each other to the undisguised delight of the private soldiers. The situation ahead was still unknown as they stopped for breakfast, drinking scalding tea and eating slabs of bread and bacon from cans heated by field kitchens. With feed, the horses seemed to improve a little but several were still limping badly.

'Mount!' As the trumpets sounded, they dragged themselves to the saddle. The air was shaking now with the boom and thud of gunfire, the light crack of field batteries, and the rattle of musketry.

They were just preparing to move forward again when a staff officer appeared. He looked exhausted, his eyes in deep hollows in his face.

'Where are you heading?' he demanded.

'Mons,' Dabney said. 'Those are the orders I have.'

'They're cancelled. Namur's gone and you should be heading back. The forward elements have run slap into the Boche and Sir John French's ordered a retreat. You'd better rejoin your regiment. And keep a sharp look-out. The Germans are somewhere on the road from Mortigny.'

The patrols were called in and sent to the flanks. Leduc's patrol, heading for Carville, was strengthened and warned to be careful. It was as well Dabney had taken precautions because they had been moving only a couple of hours when a corporal came tearing back at the gallop.

'Germans, sir,' he shouted as he drew his lathered horse to a sliding halt. 'Near Vernhout! Across the line of march.'

'Lead the way!' Dabney called for his trumpeter and the column began to move forward at a trot.

His heart was thumping. What would the first sight of the Germans be like? He was not unused to German soldiers because he had seen them when he'd stayed with Helen's family in Berlin. But then they'd been on parade and moving with the precision of toy dolls. These would be different, and eager to kill him.

The corporal from Leduc's patrol had moved ahead to find Leduc and now he came tearing back again, clods leaping from his horse's hooves.

'They've still got 'em in sight, sir.'

They came on the Germans a quarter of an hour later, men in grey uniforms wearing the same flat-topped lancer schapka they wore themselves at home on parade. Their lances appeared to be of metal, like lengths of gas-piping, and as they moved across a stubble field that stretched towards a line of woods, they looked magnificent in the morning sun, a solid line of horsemen, rising and falling in the saddle with a regular cadence as if they were all worked by the same clockwork mechanism.

Raising his arm to stop his own little column, Dabney turned to Leduc.

'How many do you think, Tim?'

'A hundred and fifty. Perhaps two hundred. I think we have them.'

'I think we have. Dismount one troop. Take the rest and work round to your left. Move out on them as soon as we've fired five rounds rapid.'

Dabney was totally confident. From what he'd discovered, the German cavalry wasn't much better than the French, whose failure so far had been calamitous. The lessons of the Boer War had been well learned by the British, however, and they were well trained, but he would need to be careful because the Germans sometimes had Jaeger infantry with them armed with machine guns.

As the Germans caught sight of Leduc, Dabney saw their pace quicken and they began to swing into line, prepared to make a fight of it.

'Hurry, hurry,' he called as horseholders moved up and a cart carrying the squadron machine guns appeared.

The Germans began to move forward, leaping into a gallop within a few strides, the lances coming down to the Engage. Aware of every eye on him, Dabney waited, then, as the Germans came nearer, he nodded and the line of dismounted men in front of him burst into a rattle of firing. Several horses went down and he saw their own mounts in the trees behind toss their heads in alarm at the noise.

The German charge was halted at once and, as the horsemen in the meadow began to mill around in confusion, Leduc's patrol appeared.

'Cease firing!'

As the musketry stopped, Leduc smashed into the Germans' flank. A horse stumbled and went down and others began to rear and stagger as the heavier English mounts shouldered them aside. Several Germans were rolling in the grass as Leduc's men broke through and circled away to the rear.

The machine guns had been set up now and the gunners began to squat behind them. Some of the Germans seemed to think that Leduc's men were all there were and that they had also been responsible for the firing, and they drew rein at the other side of the road and faced about. As they moved towards the fallen men, one of them coolly dismounted and began to go through the pockets of one of the British soldiers who was lying still in the stubble with one of the aluminium German lances in his side.

As the machine guns began to fire, they remounted hurriedly and, still unclear as to where the firing was coming from, swung across the front of Dabney's line. More horses and men went down and, as the Germans reined in, turning their horses in bewilderment, Dabney nodded to the trumpeter and, as the clear notes cut the air, he led the rest of A Squadron out of the trees. As they crashed into the fleeing Germans, Leduc, determined not to be left out, set spurs once more to his jaded mount. The German column was scattered and as the clatter and shouting died, the last of them galloped away to the north-east, leaving their dead and wounded behind them, and a dozen riderless horses cantering slowly across the field, their tails in the air.

The Germans were conscripts, all very young, and they hadn't seemed to know how to use their lances. As they were rounded up and the wounded collected, a young officer was brought to Dabney. He was a slim boy with a yellow collar on his grey uniform and a deep gash on his neck. Sergeant Ackroyd took out his field dressing and applied it to the wound.

'Name?' Dabney asked.

'Werner Raus-Willing, Leutnant.'

'Regiment?'

'I don't have to answer that.'

'I think I know.' Dabney was looking at the German's buttons. 'You're the 19th Prussian Lancers. I've seen you in Berlin.'

The German eyed him suspiciously. 'You speak excellent German, Herr Major.'

'I have German cousins.'

The German frowned. 'Then perhaps we ought not to be at war with each other.'

'Perhaps not. What do you think of it all?'

'I don't know what to make of it, Herr Major. I'm not even sure what it's all about. My men were called up for training only a few weeks before it broke out and they are not what you would call "full of fight". Some of your men even refrained from running them through because their backs were turned. I am grateful for their forebearance. I am a reserve lieutenant and I joined them when my class was called to the colours. What is the name of your cousin, Herr Major?'

'Karl-August von Hartmann.'

The young German's face broke into a smile. 'He is a good man, Herr Major. I know him well. He left the regiment for staff duties further south.'

They were all cock-a-hoop at the thought that in a war where the rifle and the machine gun were master of the field, they had not only fought a mounted action but had actually routed German cavalry.

Sending off a messenger to inform Johnson that the road was clear, they were still elated when they reached the Carville–Mortigny highway to await the arrival of the regiment. But their messenger was still there and informed them that Johnson had moved ahead during the night and was now a long way in front.

'Mount the men, Tim,' Dabney said, faintly irritated. 'We'd better push ahead and rejoin.'

Two miles further along they ran into the first column of refugees, and the sight of so much human misery immediately brought the war back into perspective. Long strings of wagons, carts and people on foot crawled through the hedge-less countryside. All along the line of march they were emerging from side roads, a whole province emptying itself into the main stream as they clung to the troops. Two great currents were forming, on the right a twenty-mile-long column of military wagons and soldiers, on the left a vast flood of civilians; huge farm carts loaded with beds, bedding and children; grandmothers dressed in their black best; drays pulled by slow-trudging oxen, mules or asses; pony-carts and dog-carts; decrepit landaus and victorias pulled by decrepit horses; bicycles and barrows; in mile after mile of flooding wretchedness, the only thing in their minds the disaster of 1870 when the French army had collapsed and the Germans had spread across the whole of France.

They looked grey like ghosts because their black clothes had become coated with dust and they poured past in stony silence, their faces expressionless with despair. Two young girls who looked like sisters were helping each other along, the blood from their torn feet oozing through low silk shoes; an old sick woman was balanced somehow on a perambulator; an elderly couple walked arm in arm as they had probably walked arm in arm round their garden for years; a small boy tried to encourage his mother who was sinking under the weight of two babies. Some of the carts must have contained the entire infant population of a village pushed aboard pell-mell, all wide-eyed and bewildered. Behind them the growing mutter of guns was interspersed with the occasional crash of a shell.

For two days it went on, a sense of shame flooding through the British, the bitterest incident of all when their horses' hooves trod underfoot a strip of cloth across a village street which had once hung in greeting – 'Welcome To Our British Saviours.' Exhaustion, already close on their heels after their prolonged advance, swept over them. The sun never let up and the dust grew thicker, filling the eyes, nostrils and mouth, clogging the pores, lying on the ungroomed coats of the horses and in the folds of uniforms. The first day the march went on far into the hours of darkness and, as they halted, the men in the saddles began to droop further and further forward in sleep until one after another fell to the road with a crash. The danger now was not from the enemy guns but from sheer weariness. The horses trudged on with their heads down and their ears drooping, listless and indifferent.

Dabney's mount had always been a spirited animal but now he had to use his spurs even to coax it to a trot. Its coat was shaggy and its shoes had worn wafer-thin; half the time the farriers' tools were missing because the 'shoeys', like the grooms, the saddlers, the bandsmen, and the signallers, were needed for other duties.

The men were dirty, their uniforms stained, their cheeks bristling with beard. Straggling increased daily as the bad characters got hold of liquor, and away in the rear trailed a little group of men whose horses had foundered, struggling along with whatever equipment they could carry. The numbers were growing horrifying and at the halts Dabney hobbled stiffly round those who remained, urging the officers to keep a tight hold on their troops, haranguing the sergeants, exhorting the weary men.

B Squadron appeared, under the command now of a lieutenant, because the captain who had taken over when Hawker had been wounded, had also been hit. They had been sent back to rejoin A squadron but they had no idea where Johnson had got to. He had forced the pace but had then announced that he must see the general again and had disappeared with C Squadron and they hadn't seen him since. They were in poor shape, as though they had been too hard-driven, but there was no possibility of rest and they tagged along behind, as relieved as A Squadron at the unexpected increase in numbers.

The retreat continued. The horses stumbled ahead like sleepwalkers, moving alongside infantry staggering along like ghosts, unconscious of what was going on around them, grey-faced, unshaven, their eyes dead, some of them supporting a man with a bandaged chest or head. In front, a sergeant was doggedly playing 'Tipperary' on a mouth organ. 'Keep the step, lads,' he kept calling. 'Keep the step. It'll 'elp. You'll get back. *I'll* get you back. Just pick up the step.'

Among them were the French, shuffling along with no attempt at military bearing, small men for the most part, red-breeched, blue-coated and often heavily bearded. Their cavalry wore breastplates, high jackboots and plumes on their cloth-covered brass helmets, and they rode small horses.

'Christ,' someone muttered. 'Any smaller and all you'd see under the saddles would be arses and 'eads.'

They passed through a town whose Mairie had been smashed by shells and was full of hurt soldiers. Around it, the pavement had been torn up and there were dead horses and dead men in every corner of the neighbouring streets, the air full of the cloying smell of burning oil from a wrecked lorry. The cheering formations of a fortnight before were depleted and exhausted and Dabney was close to tears as he saw the stumbling figures scarcely capable of advancing a yard, and the drooping heads and staring coats of the horses.

Toiling along the by-roads, trying to avoid the jam of soldiers and civilians in an attempt to find C squadron, they finally managed to make contact just as the order came to hurry. In the darkness they caught up with a troop left behind to find them just as it was dragged out of its billet in a drab French town. Mounted orderlies were already clattering over the cobbles and an order came to quicken the pace. Johnson was still missing and the lieutenant in command conferred hurriedly with Dabney about what they should do.

They moved out of the village again at a tired trot to the jingling of equipment and the squeak of leather. As they reached the countryside again in the early hours of next morning, they finally came up with the rest of C squadron and Dabney had just sent a message ahead to inform Johnson that he had rejoined when he heard a roar like an approaching express train. There was a shattering explosion and he heard a horse screaming, and a team pulling an ambulance bolted, the tail gate still down, stretchers and equipment bouncing out on to the road.

Riding forward to see what had happened, he found a smoking hole in the road, its edges seared by heat, and two horses in the ditch, one dead, its hooves sticking up stiffly like the branches of a tree, the other struggling with a broken back to drag itself away. Bulging eyes stared at him as he slid from the saddle, and froth blew across the road as the animal let out a squeal of pain and terror.

Dabney's stomach squirmed at the animal's agony then, as Ellis Ackroyd levelled his rifle and pulled the trigger, the great eyes glazed and the heavy head thumped down on the road.

'Where's the Colonel? What happened?'

Fullerton, of C Squadron, a sick look on his face, gestured to the other side of the road. By the wall of the cottage, on a patch of grass, a man lay stretched out, his chest and throat covered with blood. Nearby, Johnson was leaning against the cottage wall, with the doctor bent over him. He looked up as Dabney appeared, his expression twisted with pain.

'Where the devil have you been, Goff? You've let us down badly.'

It was manifestly unjust but Dabney put it down to the pain Johnson was suffering.

'Buggering about trying to pick up a bit more glory, I suppose,' Johnson snarled. 'Trying to add a bar to your DSO. Get back to your squadron, sir. Fullerton's going to need steady men, not glory-seekers.'

Angrily, Dabney returned to his men, watching silently as a car was stopped and Johnson pushed inside.

Fullerton moved his arm and the regiment moved forward again.

'And keep closed up, for God's sake, Dabney,' he said. 'We can't afford to have anybody else get lost.'

five

They moved off again. More shells fell, none of them close, then they passed a great gap in the road where a salvo had caught a column of wagons. Dusty carcasses sprawled across the cobbles with the wreckage of carts. The wounded had been cleared but in the hurry some of the human detritus had been missed and Dabney saw a boot, with a foot and part of a leg still in it, standing upright, a trail of puttee stretching across the cobbles. It looked as though it had been tidied up and placed there neatly out of the way.

As they reached Mortigny, a staff officer with his hand bandaged and blood on his uniform appeared on a limping horse with dilated nostrils and wild eyes.

'Halt there,' he said to Fullerton. 'Brigadier Farrar wishes to see you.'

As they waited, the horses with their heads down, too tired to whinny or stamp, a battery in a field alongside began to fire. Immediately, the wounded staff officer started to yell.

'Cease firing! Limber up and get out of it! The action's been broken off! Retire at once!'

Then a stout officer with red round his cap and a white moustache appeared on foot from one of the houses.

'Get your men dismounted,' he snapped at Fullerton. 'Have your horseholders told off. There's a gap in the front a mile wide. You're going into the line.'

'As infantry, sir?' Fullerton asked.

'Of course as infantry, man! You bloody cavalry people think you're too good for that sort of thing, I know, but I can promise you that you aren't.'

Fullerton's mouth opened to protest, but he closed it again and gave the order to dismount. Glancing at Dabney, he followed the general into a cottage and Dabney saw them leaning over a map spread on a kitchen table. When he came out, he looked slightly shocked.

'With farriers, excepted men, and one man in three to handle the horses, a cavalry regiment can produce only two hundred for a dismounted action,' he said. 'But they seem to be intending us to hold as much line as an infantry battalion. Are the machine guns up?'

The machine guns were usually given to the man with the worst seat in the regiment and the 19th were no exception. But young Quibell, who could be relied on to fall out of the saddle whenever the regiment broke into anything faster than a canter, had a mechanical turn of mind and a good eye for country and he was already working the guns forward. The horseholders, riding one horse and leading two, were bursting away to the rear and foraging parties were sent into the fields to try to find barbed wire. Barbed wire, that anathema to a horseman, was very much in demand suddenly.

Fullerton was still explaining the situation, 'We have the Buffs on our left and the West Kents on our right. They've pushed the Hussars in on the other side of the West Kents. Are we ready?'

'Everything's up. Wagons, guns, supplies, everything.'

'Right. We're to get the chaps into the trenches as fast as we can. There's no one else, it seems, and nothing behind us. If we give way, the whole front falls apart. We've been told to hold to the last man – the very last.' Fullerton's expression seemed to indicate that he knew that death was just round the corner. 'We start digging as soon as we arrive.'

'What do we dig with?' Dabney asked. 'We don't carry entrenching tools.'

Fullerton gave a weary gesture. 'I told him so. All he said was "Well, you bloody well ought to." He told me to get on with it and not argue. He's not a cavalryman, of course. Rifle Brigade, I believe.'

Still stiff from riding, they formed up on their hind legs in the village street and began to march out. The regular crunch of boots sounded strange after the irregular clatter of hooves they'd been hearing for the past fortnight. The old cavalry attitude – the need to give tone to what was otherwise a vulgar brawl – was forgotten, as was the old argument about whether a lance was better than a sword. For years it had occupied cavalrymen's minds but both seemed as out of date now as the bow and arrow. All that was wanted was men with rifles who could fire fifteen rounds to the minute. All too often before the war the cavalry officer had been regarded by the rest of the army as a figure of fun – it was said that some were so stupid even their brother officers were beginning to notice. They wore their tunics cut with longer skirts than the infantry to give them style, though they said it was necessary for riding, and they had always considered themselves a very special élite. But they were also well aware that exclusiveness had to be paid for and the gap was closed just in time.

The Germans arrived even as the 19th reached their position and extended into line. A deep ditch ran along their front under a line of poplars and they filed into it quickly as a machine gun somewhere in the distance started to clip the leaves above them. Dabney was on the right of the line and in front a beet field rose in a gentle slope. On his left he could see a village from whose church tower hung a Red Cross flag. Beyond, the ground rose in a gentle swell, cut by an avenue of pollarded trees marking the road, straight as a giant ruler across the countryside.

In the distance, tiny figures were moving, which he could only assume were Germans, then his eye fell on a dark column like a winding snake and he saw the sun glittering on it as it caught bayonet points and polished equipment. Between the column and the rise the gold and green sweep of the countryside was flecked with white and yellow smoke clouds from shrapnel and high explosive, some of them cut across with yellow flame, then what seemed to be a salvo from a whole battery of guns fell on the village on his left and he saw the houses crumbling and collapsing as if an invisible giant hand had swept across them.

Even as they divested themselves of unnecessary kit and the machine guns were set up and rifles laid along the eastern edge of the ditch, they saw small spikes sprouting over the curve of the slope in front. The spikes became cloth-covered helmets and then heads. Then the whole horizon seemed to sprout men as they came in masses across the flower-strewn fields, toiling up the slope, fully expecting to find nothing in front.

Nobody ordered firing to start. Ellis Ackroyd, who was near Dabney, was the first to pull the trigger and Dabney saw a German officer riding a horse in front of his men fall backwards over the tail of his mount. Immediately, the masses of grey-clad men seemed to move faster. They were extended to not more than two paces and keeping a very bad line, but they came forward to the music of bugles and brass bands and the loud singing of 'Deutschland Über Alles.' From the ditch it sounded like an insane chorus, and the Germans, like the Uhlans they had captured earlier, seemed from their behaviour to be new to war, and weary of marching in the hot sun.

'One thousand yards! Open fire! Rapid independent!'

The machine guns, those derided instruments that had always seemed to be no part of cavalry equipment, had been sited under a bush on the edge of the ditch where they were

173

difficult to see, and Dabney saw young Quibell's arm sweep down. As they began to stutter, the line of men in front began to waver and crumble, then the rifles began to spatter out a steady fire. The grey mass in front wavered and came on again but finally broke into groups which, in turn, shredded into single men running for cover like rabbits. Some of them threw themselves flat among the beet and, as the firing died, rose and bolted back over the crest.

'We've stopped them!'

But another wave of men came up the slope, led by officers waving swords. One after the other the officers fell but the soldiers still tried to advance, coming on in short rushes until they were almost on top of them; almost, it seemed, reaching out to climb the parapet of the ditch. Then the line crumbled, faded to nothing and vanished. Dabney was only barely aware of bullets until he heard a man cry out and saw him sit down heavily alongside him, then he realised the Germans had gone to ground and were returning their fire until reserves could be brought up.

The 19th had entered the ditch not in squadrons and troops but just as they had arrived, and now they were digging with anything they possessed. Moving along in a half-stoop behind them, Dabney found the line petered out at a point where the ditch angled backwards. Here, small groups of men were lying in the long grass, in tenuous touch with the West Kents. He was about to call some of his men up to extend the line when the machine guns started again and along the whole front, from the left of the 19th to away on the right beyond the Kents, he could once more see rolling masses of grey.

Solid blocks of men in spiked helmets were trudging forward again, their rifles held across their chests. They were so packed together it wasn't even necessary to aim, and as the firing restarted the whole mass seemed to shudder, recoil on itself, tried to struggle on, then began to fall back, leaving heaps of dead to mark where they had been.

'More conscripts called up and given a few weeks training,' Dabney said to Leduc. 'Before long, it'll occur to somebody to call up the artillery, so we'd better make our position deeper.'

The hole Dabney scraped for himself was barely big enough for his binocular case, and the bullets were whipping over him as he lay down to watch. There had been a heavy shower of rain and the men were soaked to the skin and caked with mud. The trench was already in a state of disrepair, and where attempts had been made to deepen it water had appeared. There was no proper communication with left or right and the field of fire was limited to the slope of the hill. On the right a barn was in flames but fortunately the wind was blowing the smoke away from their front and, with the aid of a battery which gave support against snipers, they were holding.

The bullets were still whipping over Dabney and he had to remain motionless until the firing died away, then he turned, and ran, bent double, for the ditch again. One of the sergeants from C Squadron met him.

'I think you'd better move along the line, sir,' he said. 'Major Fullerton's been hit.'

He scrambled along the ditch behind the troopers lying against the forward bank, the straps of their cheese-cutter caps under their chins, sucking at pipes and cigarettes, their eyes bleak as they stared across the empty ground in front that was still now and empty of Germans beyond a few squirming bodies. One of them tried to heave itself up, lifting itself on its hands, and for a horrible moment it reminded Dabney of the horse Ellis Ackroyd had shot.

Reaching Fullerton's squadron, he came upon a little group of men. In the middle of them, Fullerton was lying on his back, a small neat hole just above the bridge of his nose.

'Sniper, sir,' the subaltern said. 'You're in command.'

'Right.' Dabney glanced about him. 'Then we'll not stand round like a committee of enquiry. It doesn't require this many, I'm sure. Let's have him lifted out of the way so we can move about.'

'Where can we put him, sir?' The subaltern seemed on the point of tears. 'The ditch's not very wide.'

What the boy said was correct. But they obviously couldn't leave Fullerton where people would stumble over him.

'Lift him on to the rear parapet.'

'For God's sake, sir – ' The subaltern looked shocked. The idea of leaving his late commander's body in the open where it could be hit again by flying bullets seemed vaguely indecent to him.

'Dammit, do as you're told, man!' Dabney snapped. 'He won't object and nothing can harm him now.'

Unwillingly the boy had the body lifted and pushed out of the way on the reverse parapet. And only just in time, because as Dabney had expected, the German artillery began to open up on their positions. A Very light curved up into the sky and burst in a red glow, and almost immediately with a white star-shaped flash two shells burst just in front of the ditch. More shells fell, but they were all just short and the men at the extremities of the position used the craters to extend the line.

Experienced only in the bombardments in South Africa, Dabney couldn't believe the ferocity of the one that fell on them now. The peppery reek of high explosive was drifting back as the Germans probed for the range, then they were cowering awkwardly as the missiles came whimpering and shrieking down on them. A gale seemed to howl overhead, piling up great barriers of sound, and there was a wild eruption of the earth, clods and stones and bits of rubbish falling on top of them in a shower. The ditch side bulged with a tremendous grunting noise and another shower of pulverised earth filled Dabney's eyes and ears and mouth. A man had been buried and they scratched with their bare hands to free him, but it was difficult because of the huddling figures and the narrowness of the ditch, and when they dragged him free he was found to be dead.

This time there was no argument. In the holocaust of sound, they needed elbow room, and the corpse was lifted up and rolled over the back of the ditch without question, and they all cowered down again, flinching and ducking as the shells cracked nearby. Next to Dabney, Ellis Ackroyd was crouched, his face grim, and just beyond him Leduc, his face haggard, was blinking and gasping for breath with each crunching blow.

'Where's our artillery, for God's sake?' he demanded. 'Those bloody Germans are concentrating again behind the rise.'

Through his glasses, Dabney could see that what Leduc said was correct. It was difficult to see the Germans, but small movements, occasional glimpses of spiked helmets or crouching men indicated that they were preparing for another rush. But as they rose to their feet and came over the crest, two shells burst right among them. Bodies were flung right and left and as the smoke drifted away they saw forty or fifty men squirming or lying still among the beet tops. More shells burst along the crest and the Germans turned and bolted back out of sight, followed by rapid fire and loud cheers from the ditch.

'That's shook 'em,' somebody said. 'Didn't think nobody was in front of 'em.' There was a pause. ' 'Ow long we been 'ere, anyway?'

'Gawd knows – ' the reply came slowly ' – I reckon I was born in this bloody ditch.'

Dabney smiled. It wasn't the chatter of downhearted men.

'Have the ammunition collected from the dead and wounded,' he told Leduc. 'Together with field rations and dressings. We shall probably need every one before we've finished. And let's have patrols pushed forward in case they come again.'

As the wounded were moved back to the shelter of a cow byre where the medical officer and his orderlies were working, the supply column came up, bringing ammunition and food.

Desperate for men and remembering the extenuated flank barely in touch with the Kents, Dabney considered for a moment impressing the supply column into the trench but he realised they were probably needed to carry supplies elsewhere. The food they brought was cold bully beef and biscuits, but it was snatched up without question by the starving men.

During the evening, Brigadier Farrar arrived with the wounded staff officer, who looked by this time as though he were ready to faint, the bandage on his hand saturated with blood. The brigadier wasted no time sympathising about Fullerton, and Dabney attacked straight away. His father had always told him that if he had anything unpleasant to say it was best to say it as soon as possible and as unpleasantly as possible, so there was no mistake about how he felt.

'We need spades,' he said.

'We haven't got spades,' Farrar snapped.

'Then you might as well accept that we shall have to give this place up, sir,' Dabney retorted. 'It's not our fault the cavalry don't carry entrenching tools and, with respect, sir, nobody can hold this place unless we make it deeper.'

'And then?'

'Given spades, I'll hold it as long as you like, sir.'

Farrar stared at him for a moment then he nodded. 'I'll get you some spades up as soon as it's dark,' he said. 'Can you hang on that long?'

'Yes, sir, we can. I'd like wire, too, if there's any available. Then I can get it out in front tonight.'

'I'll do what I can.' Farrar searched his face. 'You're a Goff, aren't you?'

'Yes, sir.'

The general's severe face relaxed momentarily. 'Knew your father. Served under him in India. You've got a reputation to keep up. See that you do. I'll try to get hot food up tomorrow. In the meantime, it's up to you to do what you can. You'll have to hold on here at least for another day. I've got the Gloucesters coming up but they can't possibly be here until tomorrow night. I can scrape up a few base wallahs like cooks, clerks and so on to help. How about your horseholders?'

'I'd like them up here, sir. They belong to the Regiment and they'll do a lot better than clerks and cooks. Have you some grooms who can look after our horses?'

'I can see to that. I'll send your men up as soon as I get back. Everybody's holding, but the Hussars seem to have been hard hit. They had no shelter and God alone knows who's running the show at the moment. A wounded man brought the news back. I'm going up there to try to stiffen them. I'm also getting my clerks and cooks to prepare a strong point in the village just in case. There's a railway that runs through it and we can man the embankment. Just hold on and we shall be all right. You're doing all right so far. But you have no choice. Your orders are unequivocal. There's nothing between you and the Channel ports.'

When the 19th were relieved six days later they were mere shadows of the soldiers who had gone into the line. They moved like phantoms, a ghostly trickle of men in which the will to move struggled with the wish to sleep.

An infantry battalion whose identity Dabney didn't even bother to enquire took over from them, fresh soldiers, clean and unstained with mud or blood, their packs neat, their rifles clean.

'Well played, the Clutchers,' one of them said. 'Are we downhearted?'

The yell went up immediately from the men round him. 'NO!'

One of the exhausted Lancers lifted his head and stared at them with red-rimmed eyes from a haggard black face. 'You bloody soon will be,' he observed.

Dabney's face was foul with dirt and his clothes were torn and covered with blood. He was dazed, a hundred years older and grimmer, but unhurt. Leduc stumbled alongside him, also untouched. He was licking his lips and his tongue seemed curiously pinker and cleaner because of the filth on his face. He looked taut and distressed and he carried a pack that was full of the identity discs and pay books of the dead.

The whole place reeked of the acid fumes of high explosive, the smell of death and the stink of human excreta, because they had never been able to dig latrines. Here and there on the grass were flecks of dried blood where they had dragged a wounded man to die, and behind the line was a group of neat mounds in which they had buried the grey-faced dead. It had been a dismal job in the slow-falling rain.

'Poor devils,' Leduc had muttered as the padre intoned a prayer. 'Their graves are full of bloody water.'

As they stumbled back to Mortigny, men wearing bandages startlingly white against the grime of their faces were supported by their friends. A man with his arm in a sling had his other arm round the shoulders of a weeping boy far less badly wounded. 'There, there, mate,' he was saying. 'You'll be all right.'

Mortigny was full of relieved regiments, infantry and cavalry all mixed up together, wandering about in aimless fashion, all too tired to care. Most of them were bowed and limping, muddy ghosts who looked in their stained uniforms as if they'd been buried and dug up again. Scores had gone to sleep on the pavement, their backs against the walls, indifferent to the appeals of NCOs and officers. Food had been brought up and those who were awake munched thick sandwiches of bread and bully beef, their faces brooding and enigmatic, their mouths pursed round the stumps of Woodbines.

The wounded were being gathered in a field behind the Mairie. The anaesthesia of shock was wearing off now and pain and thirst were setting in among the torn bodies. A doctor, wearing a bloodstained apron, moved among them giving injections of morphia and anti-tetanus, and the whole area under the Red Cross flag stank of carbolic, ether and chloroform.

Gathering the regiment together, they began to call the roll. Leduc was swaying with fatigue as he stood near Ellis Ackroyd exclaiming the names in front of Sergeant-Major Waterford. They seemed not to have eaten a proper meal or slept for days and Dabney was light-headed with exhaustion. Somewhere, he knew, he would sleep and that was the only thing in his mind. For the moment, all he knew was that the cavalry corps had virtually ceased to exist.

Brigadier Farrar was moving through the crowding men. He looked worn-out and the wounded staff officer who had been with him had disappeared.

'Leave them,' he was saying to a subaltern trying to rouse a group of infantrymen. 'Let them sleep. I've arranged transport. There are buses coming to take them away.'

Ackroyd had finished calling the roll by this time. It hadn't taken long, and Sergeant-Major Waterford was now addressing the survivors.

'That lot can go in buses if they like,' he said. '*We* shall march out. I know they call us the Manure Shifters but we're more than that. We're Goff's Greens. Goff's Gamecocks. The

Clutchers. The Widowmakers. And, by God, we've made a few widows these last few days.'

It raised a smile. It was the old magic working. They weren't fighting to defend Belgium or save France. Not even to protect Britain or the King. They were fighting for the Regiment. A soldier's loyalty was always to his regiment. He knew everything about it. It was his family and it was to the regiment that he directed his energy. The British soldier's feet, like his head, were not his strong point, but they all knew what the Sergeant-Major meant. Marching out was a gesture and, while gestures could sometimes be pointless, this one was being made to indicate that they were the best regiment in the British Army, something every other single regiment in their simple faith also believed.

Recovered now, the horses were waiting two miles to the rear. Ackroyd got somebody to play the mouth organ and they marched off singing. It was poor singing but they marched in step, their boots barely leaving the cobbled road, their bodies rocking from side to side like automata, using what energy they had left to lift their legs one after the other, concentrating everything in getting each foot forward, as if that were the only way they could move.

As he watched them pass, Dabney noticed Farrar standing near to him. As the column of worn men trudged by, Leduc, who was leading, ordered them to march at attention and ordered 'Eyes right'. Somehow, the fours of shuffling men picked up the step and found their files. Shoulders were thrust back and heads clicked to the right as they plodded past.

Farrar swallowed. 'Well done, Lancers,' he said. 'Well done, well done!' He touched Dabney's arm and gestured. 'Off you go, my boy. Take care of them. They're splendid chaps.'

As the last files passed, Dabney saw dirty faces blurred by a fuzz of beard, eyes blank and staring into nothingness.

They were a resilient lot and a long sleep and a hot meal would restore them remarkably. These were his men, he thought. They had responded to everything he had asked of them. Their entry into the war as horse soldiers had been short and sweet but in their new role they had let no one down, neither their country nor their Regiment. The army, he decided, was a strange institution. Composed of hard-boiled soldiers not given to emotion, men whose minds were all too often concerned only with food, booze and women, it still had the ability to move a man to the point of tears.

s i x

The autumn fields of Yorkshire were full of blue mist that clung to the hollows and gave a ghostly look to the leafless trees. As Josh and his grandfather galloped round the curves of the hills, the sheep scattered in front of them, their resentful baas as harsh as the sound of crows in the tall oaks by the church.

Josh was riding a dappled pony he'd been given for his birthday and the old man was astride an ugly hunter with a fiddle head and a long upper lip which had carried him uncomplainingly across country for years. It was an enormous animal that looked far too strong for the old man but it was a bold jumper which never refused and though it lacked pace it never reached the end of its stamina and perfectly suited the Field Marshal who no longer wished to hurry.

They handed over the horses at the door of the Manor and clumped inside, Josh feeling twice his normal size. He had first been taken hunting by his grandfather and it always gave him pleasure to ride with him when he was not at school. The arrival of the old man's trap outside the front door of his home and the sight of the grinning face of one of the Ackroyds as he waited to drive him the few miles to where his grandfather would invariably be stamping up and down the hall of Braxby Manor expecting his arrival always set his heart thumping.

184

In the library the old man poured himself a strong whisky and soda to warm himself, singing to himself as he lifted the decanter.

'Wrap me up in my old stable jacket
And say a poor devil lies low – '

'What's that, Grandpa?' Josh asked.
'Song,' the old man said. 'Soldier's song. About cavalrymen.'
'Finish it.'

' – And six of the Lancers shall carry me
To the place where the best soldiers go.'

The old man's voice, quavery and out of tune, wavered to a stop and he looked round sheepishly at his grandson.
'That's all,' he said. 'Song about death and funerals. Not for a youngster. Old soldiers know a lot of songs like that.'
He moved to the fire and took a long pull at the whisky. 'Better than tea,' he observed. 'Tea's a flat-footed dismounted drink. Rots your inside.'
The newspaper had been left for him and as he sat down in the leather armchair he favoured, so that Josh could drag off his boots, he lifted it to read the headlines.
RETREAT HALTED, they announced. ALLIED TROOPS MOVE FORWARD ALL ALONG THE LINE. VICTORY IN SIGHT.
'Tripe,' he said. 'Rubbish!'
Placing the boots in the hall, Josh returned in his stockinged feet. 'Why is it tripe, Grandpa?'
The old man frowned. 'Ain't possible, boy. With the size of the BEF and after all the casualties we've suffered, we couldn't possibly be in sight of victory.'

Squatting on the floor near him, Josh began to study the pictures in the illustrated magazine which was delivered with the newspaper especially for his visits. Some enterprising publisher had seen a quick profit in the war, and for the most part its policy was one of unrestrained optimism.

'It says here,' he pointed out, 'that the shellfire's terrifying at first to new troops.'

'It's not all that pleasant to old ones!'

'It says the Germans ran away. Have you ever run away, Grandpa?'

'Yes. But never fast enough for me.'

'Is being afraid the worst thing about war, Grandpa?'

'Not by a long chalk.'

'What is?'

'The way it stinks. 'T ain't like a field day at Aldershot, y'know.'

Josh hadn't supposed it was. He knew Aldershot well and visited it often when the old man had been general-in-command. He was familiar with the well-kept barracks, the gravelled squares and whitewashed stones, the messes with their bright window boxes, the spick and span stables, the recruits, the sentries, the cavalry and artillery exercising in the Long Valley and the horses being schooled over the jumps.

As he became silent, the Field Marshal picked up a letter that had been laid ready for him. Putting on his glasses, he began to open the envelope. As he did so, Josh lifted his head again.

'Mother says the Regiment's been fighting on foot,' he said.

The Field Marshal grunted. 'Nothing wrong with that. A cavalryman's a maid of all work.'

'All the same – ' the boy's face was eager and excited ' – we did have a charge, didn't we? It's here in the paper. "Nineteenth Lancers' Brilliant Charge." '

'Yes –' the old man's jaws moved ' – that's something.'

'Mother says that Father wrote that he'd been in action against Uncle Karl's regiment.'

'Yes.'

'But that Uncle Karl was safe in a staff job somewhere else.'

The old man grunted again. He'd read the letter, because Fleur had brought it to him at once. It was good to hear there was little chance of Dabney and Karl-August coming face to face. That would have been too awful, but it was no certainty that a staff job was safe. There had been a great many staff officers killed in France already.

He turned over the letter in his hand. It was from Robert and, like most epistles that came from Robert these days, it immediately gave him a headache.

'Dear Father,' Robert wrote, 'I hope you have been in better health than of late, but of course none of us are getting younger…'

The old man scowled. Robert looked the picture of health and always would, because he never risked his neck at anything.

'I have been intending to come over and see you for some time,' the letter continued. 'In view of the war, there are a great many matters of property that we ought to discuss and one of these days we really must try. Elfrida complains of the problems of getting help. Already the war has affected us and I expect it's affecting you, too, because I've heard Ellis Ackroyd and one or two others have joined the forces. I think Kitchener must have been off his head when he appealed for 100,000 men.'

The old man scowled and adjusted his glasses.

'Obviously,' Robert went on, 'men won't be able to leave the mines or the steel and munitions works to join up – as I well know, because I have the problem of dealing with them and they are already beginning to demand higher wages – so that the only people free to go are those in other jobs. And this inevitably covers servants. It wasn't too bad until this stupid retreat from Mons, but now, suddenly, everybody's rushing to join the colours and we are left short. I was wondering if you couldn't use your influence with Lord Kitchener, whom I know you know well, to persuade him to put such people in reserved jobs. It isn't that I'm not patriotic. It's just that it makes life a lot more difficult for people like me.'

Difficult! The Field Marshal shifted in his chair. Life was even more difficult for the boys in the Regiment who had been mutilated in the stand at Mortigny. It was even more difficult for Chapman who'd been blinded, and more difficult still for Fullerton, who'd been killed. Robert, as usual, was thinking only of Robert. And the Field Marshal *wasn't* in better health of late. He was in worse health. He was too bloody old and in danger of dying. Bobs was already dead. He'd been visiting the Indian troops in France and had caught a chill which had turned to pleurisy. The Field Marshal grunted. The old ass ought to have known better. In his eighty-third year, he was in no state to go gallivanting round France. The Field Marshal had gone to the state funeral which had been attended by the King and even the German press had not missed the occasion. He had wondered often if Graf von Hartmann hadn't had a hand in it. He had once met Bobs at Braxby, and the report in the *Lokalanzeiger* which the Field Marshal had been shown at the War Office – 'There are in war moments when we salute the enemy with the sabre instead of destroying him' – had the touch of Von Hartmann, who, for all his self-complacency about Prussian superiority, was always a gentleman.

It was a brief flicker of chivalry and the Field Marshal had a suspicion that they wouldn't see much of it in the future. An invasion scare had brought about a spy neurosis and enemy agents were being seen behind every hedgerow.

Income tax was up, beer was up and there were alarming stories of shoddy uniforms and poor army boots – the Field Marshal often wondered how much Robert and young Cosgro were involved! – together with a great deal of shiftiness in the matter of pay and allowances. Bitter public protests had resulted and Kitchener hadn't helped with his instructions to the police to picket the public houses to make sure that wives didn't misconduct themselves. As far as the Field Marshal could see, soldiers' wives couldn't *afford* to misconduct themselves – but Kitchener was a bachelor and didn't always show a lot of sense.

He looked down again at Robert's letter. For God's sake, he thought sourly, how else did you face up to a nation with over a million men under arms except by calling for volunteers up to the number of a hundred thousand. There'd be a need for a second hundred thousand before long and probably more, and then Robert's worry about servants might have some meaning. Robert, the Field Marshal considered, had little to complain about.

Josh looked up. 'Grandpa,' he said. 'Why do the Germans kill Belgian babies?'

'They don't.' The old man's reply was short and to the point. 'Neither did the Boers. Newspaper talk, boy. That's all.'

'Don't newspapers tell the truth?'

'Truth's always the first victim of war. Newspapers are run by a set of cads who make profits out of other people dying. They call it stirring up the war effort. If you were to sit down there and write out a football team for cads, Lord Northcliffe would be the captain.'

'Would the Kaiser be in a team for cads?'

The old man grinned. 'Without a doubt. Von Kluck and a few others, too.'

'What about Lord Cosgro? I heard Mother say he was a bit of a cad.'

'The Cosgros have always been cads,' the Field Marshal growled. 'Without any doubt Cosgro would be in the team. Probably vice-captain in case Northcliffe was unable to play.'

'How about the Emperor Franz-Joseph of Austria? Is he a cad?'

'Shouldn't think so. Bit too old. Like me. But you could put him down.'

Josh reached for a piece of paper and a pencil and began to write. 'How about Joffre? After all, he lost to the Germans.'

'Why not?' The old man's humour began to improve as the boy distracted his attention from the letter in his hand. 'You could include Henry Wilson, too, for that matter.'

'Which Henry Wilson?'

'*General* Wilson. Tall feller. Moustache. Brigade major to Lyttelton at Colenso. Intriguer and mischief-maker. You could perhaps even include John French.'

'*Sir* John French.'

'That's the feller.'

'I thought he was leading the BEF.'

'Not so damn well, it seems to me. He's a bit shifty, anyway. Never liked him.'

Josh looked at what he'd written and lifted his head. 'We've nearly got a team, Grandpa. We only need three more.'

'How about Lloyd George?' The old man was thinking less of the war than of the stories he'd heard round Whitehall. 'And you could shove down that bloody man, Bottomley.'

'Which bloody man, Bottomley, Grandpa?'

'Horatio Bottomley. *John Bull.* Goes round spouting about the need for patriotism and draws a fee for doing it.'

'That's ten. I can't think of anybody else.'

For a long time there was silence as they applied their minds to the problem.

'Better put down Mrs Astor,' the old man said eventually. 'She's always going on about Women's Rights.'

'She's a woman.'

'She could play in goal.'

Josh grinned. 'That makes eleven. We've got a team.' There was a silence then he looked up. 'Grandpa?'

'Yes, boy?'

'Is Uncle Robert a cad? Mother said he was. To Father. Just before he went to France.'

The old man knew exactly what they'd been referring to. This blasted business with Lady Balmael. He'd heard rumours and had been wondering for a long time what he ought to do about it.

'Sometimes,' he conceded reluctantly.

'Is it possible for a Goff to be a cad, sir?'

'Oh, yes. Make no mistake about that. There's one in every family.'

'All the same, I don't like putting a Goff down with the Kaiser and Von Kluck.'

'Put him down as first reserve then. Then he's part of the team but he isn't in it.'

'That's a good idea.' Josh wrote for a while then he handed the list to the old man.

> 'L Northcliff (Captain),' he read.
> Kaser
> Von Cluck
> Lord Cosgro (vice-captain)
> Frans-Joseph
> Joffer
> H Willson
> J French
> L George
> H Botomly
> Mrs Aster.
> 1st Reserve R Cosgro-Goff.'

'Good team, that,' the old man said enthusiastically. 'Of course, you'll have to change it as the war goes on. Cads come and go, y'know. Some improve and become non-cads, while other people appear who qualify better. We'd better make a habit of it.'

Tyas Ackroyd appeared with a cup of tea and a muffin. The Field Marshal stared at them indignantly.

'What's this, Tyas, for God's sake?'

'Your tea, sir.'

'*One bloody muffin!*' The old man looked at Josh. 'One muffin's no good, is it?'

Ackroyd sniffed. '' 'Er Ladyship says you eat too much and don't do enough.'

'Of course I don't! It's too bloody cold. *I'*m not going to do a Lord Bobs and go inspecting the army in this weather. I can just imagine the uproar he caused in France. All right, Tyas, shove it down. How're you today?'

'Chest hurts when I cough.'

'Oh, my God, Josh, aren't we a bunch of old crocks? How's young Hedley?'

'They've turned him down, sir.'

'Who's turned him down?'

'Flying Corps, sir. They don't seem to think he's the right material for a commission as a pilot.'

The Field Marshal almost dropped his muffin. 'Jesus Christ and all His pink angels! I'd have said he was *perfect* material. Didn't he tell 'em where he came from? That I've known him all his life? That –' the old man looked up, a malicious twinkle in his eye ' – that he's chasing me granddaughter?'

'Is he, sir?' Ackroyd looked the picture of innocence.

'You know damn well he is, Tyas, you bloody old rogue, and I know damn well he's been meeting her at your cottage. Who was this idiot who turned him down?'

'A Major-General George Assheton-Smith, sir.'

'Do I know him, Tyas?'

'You once told me a story about him and rat droppings at an inspection, sir.'

The Field Marshal searched his mind. Generals all had inspection phobias. Some were concerned with cookhouses, some with latrines, some with such trivialities as bootlaces. He remembered that George Assheton-Smith was a fodder-chewer and had always considered it his duty to sample the horses' food until a roughrider sergeant, irritated by his fussiness, had warned him to look out for the little black bits. 'Them little black bits,' he had said, 'is rat shit.'

The Field Marshal grinned. 'I'll give him Major-General George Assheton-Smith,' he said. 'I'll see Mr Major-General Assheton-Bloody-Smith next time I'm in London and give him a piece of my mind. For the mean time, you can tell Hedley he'll be a pilot all right. I'll see to it.'

As Ackroyd disappeared, the old man settled back in his chair. The football team they had selected and the exchange with Tyas Ackroyd had cheered him up but he was still a bit bored and itching to do something for the war effort. Then his eye fell on Robert's letter again.

'There are matters about property that we ought to discuss,' he saw. The Field Marshal knew exactly what that meant. Robert had always had his eye on Braxby Manor. It wasn't the most beautiful of places and had draughts that could suck a cat up the chimney in a high wind, but it had a hell of a lot more dignity than that monstrous great pile the first Lord Cosgro had built when he'd been made a baron. Robert was after a title for himself and he was seeing Braxby Manor as his seat.

He glared at the letter again, his good temper gone once more. 'The war has affected us.' But not that damn much! Not with the horde of servants they employed. And if he knew Robert he'd be pulling strings like a puppet-master to prove that everybody he employed was in a necessary occupation and making it very clear to his underlings that any who volunteered needn't expect their jobs back when the war was over. 'This stupid retreat from Mons.' For God's sake – the Field Marshal's blood pressure rose – to Robert, Mons was only an inconvenience! To fifty-seven men of the Regiment it had meant the end of joy and laughter and love, the disappearance for ever into the cold and the comfortlessness and the dark. Robert was a selfish idiot. He'd always been a little that way, of course, a little dubious, a little uncertain, but since he'd joined the Cosgros, allying himself quite clearly with a family which had *always* raised the Field Marshal's blood pressure, he'd grown worse. His stupidity had become bone-headedness, his selfishness plain greed, while unfortunately his uncertainty had changed to certainty because he now knew what he wanted out of life and, as a Cosgro, was going all out to get it.

The old man swallowed his tea, burned his tongue, swore, and in disgust, almost choked on the muffin.

He stared at the letter again, feeling suddenly old and ill, then he pulled forward a pad of paper, took out his fountain pen and began to write.

'Dear Robert,' he wrote.

'Why in the name of God do you always appear to be so bloody useless? If you had one ounce of sense in that thick head of yours, you would be aware that we are in danger of losing this war and that K's demand for 100,000 men is one of the few things that are likely to save us. You can be very certain that there'll be another 100,000 and probably many more afterwards, and if this has the effect of reducing the legion of servants you keep to run errands for yourself and your fat and unhealthy family, so much the better for all of you. If I hear one more word of complaint from you I will personally inform the Prime Minister of the profits I suspect you and Cosgro are making on the side and the fact that you are undermining the war effort with treasonable dissension.

As for this business of property you wish to talk about, I am fully aware what that means. You wish to add Braxby Manor to your not inconsiderable possessions and, to do so, you are quite happy to snatch away your brother Dabney's birthright while he is not here to argue about it but is fighting to save your useless skin. Believe me, your getting this house will happen only over my dead body and, if I have anything to do with it, not even then. I wouldn't leave you a brass farthing to add to the fortune of the Cosgros.'

Writing the letter gave him immense satisfaction. At the bottom he added, 'Your father, Colby William Rollo Goff, Field Marshal.'

It pleased him. He had enjoyed signing his full name and adding his rank. Made it more official. Then he sighed, tore it up and started again.

'My dear Robert,' he wrote more calmly. 'Lord K's appeal for 100,000 men is not so silly as it sounds and, though it will undoubtedly result in inconvenience for a lot of people, it is nevertheless a far-sighted move that should be warmly applauded –'

s e v e n

Leave at Christmas came unexpectedly for Dabney.

For three weeks from October 16, there wasn't an officer or man of the cavalry division who was not fighting continuously, and for the first days they had fought alone and unsupported, not a whit of difference between them and the infantry. They had arrived in France superbly mounted and shining with the glitter of peacetime but by the middle of October the shine had all gone. Leather and brass were mud-smeared and the horses had long since been led to the rear. Dabney had washed and had his boots off twice in ten days and had almost forgotten what a horse looked like.

They had still managed to distinguish themselves, however, and one of the sergeants, sent off to deliver a message to another part of the line by horse when cut off by twenty Germans, had drawn his sabre and delivered a one-man charge that had left five Germans dead and won him a Military Medal.

They had finally been relieved by scraped-together infantry battalions and had rejoined their division to find that Indian cavalry was arriving to help. The Indian Army had formerly been considered to have no social status at all. Though the Gurkhas were good and the Sikhs not bad, the Baluchis, Punjabis, Pathans, Dogras, Rajputs, Mahrattas and Garhwalis were just infantry with black faces. The cavalry were accepted, of course, because they were good at polo. But now they were more than welcome to relieve the strain of overwork, and as they had joined the surviving cavalry regiments of the line, their dark faces, blue turbans and lances had been the most wonderful sight Dabney had ever seen, and they had moved forward together through villages where women came to cottage doors with jugs of wine, the children screaming round the horses in search of souvenirs. When pay arrived for the first time, the soldiers flooded the cafés demanding beer and complaining about its quality when they got it.

'In my opinion,' Dabney heard, 'they should pour it back in the 'orse.'

The fact that he had been among the first to be granted leave aroused in him a strong suspicion that the colonel, Johnson, was eager to be rid of him. From considering it a personal insult that the Regiment had had no casualties while under his command, he had now changed his view so much he resented not having been there when they had, and his dislike for Dabney had grown with the bar to the DSO that he had received for the defence of Mortigny.

The fact that his colonel didn't like him could not be held to be a matter for concern. As a soldier, Dabney was well aware that he ought to be able to handle the situation, but it made life a little more difficult and he was glad to get away. He left the front in darkness, moving with his group among the dim figures at the railhead waiting to climb into the train for the coast. Peaked caps and rifle barrels were caught in silhouette against the sky and the murmur of many voices came from the dusk.

Dawn revealed the train passing through the French countryside with its clumps of wind-stirred trees. Dabney was already stiff from sitting wedged into a packed compartment and was flushed with the stuffy atmosphere and the stale cigarette smoke. Midday brought them to Calais and the train began to jolt and clatter through streets and warehouses, ragged urchins running alongside it, begging in shrill voices for 'Bullee.' As the train stopped, the men poured from it, noisy, eager to be in England. A strong salt wind buffeted round the angle of a shed and then in front of him were two tall funnels and the rakish masts of the leave ship.

The day's newspapers in the saloon were full of rubbish, suggesting that only the Germans were afraid. The panegyrics nauseated Dabney because all soldiers were afraid at times and most weren't ashamed to admit it, while war correspondents were as rare at the front as generals. As he left the ship for the train to London, a line of stretchers was being lifted into ambulances. The men on them were silent, grey-faced and still. A well-dressed woman carrying a small dog indicated them to the animal.

'Look darling, wounded soldiers.'

The train north was jammed with people, and as it left the cavernous darkness of King's Cross and sped between the packed houses of London's suburbs, he found himself dropping off to sleep. As it passed through the outskirts of Sheffield, it stopped across a level crossing. Marching alongside was a battalion of Kitchener's New Army.

He studied them with interest. They were among the finest-looking men he'd ever seen wearing British uniform, and he knew they were by far the most intelligent. They included works managers, newspapermen, sons of wealthy manufacturers, stock exchange dealers, architects, lawyers, university lecturers, graduates and undergraduates, a thousand splendid men with steelworkers and miners to add the brawn to the leadership qualities of the others.

They were singing. But not the bellicose songs the Germans and French favoured. For them it wasn't 'The Watch On The Rhine' or 'The Marseillaise', but self-denigratory songs that showed their sense of humour.

'Send for the boys of the Girls' Brigade
To set old England free
Send for my mother, send for my sister,
But for God's sake, don't send me...'

Changing trains in York, he bumped into Hedley Ackroyd. He was wearing the uniform of the 19th and looked well in it, too. Recognising Dabney he slammed to attention and saluted.

'Cut that out, Hedley,' Dabney smiled. 'How are you? I seen you've joined our lot.'

Hedley smiled. 'Only temporary, sir. A ruse of the Field Marshal's to get me into the Flying Corps.'

'Been home?'

'Yes, sir.'

'Seeing Philippa, I'll be bound.'

The boy gave a sheepish grin. 'Yes, sir, I have. I start to fly in the New Year.'

He was a good-looking young man with his mother's features and the Ackroyds' strength and carriage. At least, Dabney thought, Philippa Sutton's affection wasn't a flash in the pan. It had been going on a long time now and she had never wavered.

He was talking earnestly now about the little experience he had. 'Training seems to be a bit slow,' he was saying, 'because when the wind's blowing they say it's too dangerous and when it's not they say there's no "lift" in the air. In any case, everything we use is out of date and the one thing we need is a machine with a gun to fire through the propeller. It would revolutionise war.'

Dabney smiled and headed for his train to Braxby. As he turned away, he looked back. 'I think the war's already been revolutionised, Hedley,' he said. 'As quite a few of us have found out.'

*　　*　　*

Braxby was grey and silent with winter. The stone walls had a purple-violet look about them, the lowering slopes of the hills were heavy, and the water of the Brack looked leaden. Because his leave was unexpected, there was no one to meet Dabney, but the village grocer was passing in his trap and stopped to talk.

'You won't find your family at 'ome, Mr Dabney,' he said. 'I saw 'em get on the train to York. They was all going Christmas shopping.'

'How about dropping me at my father's place then?' Dabney said. 'I can get a lift from there.'

His mother greeted him with tears in her eyes and for the first time in his life he realised she was no longer young; and that, in its turn, made him realise how old his father must be.

'Where is he?' he asked.

'Inspecting some battalion in York,' Lady Goff said. 'He likes to be part of this New Army. He thinks they're such splendid men.'

There was an unexpected tremulousness about her, a mixture of happiness and sadness that puzzled him and he wondered for a moment if his father were ill.

'Oh, no, he's all right.' His mother managed a twisted smile and brushed the tears from her eyes. 'It's a letter that came from Helen.'

It had arrived via Holland. The Hartmanns were all safe and well and Karl-August was on the staff on the Eastern front facing the Russians. The letter was full of longing for England, for the need to see her parents and be reassured through the miseries of war that she was still loved. Though she didn't say much about it, it was clear the Germans were suffering from the same sort of war fever that had gripped England and she was lonely as her neighbours regarded her askance. The children were not finding it easy at school but she was constantly reassured by the letters she received from Karl-August who remained tolerant and encouraging, while his father, the Graf, had made it clear that she was under his wing so that things had improved a little.

Though the letter was full of affection and longing, it was curiously devoid of any other news beyond her family, and Dabney realised that Helen was trying hard to be loyal to her new country and avoiding writing anything that might be of help to its opponents. It was a curious sensation to feel his own sister was withholding information because they were enemies.

He mixed himself a whisky and soda. His mother watched him anxiously.

'Your father will be home soon,' she said. 'Go into the library. I'll have tea sent in.'

Dabney held up his glass. 'This'll do me, Mother.'

In the library, everything about his background was around him. The pictures were all of cavalrymen, most of them wearing the rifle-green uniform of the 19th with its gold-striped overalls, red plastron and plumed schapka. There was a statuette of a lancer in silver which had been presented by the Regiment to his father on being made a Field Marshal; strange spears and curious firearms; pictures of officers in ceremonial dress; statuettes of horses; assegais; mounted spurs; a sabre; a rake, poker and shovel said to be made out of French cavalry swords collected by his grandfather on the field of Waterloo. As a boy he remembered his father using them to demonstrate weapon drill.

He moved about the room, looking at the books on the shelves, picking up objects with which he was familiar, among them the sword he had carried himself at Omdurman. It was bent like a question mark and, as he held it in his hand, he wondered why they had thought *that* such a terrible business. After Mortigny, Omdurman seemed no more dangerous than a Saturday night scuffle outside a public house.

On his father's desk was a letter. It was a report on an inspection the old man had made on a Kitchener battalion at Leeds, and he saw with surprise that it was addressed to Kitchener himself at the War Office.

He couldn't help reading it. His father was making his feelings very clear. 'The one thing we must never do,' he had written, 'is to allow them to go untrained into battle. One of our first tasks should be to weed out the clever and see they are given experience with regular battalions so that they can become officers. There are also far too many technical men among them who would be better using their skill in manufacturing the needs of the army. I feel it was a bad mistake not to use the Territorial Army machinery to recruit, train and equip these men...'

He knew exactly what his father was getting at. Kitchener's dislike of the Territorials – Saturday Afternoon Soldiers, he called them – was well known, but the Territorials were already acquitting themselves well in France and their organisation had been good enough to allow them to fit smoothly into the regular army.

He looked at the letter again. 'Let us have men back from France as soon as the situation there makes it possible, to train them, to give them some idea of what modern war is like. I am desperately afraid that they are likely to be sent into action in the old dangerous formations I saw as far back as the Crimea. Wounded men should not be returned to their battalions but attached to the new K battalions to give them the benefit of their experience. Whatever Douglas Haig feels about cavalry breakthroughs, I think we have to face the fact that this is going to be an infantry war of siege and entrenching, and these new men must be instilled with the knowledge of how to behave in those conditions...'

He heard a movement and looked up to see his father watching him. The old man seemed tired but he looked splendid in his uniform, his chest ablaze with medal ribbons.

'Hello, Father,' he said, as they embraced.

'Hello, my boy. How's the regiment?'

Dabney sighed. 'Fullerton's dead. You know that, of course. Hawker and Harbord are wounded. But Tim Leduc's splendid and so's young Quibell. Unfortunately, I suspect we'll be losing Quibell soon. He'll be leaving us for a machine gun battalion when they get the guns. It'll mean promotion and he deserves it.'

'What about Johnson?'

'He bothers me, Father. I don't think he's good enough. Unfortunately, a lot of people don't seem to be good enough.'

The Field Marshal indicated the desk. 'You were reading my letter to Kitchener?'

'I didn't mean to pry.'

'Don't matter, my boy. What do you think of it?'

'I absolutely agree, Father.'

'I've just come from York. They're living in shocking conditions. The local brigadier's a dug-out. Too fat, too much moustache, too rigid with regulations. Eyes like boiled marbles. I told him to forget the bloody regulations and get them properly housed before they all go down with pneumonia. There was an orderly room clerk listening at the door, I knew, but I didn't keep my voice down. I wasn't wanting them to fall on me neck in gratitude – just to know *someone* was on their side. There's already too much feeling that senior officers are stupid and that nobody cares.'

The old man sighed. 'Kitchener never did have the gift of delegating work and it's pretty obvious he's already trying to do too much. Yet everybody's terrified of him.' He poured himself a drink. 'I expect my report will be lost in the piles of paper on his desk.'

Dabney frowned. 'The whole business of asking for volunteers was wrong, Father. The bravest, the most patriotic always volunteer first and, since they're the boldest, the most intelligent who've already begun to make their mark in the world, they're the ones who can least be spared.'

The Field Marshal sipped his drink. 'It's always been the same, my boy,' he growled. 'For some god-forsaken reason I've never been able to fathom, this country backs away from conscription as if it were the plague. War's always a contest in blunders and the side that makes the least ends up the winner, but, you know, in this country the greater the inefficiency of the army, the greater seems the contentment of the politicians. I was talking to Haldane the other day about it and he had the bloody nerve to say that in the event of a great national emergency it *might well* be necessary to resort to conscription. Great God, what greater national emergency can you think of than war?'

Dabney managed a smile. 'It isn't like South Africa, is it, Father?'

'Never supposed it would be. When are we going to get moving, Dab?'

Dabney frowned and his father noticed the grey hairs and the new lines at the corner of his mouth. He gave his father a grim look and came straight to the point.

'We're not, Father,' he said. 'Mobile war's finished.'

Christmas day was a strange affair with everybody trying to be light-hearted and not mention the fighting. With his family, Dabney drove across to Braxby Manor for breakfast and they made the pilgrimage round the stables as they had for years. Both preceded and followed by elderly Ackroyds who could no longer be called upon to serve their country, they progressed past the stalls and loose boxes with their oaken buckets, dandy brushes, body brushes, water brushes, hay whisps, stable rubbers and curry combs. The horses watched them, eager for titbits, their souls in their eyes, and the youngest children were placed on their backs to make sure they knew what was expected of them when they grew up.

The Christmas service at Braxby Church followed much the same pattern as elsewhere across the country. Prayers were offered for victory and the quicker slaughter of Germans.

'God is on our side,' the Rector announced confidently.

'That's what the Germans say,' the Field Marshal growled as they headed for the trap. 'They even wear it on their belts. *Gott Mit Uns.* I expect the Austrians are saying the same, too, to say nothing of the French and the Serbs and the Russians and everybody else, too. I reckon God's got his work cut out.'

Goff relations arrived to share nuts and drinks and mince pies, among them Robert and his family.

'Were you in this retreat business, Dab?' he asked, lightly, as if what they'd gone through had been a bit of a joke.

'Yes,' Dabney said. 'I was in the retreat.'

'Doing your stuff, I suppose, in the rearguard?'

'I was on a very slow horse.'

Games and charades were played with the children, Robert sitting at the back of the room with a whisky in his hand as if it were beneath his dignity to prance about in front of the fire. Dabney entered into the spirit of the games more ardently than anyone, noisy and riotous with the excited children in a way that worried his wife and his parents. He drank more than they had ever seen him drink before and threw himself into charades as if it were the only thing on earth he wanted to do.

'You'll rupture yourself, old boy,' Robert said as he watched.

'More than you'll ever do,' Dabney snapped back.

It was unnecessarily sharp but Robert was placid enough not to notice it. It didn't go unmarked by the Field Marshal, however, and he noticed later that when the children were taken to see a Punch and Judy show put on by one of the Ackroyd boys in the nursery, Dabney went straight to the whisky decanter. The Field Marshal put his hand on it but Dabney gently pushed it away.

'No, Father,' he said. 'I need this.'

'France, boy?'

'I suppose so. It's nothing.'

'If it's important, as a senior officer of the army, don't you think I ought to know.'

Dabney stared at his father for a moment then his eyes dropped. 'I find it faintly insulting to see Robert sitting there so bloody placidly, Father,' he said deliberately, 'while my chaps in France are short of equipment and short of ammunition.'

'If you're short of ammunition, this isn't the place to air your grievances.'

'I've aired them, Father. In the right places. Not much was done. When the battles start again in the spring, we're going to have casualties because nobody's bothered.'

'*I've* bothered,' the Field Marshal said quietly. 'I'm *still* bothering. Unfortunately the fact that we're at war doesn't seem yet to have seeped through to the House of Commons. Asquith's being led by the nose by his colleagues in the Cabinet, Balfour's trying to score points all the time, and Keir Hardie's preaching peace.'

'Can't *you* stir 'em up, Father?'

'My job's to work for efficiency. At my age, that's about all I'm good for. We need someone younger. Someone who isn't going to take long lunches and is prepared to work late into the night. Winston, for instance, or this feller, Lloyd George.'

Dabney frowned. '*He* was preaching peace when we were fighting in South Africa,' he said.

The old man shrugged. 'Makes a bit of difference when you're in power,' he observed. 'He's more to lose nowadays, and I suspect he sees himself as Prime Minister.'

eight

1915 was a sad year.

It began with the realisation that the war of manoeuvre had come to a stop with the construction of trenches and that the German-occupied area of France and Belgium would have to be regarded as a fortress. It was also clear that it was too big to be invested, yet there was a feeling in France that, with national territory in enemy hands, there could be no letting up on the offensive strategy and, faintly embarrassed by the smallness of her contribution, Britain allowed herself to be dragged into a series of useless attacks, which achieved nothing but casualties.

Though the end of the war, which had been so confidently predicted by so many by the Christmas of 1914, had not come about, the new spring and summer campaigns had been expected to settle things, but nothing was changed except that the new year brought unexpected weapons such as poison gas, zeppelins which began a series of raids on London, naval hit-and-run attacks on British coastal towns and, above all, the U-boat, which up till then nobody had thought of except as an auxiliary to the fleet. The Germans had suddenly realised its potential against merchant ships and had begun to destroy on sight, their greatest success – and their greatest mistake – the sinking of the liner, *Lusitania*, which carried American passengers. Winston Churchill, an old friend of the Goff family, stopping by for the night en route for a visit to northern shipyards for the

Admiralty, put it succinctly. 'Under the official grief in Whitehall,' he admitted, 'there's also a feeling that this time they've gone too far and it'll bring the Americans in.'

It was an opinion which seemed to be shared by the German leaders because they offered to stop the sinkings if the British navy would relax its blockade. The noose, it seemed, was already tightening, as Helen's letters, still coming regularly through Holland, showed. 'Why are you trying to strangle Germany?' she asked with a note of bitterness. 'German women and children have no quarrel with you but, when food grows short, it will be they who suffer.'

A faint trace of distrust lay over all her letters these days. 'Germany has no quarrel with Britain,' she kept insisting. 'Russia is her most dangerous enemy and she asks nothing from Britain and France but to be left alone.'

'She's talking like a dyed-in-the-wool Prussian,' the Field Marshal muttered.

He was feeling old these days and was made very much aware of his age by the fact that Tyas Ackroyd had finally had to retire to one of the cottages by the Home Farm. For a while it had seemed as if the end of the world had come, because Tyas Ackroyd had been with him ever since the middle of the previous century. He had ridden alongside him at Balaclava, and had saved the Field Marshal's life when he'd been wounded at Yellow Tavern. He had never before left the Field Marshal's side and his disappearance brought home to him the fact that he, too, no longer had much time left. Though it didn't frighten him, it was a sobering thought.

If only, he felt, he could be spared to see the success of British arms. But the news from the war made him feel ill. French was proving a disaster as commander-in-chief and, still moving mercurially between enthusiasm and black despair, was blaming his failure at Neuve Chapelle on the shortage of shells.

The summer changed nothing and when French failed again at Loos as the warm weather ended, the writing seemed to be on the wall. It was clear French was trying to discredit Haig, even as Haig tried to discredit him, so that in addition to a casualty list of staggering proportions, the army was also being treated to an unedifying squabble between senior officers.

Autumn arrived with the government now a coalition and Haig getting what he wanted, the job of commander-in-chief. Even Kitchener's position was insecure now, because he had been held responsible for the shell shortage and with Northcliffe, of the *Daily Mail,* determined to bring him down, Lloyd George had been given the job of Minister of Munitions.

'Perhaps,' the Field Marshal said, 'it'll begin a new sort of war.'

Almost before they knew where they were, however, they were telling themselves the same things all over again.

1916 would settle the Germans' hash. By then the mass of the new Kitchener Armies, not a hundred thousand as had been originally intended, but vastly more, would be trained and ready for action. A few had already been in the trenches, a few had even been in battle, and, despite their inexperience, their intelligence had shown them to be adaptable and capable of learning quickly, while their fierce patriotism made them go on trying when everybody else had given up.

But the Dardanelles, the one hope of getting into the German fortress by the back door, had proved a failure. Out of office suddenly and trying to get a command in France, Churchill made his feeling clear to the Field Marshal.

'The guns and the shells and the men,' he said, 'were held back for France where they were wasted on futile frontal attacks that got us nowhere.'

Now everything was concentrated on the narrow strip of land that ran all the way across France from the sea to Switzerland, stale, covered with the rubbish of war and soured with the hundreds of bodies that were buried in it. Criss-crossed by rusty barbed wire, it represented the dead hopes of military and political leaders on both sides. The opposing armies had fought since 1914 over this same narrow area of bloodstained ground in which occasionally a salient was bitten off or another thrust out, the futile finishing point for some ambitious attack that had cost thousands of lives, and the war had sunk into a wretched stalemate from which only the New Armies could be expected to rescue it.

Studying his paper, his grandson at his feet, the Field Marshal brooded. Nobody had heeded his exhortations about the new men. They had not been intermingled in the experienced brigades and divisions of the Regular Army as he had advised, but had been formed into entirely new units with untrained NCOs and untrained officers. Apart from a few, they had not even been given the chance to learn in small trench actions, and those who had were derisive of the old army's methods.

'Does no-bloody-body have any sense these days?' he muttered.

Studying his illustrated magazine, which showed the war in a much cleaner and more honourable light than it seemed to the Field Marshal, Josh looked up.

'What did you say, Grandpa?'

'I said –' the old man paused ' – I said, that this seems to be a very dirty war, boy.'

'Aren't all wars dirty, Grandpa? You once said they were.'

'Of course they are. But most wars move about. This one stays in the same place. One long, dirty, muddy, sour, stinking strip of land that runs across the whole of Europe where men have to live like moles to survive.' The old man was more than usually bitter.

'But there were trenches in the American Civil War and trenches in the Franco-Prussian War and the Boer Wars, Grandpa. You said so.'

'Yes.' The old man sighed. 'But nobody remained in 'em long and they didn't bury their dead where they were living and eating and sleeping. By comparison, those were gentlemen's wars. This is a cads' war, boy. With submarines sinking ships without warning and zeppelins dropping bombs on women and children, there isn't even any honour any longer. And poison gas! Good God, boy, what are we coming to?' He warmed to his theme. 'In South Africa, where your father and I fought, it *was* a gentleman's war. I suppose we were still a bit old-fashioned in those days – but there was a lot of courage, boy, and headquarters weren't in a château miles behind the front. They were in the saddle. Perhaps we weren't very bright and neither were the men, but we fought together, and in the cruelty of war, men's behaviour to each other is the only thing that lifts it out of the depths of barbarism. We abandoned our wounded, knowing perfectly well they'd be cared for, and so did the Boers. We didn't contribute willingly to brutality and we never needlessly took life. For God's sake, boy, look at this war: Ypres, fifteen thousand. Neuve Chapelle, thirteen thousand. Aubers Ridge, twelve thousand. Loos, eight thousand. And that doesn't include French casualties which must run into *hundreds* of thousands by now.'

'My *War Illustrated* says our troops are always cheerful.'

The old man's eyes grew misty. 'They always are, boy,' he said. 'That's the incredible thing. They lose all their friends, they don't get fed, they have fools put in command of 'em, and they *still* remain cheerful. I'm damned if I know how they do it. I never did. Yet those bloody politicians in London have always kept 'em short of everything they ever needed.

This *is* a cads' war, boy, and no mistake, and it's time we picked another cads' team.'

Finding a pencil, Josh eagerly began to write in the margin of his magazine. 'The Kaiser, of course,' he said. 'He has to be captain.'

'Yes. Then you'd better put down Asquith. And Bottomley. He's still there. And Woodrow Wilson – '

'Who's he?'

'President of the United States. He ought to be coming to our rescue.'

'But he's an American and the Americans aren't fighting.'

'No. Better leave him out then. There are plenty better cads than he is.'

'Sir John French? Father doesn't seem to like him.'

'No. Not French. He's in nobody's team. He's out. No longer even a player. He's already forgotten. How about Haig?'

'But he's commander-in-chief in France!'

'Thanks to his own tittle-tattling. If he'd behaved like that at school, he'd have been called a sneak. I don't like Haig. Put him down.'

The boy looked bewildered but he did as he was told. 'How about Enver Pasha?' he asked. 'After the Dardanelles, we ought to have a Turk in the side.'

'Why not?'

'How about Uncle Robert? He was first reserve last time but when I told Father about our team when he was on leave he said he ought to be captain.'

The Field Marshal sighed. 'Not captain,' he said.

'Well, Father said he had no right to live the way he did when men were dying in France.'

'No boy, I suppose he oughtn't. Better make him vice-captain.'

The old man's heart was heavy. Robert's return to the army had been short-lived. When yeomanry units had been whipped abroad to take the place of the decimated regiments of the Regular cavalry, he had suddenly discovered he was too busy producing uniforms and guns to be a soldier and had resigned.

He was backing Lloyd George to the full now, had even changed his politics to Liberal because he claimed Lloyd George was the only Minister who knew what war was all about. Certainly, he was waging it at home as well as abroad and for the first time it had ceased to be a mere extra in life, because the Welshman had made it the *whole* of life. With the War Office still ordering munitions on a peacetime scale, he had regarded with contempt Haig's claim that two machine guns per battalion were enough and Kitchener's that four were enough, and told his assistants to square the number, multiply it by two, then double it again for luck. The Field Marshal had had the figures from Lloyd George's own lips. The man was a bounder, there was no doubt about that, but he didn't hesitate, and he had a broad vision of things.

Despite the changes in the government, the war didn't really improve much. Italy had come in on the side of the Allies, but she seemed to be more of a burden than a help because she had no guns and no equipment and the back door to Germany through Austria remained locked by the Alps, while Russia, defeated to the extent of having to withdraw three hundred miles eastward, had lost nearly a million men as prisoners alone and ten million of her inhabitants were refugees.

The New Year – yet another new year and the war still not ended – came with a mixture of hope and despair. Every family in the land seemed to have been involved in the butchery in France. Mourning was everywhere, with battalions of grieving women. Yet there was hope, too, because soon Kitchener's New Armies were going to break the German stranglehold before long on the Somme. Everybody knew about it.

'If *we* know about it,' the Field Marshal growled to his wife, 'I dare bet the Germans do, too. For God's sake, Gussie, the whole art of battle is to surprise your man and hit him where he isn't expecting it, but there's no surprise anywhere in this war. They're obsessed with barrages, and all *they* do is alert the enemy to the fact that we're coming and smash up the ground we're going to attack over. We need cavalry to move fast. But not horsed cavalry. Something else. Aeroplanes, God knows what, but a device to smash the machine gun. It shouldn't be beyond the power of the inventors to think of something.'

He tried the idea on Robert when he next saw him and Robert was surprisingly coy.

'Don't worry, Father,' he said. 'We've thought of it already. It's highly secret.'

'If it's that secret what the devil are you doing telling me?'

Robert ignored the comment. 'A chap called Swinton in the Engineers thought it up,' he said. 'He got Winston interested.'

'What is it? Battleships?'

Robert smiled. 'You might call them land-ships.'

'What in the name of God are land-ships?'

Robert pulled a face. 'Look here, Father, I'm going to tell you. It *is* a hell of a secret, as you say. I'm surprised you haven't heard, in fact.'

'You don't *have* to tell me,' the Field Marshal said. 'But, good God, after over fifty years in the army, I know all about keeping bloody secrets, boy!'

Robert fidgeted. 'Well, the army wasn't interested so they took the idea to Winston.'

'Winston's out of office. What can he do?'

'Nothing, now. But he got it moving with Admiralty funds. They call them tanks. It's only a code name, of course.

When somebody asked what they were, they were told they were to carry water to the troops. They're armoured tractors with machine guns on them. They can go through trenches and barbed wire entanglements. When Winston left the Admiralty, Arthur Balfour took the thing under his wing. They come in two models, one with a six-pounder, one with a machine gun. They're a bit slow, unfortunately, but we shall get over that.'

The Field Marshal eyed his son narrowly. 'And *you're* manufacturing them?'

'Just the armour plate. In Sheffield.'

'No wonder you're enthusiastic.'

Robert laughed. 'We shall certainly do well, Father. Very well. Lloyd George's delighted. He's going to put my name forward for something.'

The Field Marshal snorted but Robert placidly looked at his watch. 'In a hurry,' he said. 'Have to sit on a tribunal. Compulsory military service.'

'I know all about your damn tribunals,' the old man growled. 'The one at Market Bosworth exempted all the Hunt servants on the grounds that they had indispensable occupations. It had better not happen here.'

Robert remained unperturbed. 'I shall do my duty, Father,' he said. 'Which leads me to another subject: This house.'

'What about this house?'

'Well, look, Father – I have no wish to sound morbid or even to appear to be fishing, but I'm wondering if you've done anything about it. I hope you've made a will.'

The Field Marshal glowered. 'Of course I've made a will,' he said.

Robert smiled. 'Then that's all right. I only felt it was time we got things straight.'

'In case I dropped dead tomorrow?'

'No, of course not, Father. But as the elder son – '

' – you felt you'd like to be assured that everything would be coming to you. Well, I'm not promising that.'

Robert's smile faded and his jaw dropped. 'In this country, Father, we believe in primogeniture.'

'In this country, we *certainly* believe in primogeniture,' the Field Marshal growled. 'And the baronetcy will be handed on to you. But any wealth I have will be shared between my family.'

'I'm not worried about wealth, Father. I'm concerned about this house.'

'So that when Lloyd George gets you what he's promised, it can be your seat.'

'A titled man has to have a seat somewhere.'

The Field Marshal's eyebrows worked. 'And what would Dabney do?' he demanded. 'It's his home as much as yours. We can rule out Helen because she's in Germany and old Von Hartmann's far from poor. Jane couldn't give a damn. She's a farmer's wife, which is all she ever wants to be and John Sutton has his own land. Which leaves Dabney and you.'

'Exactly, Father. Split between two, the house would be valueless.'

'Who said I intended to split it?'

Robert's smile returned. 'That's all right then, Father. I'll arrange to see your solicitors in York, shall I?'

'Not just yet, because it isn't my intention of leaving it to *you.*'

Robert's face went pink, then white, and there was a pinched look at the corner of his nostrils. 'I'm the elder son, Father.'

'And you already have more than you need,' the old man snapped. 'When Walter Cosgro dies, you'll even have Cosgro Hall. He's got no children.'

'That's not the point, Father.'

'I think it's very much the point. Considering that you already have more than you need and the promise of Cosgro

Hall, what's your objection to Dabney – who has only his pay as a soldier and will inherit precious little because I'm far from being a rich man – having this place? The fact that you're the eldest son don't mean a thing. You've thrown in your lot with the Cosgros, taken their background, even their name. By what right do you come here making demands that your family gives up to you what you've already rejected? This place has been Goff territory for generations and, if I have anything to do with it, it will remain Goff territory.' The Field Marshal looked hard at his son. 'So you can put that in your pipe and smoke it.'

n i n e

The rumours of the push on the River Somme grew so persistent and so public, when the Field Marshal received a message that Kitchener wished to see him, he set off for London determined to voice his fears.

He caught the train at York, accompanied by his wife and daughter-in-law, who were going to the capital to shop.

'Not that there's much to choose these days,' Elfrida said. 'But Robert went off to Sheffield to inspect the plant there, so it's better than being at home alone.'

As the Field Marshal put them into a taxi at King's Cross before seeking one himself to take him to the War Office, Elfrida pushed her head through the window to kiss him. For some reason, she seemed to have a high regard for him and he returned the salute warmly. His earliest fear that Elfrida was a fool hadn't materialised. She was plump and far from clever but she seemed to be able to turn a blind eye to Robert's peccadilloes and, if nothing else, provided a good example to his children.

The War Office was full of officers seeking appointments or transfers from one command to another. There were also, the Field Marshal noticed, a great many young men in immaculately-cut uniforms who seemed sleek and well-fed, moving about with arms full of papers and an air of self-importance.

Kitchener greeted him with his usual gruff welcome and promptly derided his concern that the coming push was on everybody's tongue.

'Nobody's going to find out,' he said. 'The Germans don't have spies in every office.'

The Field Marshal had a feeling that they might well have them outside, but Kitchener was adamant.

'The Germans have plenty to do without worrying about that,' he insisted. 'They've got themselves in a mess at Verdun, and it'll keep 'em occupied while we build up our own offensive on the Somme.'

He seemed ill-tempered and liverish, his obduracy more marked. He was still a towering figure with his pale brooding eyes and red beefy face, but the famous moustache had lost some of its neatness and he had an irritated air about him, as if the fact that he'd lost a lot of his power was worrying him.

'We have plenty of other things to concern us apart from German spies,' he went on. 'Those Russian swabs have been getting themselves in trouble and the government's talking of sending me to sort things out a little.'

The Field Marshal said nothing, aware that it was nothing more than a ruse to get the great man out of the way so that the government could get on with the war.

'They need stiffening,' Kitchener went on. 'Come to that, so do the troops in France. We're sending out people to see them.'

'What sort of people?'

Kitchener's grim face relaxed in a malicious smile. 'Your sort. We want you to go out there and talk to them.'

The Field Marshal was indignant. 'They've got enough to do out there without having to spit and polish because an old fool like me's going to inspect 'em.'

'It's Lloyd George's idea. You'd better see him.'

Ellesmere, who had been wounded at Neuve Chapelle, was at the War Office, holding down an insignificant job

219

until he had recovered. He looked pale and ill but he welcomed the Field Marshal warmly.

'Yes, I've heard of the visit,' he admitted. 'Lloyd George has a feeling that the men in France are being neglected by the people at home. He wants you to go to France and let yourself be seen.'

'I'm too bloody old for that, Ned, and you know it.'

Ellesmere smiled. 'You're a remarkably fit man for your age, sir. And France can be pleasant in the spring.'

Lloyd George, handsome, energetic, romantic with his long hair, his mouth full of rhetoric, received the Field Marshal warmly.

'I don't want inspections,' he explained at once. 'That's the last thing I want.'

'It's the last thing *I* want,' the Field Marshal growled. 'I want to visit the front line.'

Lloyd George looked startled. 'If you drop dead,' he said, 'it'll be your own fault. What *I* want you to do is visit Headquarters.'

The old man's eyes narrowed. 'I'm not going to cut anybody's throat for Parliament.'

The Welshman held up his hand. 'I don't trust soldiers. I never have. War's too important to be left solely to soldiers.'

'It's certainly too important to leave it to politicians.'

Lloyd George acknowledged the rebuke. 'The obvious answer's to work in each other's pockets. Unfortunately, we suspect we're being kept in the dark. Haig has the ear of the King, as you probably know. That makes him pretty well above our reach. We have to devise other means. I want to know what's happening. That's all.'

The agreement was made and Lloyd George smiled. 'In compensation, I have something I'd like you to see. I'm going to Hatfield Park in Hertfordshire tomorrow. I'd like you to come along with me.'

The following day was cold and Hatfield Park looked bleak with the fag-end of winter. The sky was a sullen grey, the packed clouds in a thick layer over the earth so that the light was poor and thin.

Standing, cheerless and cold, near a group of officers, the Field Marshal was not surprised to see Robert among the civilian experts and politicians who had gathered. Lloyd George moved between the groups, excited, enthusiastic and full of mordant wit.

'There's nothing very surprising about what you're going to see, when you come to think of it,' he said. 'It's nothing but the logical adaptation of the automobile to trench warfare. We used cars with armour on them in 1914 at Antwerp and the idea was suggested more than once before the war, in England, Austria, and Germany. Needless to say, H G Wells thought of it, too, and just as naturally, the military rejected it and it was pushed into a pigeon hole. Fortunately the German military had the same sort of mind and they marked it "No importance for military purposes!" '

There were a few sidelong glances among the officers. Lloyd George never hesitated to make known his view of soldiers.

'Let's have the demonstration, David,' one of the politicians suggested. 'We all know what you think of the army.'

The politician gave a sly grin. 'For myself,' he went on, 'I can't imagine why, if a civilian could foresee the type of warfare we would be facing, the War Office couldn't. However –' he smiled and gestured ' – it's become very clear that we need some sort of mobile fort to overcome barbed wire and machine gun fire, something armed and armoured which is capable of crossing very rough country.'

He gestured and a tall slender officer wearing what appeared to be a leather skull cap took over.

'We're obviously not entirely happy with what we've produced,' he said. 'Because haste has been the order of the day, there's been little time for research and the perfection of design. Only by adapting existing components to meet the rough specifications we've been given have we been able to get enough machines ready for the campaign this spring.'

'If this feller knows about the coming campaign,' someone asked, 'how many others do?'

'Wait, wait!' Lloyd George gestured. 'Let him finish.'

'We tried various lines,' the man in the leather cap went on. 'Eventually we began to look at the idea of caterpillar tracks and in the end produced a pressed-steel affair which, gentlemen, was the birth of what you're going to see today.'

'And a long time it took, too,' Lloyd George murmured.

There was a little angry muttering among the group of officers and the man in the leather cap flushed. But he went on doggedly.

'We've been asked for a trench-crossing capability of eight feet,' he said, 'and the ability to climb a five-foot parapet – '

'We came to see the bloody thing in action,' one of the politicians behind him interrupted. 'Not hear people spout about it.'

They hadn't long to wait. Cars were brought up and they drove to where a mock-up of a trench system had been prepared. A deep ditch had been dug and lined with sandbags. In front of it, coils of barbed wire caught the grey gleam from the sky. Behind it a five-foot stone barrier had been constructed. Along one side of the trench was a raised mound where they could stand and watch.

'Hey, presto,' Lloyd George said. 'Here it comes!'

Emerging from the valley came a grey shape over thirty feet long, shaped like a lozenge. From sponsons on either side poked the snouts of guns, and endless caterpillar tracks moved over the top of the eight-foot-high hull. The thing looked like a grey slug as it approached the barbed wire, waddling forward through deep mud, followed by a pair of wheels with which it appeared to be steered.

It climbed the green slope slowly, cutting the turf with two dark tracks like the trail of a snail until it came to the barbed wire. Twanging and clattering, the wire gave beneath the enormous weight then the monster raised its snout over the parapet of the trench, paused, and dropped with a nerve-shattering crunch with its nose down on the other side.

'Reason for its shape,' the man in the leather hat pointed out. 'The trailing stern holds it down until the raised bow is across the trench and it can safely fall into place to bridge it.'

Scattering clods of earth, the monster was churning across the trench now, heaving its ugly snout up against the wall. The caterpillar tracks clattered and scraped and the bow lifted, then hung, poised on top, before dropping with a crash over the other side.

'Good God!' the Field Marshal said.

The tank had swung round in a wide circle and was stopped now for inspection. A door in the side opened and the crew climbed out and stood alongside. Despite the chill of the day, their clothing was thin. On their heads they wore leather helmets like the man who had explained the monster's functions, and a mask of chain mail.

The Field Marshal moved warily forward. 'What's it like in there, my boy?' he asked the commander.

The officer was a pink-faced youth, his cheeks damp with perspiration and streaked with oil.

'Hot, sir,' he said.

'Difficult?'

'There *are* difficulties, sir. We have to have four men driving and the idea's to have four others to fire the guns. It'll not be easy, but I think we've got something here and I expect we shall manage.'

'Your clothes are thin, boy.'

'That's because of the heat, sir.'

'What about the engine? She seems very slow.'

'It ought to be faster, sir. Everybody acknowledges that.'

The officer who had stage-managed the demonstration interrupted. 'The navy and the flying corps have first call on all engines,' he explained. 'We have to make do with what we can get.'

Aware of his lack of knowledge even of the car he owned, the Field Marshal turned to the tank commander again. 'I'd like to see inside.'

A few eyebrows were raised but the tank commander was more than willing.

'It's pretty dirty in there, though, sir,' he warned.

'Damn the dirt! This is the most exciting thing I've seen for months.'

The inside of the tank was stifling and stank of hot oil. There were projecting pieces of hot metal and only limited vision through open slits.

'How about communication with each other?'

'Hand signals, sir. You can't shout above the engine and the noise of the tracks.'

'How about with outside?'

'Pigeon, sir. We shove 'em out through the hole there.'

'Then how do you lead your people into action?'

The boy shrugged. 'That's something we're trying to work out, sir. So far, we can only think of the commanding officer walking in front.'

'And that,' the Field Marshal said in a flat voice, 'will be bloody dangerous.'

The demonstration was followed by lunch and drinks which made the Field Marshal wonder why it was that politicians seemed unable to decide anything without feeding their faces. Robert, he noticed, had disappeared and he decided he'd gone deliberately rather than have to offer his father a lift in his car.

Because of the late hour when he returned to London, the Field Marshal decided to eat in the West End before meeting his wife and daughter-in-law. The Cavalry Club didn't appeal because he wasn't in the mood to listen to flattery or to satisfy the old men waiting in the leather armchairs for the latest news from France or the War Office. Instead, he took a taxi to Claridge's, and he was sitting in a dark corner of the lounge drinking coffee and brandy when he saw Robert enter. He was about to rise to greet him, wondering why he was there, when he realised his son wasn't alone and that the woman with him was Lady Balmael. They spoke to the clerk at the reception desk and turned to go upstairs.

As they reached the lift, Robert's eyes met his father's. For a moment he hesitated, awkward and embarrassed, then he defiantly followed Lady Balmael.

For a long time the Field Marshal sat in silence, staring straight ahead, as if he'd seen nothing, then he rose, paid his bill, and headed for the street. Feeling he needed to be alone, he headed for the Cavalry Club. He couldn't face his daughter-in-law at that moment.

As he walked, deep in thought, he realised he was in the middle of the park and could hear sirens going. As he stopped, wondering about his safety, it occurred to him that, despite the whistles, he was probably in the safest place in the whole of London. Nothing but a direct hit from a bomb could hurt him. In the distance, he could hear the screams of women heading for the shelters and the shouts of the men with them. The street lamps had gone out and the place was in darkness but, standing in the park, he saw that searchlights had sprung up all round the city. Lifting his head, at the apex of two or three beams, he saw a long cigar-shaped object raising its nose towards the clouds that were reflecting the light of the searchlights. Guns began to fire from all directions and he saw the sparkle of shells in the sky, then over the East End several flashes lighting the sky told him bombs had fallen. Pity one couldn't fall on Robert, he thought savagely.

Next morning, he was at King's Cross before most of London was about. As he rode back north he found his mind occupied partly by Robert's stupidity and partly by what he'd seen at Hatfield Park.

Gradually, Robert faded to the back of his mind and he began to grow excited. It still bewildered him a little that the army had allowed so many months of trench warfare to pass without considering some means of overcoming its special problems. Doubtless they were too busy, like the politicians in the House, with their private squabbles; and it was typical that it was Churchill who had risked his reputation and Admiralty money on the new invention.

It was quite obvious that in the tanks they had a weapon which must not be squandered or presented to the enemy too soon. The first time they appeared on the battlefield they must appear in the largest possible numbers so that they could reintroduce the long-forgotten quality of surprise and tear a hole in the enemy front big enough to be properly exploited by fast-moving troops – even men on horses.

When his wife arrived home, she was looking worried. She kissed her husband abstractedly, and as she took her hat off, he fished a little.

'Something wrong?'

'No, nothing.'

'Come on, Gussie. You've never told fibs to me before. What's it all about?'

She sighed. 'Robert,' she said. 'All that nonsense of Elfrida's about going shopping in London was just show. She wanted to talk. She thinks Robert's carrying on with another woman.'

The Field Marshal drew a deep breath. 'He is,' he said. 'I went to Claridge's for a meal and he was there with that damned Balmael woman.'

PART THREE

one

Everywhere you looked the earth was brown with humanity. Every field seemed to be choked with men and horses, and the arrow-straight road was jammed with more guns and vehicles than the Field Marshal had ever seen.

As the Crossley car that carried him drove towards the east, convoy after convoy came past, rumbling carts with screeching axles and square-nosed, brass-bonneted ASC lorries, nose-to-tail, their drivers nodding at the wheel. Thousands of pack mules with tossing heads and wild eyes trudged southwards and westwards from the front, their legs and bellies caked with the chalky mud of the forward areas. Near every village carpenters were at work, both civilian and military, smocked and uniformed men working alongside each other to hammer bunks together outside barns and sheds.

'There'll be no mistake this time, sir –' The pink-cheeked young major with the red tabs and arm brassard who had been wished on the Field Marshal at headquarters spoke enthusiastically as his eye roved over the ranks of guns, battery on battery, that were waiting ready in the fields, the men behind them stacking great piles of shining shells into dumps.

The Field Marshal wasn't so sure. Remarkably little seemed to have been done to disguise the approach of the offensive and, as he lifted his eyes to the high ground in the distance, he was in no doubt whatsoever that the Germans were aware of it.

Listening to the soldiers, he was worried by their cynicism, sufficiently an old soldier to know what lay behind their guarded comments. The New Army men who had seen action seemed to have lost that eagerness that had led them to enlist and were now doing their job without sentiment or emotion. There was also no religious feeling, because the New Army men had sufficient intelligence to see that their God was the same as the Germans' Gott, but what appalled him most was the intense hatred for the staff that was obvious everywhere. He had always been aware of the fighting soldier's dislike for the men who mislaid his rations and got his friends killed in pointless attacks, but here in France so much fun was being poked at the red tabs, the glossy field boots and the elegant breeches it was almost a campaign of derision. Unhappily, it seemed well-deserved, because there were clearly far too many young men at the headquarters he had visited who had been selected less for their ability than for their family connections.

Among them were some splendid men, many of whom had been wounded in action, but there were others who were almost caricatures of brass-hats, and the general impression seemed to be that they lived in luxury, never missed a meal, consorted regularly with smart Frenchwomen, and seemed less concerned with fighting than with conducting distinguished visitors round the safe rear areas.

Despite the Field Marshal's wishes, his visit had been well publicised by the government and there was a major general, a brigadier, several colonels, a whole battalion of less senior officers and a posse of newspapermen to follow him around.

'I didn't ask for this, dammit,' he snapped.

'With respect, sir – ' the brigadier was a smooth man in immaculate uniform who seemed to be remarkably untouched by the war ' – it has to be done. Government instructions. War Office instructions. The people are interested. It's a morale-building exercise.'

'What damn morale can an old man like me build?' the Field Marshal snarled.

But he went along with the arrangements. Battalions were inspected at Querrieux and Bus and Coigneux, batteries in front of Albert and Sailly, and a training school for bayonet fighting at Verquemont where he listened appalled to the instructions offered to young men being inoculated with blood lust. In a South African Division facing Delville Wood, he found men with familiar names, one of them even a Burger and a grandson of the man who had been his second-in-command in the Zulu War. But no one remembered him.

Then he discovered that the North Cape Horse, his old unit, had raised a contingent which was fighting as infantry, but once again he realised he belonged to the lost age of Victoria's little wars and his connection with them was unknown.

He was equally disappointed with his visit to head-quarters. He was given a good lunch and the brandy bottle was placed so conspicuously to his hand that he was particularly watchful. The Commander-in-Chief was on a visit to French headquarters and he was attended throughout by the brigadier in charge of Intelligence, one of whose jobs seemed to be to convince everybody at home through the person of the Field Marshal that all was well. He seemed to be suffering from a sort of self-delusion that the Germans were blind and stupid and was convinced that the struggle for Verdun which was beginning at last to die down from sheer inanition, was going to be a great help.

'The Germans are worn out,' he insisted. 'Their reserves have all been swallowed up in the battle against the French. Once we get going, we can punch a hole in the front here so wide that any attempt by the Germans on the flanks to close it can only fail.'

Over the maps, he became even more enthusiastic. His hand moved across the sheets, indicating strong points and positions where German reserves were held.

'Sir Douglas would have preferred Flanders,' he said. 'But it was Joffre's claim that the land here in Picardy is far drier and more suitable than the marshy land up there. Besides, it's unfought over and undamaged and it gives us elbow room. We've built railway lines and provided water and seven weeks' lodgings for over four hundred thousand men and a hundred thousand horses. It was, of course, originally to have been a Franco-British attack but the German assault on Verdun's changed all that. It's now almost entirely British.'

In the eyes of the staff officers around him, the Field Marshal perceived an unholy glint of triumph – as though they had never wanted the French, anyway, and welcomed the slaughter at Verdun as a means of freeing them from the interference of foreigners they didn't like.

'What about the men? Can they operate in scattered groups?'

'They won't need to. We've made it clear to them they're to obey orders to the letter. All they'll have to do is go over with the bayonet and mop up the survivors of the bombardment.'

The Field Marshal had looked across the maps at the brigadier. 'Have *you* ever done any trench fighting?' he asked.

The brigadier seemed surprised at the question. 'Of course not,' he said.

'Then,' the Field Marshal had asked coldly, 'how can you be so sure?'

Sitting in the car that was taking him up to the line, the Field Marshal thought on what he had learned. The French seemed worried by the ideas coming from British headquarters and he had discovered that Rawlinson, commanding Fourth

Army, whom he had met in South Africa and considered an intelligent man, also had doubts. Rawlinson believed there was too great an optimism at headquarters and felt that the methods to be employed would exhaust the British before they had exhausted the Germans. His own suggestions had been for a more modest series of attacks instead of an attempt to finish the war at one blow. Allenby, another intelligent man who had the Third Army, was also suggesting less ambitious ventures, but neither was prepared to object too strongly, and it occurred to the Field Marshal that the Dardanelles had had its effect on all of them. Ian Hamilton, who had run that campaign, was also an intelligent man and he had been defeated, and they didn't seem prepared to set too much store by their military acumen.

As the car neared the front, the Field Marshal brooded. He had to admit that about him there was a new spirit in the air. He could sense it, could see it in all the eager faces about him. Kitchener's New Armies were arriving in their tens of thousands now, enthusiastic and, for the most part, untouched by the cynicism of the older soldiers. The shell shortage had been overcome, the ground was dry and different from the soggy marshes of Flanders. It was land where cavalry could move, good open country for the breakthrough. The Field Marshal earnestly prayed that they'd be given the chance.

The procession of cars reached Albert during the afternoon. The place had been destroyed in the early battles and hollow echoing buildings with broken windows like empty eye-sockets and smashed doorways like wailing mouths passed on either side. Heavy batteries were hidden among the trees and behind ruined houses and, as they entered the road that led to the Rue de Bapaume, the car stopped to let a battalion of marching men pass. Mouth organs were whining and they were singing the maudlin songs that had already carried them across France for two years. They were all grinning as they passed, old faces, young faces, all brown and healthy, all excited at the prospect of being in at the final victory on the Somme. They were a Kitchener battalion and they forgot to give eyes right and one or two men, seeing the Field Marshal's red hat band, even made rude noises.

The old man, huddled in his coat, said nothing. He had never been one to fuss about ceremonial. What was more important was the look of these splendid men. Four after four they came, the crunch of their heavy boots muffling their strong rough voices. They were all reduced to a common level by their khaki uniforms and were sweating under the weight of their equipment, but they were all singing, all cheerful in spite of their loads, all chivvied by new young officers, all bursting into cheers at the slightest excuse.

When the last man had passed, the car moved on again, eventually stopping at a crossroads close to the line. A tired-looking young captain with hollow eyes and a livid scar on his face that looked only newly healed, was waiting for them. He seemed quite indifferent to the Field Marshal who suspected he had done this job of conducting important people to safe areas of the line far too often to be impressed.

'Cleaver,' he introduced himself. He nodded to the pink-faced major. ' 'Morning, Horton.'

Major Horton seemed to resent his attitude, but Cleaver appeared not to notice.

'Ammunition dumps,' he pointed out, gesturing. 'Rest billets for troops.'

'I didn't come all the way from England to see ammunition dumps and rest billets,' the Field Marshal snapped. 'I've come to see the troops.'

'Sir,' Horton pointed out, 'we've seen troops all the way up here.'

'I've seen troops moving up to the line. Many of 'em. But I've not seen troops coming out of the line and I've not seen troops *in* the line. That's what I intend.'

It was noticeable that the cortège of officers and pressmen dwindled suddenly. The smooth brigadier discovered he had work to do and with profuse apologies climbed back into his car, removing with him several other officers. The press gallery disappeared at once – and far from unwillingly – as they were informed that they were not allowed, as civilians, into the area of the front line.

Cleaver stood watching the Field Marshal while all the sorting out was going on. The old man waited patiently. He was cold and tired but was still grimly determined to see what he'd come to see. Cleaver seemed to consider him mad, but he shrugged and finally led the way.

'Dangerous just here,' he said, moving quickly across the road.

Hurrying after him with Horton, back aching with stooping, knees cracking with unaccustomed exertion, the Field Marshal arrived at a wide and muddy path cut in the clay that ran through a cluster of white crosses on the edge of a wood. On one or two mouldering caps hung khaki ones among the old-fashioned French képis.

'Devons caught it here,' Cleaver remarked.

The path went downhill until they found themselves stumbling below ground level between strong parapets of clay. The going was hard because the mud was glutinous and sometimes deep, and Cleaver was clearly worried for the health of his elderly charge.

'You all right, sir?' he kept asking.

'Yes, dammit,' the Field Marshal panted, hoping to God he hadn't bitten off more than he could chew.

They passed under a plank bridge and moved round a promontory of earth and timber that forced them to make right-angled turns. The parapet was edged now with sandbags, laid header-stretcher three or four deep. Between them grass was sprouting and a poppy bloomed scarlet against the sky. A few men stood in the trench, dressed in mud-caked sheepskin jackets, and more lay asleep on the fire-step. They waited patiently as the group pushed past, a tattered crowd with hacked-off overcoats and sloppy unwired caps.

Here and there were dark caves with corrugated iron roofs with, occasionally, real curtains and little doors to give them a look of home. Above the openings were signs, 'No barrel organs, circulars or hawkers.' In the entrance to one of them a man was sitting with his shirt across his knees, delousing it.

'Just picking them out?' the Field Marshal asked.

The man looked up, his expression a little startled to see red tabs, but he made no attempt to rise. 'No, sir,' he said. 'Just taking them as they come.'

It had begun to drizzle now and the dry walls of the trenches were changing from dust to pasty white mud. Horton's splendid uniform was showing signs of heavy wear and tear.

'How much farther?' the Field Marshal asked.

Cleaver smiled. By this time, he was beginning to admire the old boy who was so persistently eager to see the conditions. He had conducted many important people to the front but very few of them had been willing to come this far.

'Any further, sir,' he said, 'and we shall be in Jerry's lap.'

The Field Marshal smiled back at him. 'I'd like to see the commanding officer.'

The young captain in command of the trench was shaving as they stumbled into his dug-out, scraping his face by the light of a candle.

'Come in,' he said cheerfully. 'Brought the reliefs?'

'This,' Cleaver said forbiddingly, 'is Field Marshal Sir Colby Goff. This, sir, is Captain Archer, 3rd/7th South Yorkshires.'

The captain put his razor down and slammed to attention, his face half-shaved.

'Finish what you're doing, my boy,' the Field Marshal growled. 'I'm sorry to intrude.'

The officer finished his face in record time and scrambled to put on his collar and tie and tunic. 'Can I offer you a drink?' he asked. 'Only whisky and it's out of mugs. But the whisky helps the water and the water helps the whisky.'

Somebody hooked a box forward with his foot and the Field Marshal sat down.

'You comfortable?' he asked.

The boy grinned. He looked tired but in good spirits. 'Hardly comfortable, sir,' he said. 'But it'll do.'

'Anything you need? I'm here to find out.'

The boy grinned again. 'Only the end of the war, sir.' He paused. 'We could do with more Mills bombs, sir. There's an awful lot of cock – that is, rubbish, sir – talked about going in with the bayonet. Bombs are much more useful.'

'Make a note of that, Horton. Anything else?'

'Rubber boots, sir. It's going to get pretty sticky when the summer ends. That's about all.'

'You sure?' It seemed a modest enough request.

The boy stared at him, and for a moment there was an aching pause as though he felt he had something to say and daren't. The Field Marshal tried to persuade him to speak further but he wouldn't, and they left as soon as they decently could.

As they moved into the communication trench, a flurry of shells dropped nearby. Cleaver grabbed the old man and dragged him under the shelter of the parapet as a shower of pulverised earth and stones came down on them.

'We'd better hurry, sir,' he said. 'We don't want anything to happen to you.'

'Dammit,' the Field Marshal pointed out, 'it would do no harm, at my age. We all owe God a death, my boy, and mine's been put off on more than one occasion.'

By the time they left the communication trench on the return journey, the Field Marshal was growing weary. As Lloyd George had said, he was no longer young and this sort of behaviour was exhausting, even for a fit old man. Besides, he was growing chilly and felt he had a cold coming on, but he insisted on seeing the 19th Lancers.

The Crossley moved under a darkening sky past long-snouted guns painted in drab browns and greens. There were military police everywhere and then, on the right, in a long sloping grass field that ran down to a crescent-shaped valley that lay like a shadow, the Field Marshal saw thousands of cavalry horses picketed, and clusters of lances, their bright blades catching the daylight above the pennants.

The 19th were nearest the road and headquarters were in a ruined cottage in a corner of the field. Dabney was there, working over a map, and he jumped to his feet as he saw his father.

'Father! Sir! Good God, what are you doing here?'

'Tour of inspection, boy. They tried to fob me off with the second line and reserve billets. I wasn't having that. How are the men?'

Dabney grinned and pushed a box forward. 'They're splendid. They never complain.'

The old man was silent for a moment, then he lifted his head. 'What do you think of the coming battle, Dab?'

Dabney's smile died. He paused then he drew a deep breath. 'I think the whole damn thing is wrong, Father,' he said. 'It's so flagrant, the Germans must be just waiting for us.'

'Military commanders in time of war,' the old man said slowly, trying hard to be tolerant, 'succeed in tasks that would make the running of a large commercial enterprise

238

seem like child's play. What's more, their decisions are often made under conditions of enormous stress, with noise, fatigue and grinding responsibility added to the ever-present threat of death.'

'It's not that, sir.' Dabney looked tired and irritable. 'There aren't enough men.'

'With five hundred thousand?'

'Numbers count only up to a point. We've begun to think in terms of numbers instead of skill. They're not trained. They haven't time to train. Their duties rotate between holding the line, labouring and rehearsing for the offensive. They don't know the meaning of rest because they're always being called on for patrols. This spirit of unlimited offensive's smiting the infantry like the Black Death. It not only keeps the Germans on the alert, it also takes a heavy toll of our own men.'

'Go on.'

'There's a vast army of conscripts in England doing nothing. They could carry railway lines. They could lay telephone wire and fill sandbags.' Dabney paused. 'Sir – Father – there's something wildly unreal about the whole thing. The Kitchener battalions are splendid men, better than I've ever seen. But they're not soldiers yet, sir, and a lot of them are going to die.'

The Field Marshal was quiet as he rode back in the Crossley. His body ached from the unaccustomed exercise and he was well aware that, despite his rank, he no longer counted for much.

A battalion of Kitchener men was waiting to allow an ammunition train to pass. They were watching with interest and barely noticed as the Crossley stopped alongside them. Then, over the silence, the Field Marshal heard someone ask:

''Oo's that with the red 'at band?'

There was some discussion because clearly nobody recognised him. Somebody suggested he was the Commander-in-Chief but, since nobody had ever seen the Commander-in-Chief, the idea was turned down. Then one man brighter than the rest recognised him.

'I've seen his picture in the papers. It's Field Marshal Goff.'

''Oo's Field Marshal Goff?'

'Sir Colby Goff. He rode with the Light Brigade at Balaclava.'

There was a long silence then a shout of laughter, and the first voice came again.

'Bala-bloody-clava? Christ, no wonder we're losing the war!'

The Field Marshal pushed himself further down in his seat. He felt old and tired and unwanted. It seemed to be time to go home.

two

The Field Marshal was in London when the Battle of the Somme started. He had arrived home, shivering and exhausted, and been promptly packed off to bed by his wife.

'You old fool,' she chided him gently. 'You ought to know you're too old to go gallivanting round the trenches.' She kissed his forehead as he looked up at her, his thin peaked nose over the sheets, his white hair in wisps round his head. 'All the same,' she added, 'I'm proud of you.'

His recovery took longer than he expected but he was on his feet and back to normal by the end of June, thankful that he hadn't dropped dead in France and given the army the trouble of carting him home. Besides, he found he was surprisingly involved in what was going on and was constantly in demand on committees in London, giving decisions on all sorts of things from new equipment, remounts, Dominion troops, trench raids, courts martial for desertion or cowardice, even aircraft.

When the Somme barrage started, there were people who swore it was possible to hear it across the Channel. The Field Marshal doubted it but, knowing its size, he thought he might well be wrong. The first intimation of the attack came within hours with press posters on the streets. GREAT BRITISH OFFENSIVE BEGINS, they said and snippets of news made great play with the names of villages that had been captured. GREAT BRITISH VICTORY appeared the next day. NEW ARMY ADVANCES MILES INTO

GERMAN LINE. On July 7th, the British were reported to be starting a new offensive and it seemed to the Field Marshal that, despite misgivings, the men in France had been right and they had smashed the door wide open.

But then he noticed that many of the names seemed to be familiar and, obtaining a Michelin map of the Somme, he studied it in his hotel room so that the great British offensive was brought into perspective. As far as he could make out, what had happened had been mere nibbles at the German line at the south end of the front, with no gains whatsoever in the north.

He telephoned his puzzled wife that he had business at the House of Commons and was likely to be delayed in London, and told the hotel porter to call him a cab. His work had taken him often to Westminster so that he was well known there and he was greeted in the corridors by the Attorney-General. He looked grave.

'Winston's on his high horse about the offensive,' he admitted. 'He doesn't see it quite in the way the newspapers do. Not that he can do much at the moment. He's not a member of the government, just an unemployed lieutenant-colonel. But he promises me a memorandum for the Cabinet. Lloyd George isn't going to be pleased.'

Lloyd George saw the Field Marshal in his office, sending out his secretary and shutting the door firmly.

'Well?' he said.

'I think you were right to suspect,' the old man said.

'You must be the only senior soldier who does,' the Welshman growled. 'Have you seen the convoys of wounded? They started on the 4th, and they've continued without stop ever since. They're immense. You can ignore the ones you see about the streets. Everybody's buying them beer and cigarettes, but they're the men with the neat bandages on their heads and arms. They aren't the ones maimed by explosions or gashed by shell splinters. Those people in

France must be curbed. If I were Prime Minister I'd make sure they *were* curbed.'

'Will you be Prime Minister?'

'Before long.' There was no doubt in the politician's voice. 'Then we shall have to see. We can't have them wasting the manpower of the country in this profligate fashion.'

Worried by the Welshman's disclosures, the Field Marshal headed for the War Office. It was a warm day and he decided to walk. His old enemy, *John Bull*, was still pushing out its scurrilous and totally ill-founded stories, he noticed, and the newspapers were suggesting that the Germans had been so hard hit they were even opening their gaols to recruit the criminals for the army.

To the Field Marshal, experienced in war, it seemed the newspapers were completely misjudging the situation. They were living through a time of historical intensity as great as the Franco-Prussian War or the American Civil War but they knew nothing of the foulness of trench life and tried to create the impression that the battle was little more than a rather rough sporting event in which a few people occasionally got hurt. Most people in London were still more concerned with the possibility of being hit by a bomb dropped by a zeppelin and by the fact that the Defence of the Realm Act restricted their drinking.

Feeling he needed to know more, he went to see Ellesmere at the War Office, but Ellesmere had vanished and he sought an interview instead with Robertson, the Chief of the Imperial General Staff.

Not unnaturally, Robertson was busy and he kept the old man waiting. When they met he was wary.

'Ellesmere felt he had to go to France,' he pointed out. 'He was given a Division.'

'Then *you'd* better tell me, Wullie,' the old man said. 'How are things going on the Somme?'

'Things are moving forward.'

'As they should?'

Robertson regarded him warily. 'There have been setbacks, of course,' he replied guardedly. 'There always are, as you know as well as anybody, sir.'

The old man regarded the CIGS carefully. They had met in the Chitral campaign and he had a liking for the blunt Scot who constantly dropped his aitches but had worked his way up from the ranks to his present position by sheer intelligence and hard work.

'Don't humbug me, Wullie,' he said. 'What are they up to in France? Intelligence seems to be pushing out stories of a great victory but I was there not long ago and I know where they were aiming. They don't seem to have got there.'

Robertson looked worried and gnawed his moustache. 'No, sir,' he said. 'They 'aven't. I might as well be frank with you, though, of course, it 'as to be kept to ourselves. It seems to have been a proper shambles.'

'What happened?'

'No gain at all in the north. Fricourt was a failure. The Irish smashed through four sets of trenches near Thiepval but they were isolated and had to come back. The Newfoundlanders were wiped out at Hamel and the South Wales Borderers at Beaumont. The Durhams were smashed at Ovillers, the Green Howards at Fricourt, and the Yorks and Lancs at Serre. All those fine fellers. Whole battalions, thousands of fine men, swept away.'

'What about the casualties?'

'First reports showed 'em to be small. Fifteen thousand. That sort of figure. Now they think they'll be more in the region of sixty thousand.'

'Sixty thousand? That means twenty thousand dead!'

'In one day,' Robertson growled. 'The first day. In the first hour or two, if we 'ave to be honest.'

There was a long silence then the Field Marshal rose. 'Thank you, Wullie,' he said. 'Thank you for being honest. I probably shan't be seeing you again. I think in future I'll stay by my own fireside.'

As he left the War Office, the old man's feet were dragging a little. He obtained a taxi with difficulty and directed it to his hotel. By the time he reached his room, his mind seemed numb and he felt as if his cold was coming back again.

Not wishing to alarm his wife, he wrote her a note to say he'd been detained again. Sixty thousand casualties! The figure hammered at his brain like a gong. Sixty *thousand!* It didn't seem possible! All those splendid young men! All those high hopes!

Going to bed, he pulled the blanket over his head and lay still, wondering if his son could possibly still be alive.

The 19th Lancers had not even been in action. The expected cavalry breakthrough had never materialised and the horsemen had been used for nothing else but to clear the dead.

The corpses filled every ditch and covered every verge, some of them kneeling, their hands groping out as if still reaching for their weapons, some with arms lifted as if playing the violin, some with one leg raised as though shot in the act of running forward. Still others, caught by blast, were mere shapeless sacks moulded only by the clothes that contained them.

In a back area facing Trônes Wood, Dabney brooded on the tragedy. Just behind where he waited with his men, the horses in a restless line, was the grey-and-red ruin of a village, nothing but charred ribs and broken walls blasted by counter fire. The street was empty apart from one or two animals and their riders who had been edged into it by the crush. Shutters hung limply, and doors and windows gaped in despair over the brick-strewn sidewalk. Letters and photographs were scattered everywhere, trampled by muddy boots, and mattresses lay in the roadway, bloodstained from the bodies that had rested on them after the attack a fortnight before. In one or two houses out of reach of shell splinters, ruined beds had been shoved aside and graves had been dug and crosses erected, the caps of the dead askew on them, and here and there were carcasses of horses, lying in clotted heaps.

By this time, the forward area of the Somme was like a moonscape, pitted with shell craters and the wreckage of the battle. Some of the dead horses had obviously kicked their team-mates to ribbons in their attempts to get free. Others, dusty and forlorn-looking, lay with their legs starkly in the air among the smashed wagons and limbers and the incredibly broken guns which showed where the German artillery had done its deadly work.

July 1st had been the disaster Dabney had prophesied. And, sickened by the bodies that lay in every grotesque attitude, their uniforms filthy with mud or stiff with blood, their horses nervous at the smell of death and the unceasing chatter of musketry, they had cleared the field with what compassion they could muster, their minds numbed by the horrors, Dabney at least convinced that their role in war was ended.

But, now, after a fortnight of bloody fighting in which futile attacks had been launched one after another to try to gain some narrow strip of blood-soaked ground so that the public at home could be given the victory they'd been promised, something new had been tried, and plans had been made for a night attack without a preliminary barrage to warn the enemy. Twenty-two thousand men had been assembled after dark in No Man's Land without the enemy suspecting and they had got through the wire without a shot being fired. Five miles of the German second line had been taken and the cavalry had finally been ordered to stand by. After the humiliation of the first days, there was a feeling that this time something might really happen because, on the left of the attack, open country – that open country the army had been seeking ever since the autumn of 1914 – lay tantalisingly before them at last.

A staff officer appeared and spoke to Johnson, warning him he was due to move off at once. 'German resistance's beginning to disintegrate,' he said. 'Rawlinson wants the cavalry to push forward.'

There was an excited stirring. In front of him Dabney could see the high ground lifting away to the sky, and he glanced back at the restless lines of horses and the men standing in groups, dragging at cigarettes, their faces bleak with anticipation. But there seemed to be some confusion over the orders and Johnson was growing more impatient by the minute.

'Cavalry action should be left to the men on the spot,' he fumed.

Storming off to see the brigadier in command, he returned livid with rage. 'The bloody fool's gone off to some infantry headquarters to find out what's going on, and he's sent his liaison officers all over the blasted countryside to see what's happening, so that now nobody knows anything.'

He had barely spoken when a message came for the move forward to begin. But the Secunderabad Brigade of Indian cavalry was still without its commanding officer and the two British regiments, the 7th Dragoon Guards and the 19th Lancers, had been told not to move without him.

'For God's sake!' Johnson fumed. 'We've already been waiting for hours! Those bloody Wogs were never any damn good at anything except polo, tent-pegging and pigsticking!'

In the end, they began to move forward without the Indians, clattering out of the village and on to a plank bridge over a trench filled with the detritus of battle. They were held up again on the edge of a shattered wood where the Germans had been dropping shells since the battle had started fourteen days before. By this time it was a mass of shell holes, with every tree broken off at the top or bottom to add to the impenetrable tangle that sliced the sun into broken dusty beams.

Nearby, the mainstream of the battle traffic passed, artillerymen sitting stiffly on tired mounts in front of long steel guns, weary infantrymen trudging along in little groups, out of step, heads heavy under helmets. Mounted officers dozed on jaded horses, nodding forward over the saddle horn, their sleeping men drooping over gun limbers, fast asleep even while hanging on. The chink of equipment and the tap of a bayonet against a petrol tin half-full of water seemed the only sound about them over the shuffle of boots.

There were a few jeers at the cavalry that served only to make Johnson more livid, but eventually, the Indians appeared, their dark faces shadowed under their helmets, and as the order came to move forward, the columns cantered ahead. But as the tarmacadamed road was left behind, they found themselves struggling in the shell-pitted, churned-up land near the original front line. Horses slithered and stumbled in the increasingly deep mud and one or two went down, horse and man rising covered with grey sludge.

As they stopped once more, the guns seemed to have grown quieter and they could hear only sporadic firing on the flanks. But no orders came and nobody seemed to have thought of food for them, so that the horses began to stamp and whinny with impatience.

The brigadier had detached several squadrons to gallop round the wood to prevent German reinforcements approaching, while other squadrons were ordered to dismount and push forward on foot from the north. The reserve squadrons were ordered forward again and as afternoon gave way to a pale sun-washed evening they found themselves on the slopes leading towards High Wood, two squadrons of the 19th, two of the 7th Dragoon Guards and two of the Deccan Horse, with Johnson in command as senior colonel.

As they thudded along the valley, ahead of them lay barley fields and the rich beauty of undamaged countryside. A field of corn sloped upwards on their right, and at the other end they could see spiked-helmeted German officers moving about. For a moment, as the six squadrons edged forward, clattering and clinking, the horses whinnying excitedly, there still seemed a little glory left in the war.

Then a machine gun opened up on them and several horses went down. At the edge of the wood, a few shells dropped close, to empty a few more saddles. Galloping along the line of men as they became unsteady under the shelling, Dabney's voice and example restored a drift to the rear. His eyes were everywhere, looking for chin straps not in place and rifles not jammed home in the bucket, as he always did, and they began to think that if he had time to think about such things it couldn't be as bad as it seemed.

As they reached the corn, German outposts rose to meet them. They were trying to mount a machine gun and, immediately, realising it demanded instant action, Dabney waved his squadron forward without waiting for orders. A German officer swung to meet him as he thundered up, raising a hand with a revolver in it to point it at Dabney. The shot went past his ear then the German staggered back, clutching at his head as Dabney's sabre crashed down on his helmet and sent him rolling under the flying hooves. As the rest of the Germans turned to run, they were speared by a group of Deccan Horse which had come up alongside.

'Hold those men, Goff!' Johnson came galloping up as they drew rein, angry that Dabney had moved without orders. 'Keep them steady, damn it! We don't want them out of hand.'

Dabney gave him a cold look, knowing perfectly well his men had been well under control, but Johnson wheeled his horse and, as they regained their place in the line, he took a position just in front, followed by his orderly and his trumpeter. It seemed an unbelievable sight, with the corn and the luxuriant green of the wood as a backcloth. But there were more Germans with machine guns waiting along the edge of the wood in a position to enfilade them. Johnson seemed blind to the danger and, feeling it his duty to point them out, Dabney edged his horse forward.

Johnson waved him away. 'We've been ordered to take the wood,' he said. 'It's our duty to take it, machine guns or no machine guns. Dammit, so far we've hardly been touched by the battle! This is a splendid moment and we mustn't fail.'

He seemed elated by the thought of action and quite unable to appreciate the danger in his eagerness. As the trumpets sounded, Dabney glanced at his men. Ellis Ackroyd's face was set and grim, but, as they began to move forward at a trot, the surge and excitement of the action gripped him, too.

As they swung into the corn, moving from column into line, the machine guns started to chatter. Immediately, the magnificent vision of a mounted action crumbled into slaughter as horse after horse went down, flung to the ground like rabbits at a farm shoot. Johnson was waving his sword, urging them forward, and his trumpeter had his head back, his trumpet in the air, sounding the Charge. But the machine guns swept across and the call ended in a despairing bray as the trumpeter's horse went down. Johnson was just turning as the bullets caught him. His head was back and his mouth open, and Dabney saw his chest and throat flower red. The raised sword fell from his hand and, after a few more strides by his mount, he drooped in the saddle and slid to the ground.

More and more horses were going down, squealing and neighing in pain. Riderless chargers were facing in every direction and as Dabney's own mount went down, he lay for a moment in the corn, dazed. Recovering his senses and rising to his feet, he began to shout, his sword in the air, trying to rally his men, but Johnson had led them into a perfect ambush, and it was impossible to make himself heard above the din. A horse crashed to the ground alongside him, frothing blood, its eyes glazing even as it stopped rolling. Its rider scrambled to his feet and stood alongside Dabney, responding instinctively to discipline. Almost immediately, however, he was hit in the face and staggered back, tripping over the neck of his own dead horse to sit down beyond it and flop over, flat on his back, his spurred boots in the air.

There seemed to be no one else near Dabney and he began to run bent double to where he could see a grey horse standing trembling in the waist-high corn, its Indian rider dead alongside it. Stumbling over the body, he reached the horse and swung himself into the saddle, only to realise that the grey had been hit, too. As it moved away, its breath came in spasmodic wheezes, and its legs were already unsteady.

The following squadrons had caught up with the first line now, and were thrown into confusion by the struggling horses and men and, as the grey finally crashed to the ground, Dabney found himself sprawling again. Struggling to his feet just as a group of Indian soldiers galloped towards him, he had to dive for safety behind the body of the horse and one of the Indians actually hurdled them in a perfect jump to pelt him with flying clods of muddy earth.

The advance had lasted a mere two or three minutes and now the flailing maelstrom of men and horses was shredding itself out into a general movement to the rear. Forced along with it, Dabney found himself alongside Ellis Ackroyd whose face was covered with blood and grey with pain.

'Get up behind, sir,' he yelled.

As Dabney swung himself up, horses were still falling, the unseated riders rolling and dodging until knocked senseless by flying hooves. One of the Indians crossing Ackroyd's front was hit by a machine gun burst and bounced from the saddle in front of them, all scattered brains and smashed teeth. Another horse barged against them, its rider dragged along screaming, one foot still in the stirrup, then Dabney became aware that Ackroyd's mount was faltering, too, and, even as he wondered what to do, it went down on its knees and he and Ackroyd were flung over its head into the trampled corn.

For a while Dabney lay still, dazed, as the field emptied of living men. All round him, wounded horses were screaming and there were moans from the dying and cries of anger and disgust from the running survivors. Dragging himself to his feet, he moved to where Ellis Ackroyd lay. His eyes were open but he seemed unable to speak, and, quite unaware of the machine guns that were still chattering by the wood, Dabney managed to drag him over his shoulder in a fireman's lift and began to stumble back down the slope. Johnson's charge had been an utter failure.

The shattered squadrons were regrouping behind the trees further along the valley, wounded men stumbling in, clinging to the stirrup of any man who still had a horse. The slope above them was scattered with dead and dying, half hidden by the corn which was now trampled to a bloody mash. A wounded horse was lying on the ground, its hooves skittering against a patch of stony ground until its rider drew his rifle from the bucket on the saddle and put a bullet through its head.

As Dabney lowered Ackroyd to the ground, a trooper of the 19th, his face bloody but still mounted, approached, leading a limping horse.

' 'Ere y'are, sir,' he said. 'Better 'ave this one. It don't seem to belong to nobody.' He looked at the shattered squadrons and the panting, dazed men, then back at Dabney. 'For God's sake, sir,' he said, 'what the 'ell did we want to go and do a soft-brained thing like that for?'

three

The newspapers were still hailing victory on the Somme in a lunatic fashion, full of reports that made the British soldier sound like a sportsman, and killing Germans a cheerful sort of affair a little like ratting.

Taking a taxi to King's Cross, the Field Marshal climbed into his compartment feeling as old as God. York station was full of soldiers and, having a long time to wait for the train to Braxby, he went into the station hotel, where he almost bumped into Hedley Ackroyd.

'Better join me,' he growled. 'You on leave?'

'A short one, sir. My grandfather's ill. We've been given new single-seater machines and brought back from France to see if we can do anything about the zeppelins.'

'What's that on your chest?'

'Croix de guerre, sir. We shot down a German machine which was worrying a Caudron carrying a French general. He was so relieved at his escape, he put me up for it.'

The old man was recovering his spirits slowly. For a man who had spent half his life in odd corners of the world fighting for the Empire, he felt a curious ageing sensation of being safe only in his own small corner of Yorkshire that he had never felt before. It was good to be surrounded by familiar sights and reassuring to see familiar faces like Hedley's.

'You been seeing my granddaughter?' he asked.

The boy stiffened and looked the old man straight in the face. 'Yes, sir, I have,' he said. 'I hope you have no objection.'

'Good God, boy, whatever made you think I might have?'

'Well, sir, my father being only your sergeant – '

'*And* my friend. As also was your grandfather. I've known your family a long time, my boy. It doesn't surprise me. What about her parents?'

'I don't think they mind, sir.'

'Shows their good sense. Perhaps I ought to congratulate you. Philippa, too. She's getting a good bargain. Are you getting engaged?'

'We'd like to, sir. But the war's a problem.'

'War's always a problem. But you might just as easily get knocked down by a brewery dray in Ripon.' The old man sighed. 'With all the people who're being killed, my boy, marriage is coming into its own more and more as an institution. I shouldn't let that put you off.'

As the cab rolled up to Braxby Manor, Lady Goff appeared on the doorstep to greet her husband with bright eyes. 'Isn't the news splendid, Coll?' she said.

'What news?'

'The battle. Do you think the end of the war's in sight at last?'

'No!' His retort was sharp and harsh and she looked hurt and puzzled enough for him to try to soften it.

'What you've been reading in the newspapers, Gussie,' he growled, 'is nothing but a lot of bloody mumbo-jumbo.'

He hadn't the courage to tell her the truth, only that it had been an infantry battle and that Dabney must be safe. During the evening, Robert arrived, pink and smiling.

'What do you think of the battle, Father?' he said. 'It's obviously a victory.'

'It's nothing of the kind,' the Field Marshal snapped.

He tried to explain without giving away the facts and Robert frowned. 'Well, anyway,' he said. 'We shall pull it off before long. They've asked for the tanks to be sent out.'

'How many?'

'Well, there aren't many ready yet. We shall send all we've got. Fifty or so.'

'And they're going to give away a secret like that for a piffling little local victory? They must be mad. And so must you.'

With Robert despatched with a flea in his ear, the old man huddled in his chair, watched by his worried wife. The following morning brought a letter from Dabney. It was enough to break his heart. Up to now, despite the losses, the battle had been impersonal, though made less so when he noticed among the casualties the names of Captain Cleaver, and Captain Archer of the 3rd/7th South Yorkshires. They had both treated him kindly, pleasant young men tired of the war, both of them anxious to tell him things he ought to know but trying to be loyal enough not to. Now Dabney's letter informed him that with the cavalry finally in action, two-thirds of the 19th Lancers had been wiped out.

The old man frowned. He had seen the picture too often not to know what it meant. In his mind's eye he saw the surge forward crumbling into butchery and the survivors stumbling back across the field among the dead. It had happened to him over sixty years before in a long valley in the Crimea.

He turned to the end of the letter. 'Johnson's dead,' Dabney wrote. 'Tim Leduc's wounded. Quibell was killed with the machine gunners. Ellis Ackroyd is gravely hurt.'

The old man's eyes filled and he remembered what old von Hartmann had once said to him of war. 'It's always the tallest poppies that are taken.'

He rose and, pouring himself a brandy, swallowed it hurriedly. Poor Ellis! Suddenly he felt desperately old and lonely and, almost without thinking, he poured another brandy and swallowed that, too. Immediately, he felt his heart begin to thump and decided he'd better swear off the damned stuff. These days it made his heart race.

'Thank God not Dabney,' he murmured.

He informed his wife and together they went down to the Home Farm in the Vauxhall to inform Ellis Ackroyd's wife. Hedley met them, his face grim.

'We've just heard,' he said.

'I can't say how sorry I am,' the old man said.

They returned to a quiet lonely house, and it was late in the evening when the doorbell rang. It was Hedley. He paused. 'I've come about my grandfather, sir,' he said. 'I thought you ought to be the first to know. He died this evening. About a couple of hours ago, to be exact. I came straight up.'

The Field Marshal turned away, blinking rapidly. Tyas Ackroyd, of all people! The old fool, going and dying like that! He drew a deep breath, aware for the first time how fond he'd been of him.

'I'm sorry, Hedley,' he said slowly, trying to control his voice and stop the tears coming. 'I had good reason to be fond of your grandfather. How's everybody taking it on top of your father?'

'Not too badly, sir. We'd been expecting it ever since he had to retire, of course. It was just as though he were tired and wanted to go to sleep.'

Lady Goff watched her husband come down the stairs. He was in full fig, in the complete panoply of the 19th Lancers. His uniform was a little tight across his stomach and his overalls were looser round the thighs than they were once, but, despite his age, he still looked an impressive figure.

'Bloody uniform,' he growled as he reached the hall.

'Dear Coll.' His wife kissed him. 'You look magnificent.'

'I'd have preferred,' he grumbled, 'to look magnificent for something other than Tyas Ackroyd's funeral.'

She handed him his sword which he clipped in place, then he put on his schapka and let the peak rest on his nose. The green and red dyed blackcock's feathers hung over his cheek with the cord that attached the helmet to his shoulder. Studying him, she was aware how little time they had together now and felt desperately close to tears.

She handed him his gauntlets which he dragged on one after the other in silence, then she held up his cloak.

'Shan't want that,' he said.

'You'll catch your death of cold.'

'No, I won't.'

'I've ordered the Vauxhall.'

'You can send it away.'

His manner was gruff but she was well aware of the hurt he felt and ignored his brusqueness.

'You'll need the car,' she said.

'No I won't.'

'You're surely not contemplating walking all the way to church?'

'Yes I am. Back, too.'

'You silly old man,' she said softly. 'You're nearly eighty, it's much too far.'

'No, it isn't! Dammit, it's only just down the lane. I'd do it for Tyas if I were a hundred and eighty. Robert turned up yet?'

His wife drew a deep breath, dreading having to tell him something she'd known for forty-eight hours.

'He can't manage it.'

The Field Marshal's head jerked round. 'What in God's name does he mean? – he can't manage it.'

'He has to go to London.'

'That bloody woman, I expect!'

Lady Goff sighed. 'Perhaps that was his intention originally, dear, but Elfrida's insisted on going with him this time. I think she's wise. She's sent her apologies.'

'He should have been present. Tyas wasn't just a servant in this house.'

'No, dear. But you can't dragoon people into it and Robert's never felt the same about the Regiment as you have.'

'Pity Dabney ain't home.'

'It's always a pity Dabney isn't home. Still, Josh says he wants to go.'

'He shall walk alongside me.'

'He's too young.'

'He's ten.'

'That's far too young.'

The Field Marshal sighed. 'Then he shall sit next to me in church. Represent his father. Future of the Regiment. I'm the past, like poor old Tyas. He'll go into the Regiment.'

'He might decide he doesn't want to.'

'Rubbish, woman. Bound to.'

'Robert didn't.'

'Robert's an ass. Always was.'

Lady Goff sighed. The Field Marshal was in his most intractable mood. She was well aware, however, that the occasion meant a lot to him. The previous year he had gone halfway across the country to attend the funeral of some old man who had died in a workhouse in London, simply because he had ridden at Balaclava, and had come back in a foul temper, demanding to know why the bloody Government let men die in poverty after they'd served their country well.

'Where does the cortège start?' she asked.

'Tyas' cottage.'

'Surely there's no reason for you to walk there? It's a good quarter of a mile. You could be driven there and then walk. It would reduce the distance a little.'

He considered for a moment. 'Very well,' he said. 'I'll do that.'

Sitting in the Vauxhall with his grandmother, Josh watched as his grandfather waited. His mother was working for the Red Cross in York and, claiming that the dead were less important than the maimed and dying, she was coming alone in her own car. Without her, Josh felt lonely. He had no idea she was thinking of her husband, whom she might also be mourning in a matter of days, and that she found it hard to be present at all. He had been crowing over a new cricket bat with which he expected to score an incredible number of runs when he had heard of Tyas Ackroyd's death. Not only had he lost a friend but he felt also that somehow a part of the past had vanished. He was shivery and chilled and he could only put it down to the sorrow he felt.

His mother's car drew up alongside the Vauxhall and he gave her a grave nod. His grandfather was a small slight figure rigid as a ramrod but swaying a little in the blustery wind.

'I'm sorry Tyas is dead, Grannie,' he said.

'Yes, dear,' his grandmother said. 'I think your grandfather is too.'

It had been Tyas Ackroyd he remembered, who had first taught him to ride.

'If you learn to ride like a Clutcher,' he had said, 'you'll have learned proper.'

The boy thought for a minute, trying once more to imagine his grandfather and Tyas Ackroyd riding down the valley at Balaclava. He'd seen pictures of the charge but somehow all he could ever imagine was the Braxby Hunt going into Rush's Meadow after a fox.

They were using a haywain from the Home Farm to carry the coffin. It had been washed and cleaned up and the two great Percherons which were to pull it, groomed to within an inch of their lives, waited now, pawing the ground, the black crêpe on their harness fluttering in the breeze.

The Field Marshal was shaking a little with the effort of keeping still. His hand lifted to the salute as the coffin appeared.

Josh stared about him, trying to stop his eyes prickling. As they waited, another small boy on a bicycle appeared. He was dressed in his best suit, with a black tie and his hair plastered down into spikes. It was Robert's son, Aubrey, Josh's cousin.

'Thought I ought to come,' he whispered as he climbed into the car on the other side of Lady Goff. 'I borrowed some of Father's brilliantine.'

Josh felt like weeping. When rotten old Aubrey could manage to turn up, it clearly meant something. He blew his nose hard. Perhaps Aubrey wasn't so bad, after all, he decided. He'd have to remember to include him more.

As the little cortège moved off behind the haywain that carried all that remained of Tyas Ackroyd, it was followed by black-coated relatives, among them a sprinkling of uniforms. The Vauxhall took its place at the rear and Josh could see his grandfather, clutching his sword in frozen fingers stumping along behind, a small figure with the schapka bouncing on his nose. Without knowing why, Josh found his eyes had finally filled with tears.

At the graveyard alongside the church, with the Percherons stamping at the ground, the Ackroyd family and relations, followed by the Field Marshal's family and anyone else who could crowd inside, moved into the pews. The two boys sat down alongside their grandmother. On her other side was Josh's mother and the Field Marshal, and just in front Hedley Ackroyd.

'We are gathered here today to say farewell to Tyas Emmott Arthur Ackroyd –' Josh was startled to realise that the old man he'd known only as Tyas had had other names as well ' – who was one of that dwindling band who rode with the fearless Lord Cardigan down that Russian valley in the Crimea nearly sixty years ago with the Light Brigade...'

Glancing at his grandfather, Josh saw his face was like stone. Turning, he looked at his grandmother, and was surprised to see there were tears on her cheeks and, in a strange moment of adult awareness, he knew they were not just for Tyas Ackroyd.

As they filed out of church again and took their places behind the coffin, Josh sidled forward until he was alongside his grandfather, trying to stand as rigidly to attention as the old man as they lowered the coffin into the hole in the earth.

'Man that is born of woman hath but a short time to live, and is full of misery – '

Josh's thoughts wandered. He had never thought of Tyas Ackroyd in that way. Until recently, Tyas had been a mischievous old man with a fund of funny stories, a fondness for helping himself to Grandpa's whisky – something which Grandpa was well aware of but said nothing about – a tendency to demonstrate sword drill with the fire irons when he should have been cleaning them, and a liking for his pretty nieces. According to Grandpa, he had been quite a boy in his youth and had certainly never seemed to be full of misery.

After it was over, Aubrey reached for his bicycle and lifted his hat to his grandmother.

'Wouldn't you like to come home for tea, dear?' she asked.

'No, I've got to get back.'

As he rode off, Josh stared after him. 'Old Auby's not bad, you know, Grannie. Better than I thought.'

'Most people are, dear.'

They talked for a few moments with the relatives, then they solemnly put on their hats and moved away as the Field Marshal headed for the Vauxhall. His wife hung back, knowing he wished to be alone.

'I'll go back with Fleur, dear,' she said. 'Josh can go with you.'

The Field Marshal nodded and they climbed into the car together. As Fleur's car moved off, the Field Marshal lifted his hand and touched his driver's shoulder.

'Just a moment, George,' he said. 'Not yet.'

They sat silently. It had begun to spot with rain and the splashes were striking the windows and sliding down the glass. The boy was surprised to realise that his grandfather was singing, half to himself in a low shaking voice. He recognised the song at once.

> 'Wrap me up in my old stable jacket
> And say a poor devil lies low.
> And six of the Lancers shall carry me
> To the place where the best soldiers go.'

The old man stopped and, without turning his head, spoke to the boy.

'When they buried my father,' he said slowly, 'that song went round and round in my mind. They played the Dead March in *Saul*, but he wasn't a fussy man and I think if he'd been asked, he'd have preferred that above all others.'

There was a long silence. 'They had a good trumpeter that day,' the old man went on in his faraway voice. 'The trumpet had its origin in heaven, boy. Did you know that? I've heard many beautiful things in my time – the slow march of the Gordons, for instance, and that heart-tearing *Lament for Culloden*. But nothing beats a good trumpeter. There was always only one thought in the darkness when I heard the Last Post at night: Military funerals, boy. Muffled drums and lonely graves in empty fields all over the world. Cavalrymen who'd gone ahead.' The old man paused. 'They're notes of loneliness, boy, and the exile of men far from home, but they're also notes of pride, for men who died defending their country.'

As he stopped speaking there was a long silence except for the blustering of the wind that shook the high-tonneaued car and the soft spatter of rain on the windows.

When the old man spoke again, his voice was thin and old.

'Josh –' he stopped, cleared his throat, then went on in a stronger voice '– should I predecease you, which I have no doubt I shall, you will remember that as a field marshal I am entitled to a little more pomp and ceremony than poor Tyas. I don't want it – bloody tiresome business for all concerned – but they'll probably insist on a band and medals and all that rot. You will therefore – assuming you're old enough and that the war is over – arrange that the band will be that of the 19th Lancers and that they will play me to my grave with the Dead March in *Saul*. That's because funerals are supposed to be sad and the Dead March in *Saul*'s the saddest thing we know. However, I don't expect *you* to be sad, my boy, because by then I shall have had a good run for me money and I've enjoyed most of it, apart from the bits where the grocers in the army took over and those people in the cads' cricket team were in the ascendant.'

'Grandpa –' the boy looked anxiously at the old man '– you're not going to die soon, are you?'

'I don't intend to hurry it along, boy,' the old man said briskly. 'It's nevertheless the one event that none of us can escape. I'm not worried. I've done most things and it'll be a new experience. There's one thing, however, I want you to do for me. I've never been of a musical turn of mind but I've always thought that *Morning* from *Peer Gynt* would be a suitable tune to go to Heaven with. A touch of sadness but also a touch of hope. I've been told more than once by the Rector that I might not get into Heaven because I haven't been much of a believer, but personally I think God's far too intelligent to blame me if I'm wrong and He might even welcome a pleasant tune as I arrive at the pearly gates. Will you arrange it for me?'

'Of course Grandpa. *Morning* from *Peer Gynt*.'

Josh was still wondering who *Peer Gynt* was when he noticed the old man had become silent again. His thoughts were clearly sombre. And Josh saw his mouth working, as if he were chewing, and caught glimpses of old brown teeth.

'It does occur to me, of course,' the Field Marshal went on slowly, 'that the band may well be engaged elsewhere. They may still be in France or serving in India, in which case it might be difficult to get them home. In that event I will settle happily for just two trumpeters, one at the head and one at the foot of the grave, to play the Last Post and the Reveille. The Last Post for my departure and the Reveille for my entry into Heaven.'

There was another long pause. 'It has also just occurred to me,' the old man continued, 'that perhaps neither the band *nor* the trumpeters will be available. In which case, anybody will do who can play an instrument. Even the first violinist from the theatre in York.' There was another long pause. 'There is *still* one final snag. Perhaps the Rector would refuse permission for such a tune to be played on such a solemn occasion. It might not meet with the mealy-mouthed attitudes of the Church. In that case, you will just have to sing something for me. Under your breath, if necessary. Think you can do that?'

'Yes, Grandpa. I'll remember.'

'Then, that would do nicely, coming from you.' The old man leaned forward and tapped the driver on the shoulder. 'I think, George,' he said, 'that we can go home now.'

f o u r

The year ended in gloom and the Somme died, mourned by no one.

It had been a victory of a sort, but it had been an empty victory because the British casualties had been higher than those of the Germans. They had gained nothing but a few miles of shell-torn ground which were of use to no one, and finally the mud, stirred up by the rain and the bombardments, had become so impassable the attack had stopped for the simple reason that it was no longer possible to move.

It was now being said the battle had been fought to relieve Verdun, but that had come to an end before the Somme had even started; and all they had to show for it were a few miles of broken trenches, ruined fields and obliterated villages with their scattered graves marked by rusting helmets, wooden crosses or bayoneted rifles, while the glowing idealism of the New Army had found its end in the hills and valleys of Picardy.

Churchill was not hoodwinked with the talk of victory, and even came to Yorkshire, full of indignation and splendid rhetoric, ostensibly to ask the Field Marshal's views but in reality to expound his own in the hope of receiving support.

'This open ground to which we struggled with such appalling loss of life,' he said, 'was entirely without strategic significance. The capture of Verdun would obviously have been of value to the Germans. But what were *we* after? There

266

was nothing beyond the German line of any military value whatsoever.'

Even Lloyd George had been to see the old man, trying to tempt him to London in an effort to topple the military hierarchy he so disliked. But the Field Marshal refused. He was too old now and he knew it. Nobody of his generation seemed to be still active. Even Kitchener was dead now, drowned when the ship taking him to Russia had been mined off the coast of Scotland.

The war seemed to be turning Europe into a form of hell. Most people were apathetic, not only towards the enemy but also towards their own political and military leaders who seemed to have no idea what to do next. The old belief that they would smash their way through had given way to the feeling that eventually there would have to be a negotiated peace, but nobody could accept anything that would leave the Germans still occupying Northern France and Belgium, something that would be tantamount to a defeat. Yet the Germans would never give them up because *that* would be tantamount to a defeat for them.

The New Year was surprisingly quiet. England was a country these days of women, because all the men were in France and everyone had become silent in a sort of sullen resignation. One no longer offered condolences about death because every family in the country seemed to have been affected by it. Everything was short, and in some of the villages round Braxby it seemed that the Somme had wiped out the whole of the male population under forty.

A few people seemed to be doing well, however. Lloyd George had become Prime Minister at last but he was curiously without the power to do what he wished. The military leaders still seemed to be making plans and, as he read about them, the Field Marshal felt a sense of guilt that he could not feel at one with them. Business was also booming and Walter Cosgro had bought a shooting box in

Scotland from some family whose sons had all disappeared in the holocaust across the Channel and no longer had need of it. Robert's fortune had also increased and he had received a knighthood for his work.

There was an uneasy feeling in the old man's mind that they were going to lose the war. The Russians were in a state of chaos and the French, bled white by their losses, were said to be mutinous. Jutland had been a disaster, the great naval victory everybody had been expecting ever since 1914 turning out instead to be a fiasco with over-caution allowing the German fleet to escape. Finally the U-boat campaign had reached a climax that left the country desperate for every kind of necessity, and the newspapers could think of nothing but to castigate the politicians who seemed far more concerned with the success of their own parties than with the result of the war.

But, while the Somme had been a disaster for Britain, there was little doubt but that it had been a disaster for Germany also. While British casualties had been enormous, German losses were very nearly equal, something apparently borne out by the fact that the Fatherland had put out peace feelers at the end of the year.

There seemed little to hope for but the entry into the war of the United States with her legions of fresh young men. Rumours that they were intending to come in on the Allied side had been circulating for three years and German-American relations had finally been severed. But the phrase, 'America on the verge of war', that the newspapers had pumped out so regularly, seemed to have grown so old and tired nobody believed there was any truth in it any more.

It was as the Field Marshal, no longer willing to go to London or be part of the war in any way, gloomily considered the future, that a letter arrived from Helen in Berlin.

It came via Holland as usual but, with the blockade round Germany growing tighter, the letters were fewer these days and there were inexplicable delays as if the Dutch, with no wish to be embroiled, were behaving with extreme caution. The letter had been forwarded to Switzerland and finally to France. The date was December and to their surprise it was not addressed to both parents as Helen's letters usually were, but to the Field Marshal alone, and it bore his full rank and every one of his decorations, so that it had a derisory, sarcastic look about it. The old man opened it warily, conscious that it contained a shock.

Karl-August had been killed commanding a Bavarian brigade on the Somme and Helen's resentment, already showing against her own country since the previous year, had suddenly become deep-seated and passionate.

'Why did you kill him?' she wrote. 'How could you kill your own son-in-law?' With the letter addressed only to him, the accusation was thrust directly at the old man. He was a British soldier and, in his daughter's wretchedness, was therefore alone responsible for the death of her husband.

He read the letter slowly, watched by his wife. There was no sign of forgiveness in it, no sign of understanding. Helen's grief had embittered her and there was only accusation and anger.

'I no longer wish to call England my country,' she announced. 'Until now, I could never forget where I came from, despite the blows that have been delivered against my adopted country. I even tried to forgive the blockade that is forcing German people to go hungry and has caused my children to do without many of the things they need. Now all I can be aware of is that England has killed my husband and left his children fatherless. I wish to have nothing more to do with you.'

The old man read the letter in silence then, without a word, he passed it to his wife. His eyes bleak, he saw the tears come into her eyes and roll down her cheeks.

'Oh, Coll – !' She tried to speak, but was unable to and she broke off and hurried from the room, her hand to her eyes.

The old man sat in silence as the door slammed behind her, his eyes on the folded sheet of paper on the floor. His thoughts were confused and he was totally unable to put them in order. He had no idea even where to start. He had long been aware that the war had become a watershed in the lives of everyone. The Empire would never be the same again. It would end up impoverished, its classes – those societies on which it had been so securely built – destroyed. No one would ever trust anyone again. The old honest calm life would have vanished and in its place would come a new raucous existence that might satisfy the young but could never satisfy people brought up in a more gracious age.

He tried to think of his daughter and her family, but it was so long since he'd seen them he couldn't even remember properly what they looked like and he rose hurriedly and fumbled clumsily in a drawer until he found a photograph. As he stood staring at it, his heart thumping wildly, oppressed by the weight of misery, the door burst open and Josh appeared at a rush. Seeing the old man, he stopped dead.

'Grandpa, what's the matter?'

The old man thrust the photograph away and sat down hurriedly. 'Your Uncle Karl's been killed.'

The boy started to say something, then sensing that his grandfather was racked with unhappiness, he changed his mind and, instead, crossed to the old man to do the only thing he could think of. As he patted the old veined hand, for a moment the old man seemed unaware of it, then he grasped the boy's fingers and clutched them tightly.

'There must be no more war, boy,' he said fiercely. 'There *cannot* be any more war. Let us finish this one as soon as possible and then forswear it for ever.' He suddenly became aware that the boy held the daily paper. It had to come from York and arrived in Braxby on the nine o'clock train so that it never appeared at the house until mid-morning.

'What is it, boy?' He made an effort to thrust aside his wretchedness. This child was the future and must be treated as if he were. 'What have you there?'

The boy smiled, a little uncertainly before the old man's bleak look. It was so long since he'd seen his German relations, he'd almost forgotten them. Indeed, at school it had sometimes been wiser to do so, and he was glad now of the opportunity to push the matter from his mind.

He lifted the paper up, opening it wide and holding it in front of him. 'America Joins With All Her Resources,' the headline announced.

The boy's smile widened. 'The United States have come in,' he said.

It gave them something to talk about and took their minds off Helen's bitterness, and to the surprise of the household the first result of the news was the arrival of a letter from Virginia.

It was from Richmond, was addressed to the Field Marshal via the War Office, and was signed 'Micah Burtle Love, Lieutenant, 12th Cavalry.'

For a moment it jabbed at the old man's liver with the memories it raised. Over fifty years before he had been captured by a Micah Burtle Love in Maryland and helped a wounded Micah Burtle Love off the field near Parks' Bridge before taking over his command for the Wilderness and Yellow Tavern. His mind, occupied with the grey despair of No Man's Land in France, was suddenly filled with memories of a long-forgotten campaign where men fought hand-to-hand and were not butchered in thousands by enemies they never saw. There was a swirl and a romance to the name even. Micah Burtle Love. The old man's mind swung back over the years to Jeb Stuart and the frail glory of a war where men had still gone into battle carrying flags and wearing cloaks; where, dammit, his own wife, Augusta, had appeared before him carrying a sash, a plume and a locket containing one of her curls, which he'd carried with him then and ever since wherever he went.

His eyes were faraway when his wife appeared. The letter had made him realise just how old he was. His contemporaries were all dead now. Only Evelyn Wood seemed to be alive and these days they never met, two old men who had fought in forgotten wars living on their memories. 'Bala-bloody-clava? Christ, no wonder we're losing the war!' The laughter and the derision jerked at his liver again.

'Who is it?'

The sharp question as his wife appeared at the door cut across the memories, carving like a knife through his emotions.

He thrust the letter at her and she stopped dead.

'It must be – no, it couldn't be – my cousin, Micah, died in 1912. It must be his grandson.'

The old man looked again at the letter. 'American soldiers will very soon be in Europe, sir,' he read. 'But I shall be arriving ahead of them. A great many young men joined the United States Air Service when war broke out in 1914 and we have now volunteered for immediate service abroad. Some will go to France to be trained by our new allies and fight with them until our army can supply us with airplanes, some will go to Italy, some to Canada. I requested that I might be sent with the batch that will come to England, because, I said, I had English relatives. I trust you will not mind this, sir, nor the hope I have that I may call on you...'

'Good God,' the Field Marshal said. 'He's coming here.'

It was clear that new battles were brewing up and, through his contacts, chief of whom he rated his grandfather, who had contacts of his own far more illustrious and reliable than the contacts of any other boy at school, Josh was aware that the war had entered a new phase.

But before that happened, his father returned from France on leave. It startled Josh to see how he had changed. He was a colonel now, in command of the Regiment – the only regiment that Josh acknowledged – but he suddenly seemed like an old man. There were lines on his face that the boy had never seen before and grey streaks in his hair. It gave him a faded look, though his manner was as brisk as ever.

It startled him, too, to see the passionate way his mother clutched this almost strange officer with the row of ribbons on his chest. He could understand that she was glad to have him home but, remembering how several of his friends at school had lost their fathers, he could only put down the way she clung to him as springing from a fear that he might not have come at all.

As he swung his small daughter into his arms, Dabney saw his son watching him gravely.

'Hello, Josh,' he said.

Hugging his father, Josh was aware of the strange smell about him. His uniform was stained and seemed to have absorbed some of the stink of France.

'How are you doing at school?'

'All right, Father. I'm not at the bottom of the form.'

Dabney's face wrinkled in a smile that was as the boy remembered. 'I'll bet you're not at the top either.'

'No, Father. About half way. Top half, in fact. That's not too bad, is it?'

Dinner was a quiet affair and Josh noticed that his parents hardly took their eyes off each other.

'What's it like in France, Father?' The silence was becoming intolerable.

At first his father didn't seem to hear him, then he started and turned. 'What's that?'

'I said, what's it like in France?'

There was a pause. 'Not very comfortable, Josh. But a damn sight less comfortable for the infantry than for us.'

'I had a fight at school last week. Reeves Major said the cavalry weren't pulling their weight.'

'Did he? I take it that Reeves Major has a father in the infantry.'

'No, sir, a brother. His father was killed in 1914. He was in the Rifle Brigade.'

Dabney looked down at his hands where they rested on the table beside his plate. 'And what did *you* say, Josh, in reply to this calumny?'

'I didn't say anything, Father. I hit him in the eye. It was all right afterwards, of course. We're quite good friends really, and Grandpa being in the Light Brigade at Balaclava carries a lot of weight. I also told him you were at Omdurman and got the DSO in South Africa, and another in 1914. That took the wind out of his sails, I can tell you.'

'Did he have any answer to that?'

Josh hesitated. 'Well, yes,' he admitted. 'He said you hadn't done much since.'

Dabney paused. His son was looking at him, begging him to tell him that it wasn't true.

'Perhaps Reeves Major's right, Josh,' he said. 'But it's not our fault. After the South African War, which was all horses, everybody felt certain that this war would be the same. But it turned out to be more different than anyone expected and it just happened to be our bad luck – or good luck, whichever way you see it – ' he glanced at his wife who was watching him with tragic eyes ' – that we were horsed soldiers and that we rode to war in a saddle instead of marching on our own hind legs.'

'Does that mean, sir, that he's right?'

'I'm rather afraid he is, Josh. We had our day in 1914 and we didn't do too badly. But since then, we've not done much. Sir Douglas Haig's always hoped we'll get our chance and that there'll be a gap in the line we can go through, but it's not happened yet and we're still waiting.'

'I see.'

Dabney studied his son. The boy was growing fast but he looked like taking after himself and his grandfather and would not be big. He hadn't the shoulders and strength of Robert's boy, Aubrey, not tall but sturdy, slim-hipped and strong-legged. His hands were fine but they were going to be strong, too. He was going to end up with a perfect cavalryman's figure. It was a pity he would never be a true cavalryman.

His son was still watching him with troubled eyes. '*Will* it happen, Father? Will you get your chance?'

'We all hope so, though I'm inclined to doubt it. War's changed, Josh. The rifle, you see. It gave birth to the rifle pit and the trench, and that made the bayonet a pointless weapon, blunted the sword and the lance and forced artillerymen to place their guns beyond reach. Which meant that artillery had to grow heavier with a longer range.' He paused. 'It also dismounted the cavalryman. We fought in trenches in 1914, as you know. Nowadays, they prefer to let the trench fighting be done by men who're experienced at it, and keep us in reserve for when the breakthrough comes.'

'Suppose it never does, Father?'

There was a long silence. 'That is the question,' Dabney said gravely. 'Sir Douglas Haig thinks it will. I'm inclined to doubt it.'

'That means you'll not be in the war?'

'It does indeed.'

Josh was not too young to miss the glance of gratitude in his mother's eyes.

'It seems a bit unfair, Father.'

'I'm afraid it does. On the other hand, all isn't lost. We have a new arm you'll have read about. Tanks.'

The boy was silent for a long time. 'And will the cavalry *never* do anything?'

Dabney was silent again, then he sighed. 'The cavalry,' he said slowly, 'has been superseded for its reconnaissance duties by the air, and if there are to be breakthroughs they'll be made by tanks. I suspect, in fact, that they're the cavalry of the future and when this business is over I intend to find out if they'll give me a job.'

'But, Father, Reeves Major says they only go at five miles an hour. A Sopwith Camel can fly at over a hundred. Even a horse can gallop faster than five miles an hour. What about the charge, Father? You can't charge at five miles an hour and charges are what cavalry's for, aren't they?'

Dabney shook his head and his voice grew harsher. 'Horsed charges are gone forever, Josh,' he said. 'Cavalry is finished and I'm ashamed to sit behind the lines with thousands of others with nothing else to do but tend our animals while men die every day in the trenches.'

As he finished speaking, Dabney tossed down his napkin, finished his wine, rose and stamped towards the door. For a moment his wife stared after him, then at Josh, then she rose herself and ran after him. For a long time, Josh stared uncomprehendingly across the table at his sister, his eyes full of tears. Something, he felt, was dreadfully wrong. Idols he had believed in all his life had toppled. His father, whom he adored, could find no joy in his service. It left him wretched and miserable and bewildered. There seemed a desperate need for something to be done.

'Grandpa, I'm ten now. How old do I have to be to enlist?'

The old man moved restlessly. 'A damn sight older than you are now, boy,' he growled.

Joshua studied the Field Marshal as he huddled in his chair in the library among the silver statuettes of cavalrymen and the pictures of soldiers in gaudy uniforms. A clock ticked and the room seemed as silent, gloomy and dead as the graveyard where they'd buried Tyas Ackroyd.

There was a faint sun and it shone on his grandfather's head which in the last few months seemed suddenly to have grown bald. The old man, inert as the stuffed pike on the wall, stared with puffy eyes at the newspaper. The headlines struck Josh. 'French Attack Punches Hole in German Line.' Since they'd announced only about a fortnight before that the British had punched a hole in the German line at Arras, this new French attack on the Chemin des Dames, or whatever it was called, seemed to him to presage the end of the war. The Germans couldn't go on having holes punched in their lines as often as all that.

Rather to his surprise, his grandfather had not seemed impressed, which was why he had asked his question.

'I could do exercises, Grandpa,' he suggested.

The old man heaved in his chair. 'Wassat?'

'I could do exercises.'

'What for?'

'Build up my strength.'

'What do you want to build up your strength for?'

'Join the army, Grandpa.'

'Too young. Have to be eighteen at least.'

'Reeves Major had a cousin who joined up in 1915 when he was only sixteen.'

The old man shifted in his chair. 'Then the people who accepted him ought to be ashamed of themselves. Boys of that age are nothing but a nuisance. Haven't the stamina.'

'He was nearly six foot tall, Reeves Major said.'

'And as muscled as the pith of an orange, I expect.' The old man grunted. 'Bet he didn't last long.'

'Reeves Major said he was killed on the first day of the Somme.'

The old man was silent for a while. Poor little bugger, he was thinking. Josh was watching him closely and he felt obliged to go on.

'I'd never have under-age boys in the Regiment when I was running it,' he said. 'Used to send them home and tell 'em to grow a bit. A few colonels turned a blind eye to keep the numbers up, though. Didn't pay. Didn't last. When the cholera was knocking us over like ninepins in the Crimea, it was always the youngsters who went first. Same in South Africa. Most of those who died of enteric were young. No lasting power, y'see. Strength gives out. Besides, a boy of that age doesn't have the same *moral* strength as a man of twenty-odd.'

'What's moral strength?'

'Guts. Ability to keep going when all the rest have stopped. The ability to make decisions when they're alone instead of hanging on to everybody else's coat-tails. Your father showed he had it at the Graafberg. I suppose I must have had it, too, or the Regiment would never have been represented in the Light Brigade at Balaclava.'

'Have I got it, Grandpa?'

'I expect so. Runs in the family. Didn't you punch that Reeves boy in the eye?'

'Yes, I did. He said Father wasn't doing his share.' Josh frowned. 'But when I asked Father, *he* said he wasn't, too. He said he wanted to join the Tank Corps. He said they were the cavalry of the future.'

The old man considered. 'That's a shrewd assessment,' he said. 'Perhaps he's right. If they could only get the damn things to go as fast as a horse.'

278

'Should *I* join the Tank Corps when I'm old enough to go to the war?'

'Do you want to?'

'I'd rather join the Regiment.'

'Then don't be in too big a hurry, boy. By the time you're old enough they'll probably have got 'em to go as fast as horses and then you'll do your charging in a tank. Now you'd better push off. I'm tired and I want to go to sleep.'

Leaving his grandfather with his head sunk on his chest Josh wandered through the house. Since his father had gone back to France, he rarely spent his time at home. His grandfather was invariably pleased to see him and, with the Ackroyd men about the Home Farm, he was in male company such as he rarely saw at home. His mother always seemed abstracted these days and his younger sister was too small to occupy his attention for long.

Looking for his grandmother in the kitchen, he was informed by the maid who was making scones for tea that she had gone to lie down. Bored, he wondered why it was old people always had to lie down or have a nap in the afternoon.

Wandering into the hall, he stood before the portrait of his grandfather on the stairs. It had been painted to celebrate the fact that he was safe home from the Indian Mutiny.

'Habit people had,' his grandfather had once said. 'People died a lot in those days, y'see. Typhoid. Pneumonia. That sort of thing. Sanitation was a bit indifferent and people caught things. When soldiers came home safe, there was always the feeling that they might drop dead of the plague any day, so their parents got 'em on canvas just in case.'

Studying the picture, sitting in a chair opposite by the fireplace, Josh decided once more that the figure was far too tall. But his grandfather had explained that away, too. 'Always made you tall,' he had said. 'Looked better.

279

Especially with shrimps like me.' The figure was standing alongside a chestnut charger carrying a leopard skin and the gold-embossed shabraque of the 19th. The horse, he'd been told, had been called Bess, after his great-grandmother, because, so his great-grandfather had said, 'she had the same sweet temper but was just as bloody stubborn if she wanted to be.' He knew all about the mare, how she had been one of a string of three, of which one had died when the transport carrying her from England had caught fire, and one had died of disease in some place on the shores of the Black Sea. Bess, herself, having carried his grandfather down the valley to the Russian guns, had then borne the wounded Tyas Ackroyd to safety. Despite two bad cuts from shell splinters, she had been nursed back to health only to die during the winter when starving horses had been driven to eating each other's manes and tails.

Sitting still, staring at the picture, he tried in vain to associate the dozing old man in the library with his watery eyes and bent knees with this brash virile youngster. Behind him were men of the 19th Lancers, their lance points gleaming dully against a grey sky. His grandfather was black-haired, as fierce-eyed as his charger, curly-whiskered and with his hand on the handle of his sabre. On his head was the flat-topped schapka, made of metal and basketwork, with the enormous clutching eagle that gave the Regiment its name, worked into the decoration on the front above the motto, Aut Nullus Aut Primus – The Best or Nothing.

The posturing figure was splendid in rifle green, a scarlet plastron covering its breast, a double gold stripe running down the wide overalls to its polished boots. Behind was a narrow inlet between two high hills on one of which was the shape of a fort.

'Meant to be Balaclava,' his grandfather had once told him. 'Same chap did the head and shoulders that hangs in the Mess at Ripon. Makes me look as if I'm ruptured.'

The boy continued to stare at the picture, studying every detail of it, and it was only when a shadow fell across his face that he became aware that he'd been joined by a young man in khaki. He turned, realising that the uniform was different from a British uniform and that the cap he held in his hand had a brown polished peak instead of a British officer's khaki cloth one.

'Who's that?' the young man asked.

'That's my grandfather,' Josh said. 'He was in the charge of the Light Brigade. He's in the library.'

'Is he now? Well, that's great because I've come to see him. My name's Micah Burtle Love. I guess we're related.'

'Oh!' Josh was unimpressed.

'Your grandmother was a Dabney and she was related to my grandfather who was also called Micah Burtle Love. I've heard it said that your grandmother met your grandfather in one of the Burtle houses and that he actually went from her side to fight in the Wilderness and at Yellow Tavern. It's quite a story where I come from.'

Josh rose to his feet. 'I'm Joshua Loftus Colby Goff,' he said. 'I'm called after my grandfather and my great-grandfather, and also after my great-great-great-grandfather Joshua Pellew Goff, who founded our regiment.' He jerked a finger at the portrait. '*That* regiment. The 19th Lancers.'

The young man smiled. 'Well, I guess that's interesting. Do you think I could see your grandfather?'

'Shouldn't think so. He always goes to sleep in the afternoon.'

'How about your grandmother?'

'So does she.'

Micah Love looked faintly disappointed. 'That sure is a pity,' he said. 'How about you? Do you-all go to sleep in the afternoon, too?'

'Not me, sir. It's because they're old, you see. Have you come specially to see them?'

'I guess I have. All the way from London.'

Joshua considered. 'I'd take you home,' he offered, 'but Mother's at Red Cross this afternoon. She goes to the hospital. And my sister Chloe's out to tea. There's nobody there.' He smiled. 'Still, there's Uncle John at the farm. And Aunt Jane. They're always at home because of the animals.'

'Why, how about going to see them, then?'

'It's a long way.'

'I've got an automobile.'

The automobile was a small yellow runabout with a round brass bonnet and a dickey seat.

'Is it fast?' Josh asked.

'Not as fast as an aeroplane. Soon I hope I'll be flying one. I'll loop the loop over the house if I come to see you by air. Then you'll know it's me.'

'Father says that aeroplanes have taken over reconnaissance duties from the cavalry.'

'I guess they have. Does he mind?'

'I think he does a bit.'

As they rattled through Braxby, Joshua pointed out the Home Farm and the cottage where Tyas Ackroyd had lived. 'He was in the Light Brigade, too,' he said. 'He's just died. That cottage belongs to his son, Ellis Ackroyd. He was wounded last year.'

Just ahead of them a girl was struggling along with a basket.

'That's my cousin Rachel,' Josh said. 'She's older than me. She helps at the farm since she left school and does part-time work at the hospital in York. I expect she's on her way home.'

'I guess we'd better give her a lift.'

Rachel's head turned as the car squeaked to a stop alongside her. Her first reaction at the sight of the uniformed young man smiling at her was one of indignation, then she saw Josh sitting alongside him.

'Hello, Josh,' she said. 'What are you up to?'

'We're just going to the farm, because Mother's at the hospital, Chloe's out to tea and Grannie and Grandpa are having their afternoon nap. This is – '

As he paused, uncertain, the young man jumped from the car.

'Micah Burtle Love.'

'He's some sort of relation, I think,' Josh said. 'He says Grannie was a Burtle or a Love or something and that Grandpa met her at his house while he was fighting the Battle of Yellow Tavern.'

Love grinned. 'Not quite, but I guess it's near enough. It makes us cousins about four times removed.'

By the look on Rachel's face, it seemed to Josh she wouldn't have minded if they'd been cousins eighty times removed and she climbed into the little yellow car cheerfully, pushing Josh hard up against Lieutenant Love and proceeding to talk over his head in the usual manner of self-important older girl cousins.

'I had to come and look you up,' Love said. 'I'd heard of all you-all from my Grandfather. Why, he was always talking about the English branch of the family.'

'He's going to be a pilot,' Josh said helpfully. He got on well with Rachel and he could see she was already smitten by this young man from America. Micah Love was tall and strong-looking with a straight nose, dark curling hair and a firm chin. Above all he had a yellow sports car and Josh could see that had possibilities as far as he himself was concerned.

Rachel was looking at Micah Love excitedly. 'Philippa's boyfriend's a pilot,' she said. 'He's a captain now and a flight leader or something. He's already got two medals. Hedley Ackroyd. Do you know him?'

'I guess not.'

'Everybody knows the Ackroyds. They've lived here for years. Hedley's the one with the brains. Philippa's absolutely gone on him. She spends all her time looking at his photograph and writing letters to him. She says he's been wounded.'

It was the first Josh had heard of it. 'Where?' he asked.

'In the –' Rachel giggled '– in the bottom. It's not serious.'

'I meant, where was he flying?' Josh said sternly, feeling she wasn't paying sufficient attention.

'Oh! Near Arras, I think. He's coming home. She says he won't be going back for a bit, either. She's absolutely head over heels about it.'

'Of course she is,' Josh said. 'He's shot down seventeen German planes.'

John Sutton was standing by the gate of the farm when they arrived, watching a herd of cows amble through into a field. His wife, Josh's Aunt Jane, was watching from the door.

'I've got a German aunt, too,' Josh said.

'Sssh,' Rachel said. 'Mr Love won't want to hear about them.'

'Why not?'

'Well, they're Germans, aren't they?'

'Grandpa always says it doesn't matter,' Josh said. 'I liked Uncle Karl. He was killed last year.'

'I'm sorry,' Love said.

'I think Grandpa was, too.'

When Josh returned to the Manor, the postman was just cycling away and there was a large Daimler outside with a liveried chauffeur sitting at the wheel. Sitting in the hall was Aubrey.

' 'Lo, Aubrey,' Josh said.

' 'Lo, Josh.'

'What are you doing here?'

'Father's come to see Grandpa. But he's still asleep so he's talking to Grannie in the drawing-room.' Aubrey faced his cousin proudly. 'My sister May's got engaged to a lord,' he said. 'Lord Tinsley. He's Lord Lemprier's son.'

'What about it?'

'Well, he's a lord, isn't he?'

'I wouldn't marry a lord.'

Aubrey eyed Josh doubtfully. Up to that moment, he'd never had any qualms, but from the way his cousin spoke it seemed there were grave dangers in marrying a lord.

'Why not?'

'Well, who wants to marry a lord, anyway?'

Aubrey smiled. Josh's objection clearly wasn't based on very sound foundations. 'Father says I can join the Regiment when I'm eighteen,' he went on. 'He says it'll be useful. Meeting people. That sort of thing.'

'Is that the only reason? I shan't join the Regiment because of that.'

'Why will you join?'

'To serve my King and Country.' Josh had a feeling he was being priggish but it was a good closing line and he headed for the drawing-room, leaving Aubrey still waiting for his father.

As he reached the door, he saw it was open and his Uncle Robert seemed to be angry.

'Look, Mother,' he was saying. 'You can say what you like, but I feel something should be done. The house can't be split down the middle. My chap, Sleete, could make the arrangements.'

Lady Goff answered quietly and she seemed to be hanging on to her temper with difficulty. 'Your father,' she said, 'will do what he thinks fit, I'm sure.'

'But it can't be left in the air for ever, can it? Dammit, Mother, he's getting old. I've noticed it particularly in the last year.'

'So you've come to me?'

'Well, you're a lot younger, aren't you? I expect you make the decisions these days.'

Lady Goff's chin lifted. 'I have never made the decisions except in my own department.'

Robert laughed. 'Then you ought to start, Mother,' he said. 'I always thought Americans believed in get-up-and-go.' He lit a cigar and puffed blue smoke. 'Something's got to be decided, and, as I say, Father's getting old – '

'I hope you're not suggesting he's non compos mentis.'

Josh looked round. Aubrey was watching him from the hall. 'What's non compos mentis?' he whispered.

'Dunno. What are they going on about?'

'Dunno. This place, I think.'

'Why?'

'I think Uncle Robert wants it.'

'Why?' Aubrey looked puzzled. 'We've already got a house.'

Inside the drawing-room, Robert was speaking again, trying to reassure his mother. 'Of course he's not non compos mentis,' he said. 'But I don't think he has the same grasp on things he used to have. Not since the Regiment was cut up. The Somme seems to have knocked the stuffing out of him.'

'It might have knocked the stuffing out of you, Robert – ' Josh noticed how cold his grandmother's voice had become ' – if you'd been part of it.'

'Oh, Mother, surely you don't believe all that tradition nonsense they preach, do you? You're American – '

'We had our traditions, I remember, even in America.'

'Well, I think I ought to talk to him.'

'Not today, you will not, Robert!' The old woman's voice was frigid with anger. 'Certainly not today!' She held out a letter. 'I've just heard from Lucy Ellesmere that Ned's been killed. Your father doesn't know yet but he soon will.'

Robert was taken sufficiently aback not to argue. 'When shall I call again then?' he asked.

'When he's ready to see you. Your father's a man capable of great feelings, Robert, something I sometimes feel you're not. And if you dare say a word to him about financial matters until he wishes to hear you I'll never forgive you.'

As Robert went out of the drawing-room, he was frowning deeply and chewing at his cigar so much he never noticed Josh standing beside the monk's chest that graced the wall by the door as he snatched up his son.

Josh stared after him, troubled. Inside the drawing-room his grandmother was staring out of the window, her back straight, a small rigid figure with a face stricken with misery. It bothered him so much, he crept through the open door.

'Grannie,' he said. 'Micah Burtle Love's come.'

She started and turned. 'Who?'

'Micah Burtle Love. He's over at Uncle John's and Aunt Jane's. We had tea there. I think Rachel's gone on him already.'

five

The war continued to stagger from crisis to crisis. The summer weather was appalling and leading the 19th Lancers through the steadily falling rain, Dabney's eyes were bleak as the wind blew the drops of water from the rim of his steel helmet on to his cheeks.

Behind him the column of horsemen splashed along the muddy road, occupying most of its surface so that men on their own two feet had to step aside. The road seemed to be packed with troops, shuffling infantrymen, transport units, artillerymen, ambulances, all edging out of the way as the Lancers slogged back to their camp after yet another false alarm, yet another false hope of a breakthrough that would permit them to charge to Berlin. Instead of a charge there had been only a weary wait in the rain, cold and hungry and soaked to the skin, with a few horses and men killed for nothing by shellfire, and then the tramp back again, shapeless figures under the shining rain-wet capes, faces shadowed by heavy helmets, their horses weary, their ears drooping, their coats streaked with water, their legs splashed with mud.

The Flanders countryside looked grey and sodden. Somewhere up ahead where the guns rumbled, soldiers were trying to push forward through the waist-deep morass. Off the road, mules and horses, their coats plastered with mud, were struggling fetlock-deep, and guns were sinking beyond their wheel-hubs as they fired and having to be abandoned because nothing on earth could manage to drag them free. Lorries sent to help, tractors even, sank with them in the increasing wilderness of mud and water.

The rain had laid a thick mist over the land and because the earth was grey, everything else in the sodden landscape was grey, too. Lorries were grey. Guns were grey. Horses were grey. Men were grey. War, Dabney supposed, was a grey business. There was nothing to relieve the monotony of the drabness as far as he could see, nothing but a flat, soaked landscape with broken houses, their shattered rafters sticking up like the ribs of some long-dead animal among the stark and mutilated trees. Already it took nine hours to bring a wounded man from the front line back to safety.

Yet the newspapers continued to call what was happening a success, hailing advances that seemed to bring only casualties but no sign of victory. *The Spectator* had even congratulated the General Staff on the new blows that were being delivered and was suggesting that all the lessons of the past three years had been well learned and were now being applied with science and resolution. Staff work, they claimed, was irreproachable.

At a bleak crossroads – as bare as a Lincolnshire railway halt – a group of tanks had gathered just off the hard surface. There was a strong smell of petrol fumes and hot oil in the damp air and the ears were filled with the throb of engines as the grey mud-plastered monsters waited.

A colonel wearing the badges of the tank corps was sitting in a car shouting at a young staff officer in an immaculate uniform who stood alongside. It was clear from the cleanness of his uniform that the younger officer had come from headquarters. After this waste of ugliness, headquarters always seemed achingly, spotlessly clean.

'It won't work,' the colonel was raging. 'I've said so before and I'm prepared to say so again! To whoever wants to know! It's impossible!'

As the staff officer turned away, his face pink with anger, the colonel lifted his head and Dabney saw it was a man he had known at Colchester. He looked up and managed a twisted grin.

'Hello, Dab,' he said. 'You people been trying to charge through the gap again?'

Dabney gave him a bleak smile and the colonel gestured angrily. 'It's pathetic, isn't it? They try on this breakthrough-with-a-charge-into-the-gap thing about once a month, when it ought to be obvious that as far as the tanks are concerned this bloody battle's finished and done with.' He gestured at the weeping sky. 'Flying Corps and cavalry, too, it would seem to me. Can't you knock some sense into those idiots at headquarters?'

'I've long since stopped trying,' Dabney said. 'Is there something new on?'

The colonel drew a hand across his face. 'They want us to put on another show. You'll be hearing, I expect. They simply won't believe it when we tell 'em these monsters of ours are useless in that bloody bog out there.' He gestured at the grey lozenge shapes just off the road. 'We could win the war with those beauties you know, given the right conditions – and if *we* were allowed to say what *are* the right conditions. The bloody money spent on the initial barrage at Passchendaele would have built over four thousand of those machines. Enough to win any war. At the very least it would have provided the aeroplane engines we need to make 'em go faster. But nobody bothers! All they ask for is another attempt at a breakthrough to exploit your horses.'

'The idea of a cavalry attack's mad,' Dabney snapped. 'A man on a horse sticks out like a pea on a drum. If they try to launch us in any numbers the slaughter will make Balaclava look silly. For a commander even to gallop round his squadrons when they're deployed's courting suicide.'

The colonel lit a pipe. 'Given dry ground and sufficient numbers we could give them their bloody breakthrough,' he said. 'But not here. Never here. Here it'll be just like last time. The bloody things'll sink into the mud. You still keen on joining us?'

Dabney nodded.

'You'd lose rank.'

'I might gain some self-respect. I'm only a captain, anyway, by rights, and we'll all go back to pre-war ranks when it's over.'

'*If we survive*. Well, I'll push it. It's just possible you'll be in on the ground floor for the first real tank attack the world's ever seen. We've picked the spot: Cambrai. Clean, undamaged land. We'll make 'em the gap they want. So long as they don't wreck it first with one of these bloody barrages they're so keen on.' The colonel frowned. 'I just hope they know what to do with it when they get it.'

Continuing through the rain, Dabney was aware of the resentment about him. To the rest of the army the cavalry had come to represent nothing. Nothing at all. They not only failed to help the war, they even impeded it, because their horses and equipment filled acres of cramped countryside and their fodder trains jammed the roads.

Passing alongside a ruined village, they skirted a broken lorry and a group of clotted carcasses where shellfire had destroyed a gun team. The sight made Dabney wince. He wasn't a squeamish man but the way dead horses were allowed to remain unburied troubled him. He had grown up with horses and these muddy lumps looked like nothing else but mounds of earth, their limbs entangled in their death throes – with each other, with their harness leathers, even with the wreckage of the limber they had been pulling.

On the edge of the village a battalion of infantrymen were just coming out of the line. Their boots barely left the ground, merely sloughing through the thin mud that covered the surface of the road like a flood. Their bodies moved stiffly like clockwork dolls. Their faces were filthy and the eyes that stared from them appeared to gaze into space as if they were bending all their attention only on using the last ounce of energy they possessed to shuffle forward. They stumbled past the horsemen in the downpour, their uniforms plastered to their bodies as if they'd been dipped in water, their rifles tied round the bolt mechanism with rags to keep out the mud. Their expressions were as grey as the landscape with exhaustion.

Another battalion had been halted by the roadside, whole groups of men fallen asleep in spite of the mud and the passing lorries that threw sheets of grey-brown water over them. An officer was moving among them trying to kick them to life and they were stirring and dragging themselves upright, so dazed with weariness they didn't appear to know what they were doing. Then one of them saw the column of horsemen clattering past and made a noise of disgust and contempt.

'Silly peacock ba-a-astards!'

The voice came from the back of the group, full of derision and contempt, and immediately the whole lot came to life and weary faces became twisted with bitterness as they worked out on the cavalry the anger and frustration they felt against their leaders. Men scrambled to their feet, and those who were waiting under their loads like patient mules turned to join the catcalling.

'Git orf them bleedin' mokes and come and 'elp us sort Jerry out!'

The jeering started muttering among the riders and Dabney's face set grimly. It was something they had constantly to endure. He knew how the infantrymen felt. As they moved to and from the line they saw thousands of cavalrymen, thousands of horses, all apparently doing nothing but wait for the weary footsloggers to make a gap they could exploit. Their attitude was traditional. Dabney had heard his father say it had been the same in the Crimea. Now, because of the Commander-in-Chief's obsession with cavalry, because he was applying the lessons of the Boer War to a war that bore no relation to that struggle, the old derision had changed even to hatred.

He wasn't sure he could accept much more of it.

The anger Dabney felt mounted. When he next arrived on leave he shocked his son by announcing that he'd had enough of France and setting off at once to see his father. His anger was so obvious, Josh begged a lift, pretending he wished to see his grandmother when all he wanted was to know what was in his father's mind.

At Braxby Manor, Dabney stalked to the library, his son trailing behind. The Field Marshal was just tucking into his tea and muffin, huddled in his chair in front of the fire, and, feeling out of it and totally unnoticed, Josh sat quietly by the door.

His father didn't waste time and he didn't mince his words. 'Passchendaele's no place to wage war, Father,' he said angrily, and as Josh listened he unfolded a story of marshy Flanders fields turned into a morass by water from dykes and ditches broken by the vast barrages thrown at the Germans.

'In August, Father!' Dabney said. 'What will it be like in winter?'

Sitting quietly out of sight, Josh was startled by the intensity of his father's rage.

'For sheer lack of imagination,' he was saying, 'this war's never been equalled! When you look at them, it's hard for a connoisseur of generalship to single out anyone as being especially bad because they're all so awful. Allenby's all right and so's Plumer. As for the rest, God help us! While the men in the trenches wallow in blood the generals wallow only in ink. The infantry at Waterloo didn't budge, Father, because their generals were there with them. Ours are phantoms twenty miles behind the line.

'It could be forgiven,' Dabney went on, 'if it were part of a plan. If they knew of the conditions and were accepting them as part of the battle. But they *didn't* know, Father! They didn't know! They never move out of their damned châteaux! They never see it! Yet I've seen them pull up exhausted men coming out of the trenches for slovenly marching, or order them to push a bogged staff car free. Father, what's come over the bloody army?'

The old man seemed too shocked to answer and merely silently shook his head from side to side.

'Can't you do anything, Father?'

'Dab, I'm eighty now! I'm a fossil from a bygone age. I rode at Balaclava. That makes me deader than the dodo. People don't take any notice of me any more.'

'You know Wullie Robertson, the CIGS.'

'Robertson isn't all-powerful. Lloyd George would even like to be rid of him. He'd like to be rid of Haig, too, but he's not strong enough. I sometimes wish he were.'

Dabney sat in silence for a moment, his anger surging inside him, while the old man hunched miserably in his chair. Aware that he was hearing things he should not have been hearing, Josh cowered in his place, conscious that this concerned no one but his father, his grandfather, and him. This wasn't news to be spread at school. This was 'family.'

The old man lifted an anguished face. 'What about the Americans?' he asked. 'Won't they make a difference?'

'They haven't arrived yet.'

'One of them has. Micah Burtle Love's grandson. You'll have heard of him, of course.'

Dabney managed a bleak smile at last. 'Fleur wrote to me about him. He stayed the weekend, she said.'

'He's transferred his affection now to Jane's girls. Rachel's gone overboard for him. He's learning to fly at Colney Hatch, but he still manages to get up here a surprising amount. Jane's worried because it seems to be getting serious.'

Dabney frowned. 'Father, tell her that people of young Love's age *have* to start getting serious quickly. A pilot's life at the front isn't much more than three weeks.' He paused. 'How's Robert?'

'Growing fatter. He's a K now, of course.'

Dabney's face was bitter. 'A knighthood for churning out uniforms and guns?'

'Somebody has to do it, Dab.'

There was a long silence, then Dabney spoke again. 'Father, I'm going to try to get into this war more. I can't look people in the face. But I want you to promise me something. Just in case anything happens to me.'

Listening, Josh felt the tears spring to his eyes. Up to that moment it had never occurred to him that something might happen to his father. Other fathers were wounded or killed, but somehow he couldn't imagine it happening to his. His grandfather had gone through half a dozen campaigns and had suffered little more than flesh wounds, and it had left him with a feeling that Goffs didn't die. Now, suddenly, he wasn't so sure.

'Dabney –' his grandfather was speaking in that funny quavering voice that had developed over the last week or two '– I think you'd better ask somebody else. The chances are that at my age it'll probably happen to me first.'

'I don't believe it, Father, and I'm worried for Fleur and for Josh and Chloe. I want them to be secure just in case.'

The old man shifted restlessly. 'I've already thought of that, Dab. There isn't much money because I've never been rich, but this house and this land and the properties on it will be yours when I go.'

Dabney was silent for a moment. 'What about Robert?'

'Robert already has more than he needs. He can do without this place. He'll get the Cosgro fortune through Elfrida because Walter isn't married and is never likely to be now. Braxby Manor will come to you and eventually to Josh. That way it'll remain Goff land. I haven't much else to offer, Dab, but I can do that. Your mother knows my wishes and a will's made. The Suttons are well enough off and so are the Hartmanns, though God knows what'll happen to Helen. We've not heard. It seems to me best to leave what I have where it's most needed. And that seems to mean Josh. Robert's children are well provided for.'

Dabney frowned. 'So long as they're not deprived of their rights, Father. Aubrey's not a bad kid.'

'Better than Robert deserves,' the old man growled. 'Elfrida's made a better job of them than we ever expected, certainly better than we could have expected from a Cosgro. It's a pity Robert doesn't behave as he should.'

There was a pause then Dabney asked softly, 'The Balmael woman?'

Josh wondered who the Balmael woman was and, as his father and grandfather dropped their voices, he decided it was time he made his exit. Moving softly from the chair, he crept through the door and closed it quietly behind him.

For the next few days, the house was depressing. With his father angry and his mother clearly in a torment of fear, Josh wasn't sure how to behave. He was doubly kind to his smaller sister and occasionally cycled over to see his cousin, Aubrey, who swam with him in the Brack, or went ferreting with one of the Ackroyd boys in the meadows under the hills.

Then, just when they were all trying to steel themselves to Dabney's return to France, a telegram arrived. At first they thought it was to announce the death of yet another friend but instead it called Dabney to London.

Suddenly excited, Dabney telephoned his father and got one of the Ackroyds to drive him to York. During the afternoon, there was a telephone call that made his mother cry out with delight and swing Josh into her arms.

'What is it?' he asked.

'Your father,' she said.

'What's happened?'

'He'll tell you himself when he gets home.'

When Dabney arrived, he was consumed by excitement that told them he had news.

'I'm leaving France,' he said. 'I'm going to the Middle East!'

To Josh it seemed a demotion. The war seemed only to be in France, but they all climbed into the car and headed for Braxby Manor. Dabney was bubbling with an enthusiasm which his wife shared. Josh had heard them talking together eagerly and heard his mother's cry of joy, so he could only guess that something tremendous had happened.

At his grandfather's, his mother disappeared with Chloe into the drawing-room to tell his grandmother the news while his father headed for the library.

'It was Allenby, Father,' he said. 'He was at the War Office. I was just about in despair and thinking of applying for the Tank Corps, quite prepared to drop a rank, but, as it happens, it's turned out to be unnecessary. They've given me a brigade.'

This was unexpected. A field marshal and a brigadier in the same family was better than anything Reeves Major could produce! Josh beamed with pride.

His grandfather had sat bolt upright. 'That's good news, Dab,' he said eagerly. 'Infantry?'

'No, Father! Cavalry! Men on horses!'

'Regulars?'

'Of course not. That would be too much to expect.'

'Yeomanry?'

'Not even that. Mostly they're Australians and New Zealanders.'

'I didn't know we had Australian and New Zealand cavalry in France.'

'We haven't. This is Palestine, Father. Open country. Cavalry country. I'm to leave at once. Allenby believes in movement and it's his ambition to break through the Gaza-Beersheba line and get to Jerusalem and Damascus and into Turkey. They're already using cavalry out there and, with the Arabs in revolt against the Turks, he has firm hopes of success. I'd come to the conclusion that if there were promotion to be won out of this mess it wasn't going to come sitting astride a horse, but it seems I was wrong.'

There was a long silence. 'You'll find Australians bloody difficult,' the Field Marshal said slowly. 'They always were.'

'I'm fully aware of that, Father. They have a way with brigadiers they don't like. There was an Australian regiment near us who swamped their brigadier in sewage when they were in the line. They'd spend the morning penning up a mass of slime behind a temporary barrier while they built a new outflow and when they learned he was on his way, they picked their moment just as he was half-way down a deep trench and broke down the dam. It washed him away like the Egyptians in the Red Sea.'

There was a thin chuckle of laughter from the Field Marshal and Dabney went on eagerly.

'Allenby's on his way out at once,' he said. 'The idea's to knock the Turks out of the war and he asked for me. I think that little affair of ours against the Uhlans in 1914 helped. He's always been particularly pleasant to me.' Dabney grinned, unable to contain his pleasure, more alive than Josh had seen him for months. 'I could have kissed him when he told me. A cavalry brigade, Father! Think of it! In country where cavalry can work. No mud. No barbed wire.'

'Who else have you got out there? What regular cavalry?'

Dabney smiled. 'None, Father. Not a single regiment. The only regular regiments are Indian. The rest are all Yeomanry from Britain and light horse regiments from Australia and New Zealand – hostilities-only soldiers with rifles and bayonets instead of swords.'

'If they don't like you, they'll make it very clear.'

'I'll win 'em round. Jasper Capell was given a battalion. You remember Jasper. Blind as a bat in one eye and wore a monocle. His Aussies thought it a great joke and the second day he was with them every man in the battalion was also wearing a monocle. God knows where they got them. But he beat 'em at their own game. He took out his eyeglass, tossed it in the air, caught it in his eye and said "Bet you can't do that." From then on he could do anything with 'em.'

The war persisted in intruding. A cousin was reported missing and another of the Ackroyd boys was killed in France. For Josh, school became merely a repetition of what he heard at home, and, having a grandfather who was a field marshal, what they were told by enthusiastic and elderly teachers – many of them out of retirement to take the places of men who had joined the army – he had already learned several days before.

Things seemed to be short everywhere. Clothes that would normally have been cast off were worn just a little longer, and in addition to their normal work, everybody was cultivating vegetable plots, even at school. Having a farmer in the family was a help but his mother was keeping goats to provide milk because they could hardly expect John Sutton to help them all.

In November, with the stories from Flanders becoming discreetly uninformative, there was a runaway victory at Cambrai. Tanks in large numbers had broken through the German lines and for a trifling cost had captured ten thousand German prisoners and two hundred guns. The newspapers went wild and church bells were rung as talk of an advance to Berlin started. But something seemed to go wrong and, listening to his grandfather's mutterings, Josh learned that the victory had been wasted because no one had known what to do with it. The infantry had not been able to keep up with the tanks and the cavalry were destroyed once more by German machine guns and, with the reserves wasted in the abortive struggle at Passchendaele, the Germans had counter-attacked and pushed the allies right back to where they had started.

Just when they were all despondent, however, a jubilant letter arrived from Dabney to say the British had smashed through the Turkish Gaza line, chiefly thanks to an attack by the Australian Light Horse Brigade.

'I've never seen anything like it,' he wrote. 'It just shows that under the right circumstances cavalry can still be used for shock action.'

From time to time, Josh bumped into Hedley Akroyd, still limping a little but fit again and no longer wearing the taut, tired expression he had brought home the previous year. Micah Love appeared surprisingly often with his little yellow car, which he kept these days not in London but in York so that he could catch a train north and pick it up for the last part of the journey. He wore wings now and considered himself a fully qualified pilot. His ambition was to join the squadron that Hedley was expecting to take to France.

To Josh the world was a strange place. Though Braxby had not altered much, everywhere else it had. The Russian Tsar was a prisoner of the Bolsheviks, rationing had started, the papers were full of pictures of American soldiers landing in France, tall men wearing Boy Scout hats and long gaiters instead of puttees, and behind it all there was a curious nervous feeling that touched even Josh that the Germans had something up their sleeve.

Early in March, they were all invited to Hounslow in London to see Hedley Ackroyd's squadron leave for France. The Field Marshal decided that the journey would be too exhausting and Josh, who was home for half-term, was horrified when his mother claimed that the demands of the hospital precluded her going, too. Just when he was fully expecting that this magnificent opportunity to see the Flying Corps going into action was to be denied him, Rachel and Philippa took pity on him and offered to take him with them.

'So long as you keep out of the way when we're saying goodbye,' Rachel said.

There was a little argument with parents about the two girls going unchaperoned but in the end objection was withdrawn since, with a growing boy of eleven to look after, they could hardly get up to mischief, and they all set off from Braxby carrying small cases for their trip to London. There were messages at the hotel where they had booked and disgusted looks from Rachel and Philippa when they learned they had been invited to a last-minute party.

'I'll stay in my room,' Josh promised. 'Honest.'

'You can go down to the dining-room,' Rachel said, her words tumbling over themselves in her excitement. 'So long as you don't tell tales.'

They left him at seven o'clock to pick up a taxi and he went gravely downstairs to the dining-room. It was full of women with men in uniform and he solemnly waded through four courses then ordered a lemonade to be sent to his room. The hotel was so warm, he fell asleep on his bed and was only vaguely conscious of the door clicking as someone put their head round.

The following morning, Rachel woke him. She was frowning as though she had a headache.

'Come on,' she said. 'We haven't all day.'

The take-off at Hounslow was chaotic. The squadron contained several other Americans besides Micah Love, and they seemed to know every girl in London, all of whom appeared to be present to see them off. There were also a few staff officers from American headquarters, a few civilians and an American colonel called Mitchell who gravely told Josh that, used properly, the aeroplane could win the war and any other wars that might follow.

There was another boy of Josh's age, who was some relation to one of the pilots and they studied the aeroplanes with interest.

'SE5s,' the other boy pointed out.

'They're supposed to be better than Camels,' Josh said.

'Camels turn better. And they're terrifically manoeuvrable. But they're not so fast. They use SEs for chasing the Germans over their own lines.'

They spent a good half hour trying to beat each other at airing their knowledge, then they noticed that everybody seemed to be kissing.

'They're off, I think,' Josh said.

There were tears in Rachel's eyes as she clutched Micah Love; and Philippa, standing with Hedley Ackroyd, her head on his chest, was uttering little muted whimpering noises that made Josh turn away, faintly embarrassed.

There were nineteen aeroplanes and they were all arranged in position for taking off in formation with the engines already warmed up, with Hedley Ackroyd's machine out in front and the three flights arranged in a V behind him.

'Just far enough away from each other so they can't hit each other's backwash,' Josh said knowledgeably.

Hedley lined up his men and someone made a speech, then they climbed into their machines and the engines were started up. The air was full of noise and the smell of hot oil, then a red Very light soared into the air and Hedley's machine moved forward. Behind it, all the others moved too, until they were all rolling and lurching across the grass. One by one they became airborne and grew smaller until they were merely a line of dots heading towards the east.

Riding towards the station in the taxi, they all sat in silence. A strand of Philippa's hair had come down and was hanging over her ear, and Rachel's hat was no longer quite straight. But they seemed unaware of the disorder and stared in front of them with stricken looks on their faces.

On the little jump seat opposite, Josh studied their distress. 'They were flying SEs,' he said helpfully. 'They're supposed to be the best aeroplanes there are.'

six

It seemed to Josh that he had hardly been back at school more than a day or two when the newspapers were full of a huge new German attack on the Somme.

Helped by the dense fog, the Germans had overrun the forward British positions almost unobserved and at once the line had begun to crumble. The British troops, most of them conscripts, had been taught how to hold a trench and how to attack it but had no idea what to do when they were faced with what they had been fighting for four years to achieve – open warfare. Doing the only thing they could think of, they retreated and, watching the newspapers, it seemed to the numbed Josh that the Allied armies in France were in desperate trouble and he even began to wonder when the Kaiser would arrive in London to be proclaimed Emperor of the British.

As spring advanced into summer, however, the fears subsided a little because the push seemed to be crumbling and there appeared to be an undercurrent of hope that the war might even finish the following year. The Germans, it seemed, had finally become aware that their advance was doomed and were making preparations to retire on their own lines of communication. In the Middle East, with Allenby in hot pursuit, the British, Australian and New Zealand forces were pushing rapidly north from Jerusalem and the Turkish empire was clearly in danger of crumbling. Austria and Bulgaria were tottering and as the old man at Braxby huddled over his *Times* a letter arrived from Berlin via Holland which indicated that Germany's days were numbered. Helen had recovered from her husband's death. The letter was strangely devoid of the affection she had previously shown but it seemed she was still in need of contact with her parents, with England, with Braxby, with her roots.

She described how difficult it was to buy food, and how in the poorer quarters of Berlin the children were grey with under-nourishment. Queues were everywhere, the colourless women, bent with misery, crowding for hours in the hope of finding something. Sugar was necessary to make the ersatz-kaffee drinkable and to think of milk or eggs was ridiculous. Half of Berlin, she claimed, was subsisting on a greenish pulp which was the indigestible ruins of potatoes spoiled by the winter.

Ellis Ackroyd returned to Braxby, recovered from his wounds but suddenly old and slow and uncertain. In May Josh heard that Micah Love had been wounded and Rachel vanished to London, and a few weeks later, with the summer heat arriving, he turned up in Braxby in his yellow roadster, driving with the hand brake and the hand throttle, because his left leg was stiff where it had been hit by a bullet over St Quentin. Contrary to everybody's expectations, he wasn't the slightest bit depressed by the continual retreat in France.

'It's all under control,' he announced. 'All the Germans have done is advance into a sack. No reserves on our side have been committed, and we have absolute command in the air.'

Two days later he and Rachel announced their engagement and everybody went round to the Suttons to celebrate. Rachel had a new ring on her finger and a smug look on her face, but it was clear her sister was not to be outdone because she was letting it be known that she too was expecting to sport a diamond as soon as Hedley Ackroyd came home.

Toasts were drunk to the happy couple and another one, a little more subdued, to Helen in Berlin. Afterwards, Robert drew his father on one side. His manner was hesitant and uncertain.

'I'm having a bit of trouble, Father,' he announced.

'What sort of trouble?' the old man asked warily.

'You have no idea?'

The old man eyed his son. It was sad, he thought, that it was possible to dislike one's own offspring. What strange genes in his own family and the family of his wife, both of which had always seemed entirely normal, had produced Robert, he couldn't think. It couldn't surely, he felt, be his environment or his upbringing, because Dabney, Jane and Helen had had exactly the same and had turned out quite differently. Perhaps somewhere, with Robert, the oldest child, they had gone wrong and, profiting by their errors, had made no mistakes with their other children.

Yet he didn't think so. They had never been conscious of behaving differently with their first-born and he could only put it down to the fact that, somewhere in the past, there had been the facets of character which Robert showed, tucked away out of sight in the background of both of them and in Robert they had met and made him what he was. He was a moral coward; he was shallow; he was devious and untrustworthy; he was mean and money-grubbing; and he was totally without the humour with which the rest of them all seemed to be blessed. Again and again, the old man had told himself he would change but he never had. He was ambitious and energetic, yet not totally honest, and he'd heard rumours that he'd even been warned about hoarding food at a time when food was short. He had no proof, but it was entirely in keeping and now he knew that Robert's character had produced some new crisis.

'I haven't the foggiest what it's all about,' he snapped. 'Unless, as I suspect, you've been working a fiddle with your income tax.'

Robert gave the old man a sour look. 'It's not my income tax,' he said. 'That's all in order. It's something rather more than that.'

'Go on,' the old man said coldly.

'Well, I suspect that you're well aware of what it might be. You saw me in London at Claridge's with Daisy Balmael – '

'Ah! And you want me to be a party to your half-baked liaison?'

'Elfrida doesn't know.'

'And since most of your money is hers, you're not anxious that she should.'

'Look, Father, if you're going to be difficult – '

'You've got a nerve to tell *me* not to be difficult!' the old man snapped back spiritedly. 'You've always been a gutless character, Robert! When you decided to marry Elfrida, I was entirely against it because she was a Cosgro and I've never trusted a Cosgro. However, she's turned out a damn sight better than you deserve and, as far as she's concerned, I'm prepared to eat my words. However, *you* threw in your lot with Walter Cosgro and even changed your name to theirs and rejected ours completely. So don't tell *me* not to be difficult!'

For a while, Robert stared angrily at his father, and he seemed almost about to turn and stalk from the room, but he swallowed his pride and drew a deep breath.

'Balmael's found out about his wife,' he said.

'And?'

'He's suing for divorce.'

The old man studied his son. Robert, he well knew, wouldn't want to be involved. If Lord Balmael divorced his wife it would undoubtedly end with problems for Robert, perhaps even a divorce of his own, something he would never want because it would put him beyond the reach of the Cosgro money.

'I suppose it doesn't surprise me,' he said. 'What does Balmael intend?'

'He's cited George Cotton-Sampson and a feller in the Guards – John Lecquerier. He's on the point of citing me also.'

'And you've denied it, of course?' The old man studied his son with contempt. 'You never had the courage of your convictions, did you, Robert?'

'I'm thinking of Elfrida and the children.'

'Pity you didn't do that earlier. When you push your fingers into other people's pies, you must expect them to emerge sticky!'

'Dammit, Father, there were others!' Robert was using the fact as an excuse and his father rounded on him.

'I knew there were and I dare bet you did, too. All I can say is that you're not very particular. What are you after, Robert?'

'I've told Balmael's solicitor I'm not involved. I said I was with you that weekend. The *whole* weekend. It was the weekend we went to watch the tank demonstration at Hatfield Park. There's plenty of proof that I was there and your word would be good enough to get me off the hook.'

The old man's eyes were cold. 'I don't normally tell lies,' he said.

They began to argue, their tempers mounting. It was the old man's feeling that he should ignore the request, but for once he sensed he had a grip on his slippery son.

'Look, Father,' Robert blurted out. 'We've done well with the tanks. We churned out steel and armour plate in enormous quantities. I think we've helped the army.'

The old man exploded. 'Don't tell me you did it merely for your country!' he snapped. 'You did it for money! You've been well paid and you and Walter Cosgro have made a fortune out of them – as you did out of those shoddy uniforms you supplied for the New Armies in 1914.'

Robert stopped dead and drew another deep breath. 'Lloyd George has indicated that he intends to see I get something for it.'

'A title?'

Robert paused, his face red, then he nodded. 'Yes.'

'How much did it cost you?'

'Titles aren't bought.'

'A contribution to a political party goes a long way.'

'I can't discuss it, Father. You know I can't.'

'Doubtless, because of your steel and uniforms, they considered they could let you have it more cheaply than some of the other rogues who're getting them.'

'Dammit, Father – !'

'Don't you "dammit" me, Robert,' the old man blazed. 'You're in no position to! I'll tell Balmael's solicitor you were with me, if you wish. But it won't be for *your* sake! It'll be for Elfrida and the children! The credit they bestow on you's not due to you, but to Elfrida, who's probably the best Cosgro it's ever been my pleasure to meet. If it'll save her some unhappiness, then I'll tell Balmael's solicitor what you wish me to say. But certainly not to save your bloody Lady Balmael. I don't give a damn for her, and Balmael's well shot of her. He's a soldier serving in France and he had a right to expect honesty from his wife. As for you, in return for not involving you with the Balmael divorce case, I'll expect you to behave yourself in future.'

There was a look of relief on Robert's face. 'Of course, Father.'

The old man didn't believe him for a moment but at least it might make him more careful.

'The slightest suggestion that you're back with this woman – or any other woman, for that matter – and I'm prepared to let it be known that I was wrong and you weren't with me.'

'You could hardly do that, Father,' Robert said comfortably. 'It would seem like perjury.'

The old man eyed him coldly. 'You think of everything, don't you, Robert? But you forget, old men are excused a great deal. I could say age had made me confused and they'd accept it. However – '

The relieved look on his son's face changed.

'However,' the old man went on maliciously, 'I'd better make it clear before that smug look on your face becomes a smile, that I'm not doing it for nothing.'

Robert's face became wary again. 'What are you getting at, Father?'

'I've told you I don't give a damn for you. So that, in return, you'll do something for me. You'll renounce all claims on this house.'

'What?' Robert's face grew red. 'I'm damned if I'll do that, Father!'

The old man faced him coolly. 'It's your choice.'

'Dammit, Father, this is my home! This is where my roots lie.'

'You transferred your roots long since to Cosgro territory. You have everything you need. Dabney has precious little.'

'I can't do it, Father.'

'Then I'm damned if I'll swear you were with me in London.'

'Father, this house and its contents, everything the family possesses, belong both to me and to Dabney.'

'It's not so long ago when you were saying it *all* belonged to you.'

'That wasn't my intention.'

'I know damn well it was! But never mind, I've decided what I want to do. I shall make a new will.'

Robert hesitated then he nodded. The old man eyed him.

'I haven't finished, Robert,' he said slowly. 'I know what's in your mind. You're thinking it shouldn't be difficult to overturn it, to suggest I'm not of sound mind. You will argue that it should be shared between you and Dabney, then you'll use your ill-gotten wealth to push Dabney out. No, Robert – ' the old man smiled ' – it won't be like that. You'll come with me to my solicitors to *witness* the will. Then it must be accepted that you agreed with it.'

Robert stared at his father, his eyes glowing angrily. But he had no choice.

The old man turned away, as if he had had enough of his son. 'I'll make the arrangements and I shall inform you when to be present. And you *will* be present. Nothing will stand in your way. Neither your money or the government or Lloyd George or the Lord God Almighty. If you are not there, I shall assume you've backed out of the deal and I shall go immediately to Balmael's solicitors. Is that understood?'

Robert swallowed. 'Yes, Father. I understand.'

The old man headed for the door. 'Then I think we had better join the others before they wonder what's happening.'

The following morning when Josh arrived, he found his grandfather in a strange subdued mood, making notes on a sheet of paper.

'What are you doing, Grandpa?' he asked.

'Making me will.'

'Why?'

'Because eventually I shall die, and you make wills so that you can go on bossing your family about after you're dead.'

The boy looked puzzled and the old man gestured. 'This house,' he said. 'Everything in it. That – that – and that – ' the old hand with its gnarled fingers gestured at the silverware, the statuettes, the spears, the assegais, the banners and the strange weapons which had been collected during a

311

lifetime of fighting ' – I want them to go to your father and then to you.'

'Why?'

'Because they're no use to your Uncle Robert. He doesn't understand them. Your father does. I think *you* will. I want them to go to someone who won't merely stick them in the attic or throw them away.'

'I'll have 'em, Grandpa! I'll look after 'em!' The boy paused. 'Grandpa, do you think we're winning the war?'

'It begins to look like it.'

'When will it end?'

'Next year. 1919. 1920. Something like that.'

'Could it end before?'

'Could. We seem to have 'em on the run. Why?'

'I don't think I'll be old enough to join the army before it's over.'

'Your time will come, my boy. There are always enough cads in the world to start decent people killing each other. Trotsky's one. Ludendorff's one. Horatio Bottomley's one. Come to that, your Uncle Robert's one. If we had a cads' team for 1918, he'd be captain.'

'Why, Grandpa?'

'Never mind why. Just write him down.' The old man tore off a sheet of paper from the pad he was holding. 'Put 'em down, boy. Cads' Team, 1918. R Cosgro-Goff, captain.'

The boy did as he was told and looked up.

'Who's vice-captain, Grandpa?'

'Bottomley, I think. He's another who – ' the old man stopped, coughed and left it at that. 'Bottomley for vice-captain.'

'Better cad than the Kaiser?'

'I think so. The Kaiser's lost his form. Bit pathetic, now, I think. He's well down the list.'

'Hindenburg?'

'Oh, yes. Ludendorff, too. Better put down Henry Wilson. He's still not as shiny white as he ought to be. Lloyd George, too. Then Lenin and Trotsky and that lot.'

'That's only eight.'

'Well, what about Ferdinand of Bulgaria. He'd do. He came into the war hoping to get something out of it. You could also put down this Turkish Johnny, Kemal Whatever-his-name-is.'

The boy looked at what he'd written.

> *R Cosgro-Goff* (captain)
> *H Bottomley* (vice-captain)
> *Kaiser W*
> *Hindenberg*
> *Lewdendorff*
> *H Wilson*
> *Ferdinand*
> *Kemal?*
> *Lenin*
> *Trotski*

'That's only ten, Grandpa. We need one more.'

'Put down A N Other. I'm sure we'll find someone. There are plenty of 'em about.'

The boy studied the names for a moment. 'I'm glad we've never had to put down Father's name,' he said.

'Oh, no!' The old man smiled. 'Not your father's. He wouldn't have a chance in a team like that. Not even at the bottom of the list.'

The boy thought for a moment. 'I wonder what he's doing,' he said.

seven

It seemed to Dabney that the war in the Middle East was as good as won.

The Australians and the New Zealanders were always difficult and their antics in Cairo were already a legend, but, like the men of the Yeomanry and the sowars of the Indian cavalry, most of them were farmers who were unafraid of a wide countryside and had grown up among horses since childhood. Their roots were deep in the soil and they were sufficiently good to have been issued with swords.

At first they were inclined to be derisive about them but they'd gone into action at Beersheba with nothing in their fists but bayonets, and the sword, in spite of what they said, had a tremendous moral effect both on them and on the enemy. The result inevitably was that there were officers who began to insist once more that mechanical contrivances like the tank and the aeroplane would never take the place of a man on a horse armed with a sabre but, certainly, even if horsed cavalry was having its last fling, it was having it under Allenby in a resounding crescendo that had never been seen since it had first arrived with a shock that upset all calculations on its first battlefield two thousand years before. Beersheba had set the pattern and had raised the curtain on a magnificent reappearance. The Arabs had risen in revolt under a man called Lawrence who was disliked at headquarters because he preferred Arab dress and sandals to uniform, but Allenby had seen the possibilities and Dabney was expecting at any moment to see the campaign brought to a conclusion.

He was still making his preparations when, to his surprise, Hedley Ackroyd turned up, a lieutenant-colonel running a bomber wing of the new Royal Air Force, with the news that he and Philippa were engaged.

'They offered me the choice of a fighter squadron in France or a bomber wing out here,' he said. 'The Field Marshal's advice was succinct: Take the wing.'

There was a rash of promotions and Dabney became an acting major general. Fresh bombers had also been flown out for Hedley Ackroyd, and, with the Indian cavalry regiments all armed with sword or lance, the cavalry were cavalry again in the true sense of the word.

The heat was searing and they were plagued by mosquitoes, centipedes and spiders, to say nothing of malaria and sandfly fever which had turned them all into ghosts poor as crows, their horses gaunt from picking up sand with their scanty feed. But they were well led and Dabney's troopers were splendid men, tall, strong, independent and full of spirit. Their first reaction to him had been one of wariness because they had no love for British generals. But everything went well from the day when Dabney, wearing only breeches and shirt and riding alone, without any badges of rank, had found a group of them watering horses at a stream. Believing in making contact quickly, he had stopped to talk to them.

'What are you lot?' he asked.

One of the Australians, tall, lean and leathery-skinned, eyed him up and down, alerted by his English accent.

'I'm what's known as a bleedin' Light 'Orseman, cobber,' he said sharply. 'What might you be?'

Dabney grinned at the reply. 'I'm what's known as a bleedin' general,' he said.

As he clattered away, he heard a shout of laughter go up behind him and the following afternoon, reviewing a regiment of Mounted Rifles, he became aware that the leading horseman was the Australian of the day before and that he was carrying a banner on which was printed 'Goff's Bleeding Own.'

Apart from their tendency to wear shorts – and hot men on hot horses with bare knees rubbed raw on horses' flanks led to sores and blood poisoning – they gave him remarkably little trouble. The old hunting maxim, 'Care for your horse in the stable as if he were worth five hundred pounds and ride him in the field as if he were not worth half a crown', was still a good one and Dabney taught them that to a horse rubbing down was as massage was to a man, and eventually he had them so they would spend long over the regulation time at the job and walk miles for the chance of acquiring a bundle of green fodder.

For the most part they accepted his demands without a murmur because he had arrived with Allenby, and Allenby had gone through the camps like a strong reviving wind when everybody was discouraged and cynical. During the long hot months of the summer the army had languished, its problems chiefly medical, but now they were pushing north in an extraordinarily bold conception involving the largest mass of cavalry since Napoleon.

Deception was practised with wireless traffic, thousands of dummy horses made of canvas, and men marching during the day and counter-marching at night to give the impression of a vast mass movement. False headquarters were built and the Arabs under Lawrence spread wrong information, while Hedley Ackroyd's bomber wing bombarded the Turks from the air with propaganda leaflets which had the effect of setting thousands of deserters on the move south.

By the beginning of September they were well on their way, hard, lean Australians and New Zealanders alongside dark-faced Indians, British Yeomanry and the picturesque French Spahis. Overhead, Bristol fighters and an occasional Handley Page dropped bombs to the north. As the artillery barrage fell on the startled Turks, the infantry rose and began to advance. Within minutes a breach had been made and a message came back to where Dabney was waiting with his brigade. As he waved his arm, the trumpets shrilled and, led by 'Goff's Bleeding Own', thousands of horsemen began to thunder through the gap. In ten minutes they were well beyond the Turkish line and heading up the coast. Within an hour two divisions of mounted men had poured through the break and were thundering across the plain towards Megiddo and Caesarea. Within two days they had captured Nazareth, the roads and defiles of the mountains encumbered with guns, wagons, motor lorries and all sorts of stores all moving north. Two Turkish armies had vanished in thirty-six hours.

There was no stopping. Pressing on, Hedley Ackroyd's bombers caught the Turks in a ravine. Truck drivers jumped out, leaving engines running so that the vehicles ran into the tail of the artillery in front, and the guns were carried on into the transport wagons, until finally an accumulation of dead horses and wreckage brought the avalanche to a stop. It took them days to extricate the guns and burn the carts.

North of the Sea of Galilee the Turks were routed again and the great column continued to stream northwards, the light armoured cars in the van, the cavalry moving at a speed that combined haste with the preservation of horseflesh – trotting twenty minutes, walking twenty and halted five. The cavalry had come into its own again and it was a paradox that a war which had seen them reduced to virtual impotence was also seeing one of the greatest cavalry campaigns in history as Allenby's men advanced from the frontiers of Egypt towards the borders of Turkey in a movement that was classic in conception and superb in execution.

Outside Haifa, the advance came to a stop as they blundered into quicksand and Dabney came across Australians struggling on foot to drag their mounts clear, filling the air as they did so with a tremendous barrage of oaths. The Turks had to be given no chance to consolidate, however, and, galloping across the front of his Indian regiments, he led them past the cursing Australians into the city centre. Fire was coming from roofs and corners and here and there strong points had been set up. A few horses crashed to the ground but there was no stopping them.

As they galloped down the dusty street between the mud-coloured houses, a Turkish officer in a fez and waving a sabre hurtled from a side street directly in front. Dabney's horse came to a tearing halt, ploughing up the dust, forefeet extended, muscles bunched. Before the parry was completed, Dabney's right leg was urging, the rein caressing. The Turk came round to his offside and lunged, but the sword was still in the air as Dabney bore in with his blade and the Turk rolled over the tail of his horse to disappear among the flying hooves.

As the Turkish soldiers rose to meet them, they were knocked over by the galloping horses and speared as they tried to run. Up ahead the sky was full of brown smoke where Hedley Ackroyd's bombers were pulverising the reserves near the Jordan.

Their next action was at Shehba when the Indians, light, spare men with an advantage of weight over their white comrades, charged at full gallop a Turkish line established behind a cactus hedge. The red swords and lances showed how many they had killed. At El Affule, they captured seventy-five Germans, two hundred Turks, ten engines, a hundred lorries and three aircraft, marching seventy miles in thirty-four hours for a loss of only twenty-six foundered horses. It was a stupendous feat, most of the march being made in the cool of the Palestinian early light. At Jenin, the

Australians burst into the town and found a store of champagne which they proceeded to demolish before a guard could be put on it, while men, women and children, screaming 'Arab, Arab' to let them know they weren't Turks, ran before them to fling themselves on the stores of food, clothing and equipment the Turks had left behind.

There was charge after charge as they moved north. In one, owing to the number of lamed horses that had dropped out after climbing a steep ridge, there were only fifteen mounted men, yet they routed the defence. The fleeing Turks were butchered in the desert by the Arabs and the following horsemen heard shrieks in the night and saw the vultures that were always in the air, gathering ahead of them where they'd been caught.

Acre fell, then Amman. At Nahr Barbar, the charge was delivered by Australians, Spahis and Chasseurs d'Afrique. At Irbid, there was a disaster as bad as Balaclava when the Indians, facing five thousand Turks, failed to pull off their charge. Deraa was in flames when they arrived, with Turks, stripped of every scrap of clothing they possessed, lying dead in the streets among the litter of smashed equipment, burned documents and ruined machinery.

Damascus was next. Lawrence's men were the first to reach the city and, as Dabney led his men in, the place was in a state of anarchy, with the Arabs arguing and squabbling among themselves, the place mismanaged and containing a ghastly hospital with every disease known to man within its walls and not a scrap of bandage, drug or disinfectant.

There were Turkish troops to the north, however, still capable of fighting, and the farther they retreated, the worse became the difficulties for their pursuers. There was an increase in malaria, to which was added the deadly Spanish influenza which was sweeping a world undernourished and tired after a long war. Aleppo was now the target and then the Turkish border. Tyre, Sidon and Beirut were occupied and the cavalry moved north yet again.

The shock actions continued, the losses in horses always higher than the losses in men, because they were sacrificed to stop the Turks escaping. Almost every charge was delivered in extended formation and forced home at a gallop.

His command reduced by a worrying sick list, Dabney pushed on in hot, turgid weather. Though ordered to halt, he pressed forward until they heard Aleppo had fallen. The war seemed to be virtually over in the Middle East but even as he prepared to halt, instructions came to press on again.

By this time one of his brigadiers was sick and the weary horses were staggering, the tired troopers gaunt, their faces burnt almost black by the sun. Half the time they slept in the saddle, snatching food when they could. When they halted they were almost too weary to pull themselves back on to their stumbling mounts and often fell asleep standing alongside them.

Called back to a staff conference, Dabney found himself sitting next to Hedley Ackroyd.

'An attempt's being made to stand at Ain 'Aalab,' the corps commander informed them. 'It's up to you people to see they don't. Their right flank rests on the river and their left on the hills. The only way past them's through the middle, and the wells in the area have been destroyed.'

With the surviving wells beyond the Ain 'Aalab line, the cavalry was in trouble. The area was surrounded by a tangled mass of rocky hills, steep, seamed with deep wadis, often impenetrable and entirely without water. Not a tree broke the skyline and the sun was beating down like a brass gong on a plain devoid of shade. Two lines of defences had been constructed to add to the obstacles provided by nature, and Ain 'Aalab was surrounded by freshly-dug trenches.

The town itself was a drab little settlement that hardly seemed worth attacking, but it owed its importance to the wells to the north and to the fact that it lay on the railway line that ran into the heart of Turkey. As the infantry began to arrive, the cavalry were deployed to the west to keep the Turks busy. Once the Turks were forced to withdraw, it would be the turn once more of the horsemen.

Waiting as Hedley Ackroyd's bombers roared overhead, Dabney made his plans carefully. The Turks were expecting the attack to come from the south because a small squadron of Goff's Bleeding Own had been fired on, leaving one of their horses dead as they fled, its saddlebags containing the information that the Turks sought as to the direction of the attack. Unknown to the Turks, however, the documents they had captured had been specially prepared, and as the bombardment started, Dabney was standing on top of a ridge watching them face the wrong way.

His men were feeding their horses just behind. The heat, the flies and thirst were driving everybody crazy and they were all dreaming in the stony wadis of long cool beers. As the message to move forward arrived, they spent a back-breaking two hours pushing from one boulder-strewn slope to the next, until they could see Ain 'Aalab, with its shelter and precious water, three miles away across the plain in front. Though the infantry had made progress, the inner line of defences still held and it would soon be dark enough to cheat them of their prize.

As Dabney watched the dismounted troopers working their way forward over the broken terrain the corps commander appeared behind him, scrambling up to the ridge. He grinned as Dabney turned.

'I think we're going to have to make an all-out assault,' he said. 'I'm going to use your people to take the town before dark.'

As he left, he made it clear he was expecting a dismounted action, but it occurred to Dabney that, with darkness almost upon them and little more than an hour of daylight left, there was barely time.

'Saddle up,' he ordered. 'Have the Jawarlis and the Baratpore Lancers brought forward and assembled south of the track.'

As the men scrambled to the saddles, he galloped forward with the two commanding officers, his staff, trumpeter and orderlies to look for an assembly area that couldn't be overlooked and shelled from Ain 'Aalab. His horses were already in poor condition and it was essential that they shouldn't be panicked by enemy shelling. His mind was full of questions. He knew they had to move quickly but what if the Turkish trenches were protected by wire? Would it result in the same chaos that had befallen the 19th Lancers on the Somme? Would it end in a welter of blood and struggling horses and men? In front of them, he knew, there was a wadi and they had no idea whether its banks were steep or the wadi as deep as some of those they had crossed on their night march. He'd read of Waterloo, had even seen his own grandfather's letters written from Paris after that campaign, telling of the disaster that had befallen the French cavalry at the sunken road of Ohain. Could he expect the same disaster, with his wave of horsemen crashing to ruin in a wild tangle of broken legs, screaming horses and shattered bodies? His first experience of war had been at Omdurman and that, too, had come close to disaster in a ditch.

There was no time for a detailed reconnaissance or to bring up machine guns or artillery so he ordered the nearest batteries of horse artillery to do what they could to help. The artillerymen limbered up and galloped forward and, with their guns gouging great scars in the dusty earth, swung round to face the enemy. Within a minute the first round crashed out.

'Right,' Dabney said to the commanding officers of the two waiting regiments. 'Now's your chance! Off you go!'

As the Indian brigade, under the command of the senior colonel, trotted forward in column of squadrons, they looked a splendid sight, sitting bolt upright with their lances and swords, the dark faces tense and expectant. But their reputation was founded mainly on ceremonial duties and they were by no means as good as they looked. As they swept out of their assembly area, they were spotted at once by the machine guns on the hills and, as the enemy artillery joined in, shells began to explode among the moving horsemen.

As the advance slowed and halted and the groups of dark-faced horsemen began to scatter across the plains, the Turkish guns lifted and shells began to fall among the Australians in the rear. Spurring his horse, Dabney was just moving down from the ridge when the Australian brigade major appeared. He had blood on his uniform and was bare-headed.

'The brigadier's down, sir,' he said.

Glancing across the plain, Dabney saw that evening was already on them and that any hesitation would allow the Turks to retreat through the wells, destroying them as they went. Making up his mind, he galloped to where the Australians were waiting, sending the brigade major ahead.

'Bring 'em on,' he said.

As the Australians halted again, a column of orderly confusion with tossing heads, he took up his position in front of them.

'Troops into line!'

The evolution was mechanical, carried out in silence and without undue haste. There was a thudding of hooves on the flank as a horse plunged, and a few curses. Each troop, as though on a ceremonial parade, swung round on a pivot to front the enemy.

Calling the colonels to him, Dabney told them his plans. 'We go straight in,' he said. 'No waiting. No hesitating. Understand?'

The Australians nodded. One regiment was armed with swords, the other only with bayonets, their rifles still in the leather buckets.

Placing himself at the head of Goff's Bleeding Own, Dabney waited for the order to draw swords, then waved his arm and kicked at his horse's flanks. The whole line immediately swept into a gallop behind him. As they appeared, the Turkish artillery switched to the new target, but the Australians were moving too fast and the shells exploded behind them. As the machine guns opened up, a few horses fell, but the horse artillery had swung round on the flank and begun to hammer the strong points on the hills. In a cheering mass, the Australians thundered forward, scooping up the hesitant Indians as they passed, to surge on towards the Turkish trenches. The short Eastern twilight had almost ended and the flash of rifles and artillery and exploding shrapnel filled the dusk. Above the charging mass of cheering horsemen there was an enormous cloud of yellow dust that reduced visibility and hid what lay ahead.

It was almost dark now and Dabney could barely see the men thundering along behind him. By the grace of God, there was no wire and as he reached the Turkish trench, he could see no alternative but to put spurs to his mount and leap the obstacle like a steeple-chaser. The men behind him were as used to horses and riding as he was and they followed suit enthusiastically in a wave of leaping animals, then, without waiting for orders, sprang from the saddle and lunged into the trench with sword and bayonet. The increasing darkness was filled with shouts and screams, while the Indian regiments rode up and down on the flanks, spearing any Turk who managed to scramble to safety. Within five minutes the position was in their hands, and the Australian officers were rallying their men.

'Into the town,' Dabney ordered. 'Take as many prisoners as possible!'

With Goff's Bleeding Own leading the way through the darkness, they swept through the streets. Scattered bunches of Turks tried to stop them, but the horsemen rode them down, driving them like partridges and keeping them on the run. As they rallied and began to reform, they were half-blinded as great gouts of flame leapt skyward.

'They're blowing up the dumps,' Dabney yelled. 'Keep going! Keep going! Get the wells!'

As the Australians swept on, he gave orders for the Indians to chase the Turks from the town and, leaving the Baratpores and Jawarlis trotting up and down looking for victims, he galloped after his leading elements.

The railway station was on fire, the flames lighting up the darkness and silhouetting the running figures of Turks as they fled into the houses and narrow streets. They had achieved their object. Ain 'Aalab was securely in their hands; and it had been achieved solely by cavalry action, even if not by traditional cavalry methods. There seemed to be dead men, dead horses and shell holes everywhere. Already, great hordes of prisoners were being rounded up and it was clear they had captured a vast quantity of guns, stores and animals. Riding forward to rally the Australians, Dabney found them already grouping together, but the Turks, knowing the importance of the wells, had established themselves behind a wall and, as he galloped up, a machine gun began to fire. A horse went down with a crash and two men rolled from their saddles. Immediately the Australians began to scatter.

Turning, Dabney saw the machine gun and the dark faces of the Turks behind it and, without thinking, he clapped his spurs into his jaded horse's flanks. As he moved forward, the startled Australians recovered from their surprise and began to swing round to form a line. Their faces, in the dancing red of the fires, were elated, lean, leathery, and hungry for victory.

As he watched the flickering flame of the machine gun, Dabney felt something crash against his left leg that almost tore him from the saddle. An over-excited trooper, bursting away from the swirling mass, urged his horse into a gallop. As it reached the wall it hesitated then, trying to leap, faltered, straddled the wall, flinging its rider from the saddle, and crashed down on top of the machine gun.

Scrambling from beneath the kicking hooves, the Turks snatched at rifles as the Australians arrived.

'Come on, the Bleeders!' someone yelled.

As they sorted themselves out into a surging wave of tossing heads, flowing manes and fierce Australian faces under wide-brimmed hats, Dabney, dizzy with the pain in his leg, spurred in front to give them the line.

Struggling, with his frantic horse, he raised his sword and shouted – 'Troops into line! Charge!' – and the flood of horse-men crashed on to scatter the Turks who turned tail and began to bolt into the darkness.

The war was clearly almost over. They all knew it. It became clearer every day and, in France, the Germans – faced now with a fresh new army from America – were in full retreat.

The attacks were coming now in sharp succession, one after the other in different parts of the front, so there was no chance for them to move reserves. The huge salient at Verdun had been pinched out and the line had now reached the Ardennes so that Paris was no longer in danger. The old obstacle, the mud, continued to hold up the advance, but, suddenly, the front in Salonika blazed into life and the Bulgarians were suing for peace because the Germans were too heavily involved to plug the hole that had been made and there were rumours of a budding revolution in Germany.

It was suddenly beginning to look as if the end of the war was going to take them all by surprise. Rachel, who was intending to go back to Virginia with Micah Love and was already trying to cultivate a Southern drawl, had set her wedding for the middle of November but, with the Ottoman Empire collapsing and taking down with it the Austro-Hungarian edifice, it looked very much as though the end of the war was going to interrupt. People in Prague and Zagreb had gone to bed as subjects of the Habsburgs and awakened to find themselves independent, while the Czechs, the South Slavs, the Poles and the Rumanians became allies instead of enemies. Hungary broke away and, with the Austrians seeking an armistice, the Germans had found their rear wide open and the Allied armies preparing to advance into Southern Germany. At the end of October, the German fleet mutinied and within a day or two the Kaiser had abdicated.

'Thank God I managed to live to see the victory,' the Field Marshal said.

He had not been well for some time. Spanish flu had appeared in Europe and was said to be in epidemic proportions in London where people were collapsing in the streets. Schools and offices had been closed, there were swelling obituary columns in *The Times*, and the hospitals were so full ordinary patients couldn't be admitted. In Germany, people were said to be dying like flies.

Two of the older and more frail of the Ackroyds and a Goff cousin had gone, but Braxby seemed not to have been hard hit until the news came that Walter Cosgro had been struck down. With his wealth and the care he could summon in the shape of the best nurses and doctors in the country, they hadn't even thought he *could* die, but he had surprised them all by succumbing remarkably quickly, leaving Robert in complete charge of the vast business empire.

The armistice was signed two days before Rachel's wedding and on the 11th the guns stopped firing. Suddenly Europe was silent. After a brief flare-up of noisy celebration, the desolated lanes of Northern France became even more desolate under the heavy hand of winter.

It was Josh who brought the news. His school closed because of the influenza epidemic, he was at home, and he tore up on his bicycle and clattered through the echoing corridors to find his grandfather.

'Grandpa! Grandpa! It's over. The war's over!'

Immediately, the whole household flooded into the drawing room and champagne was opened and they all stood round in excited groups, uncertain what to say or think or do, because what it had been like to be at peace was almost forgotten after four years. The noise and the excitement tired the Field Marshal but he gave Josh a sovereign for being first with the news.

He watched the boy with a warm feeling of affection. Ever since 1914, he had been his constant companion, drawing on the old man's fund of experience, building knowledge in his mind for the future, just as his father, Dabney, had done. Already he believed in the Regiment, not with the blind faith of a man who saw nothing but ceremonial, to whom the colour of a saddle blanket was more important than the health of the horse and the man riding it, but because his heart was with it. His belief would be the one thing that would support him in adversity. He was barely old enough to understand it yet, but already his mind ran on the same lines as his father's. The Regiment was his religion after God, its sorrows and its triumphs his own. The successes they had scored at Vernhout and Mortigny in 1914 had brought him joy just as the disaster on the Somme had brought him sadness. He was set in the same mould as his father and his grandfather, and those forefathers who had fought at Waterloo, with Wolfe, and with Eyre Coote at Wandewash, and even beyond the Regiment's foundation.

As the Field Marshal stood in front of the library fire, deep in thought, a wave of sadness swept over him as he remembered why Josh had come, what the celebration had been about, and he tried to decide what, after four years of bloodshed and suffering, had been achieved. He crossed to the table to study the map. He had been told the influenza had left his heart weak and had been warned to take things easy but he preferred to go on as before rather than live out his life as a cabbage.

It was sad, he thought, that Helen could not be with them, sadder still that Karl-August was dead like his father, who had gone in 1916. But Jane had done well for herself and had two splendid daughters. Micah Love was an excellent fellow, part of the family by habit now and certainly by tradition, while Hedley was clearly a son-in-law they were going to be proud of. His sons? Robert? The old man pushed Robert hurriedly to the back of his mind. Robert was best forgotten, though by the grace of God, his sons, Aubrey and Claude, thanks to Elfrida, seemed to be turning out well. Dabney? Ah, Dabney!

It always pleased a man to see himself in his son and in Dabney the Field Marshal saw his own image, his own moods, his own beliefs, his own faiths. Dabney was brave without being stupid, with a courage that was tempered by common sense and a feeling for his men who, as always, were going to win the medals their commanding officer wore. 'It is the common soldier's blood that makes the general a great man.' It was something he'd heard from his father who had heard it before Waterloo, and it remained as true in 1918 as it had been then. A good officer was never a glory seeker. He was a man who did his duty with imagination but with care for his men's lives. And this kind of sense Dabney had to a large degree.

He was a thinking soldier and would go far. The Field Marshal had decided so in South Africa. He had heard it from Morby-Smith, who had been killed at the Graafberg. He had heard it from Ellesmere, from Haig, from French, from Allenby. His tenets were simple. He believed in preparation and deception, not in casualties. The old man gave a secret smile. The future lay with Dabney and with his son, Josh.

Rachel's wedding was like all weddings in Braxby, not a private affair but one which belonged to the whole village. Like Tyas Ackroyd's funeral, it attracted everybody, and since Micah Love had no immediate family present, the Field Marshal and his wife sat with Fleur and her children on the right of the church with the Ackroyds, while the other side was packed with Suttons from North Yorkshire and the Dales. Begged by Rachel to appear in full uniform, the Field Marshal walked into the church, a green, red and gold toy soldier, his legs stiff and brittle, his face pale, his eyes bright, two pink feverish spots on his cheeks. His wife by his side, he moved slowly, putting his feet down with care so that no one should realise that these days he could barely see them without the glasses he had no intention of wearing on this day of all days. He was well aware that he was growing frail but he was still straight, his head held high, his shoulders back, a stiff doll-like figure from another age.

A story in the *Yorkshire Post* had ensured that the village would be full of people. Although the war was over, the weeping had not yet stopped and the ceremonial had been kept to a minimum. A canon from York conducted the service because he was a distant relative and a grandson of the bishop who had married the Field Marshal himself. Micah Love's soft voice drawled the responses which were answered by Rachel in a whisper, then they all lined up, with the Field Marshal insisting on keeping well to the rear, for the procession out of church. Though the smiles were for the bride and groom, there was also a little subdued clapping when the Field Marshal appeared.

Legs aching, he endured the business of the reception, wondering all the time when he could get away from the uniforms and the morning coats and large hats. In her happiness, his wife's eyes were sparkling and she reminded him of the girl he had first met in America during the Civil War. Fleur stopped in front of him and kissed him. She had a tranquil expression that spoke of subdued fears now dispersed.

'It's over, my dear,' he said quietly. 'Thank God, it's all over,' and she knew he wasn't referring to the wedding.

Rachel hugged him and Jane kissed him but when he found himself close to Robert he studiously ignored him. Eventually, at John Sutton's prompting, Josh brought him a chair but he shook his head, trying to ignore the trembling in his weary legs.

'No, boy,' he barked. 'I'll stand through this at least.'

By the time the toasts had been drunk, however, he was longing to sit down and after a while he managed to slip away. But he was not unseen and, as he moved quietly down the corridors towards John Sutton's office, he heard a voice call.

Turning, he saw it was Josh, wearing his best suit, his hair plastered down across his head.

'Going for a bit of a sit-down,' the old man explained. 'Keep it to yourself, my boy.'

'Would you like a drink, Grandpa?'

The old man considered. 'Might be a good idea,' he said. 'Not champagne. Blows you up. See if you can get your Uncle John to give you a quiet whisky and soda for me. I'll be in his office.'

Three minutes later, the boy appeared with a glass, and the old man made himself comfortable.

On the wall was a calendar put out by a seed merchant and on the desk were spikes holding the bills for the farm. It was here that his son-in-law did his paper work and there was a deep leather armchair. Seating himself, he lit a cigar and leaned back to enjoy himself.

'Shall I stay with you, Grandpa?'

'No. You run off. Find your cousin, Aubrey. Not a bad chap for a Cosgro.'

'I don't mind staying.'

The old man eyed his grandson approvingly. 'Yes. Know that. But I'll probably fall asleep on you. Off you go.'

An hour later, after Micah Love and Rachel had disappeared for their honeymoon and everybody was looking for the Field Marshal, Josh was at the front door with Aubrey when one of the Ackroyd maids appeared on her bicycle from Braxby Manor. She carried a telegram.

'It's for the old gentleman,' she said.

'I know where he is,' Josh said. 'I'll take it to him.'

The old man had just started awake and was staring at his hands, aware for the first time of their near-transparency. Good God, he thought, no flesh on him anywhere these days! He was growing damned old! Fell asleep when he didn't want to. Forgot things. Eyes bad. Teeth going. But it still seemed only like yesterday when he'd been thundering down the North Valley at Balaclava after that ass, Cardigan. He found it hard to believe it was so long ago. Where had all the years gone?

With a bitter reflection that jerked at his sciatica, he thought of Robert, sitting at home throughout the whole bloody war, while everybody else was doing their bit. Robert was an ass. Robert was lazy. Robert was fat. Robert was a coward, a fornicator and probably even a crook. Thank God for Dabney, he thought. Pity he couldn't have been here today. He sniffed and knocked a tear from his cheek with a clumsy hand.

He was about to rise but his legs seemed to give way and he flopped back into the chair. God damn it, that confounded flu had knocked the stuffing out of him! He was still trying to pull himself together when Josh's face appeared round the door.

'Hello, young feller,' he said. 'What do you want?'

'Just wondered if you were awake, Grandpa. There's a letter for you.'

'For me? Well, you were right to bring it here instead of interrupting the party. Let's have it!'

Josh held out the envelope, and it was then that the old man realised it was a telegram and guessed what it contained. Who the devil could it be, he thought. The war was over and he had no one in France now.

Slitting the envelope with a gnarled thumb nail, he stared at the contents.

'...regret to inform you...'

He was puzzled and suddenly his heart started thumping inside his chest until it seemed it was going to burst.

'Grandpa, is something the matter?'

Only dimly, he heard Josh's voice, anxious now and concerned for him, and managed to wave a hand to indicate that he was all right. He looked again at the words on the sheet of buff-paper, still unable to comprehend. Someone must have made a mistake. Dabney wasn't in France. And, anyway, telegrams went to wives not to fathers.

He looked again at the paper in his hand and realised that someone at the War Office, remembering who he was, had been considerate enough to inform him, and that a similar telegram would be waiting for Fleur when she returned from the reception. Struggling to make sense out of what seemed madness, he read the telegram again.

'...regret to inform you that your son, Major-General DAR Goff, DSO, has died from wounds received during the fighting at Ain 'Aalab on October 30th.'

Suddenly it dawned on him what it meant and, even in his distress, he remembered Fleur and was concerned that someone should be with her when she returned home. But as he struggled for the door, things began to grow dark and he felt as if he were choking. He must loosen his collar. Let in the air. The light had grown strange and was becoming brighter...

'Not Dabney,' he managed to say. 'Not Dabney!'

He tried to read the telegram again. 'Let's have another look,' he mumbled, his heart pounding in a way that made him dizzy. 'Died of wounds...' It was true then. His son wouldn't be coming home. Never.

Only the tallest poppies were taken. Poor old Brosy. In his extremity of misery, he confused his son with Fleur's father, Brosy la Dell, who had died in his arms in Zululand forty years before. Then he stared at the letter again, puzzled, disbelieving, and the thing finally became clear. My son! My favourite! Oh, God, I think I'd like to die!

eight

Standing outside Braxby Manor, Josh watched in silence as the coffin was placed on the gun carriage and strapped in place. The day was bitterly cold and the rooks in the oaks were croaking their mournful calls into the blustery air. The sky was steely grey and the draughts moaned and whistled along the chilly corridors and through the hall.

It was almost beyond Josh's comprehension that, screwed down inside that squarish-looking box in front of him, lying on its back, beaky nose cutting the darkness like a scimitar, was all that remained of his grandfather.

It was as though the world had grown a little darker and, with his limited knowledge, he could only feel that it must have been like this when Queen Victoria had been laid to rest. Those who were left seemed curiously diminished by contrast.

He felt cold, yet he knew it wasn't the weather that made him feel chilled. It was because something had gone from his life. As long as he could remember he had regarded his Grandfather as God, and his grandparents as jointly running the world and everybody in it, with his parents administering the law somewhere just beneath, hearing everything, seeing everything, missing nothing, while his sister Chloe and himself, his cousins and aunts and uncles and various other relations hovered in the depths below. Now the very fountain-head of his life had been snatched away, because he was never going to see his father again either.

A letter had arrived by air from Hedley Ackroyd which had told them what had happened and, soon afterwards, one in Allenby's own hand which had stated that the action of the Indian and Australian cavalry had resulted in the fall of Ain 'Aalab and destroyed the last Turkish resistance, and that its success had been entirely due to Dabney's example. With them were a few ill-spelt letters from Goff's Bleeding Own and the men he had commanded, men not given to emotion who were trying to make clear what they felt.

The double loss had rocked Josh on his heels but, curiously, because he had seen so little of his father over the last four years, it was his grandfather's death that had shocked him most. He had loved his father but, deprived of his presence, he had instinctively transferred all his affection to the old man.

His grandfather had known everything, had experienced everything. He was wise with the wisdom of old age. But curiously, Josh had never ever expected him to disappear like this. He had come to regard him as part of his surroundings, confident that he would always be there.

That morning, he had written out his cads' team for the last time. He knew he would never do it again because it was too painful and reminded him too much of his grandfather. Without the old man's help, it had been a poor effort. He had felt reasonably safe with some of the names he had set down because they were still around but it had remained incomplete and, for safety, he had removed his Uncle Robert from the captaincy, feeling he should be given the benefit of the doubt without the old man to advise. Because his experience was insufficiently broad, he had also had to bring in two of the school bullies and leave the last place open.

Shivering a little, he watched the ceremony going on just outside the door. His grandmother, straight-backed and in mourning, was standing with his mother, behind them all the Suttons and the Cosgro-Goffs, except Aubrey, the new Lord Cosgro, who had sneaked forward to be near Josh.

'What are they doing?' he whispered.

'Securing it to the gun carriage.'

'Why?'

'So it won't fall off.'

With the Regiment in France, it had been difficult to raise an escort, but a field marshal was a field marshal and the Royal Horse Artillery had provided a gun carriage drawn by six horses in the charge of a sergeant and six men. They were New Army men and they wore khaki but, under the circumstances, it was agreed that the dead man wouldn't have minded. The 19th had managed to raise an officer, a sergeant, a bearer party and a dozen men from the depot, and had even managed to equip them with full dress uniform, rifle-green overalls, jackets with red plastrons, and schapkas with dyed horse-hair plumes. They were all newly-conscripted men but they had been drilled to the point of collapse and knew exactly what to do. The band of a Territorial battalion waited to one side, with a full company of the same battalion under the command of a York lawyer who was their officer.

The arrangements had troubled Josh as he had enquired anxiously about them.

'Will the band of the 19th be there?' he had asked his mother.

Her face pale with sorrow, she had answered him gently. 'No, darling. The war's only just over. They're using a Territorial band.'

'But he wanted the *regimental* band. He asked for it.'

'I think everyone's done their best and I think he'd approve, Josh.' Fleur's voice was quiet because she knew the boy's warm affection for the old soldier.

'What'll they play?'

'The Dead March in *Saul*, I expect.' Fleur was thinking that her own man had not had that privilege and lay buried in some sandy graveyard on the Turkish border. 'That's what they usually play.'

'He wanted them to play *Morning* from something or other. I can't remember it now. That's what he said.'

'I expect they'll play something fitting, darling.'

'He said if he couldn't have the band, he'd settle for two trumpeters from the Regiment to play Reveille and the Last Post. He said even that wouldn't really matter and that a violinist from the theatre in York would do.'

No one had taken any notice of him and now, deeply troubled, he watched the sergeant of the escort twitching the Union Jack into place over the coffin, with a feeling that somehow he had let down his grandfather and, through him, his father, too.

The red, white and blue of the flag looked garish in the grey light as the men of the 19th took their places behind the gun carriage, their rifles reversed. The officer moved in front of them, just ahead of the sergeant. He moved stiffly, his face pale and blank-looking.

The high scream of the commands lifted Josh's head and set the rooks cawing again. Curtains were drawn in the village for the passing of the cortège and doors had bows of black crêpe hanging from the knockers. Under the cold sky that silhouetted the hills above Brackdale, the carriages and cars took their place behind the marching men. Alongside his mother and grandmother, Josh felt the awfulness of the occasion, and tried to sit a little straighter.

The sound of muffled drums and brass instruments beat against his mind as the notes of the Dead March, carried away on the wind, were lost in the wide spaces of the Dales. The village street was lined with people and among them he noticed a few old men standing stiffly at attention. Some of them were shabby-looking but they wore medals on their chests and he knew they were old Clutchers who had managed to make their way to Braxby for the occasion. As the coffin moved past, hats tumbled like a small wave running up the street.

Balaclava! Shalipore! Ransi! The Wilderness! Yellow Tavern! Ashanti! Isandhlwana! Tel-el-Kebir! Chitral! Ulundi! Omdurman! Graafberg! The boy knew them all because he'd often sat in Tyas Ackroyd's pantry and recited them, the names of the battles where one of the Ackroyds had always followed the Field Marshal. They sounded to him like signal guns from an age of vanished armies.

He tried to imagine the old man as he had been at Balaclava but the only picture he could conjure up was as he had last seen him, stiff and old with veined cheeks and white whiskers wearing a rifle-green uniform that no longer fitted perfectly, accompanied by Tyas Ackroyd in a black jacket and green baize apron, as he had looked when he polished the silver.

The Rector was standing by the church gate as the procession came to a halt.

'I am the resurrection and the life saith the Lord; he that believeth in me, though he were dead, yet shall he live –'

While the boy was trying to work out this apparent paradox, they slid the coffin from the gun carriage on to the shoulders of the bearers. It was done in silence, though the boy could see the sergeant's lips moving and guessed he was whispering instructions.

The lesson was read by Ellis Ackroyd, a pale shadow of the ruddy-faced soldier Josh had known. There was moisture in his eyes and Josh realised that it was not only for the Field Marshal but also for his son, whom Ellis had followed to war.

The service over, by a miracle the bearer party got the coffin on to their shoulders again without dropping it and began to move out of the church to the graveside behind the

Rector, stumbling between the crooked gravestones to the corner where all the other Goffs were buried, one who had fought at Waterloo, others who had been at Quebec and Wandewash and Fontenoy and other long-forgotten battles. Josh followed unwillingly. He dreaded the graveside, remembering from Tyas Ackroyd's funeral the hollow sound as the handfuls of soil were tossed on to the coffin. The thought that the man in the grave would soon be covered by several feet of damp earth and that the grass and the flowers would eventually grow over him, and the trees wind their roots around him was all a little beyond him, but he was aware of a restriction in his chest and the effort he was making not to cry.

As they stopped, Goffs, Suttons and Ackroyds, all standing in an untidy group, the sergeant in command of the firing party got his men lined up on either side of the grave. As they filed round, one of the young soldiers slipped on the damp earth and Josh was quite certain he was going to disappear into the open grave before the coffin. Pink-faced and embarrassed, he managed to reach his place with nothing more than a glare from the sergeant.

As everybody moved forward, Josh sidled up with Aubrey to stand alongside Ellis Ackroyd and he noticed that with him were all the old men he'd seen in the village street, the straight gnarled-faced old men with big moustaches and medals on the breasts of their shabby suits. They were stiff, their faces like granite, and he tried to stand as still as they did as the coffin was lowered into the hole.

They'd managed to get a trumpeter from the 16th Lancers, the Scarlet Lancers, and he was wearing full uniform, blue overalls, red jacket with blue plastron, and the Lancers' shapka, licking and lapping at his lips, preparing himself. As the Rector's voice stopped, he lifted the silver instrument to his mouth.

The high plaintive notes cut across the air like whiplashes. Josh knew the difference between a good trumpeter and a bad one because his grandfather had often explained, had even made him listen when they were sounding at the barracks. This trumpeter was a good one, as if the Lancer regiments had found their very best for a man who was a field marshal and, above all, had ridden at Balaclava.

He remembered things his grandfather had said about the Last Post. Military funerals. Muffled drums and lonely graves in empty fields all over the world. Cavalrymen who'd gone ahead. Notes of loneliness and the exile of men far from home. As he fought to hold back the tears, he noticed that the old men alongside him were stiffer than ever, their faces bleak, their mouths taut as they listened. 'A trumpet can play puck with your inside,' his grandfather had once said, and as he saw a tear steal out of Ellis Ackroyd's eye and trickle down his cheek, Josh knew that it was playing puck with at least one man there that day.

When it was all over, Josh requested permission to remain behind. His mother gave him a curious look but she didn't object. She knew how attached he had been to the old man and he was old enough now to know what he was doing. As the cars drove off and the gun carriage clattered away, he stood with Aubrey by the lych gate of the church, two boys uncomfortable in their best suits, their hair plastered down in spikes.

There were things to do. Josh had thought about his problem for a long time before putting it to Aubrey. Somehow, he felt, the adults had betrayed the two dead men. It had not been as his grandfather had suggested. They had done the thing as they'd pleased and hadn't bothered to consult him, the only one, he felt, who knew what the dead man had wanted.

As the Rector disappeared and the lane emptied, he looked at Aubrey. Good old Auby, he thought warmly. It hadn't made any difference, his becoming a lord. He was still a little shy and a little overweight, and still anxious to be friendly with the younger, more forceful Josh.

'There were things he wanted that weren't done,' Josh said, faintly self-important. 'I knew exactly what he asked for, but when I told them they just said "We'd better leave it to the authorities." It's up to us to put it right.'

They re-entered the church silently, both a little nervous at being there alone now that everyone had gone, still faintly awed by the pomp and ceremonial that had attended the funeral.

'It'll do for them both,' Josh whispered. 'Grandpa always used to say that a real cavalryman wasn't fussy about all that band-playing and rifle-firing over the grave. It's for my father and our grandfather.'

'What do we do?' Aubrey whispered.

A sheet of paper changed hands and Aubrey stared at it.

'Is that it?'

'Yes.'

'What do we do with it?'

'Sing it.'

'I don't know the tune.'

It had never occurred to Josh that Aubrey wouldn't know the song. Because he had grown up with it, he had assumed that everybody knew it.

'Well,' he said. 'You'll just have to do your best. I don't think he'd mind. Are you ready?'

Standing together at the back of the church, in the darkest corner they could find because they were faintly embarrassed by what they were doing, the two boys began to sing, Josh's voice skating up and down because it was just beginning to break.

'Wrap me up in my old stable jacket
And say a poor devil lies low,
And six of the Lancers shall carry me
To the place where the best soldiers go.'

As they finished, Aubrey looked at Josh. 'Is that it?'
'Yes.'
'All of it?'
'All he wanted.' Josh rose and headed for the church door.
'I think it'll be all right now.'

Max Hennessy

Back to Battle

Commander Kelly Maguire, leader of men with the British Navy, finds himself plunged into blistering attacks at the battle of Dunkirk, from bitter fighting in the Mediterranean, to the landings at Normandy. Against a background of personal tragedy, this is a compelling, action-packed saga of love and adventure.

The Bright Blue Sky

The reckless, heady days of early aviation are brought to life in a tale of daring, dashing young pilots waging war, and of the raging struggle between the hearts of two brave men for the heart of a beautiful woman. This is the tale of Corporal Quinney, an air ace in the RAF; a hero blazing through the skies to dogfight high above the Italian front, confronting deadly foes and challenging a treacherous rival in love and war.

'Very exciting...' – *Sunday Times*

Max Hennessy

The Challenging Heights

Dicken Quinney, a brilliant, heroic character, comes to life in this turbulent action novel. Quinney finds himself flying in the Baltic in a fight against the Bolsheviks. But tragedy mixes with adventure as Quinney loses his lover, Zoë. This is the second novel in the trilogy involving the air ace, Dicken Quinney.

The Iron Stallions

The Goff family have lived and died for the 19th Lancers for generations but when Josh Goff runs away from school to enlist in the ranks of the cavalry under a false name, heavy artillery pummels the landscape around him as he fights on the D-Day beaches of France in the Second World War. As he learns, the cavalry is still expected to save the day, and die bravely in the attempt.

Max Hennessy

Once More the Hawks

Last in the RAF trilogy, this story charts the exploits of world-class fighter pilot Dicken Quinney. It is the summer of 1939 and when war breaks out, Quinney finds himself flying through the skies of France, shot down over a cemetery and forced to make a breath-taking escape across Nazi Europe, into the hands of his nemesis, General Lee Tse Liu.

Soldier of the Queen

Charting the heroism of a young and talented cavalry officer, Colby Goff, this story takes the reader from Balaclava to the Zulu War, and the ruthless glinting spears of Impis. Through the tide of Imperial history, Colby progresses from a raw, wilful soldier to a laudable officer, fighting from continent to continent, engaging in the Franco-Prussian and American civil war and proving himself to be a man of passion and of steel.

TITLES BY MAX HENNESSY AVAILABLE DIRECT
FROM HOUSE OF STRATUS

Quantity	£	$(US)	$(CAN)	€
☐ BACK TO BATTLE	6.99	12.95	19.95	13.50
☐ THE BRIGHT BLUE SKY	6.99	12.95	19.95	13.50
☐ THE CHALLENGING HEIGHTS	6.99	12.95	19.95	13.50
☐ THE DANGEROUS YEARS	6.99	12.95	19.95	13.50
☐ THE IRON STALLIONS	6.99	12.95	19.95	13.50
☐ THE LION AT SEA	6.99	12.95	19.95	13.50
☐ ONCE MORE THE HAWKS	6.99	12.95	19.95	13.50
☐ SOLDIER OF THE QUEEN	6.99	12.95	19.95	13.50

ALL HOUSE OF STRATUS BOOKS ARE AVAILABLE FROM GOOD BOOKSHOPS
OR DIRECT FROM THE PUBLISHER:

Internet: www.houseofstratus.com including synopses and features.

Email: sales@houseofstratus.com please quote author, title and credit card details.

Order Line: UK: 0800 169 1780,
USA: 1 800 509 9942
INTERNATIONAL: +44 (0) 20 7494 6400 (UK)
or +01 212 218 7649
(please quote author, title, and credit card details.)

Send to: House of Stratus Sales Department
24c Old Burlington Street
London
W1X 1RL
UK

House of Stratus Inc.
Suite 210
1270 Avenue of the Americas
New York • NY 10020
USA

PAYMENT

Please tick currency you wish to use:

☐ £ (Sterling)   ☐ $ (US)   ☐ $ (CAN)   ☐ € (Euros)

Allow for shipping costs charged per order plus an amount per book as set out in the tables below:

CURRENCY/DESTINATION

	£(Sterling)	$(US)	$(CAN)	€(Euros)
Cost per order				
UK	1.50	2.25	3.50	2.50
Europe	3.00	4.50	6.75	5.00
North America	3.00	3.50	5.25	5.00
Rest of World	3.00	4.50	6.75	5.00
Additional cost per book				
UK	0.50	0.75	1.15	0.85
Europe	1.00	1.50	2.25	1.70
North America	1.00	1.00	1.50	1.70
Rest of World	1.50	2.25	3.50	3.00

PLEASE SEND CHEQUE OR INTERNATIONAL MONEY ORDER.
payable to: STRATUS HOLDINGS plc or HOUSE OF STRATUS INC. or card payment as indicated

STERLING EXAMPLE

Cost of book(s):..................... Example: 3 x books at £6.99 each: £20.97
Cost of order: .... Example: £1.50 (Delivery to UK address)
Additional cost per book:.............. Example: 3 x £0.50: £1.50
Order total including shipping:.......... Example: £23.97

VISA, MASTERCARD, SWITCH, AMEX:

☐☐☐☐☐☐☐☐☐☐☐☐☐☐☐☐☐☐☐☐

Issue number (Switch only):

☐☐☐

Start Date: **Expiry Date:**

☐☐/☐☐   ☐☐/☐☐

Signature: _____

NAME: _____

ADDRESS: _____

COUNTRY: _____

ZIP/POSTCODE: _____

Please allow 28 days for delivery. Despatch normally within 48 hours.

Prices subject to change without notice.
Please tick box if you do not wish to receive any additional information. ☐

House of Stratus publishes many other titles in this genre; please check our website (**www.houseofstratus.com**) for more details.